The Chinese Assassin

Also by Anthony Grey

Hostage in Peking
A Man Alone
Some Put Their Trust in Chariots
The Bulgarian Exclusive

The Chinese Assassin

Anthony Grey

HOLT, RINEHART AND WINSTON
NEW YORK

c. √

S

Library of Congress Cataloging in Publication Data
Grey, Anthony.
The Chinese assassin.
I.   Title.
PZ4.G828Ch   1979   [PR6057.R454]   823'.9'14
ISBN 0-03-046786-1   78-14163

First published in the United States of America in 1979
by Holt, Rinehart and Winston, 383 Madison Ave.,
New York, N.Y. 10017.
Printed in the United States of America
1 3 5 7 9 10 8 6 4 2

For Clarissa Jane and Shirley
the inspiration and the reward

First in China comes Mao Tse-tung. Then comes
Mao Tse-tung again. Next comes Mao Tse-tung
once more. Then there is a lot of nothing.
And then, and only then come all the others—
with Lin Piao leading the procession.

Peking colloquialism 1970

PART ONE

The Death of Lin Piao

FOLIO NUMBER ONE

A train of fifty camels was passing that night, black shapes swaying through the wind, darker than the distant mountains. The pale northern light that glimmers all through the sleeping hours in summer and early autumn on those steppes was already brightening the bottom of the sky across the Soviet border to the north.

Old Tsereng Toktokho, wrapped against the cold lash of the night wind in his peaked hat of fur and the heavy sheepskin coat that was almost as old as he was, sat astride his restless horse watching the camels go. His eyes never scanned his herds directly as they shifted around him. His gaze, even in darkness, seemed always to sweep the deep distances of the harsh and endless tundra that he loved. His face was like the saddle on which he sat, creased and tanned almost black by years of merciless beating from wind and sun. But though old, he was stubborn and still brave. That's how he came to be among the last *arats* in Mongolia living outside the communal co-operatives. And that's how he came to save my life.

He had just tipped a long draught of *kumiss* into his great throat from the leather bottle that always hung at his belt, when he heard the first sound of our Trident far away down the sky to the south. There was nothing like *kumiss* for keeping out the chill Mongolian wind, he told me many times in the months he hid me and sheltered me from death. But although I helped him with the milking of the mares in June and drank it to please him, I never learned to love *kumiss* like old Tsereng. Although it resembled strong beer, it was too fizzy for me. It had a sour taste that reminded me of burned almonds and to my nostrils it always reeked unpleasantly of the stables.

His horse had picked up the unfamiliar sound of the jet engines first. It was the twitching of the animal's ears and his sudden stamping that alerted the old man. Immediately he loosened the ear flaps of his fur hat to hear better. I know all this because he told me every detail a thousand times during the long winter nights as we lay on the piled furs in his yurt, warmed by the

8

pungent breath and body heat of the sheep, goats and yaks crowded in all around us, some pregnant, some already with their bleating young. I always concentrated on every word he said, even when I'd heard it all before. I had to, to prevent my eyes wandering to the stocky bodies of his wife and daughter, who invariably threw off all their clothes and sprawled naked on their furs among the animals in the stifling heat. Only when the wind really howled through the seams in the felt walls did they wrap themselves in their fur coats for the night.

The Trident had been specially equipped with military radar when it was in service with the Pakistan Air Force and that enabled us to fly at a very low level under the Soviet detection scanners. We roared over the Kerulen River, flying at little more than two hundred feet, heading north-west. The border of our beloved People's Republic of China was 400 miles behind us and we had crossed it just before two o'clock in the morning, at an even lower altitude.

It was almost three o'clock when Toktokho detected the first sounds of our approach. He was deeply mystified, because the few scheduled air services from Peking to Ulan Bator never passed that far to the east. Our track, although most of us inside the aircraft were then ignorant of the fact, was taking us directly from Peitaiho on the coast near Peking toward Irkutsk on the far shore of Lake Baikal in the Soviet Union. Toktokho strained his eyes into the darkened sky as the roar of our jet engines grew louder, scattering his terrified herds in all directions around him.

The *arats* of Khentiiaimat are simple nomads, little touched by the passage of time. They are deeply fearful of the great extremes of the elements in one of the remotest regions of the vast bowl of Central Asia. Many of the elderly among them still even worship secretly at the ancient shrine on Delger Haan, in defiance of the principles of Marxism-Leninism under which the revisionist puppet state of the People's Republic of Mongolia is supposedly governed.

So the terrible roar of our low passage through the silence of that night stampeded not only the herds of sheep, yak and cattle beneath our track. The *arats*, blind with panic too, were also put to headlong flight, the fear of an unknown death riding close at their backs. Only old Tsereng Toktokho was different. He

9

wrestled his horse to a standstill and stood up high in his stirrups, staring into the black heavens as our Trident passed low overhead. The great din of its engines faded gradually into the night. But it was not long before he heard them beginning to grow loud again. He was not to know then that we had just uncovered the treacherous plot and had forced the pilot at gunpoint to turn towards the south once more.

Until then, because we were flying without navigation lights, he had only heard, not seen, our coming. But then an explosion from the darkness above his head suddenly produced a mighty burgeoning fist of orange flame. It grew quickly bigger as we swung down towards him through the black sky. By its fierce light he saw for the first time the wings and fuselage of our crippled Trident as it slid helplessly towards the earth. When the aircraft struck the ground a half mile from him, a second and more terrible explosion sent Toktokho's terrified horse bolting into a headlong gallop that, great horseman in the tradition of his ancestors though he was, he couldn't turn for two miles.

By the time he had pacified the fear-crazed animal and walked it back in the direction of the crash, the flames were burning with great intensity. Their heat halted him a hundred yards from the blaze and he reined in his mount and sat watching the terrible inferno that was by then lighting up the whole plain. His horse shied again and almost threw him off when I crawled blindly out of the scorched grass underneath its very hooves.

But Toktokho stayed in the saddle long enough to soothe the horse. Then he leapt down to beat out my smouldering clothes with his bare hands. Close to death, I lapsed into unconsciousness while still on the ground and he had to pick me up bodily and sling me across the neck of his horse. I remembered nothing of the jolting journey to his family yurt that was pitched then near the spring at Jibhalantayn Bulag.

ULAN BATOR, Wednesday—Early in the morning of September 13 a jet aircraft belonging to the People's Republic of China violated the airspace of the Mongolian People's Republic and, continuing its flight towards the interior of the territory, crashed in the Hinteyn region. The semi-carbonised bodies of nine persons, firearms, documents and equipment proving that the aircraft belonged to the Chinese Air Force were found on the scene of the catastrophe.

MONTSAME, the Mongolian News Agency,
30 September 1971

1

When the ancient, rickety lift finally ceased its anguished groaning and shuddered to a halt at the fourth floor, Richard Scholefield heard that the bell of the telephone was already jangling behind the locked door of his flat. It was still ringing a minute and a half later when, drenched with perspiration, he finally extricated himself, his suitcase, his hand luggage, his portable typewriter and his plastic carrier bag of duty-free liquor from the clutches of the two spring-loaded latticed-iron gates that daily threatened the life and limb of all the tenants in the block.

The bulb on the windowless landing was out again and Scholefield stumbled in the darkness over a loose stair rod on the two steps leading up to his door. He was cursing softly to himself when he felt a hand on his arm. He started back in alarm. 'It's been ringing for a week. It's never stopped.'

Scholefield, still cursing, bent to fumble on the floor in the darkness for the plastic bag of duty-frees he'd dropped in the confusion. The stifling heat lent a sharp edge of irritation to his voice. 'Moynahan, if you spent your time fixing the stair rods and the light bulbs around here instead of listening through a keyhole to my bloody telephone ringing—'

The new Irish porter suddenly leaned closer in the darkness and Scholefield recoiled as he inhaled the pungent whisky fumes on his breath. 'I mean it literally, Mr. Scholefield. I'm not employin' the words to mean that your telephone has been ringin' all week in the sense that it's just been quite busy. I really mean that it's never stopped. Not for a moment. Not once.'

Scholefield stood still and listened in the darkness. The telephone was still ringing inside the flat.

'Eight days it's been goin'. Just like that. Eight days—without a moment's cease.'

Scholefield put down his cases slowly and fumbled in his pockets for keys.

'I first noticed last Thursday morning, Mr. Scholefield. When I was doin' my rounds.' He stopped and peered closely at the luminous dial of his wristwatch, holding it against the end of his nose. 'It's the twenty-second, today, right? So Thursday July the fifteenth, it was, okay?'

Scholefield tried to elbow his way past him but the porter lurched sideways knocking him against the wall. 'Terribly sorry, Mr. Scholefield—you all right?—by Sunday old Mrs. Thompson upstairs was complainin' that it was keepin' her awake nights. It's rung right through the nights y' see. I told her there was nothin' I could do. We porters aren't allowed to enter flats when the tenants are away, I says. Did you have a good trip to Ottawa, Mr. Scholefield? You and your China-watchin' colleagues got the yellow peril under control at last, have you?'

'Good night, Moynahan.' Scholefield edged slowly round the porter, speaking with exaggerated patience and inserted his Yale key in the lock. Behind the door the telephone continued its relentless clamour.

'Who do you think it could be callin' you all this time, Mr. Scholefield?'

'If it's Her Majesty, the Prime Minister, or the Secretary General of the United Nations, Moynahan, I promise to let you know.' He opened the door and carried his luggage into the darkened hallway.

'More likely that actress ladyfriend of yours. Desperate to see you the first minute you're back, eh?' The reek of whiskied breath assailed Scholefield's nostrils again and the porter laughed coarsely close behind him in the darkness. 'How d'yer like this heat, Mr. Scholefield? Hottest summer in London since records were kept, eh? Did ya know that? The summer of '76 will be one to remember, eh?'

'Forgive me, Moynahan, I'm jetlagged.' Scholefield switched on the light in the hall and closed the door quickly in the porter's leering face. He stood looking down at the telephone on the hall table. Its ringing echoed loudly through the empty rooms, jarring his sleep-starved nerves. The heat inside the airless flat was stifling and he felt the sweat running in rivulets down the sides of his face. He stared at the telephone for a moment then turned away deliberately and picked up his typewriter and briefcase and carried them through to the desk in his study. He returned and took the two duty-free bottles of Polish Vodka from the plastic carrier bag and stood them on the hall table beside the ringing telephone. Then he took off his jacket, hung it up, and carried his suitcase into the bedroom at the far end of the hall. The extension telephone on the bedside table was ringing there too.

Scholefield took the used underclothes from his suitcase and threw them into a linen basket, then hung up his suits. He opened several windows but the air outside seemed equally fetid. He took off his tie, and the shirt that was sticking to his back, undressed, and went to the bathroom and turned on the shower. He stood motionless under the cold water jet for several minutes with his eyes closed, listening absently to the shrill of the telephone. Then he towelled himself vigorously, threw the towel aside and went back to the bedroom.

He hesitated by the bedside table for a moment before lifting the receiver. When he did the abrupt return of quiet to the flat was startling. He held the instrument to his ear and listened without speaking. There was a long moment of silence. Then a diffident, barely audible foreign voice came on the line.

'Mr. Richard Scholefield?'

The blurred consonants and the inability to pronounce the 'R' sound of his first name betrayed a Chinese speaking English.

'Yes, this is Scholefield.'

There was another silence, then the sound of a long breath being drawn. When the voice spoke again, it had switched to Chinese.

'Mr. Scholefield, you don't know me. But I must see you very urgently.'

Almost as a reflex Scholefield found himself mentally categorising the speaker's nasal accent. Before he spoke again he'd placed it, in one of the Yangtze provinces of central China, probably Hupeh or East Szechuan. 'Who are you? What do you want to see me about?'

'It is not possible for me to say on the telephone. But I have something to tell you that would be of great significance for your work.'

'Who are you?'

'My name is Yang. But I am not important. What I have to reveal could be a matter of life and death for somebody much more important than me.' The man paused and drew another long breath. 'In China.'

Scholefield frowned irritably into the receiver. 'I've just this minute come off a plane from Canada—' Then he stopped. 'Mr. Yang, have you been telephoning day and night for the past eight days?'

'Yes.' The voice of the Chinese was tight with tension. 'May I come this evening?'

Scholefield rubbed a hand wearily across his eyes. 'All right. Do you know where I live?'

'Yes!' The answer was a shout of relief. 'I will be there in half an hour.'

The line went dead immediately. Scholefield shrugged, put on a fresh shirt and a pair of tennis shorts and wandered barefoot into the hall, wiping fresh perspiration from his brow. He picked up a bottle of vodka, broke the seal and was on the way to the study where he kept a cabinet of glasses when the telephone began ringing again. He pushed a pile of last year's *Peking Review* irritably onto the floor to make room for the bottle and glass on his desk, then went to the hall to answer it. He lost the battle to stifle an enormous yawn as he picked up the receiver.

'Darling, at last! I've been ringing for simply ages. I couldn't get through. Are you all right? Was your plane late? When did you get in? That is you, isn't it darling?'

Scholefield closed his eyes and smiled. 'Yes, sweetheart. Yes, three hours late. About ten minutes ago. And yes, sweetheart— in that order.'

'Don't be so bloody unfeeling, Richard. You know I hate it when you fly.'

'Not as much as I do. And I'm not being "unfeeling". It's a mixture of jet lag and this heat. The road in from the airport is littered for miles with abandoned, boiled-up cars. It's like a scene from *The Day the Earth Caught Fire*. A bit eerie.'

'I know. It's been terrible.'

'That's why I can't match Hedda Gabler's stream of lively histrionics—it still is Hedda this week, is it?'

'Yes. Nina Murphy—remember her?—has got to be at the un-air-conditioned theatre in an hour to do her twice-nightly impersonation of a disappearing grease-spot. But she might just find time for a breathless, welcome-home nude sequence at your flat at twice the speed of sound on her way there—if you want, of course.'

'Nina, you know damned well I want,' he began, 'but—'

'Then I'll be there in twenty minutes. Starting from now!'

The dialling tone resumed abruptly and Scholefield replaced the receiver, grinning broadly to himself. He bent and began picking up the airmail editions of *The People's Daily* that had been faithfully forwarded during his absence by the little Communist bookshop behind the British Museum. In his study he threw them on a leather chesterfield by his desk, fetched ice from the kitchen and poured himself a large measure of neat vodka. Then he sank down on the chesterfield and began removing the wrappers and glancing at the heavy black type of the headline ideograms, sipping the vodka as he read. But before he had drunk half of it the telephone began ringing again and he dragged himself reluctantly back to the hall.

'Richard?'

He took another swallow from the glass in his hand to fortify himself against the calculated hostility of his ex-wife's voice. 'Hello, Sarah. How nice to hear from you.'

'I'm only calling to ask when you intend visiting Matthew again.' Her tone had descended immediately to heavy sarcasm. 'It's nearly a month since you saw him. A boy of his age needs a father's attention. Even if it is only very occasionally.'

Scholefield felt his anger rising despite himself, but tried to speak slowly. 'I've been very busy, Sarah. There's been rather a lot going on in China. Mao really may be dying at last. Or have you stopped reading the papers?'

A snort of contemptuous laughter came down the line. 'I suppose I should have cited Mao Tse-tung and Chou En-lai in my divorce petition, shouldn't I, instead of your Shaftesbury Avenue whore! I don't imagine you've missed out on seeing her often in the past month.'

Scholefield gritted his teeth. 'I've been away in Ottawa at a military symposium on the PLA for the past ten days. I've got an important article for one of the monthlies to finish by tomorrow night and the BBC have asked me to script a programme by the weekend on the Peking power struggle—'

She ignored the explanation as though he hadn't spoken. 'All I want to know is whether you want to see him on Saturday or Sunday. The court granted you access once a month, unless you've forgotten. If you don't intend seeing him I shall be taking him away for the weekend. That's all I'm ringing for.'

A cold silence lengthened between them and threatened to become interminable. 'I'll be over at three o'clock on Saturday,' he said at last, drawing his words out, 'to take him out for a couple of hours.'

'Thank you. I'm sure Matthew will appreciate that enormously. It'll be just to the zoo again, will it?'

Scholefield banged the receiver savagely back on its rest without responding and drained the remaining vodka in his glass at a gulp. He was still standing indecisively in the hall when the sudden ringing of the doorbell startled him. He put down his glass and opened the door. The passageway outside was empty. He leaned out to look up the stairs and found himself staring into the glowing red eyes of a hideous dragon's head. Blue smoke streamed from its flared nostrils and the grotesque fanged jaws emitted a sudden moaning shriek. He flinched and started back just as Nina's face appeared from behind the mask, puffing furiously on a cigarette. She snatched the cigarette from her mouth laughing uproariously, then flung an arm around his neck, pulling his face close to hers.

'Did I give you a fright, darling? I'm sorry. It *is* the year of the dragon, remember. I found him in Gerrard Street. Couldn't resist him.'

She pulled away from him suddenly in alarm and stared at his unsmiling face. 'Richard! Are you all right?'

He took the dragon's head from her and placed it carefully on the hall table. He looked expressionlessly into her eyes, now clouded with worry. 'Of course I'm all right, you crazy bitch.' He spoke very quietly—then smiled suddenly. 'Just a little tired, that's all. Come here.'

She wore flared blue jeans, a loose cheesecloth smock with nothing beneath it and a square of turquoise silk tied gypsy-fashion round her hair. He wrapped his arms around her and they stood pressed close against each other for a long time in the doorway without speaking or kissing.

'We'd better shut it. I passed your prurient new porter on the stairs.' She disentangled herself, and closed and locked the door. In the study she refused a drink and took his hand. 'I have a very good remedy for tenseness and tiredness.' She smiled and with both hands pressed his fingers gently against the thin stuff covering her breasts. He sighed and kissed her quickly on the ear.

'I'm sorry, Nina, but I've got somebody arriving any minute.' He shook his head wearily. 'A mysterious Chinese. You didn't give me a chance to explain on the phone.'

She dropped his hand abruptly and sat down. 'Oh shit!'

In the silence that followed she pouted and stared up at him sulkily. 'You might have waited five minutes after you got home before re-opening your appointments book.' She flapped her hand in front of her face like a fan, bent over and began rolling her wide-bottomed jeans up her bare legs to turn them into shorts.

'I don't know who he is and I wouldn't have agreed to him coming tonight except he's been ringing the flat constantly for the past week. He dialled my number last Thursday morning and sat listening to it ring out for eight whole days until I picked it up twenty minutes ago.'

She stopped and stared up at him open-mouthed. 'You're joking!'

'No, I'm not.'

The doorbell interrupted them and Nina stood up quickly, her face suddenly tense. 'You don't think you're in any danger, do you?'

Scholefield laughed. 'From the Chinese—in W.1?'

She barred his way to the door, and put a hand on his arm, looking at him wide-eyed. 'Do you want me to go?'

'Let's just see, shall we?' She sank back onto the chesterfield, fanning herself with one hand again, as he walked into the hall and opened the door.

FOLIO NUMBER TWO

My senses swam for many days. From the mists of my delirium I remember above all else the giant communal feeding bowls. Fresh milk, salt, butter, green Chinese tea and mutton fat were stirred together in steaming cauldrons that seemed to rise up regularly before my eyes like shapeless, disembodied ghosts. The cloying, tepid liquid was always forced into my open throat but often, writhing with the heat of my fever, my whole body violently rejected this staple nourishment of the nomads.

My eyes saw only the vague shapes of Toktokho and his wife and daughter. Sometimes booted and wrapped in their long *deli* with broad belts wound many times round their waists, and sometimes naked, they moved like disembodied wraiths around the open fireplace in the centre of the yurt. As they ministered to me they were always careful to pay respect to the high wooden box against the felt wall on which stood their revered images and statues. When the sun went down the yurt filled gradually with the noise and the stink and the heat of pregnant and new-born animals. All the *arats* suffered piles from their incessant horse-riding and each night by the light of the fire the family unashamedly tended their discomforts with mutton grease.

I knew much pain in those first days. But it always seemed far away, as though afflicting somebody else at a great distance outside the walls of my body. Both my thighs and one arm were fractured and my neck and shoulders were severely burned. I could not move my head or upper body for many days and when Toktokho approached to moisten my mouth and lips or dress my injuries, the ornaments on his belt always danced close before my eyes in a gaudy mirage. A silver-mounted flint steel, and a long narrow embroidered tobacco pouch with a silver clasp, hung from a leather strap along with a lacquered tinder box and a small bag of tinder. He was proud still to be able to employ this old art of his forefathers. There was a tinkling silver bell too, attached by a silver chain to a metal knob which he used to knock out his pipe. I came to know every stitch of the prancing blue and gold horses embroidered on these ornaments and later I

19

learned that Toktokho had taken them as the spoils of victory from the body of the leader of a camel train, whom he had fought and killed in a fair fight before liberation. Every night without fail he put them on ceremonially, like battle honours, when he returned from his riding. He also wore two sheaths on the belt— a large one for his dagger and a small one for a steel tooth pick which he used to fork lumps of mutton fat from the feeding bowls.

In those fevered times while the second sheep-shearing was taking place outside I slipped, without caring, from wakefulness to unconsciousness—and sometimes approached equally carelessly near to death! Each day throughout this period, I learned later, old Tsereng was riding the five miles to the scene of the crashed Trident to watch the flurry of activity taking place there.

The dried saltmarsh in which the wreckage had come to rest was cordoned off with ropes and guarded by large contingents of armed Soviet troops. Toktokho did not approach the cordons but watched discreetly from behind an outcrop of rock on a rise in the ground several hundred yards away. Though he was old, his eyes were still almost as keen as in his youth and when I recovered he reported faithfully to me all that he had seen.

He was out at dawn on the first morning when they began hauling the blackened and charred bodies of Marshall Lin Piao and the others from the still-smouldering skeleton of the aircraft. They were loaded immediately and without ceremony into a covered military lorry which remained at the scene without moving for several days. A constant stream of vehicles jolted back and forth across the roadless steppe from Ulan Bator in great clouds of dust, bringing high-ranking Soviet military officers and civilians to the site along with frequent groups of Mongolian party and government leaders. An encampment of military tents was eventually set up close by.

By night the area was lit by huge arc-lights. The Russian troops, who had ordered all curious *arats* away from the cordon ropes in the first few days with much shouting and menaces, fired off their guns indiscriminately into the surrounding darkness every night, laughing loudly as they did so.

On the third day after the crash, Toktokho saw a sudden and astonishing change in the pattern of activity at the site. By then he was watching through binoculars from the rock knoll which rose from the plain quite near to where he had found me. Just before noon, he saw the soldiers begin unloading the nine charred bodies again from the lorry. They removed them from their canvas bags and laid them out carefully on the ground, side by side on white sheets. Then the tented camp, which had grown quite large by this time, was struck in great haste and all the Russian troops on guard were marshalled quickly into transport trucks and driven away. Only four high-ranking officers from the Soviet Union remained talking to the Mongolian officials for a few minutes. Then they, too, drove slowly away across the steppe, but in the opposite direction to that taken by their troops, leaving the Mongolians alone. Through his binoculars Toktokho saw the Russian officers halt their vehicle in a slight depression in the ground about two miles away. They then climbed on top of it and, like him, continued to survey the site through their field glasses.

A few minutes later a contingent of soldiers in uniforms of the army of the Mongolian People's Republic arrived and took up guard positions around the perimeter of the cordoned-off area and the larger sections of the remaining wreckage. A special concentration of troops was stationed shoulder to shoulder in a square around the spot where the row of corpses was laid out. They stood to attention, their weapons held clenched across their chests.

For an hour nothing happened. Then a convoy of black cars arrived, driving slowly across the grassland in a cloud of dust from the direction of Ulan Bator. The men who alighted were obviously, Toktokho said, from my own country, the People's Republic of China. They wore the formal tunic suits of official cadres, buttoned high at the neck. Toktokho reported that they behaved very nervously. For a long time they stood rooted to the spot, staring apprehensively about them at the blackened wreckage of the Trident and at the soldiers. Then they began walking hesitantly among the debris. They often gazed distractedly at the sky and barely looked at the ground, he said, as though they were anxious to be done with their observations as quickly and with as little trouble as possible.

From their cars the Mongolian officials brought two boxes of relics apparently recovered from the wreckage. They placed them on the ground and took out partly-charred documents which Toktokho had noticed scattered in the scorched grass at dawn on the first day. The Chinese did not inspect these closely but had them transferred immediately to their own vehicles. Toktokho also saw the leading Mongolian hold up a silver-plated pistol. The head of the Chinese delegation snatched this from him, almost with glee, Toktokho said. Because of his love of silver ornaments like those he wore nightly on his belt, he remembered this very vividly. It flashed brightly and pleasingly in the autumn sun, he said. This pistol was in fact a souvenir of Marshall Lin Piao's stay in Moscow from 1938 to 1942 which he had valued highly. It had been presented to him by Stalin in gratitude for his strategic advice on revising the Soviet plan of national defence. While recovering in a Moscow hospital from grave wounds received fighting the invading Japanese forces in China, Marshall Lin had time then to apply his brilliant military mind to the Soviet Union's strategic planning in its great hour of crisis.

He had concluded that the German attack directed at Leningrad was intended as a turning movement towards Moscow and therefore he advised Stalin to reinforce the defence of his general headquarters, and also to hold a sufficient force in reserve for this purpose. Those in Peking who ruthlessly sent Lin Piao to his well-planned death planted this famous and much-loved memento on the plane to help identify his burned body and so compound the 'irrefutable evidence' of his intended treachery. I had noticed it lying on a seat, during the last moments of the flight, when I burst into the closed forward compartment in which the unconscious Marshall Lin and his wife Yeh Chun had been transported. But by that time it was too late to do anything about it, or the other false and damning evidence planted against us.

When this silver pistol had been stowed in their car the Chinese delegation was conducted to the spot where the soldiers were drawn up around the line of dead bodies. On a sudden command the soldiers were marched back several paces but still stood guard at a distance, with their weapons at the ready. The delegation then moved forward and stared down at the corpses, walking quickly back and forth along the line.

The Chinese, Toktokho said, seemed puzzled at first. Gradually they began arguing among themselves, casting occasional angry looks over their shoulders at the Mongolians. Then the two leading Chinese approached the Mongolian government officials and another, more violent argument ensued. The Chinese waved their arms agitatedly in the air and became very irate, pointing repeatedly back at the row of incinerated bodies lying on the ground. Toktokho said he could hear their raised voices clearly from his hiding place among the rocks.

The Mongolians at first shouted back. But when the visitors refused to calm down they turned their backs, walked away to their cars, wound up their windows and refused to co-operate further. At this point those Chinese who had been carrying shoulder cases took out cameras and began photographing the bodies. Although the sunshine was bright they used flashbulb equipment and took many hundreds of pictures from every angle. While this was being done the leading Chinese called their whole party to a hurried conference at a distance from the troops and the cars.

Then, after some discussion, they began to spread out around the scene of the crash, scouring the ground minutely with their eyes. This meticulous search went on for an hour, the Chinese pacing carefully back and forth in a long line across an ever widening area of the grassland beyond the rope cordons that marked the limits of the site itself.

Toktokho grew alarmed when it became clear that the line was moving slowly but steadily towards the knoll on which he was hidden. His horse stood tethered a quarter of a mile away and he was afraid it might make a noise as the line of Chinese drew near, and betray his presence. He was struggling in an agony of indecision, unsure whether to make a dash for his horse or remain hidden, when the Chinese heading directly for his hiding place stopped at the foot of the knoll and let out a loud cry. He turned and held up something in his hand and the others in the line all ran to him.

It was my left shoe!

All the Chinese gathered round and began stamping through the tussocks of coarse grass in the area, jabbering excitedly among themselves. They searched the small area intensively for a further quarter of an hour but found nothing more. Toktokho was relieved when at last they returned to their line of cars.

After another conference with the Mongolian officials, orders were shouted to the soldiers and they immediately began digging beside the Trident's wreckage with their bivouac shovels. The Mongolian representatives appeared to be astonished by the behaviour of the Chinese who sat silently in their cars during the digging. Two hours later, when a large hole had been dug, the Chinese climbed out of their vehicles and stood in a silent group watching as the soldiers lowered the nine bodies, wrapped again in their canvas shrouds, into the makeshift mass grave.

They showed no emotion, uttered no words, but just stood sullenly waiting while the earth was shovelled in on top of the bodies. Some more photographs were taken, then the Chinese, satisfied that the land was flattened over the grave, without a further word to their hosts returned to their cars and drove away rapidly in the direction of the capital.

Old Tsereng was becoming stiff and cramped by this time. He had been crouched behind the rocks for nearly six hours. But just as he was rising to return to his herds he saw the four Russian officers coming back to the site from their sunken vantage point two miles away. They quickly dismissed the Mongolian troops who moved out in a convoy within five minutes. The light was beginning to fade but the sound of their vehicles had hardly died away before the much larger convoy of Russian vehicles re-appeared, rumbling back across the tundra.

The soldiers disembarked and immediately began pitching camp again. Toktokho watched in astonishment as new orders were shouted and a detachment of Russian troops set to with their trenching shovels to open up the newly-dug mass grave. The nine bodies in their canvas bags were lifted out without ceremony and loaded once more, one by one, onto the same lorry in which they had been preserved since the crash.

As dusk fell, Toktokho watched the army lorry trundle slowly away across the darkening grassland bearing its terrible cargo of burned human flesh and bones.

NEW YORK, Monday—The Columbia Broadcasting System has reported that the United States Government has intercepted a secret message from Peking to all China's foreign embassies alerting them to 'prepare for war'.

Jersey Evening Post, 23 September 1971

2

A thickset Chinese with close-cropped hair and a round, moonlike face blinked quickly in the sudden light from the hall. Despite the heat he wore a cheap fawn raincoat that was frayed at the cuffs and greasy round the inside of the collar. He carried a large box of Cellophane-wrapped 'Good News' chocolates ostentatiously in front of him. He bared his teeth in a sudden, automatic smile and raised his eyebrows. 'Mr. Scholefield?'

Scholefield nodded. 'Mr. Yang?'

The Chinese laughed nervously and stepped inside without waiting to be invited. He moved quickly past Scholefield and walked unsteadily into the lighted study, limping as though from some injury or deformity. Scholefield closed the door and followed him in. He found Yang standing uncertainly in the middle of the room looking down at Nina Murphy. Taken by surprise, she was sprawled back on the chesterfield, her legs splayed across the carpet, the jeans still rolled back halfway up her long thighs. Yang let out a strangled laugh of embarrassment and ducked his head uncertainly in her direction in greeting. He nodded diffidently towards the box of chocolates in his hand and held them towards her. 'It was customary once in China to arrive bearing a gift.'

Nina smiled and reddened in uncharacteristic confusion. She hurriedly rolled down her jeans and began to stand up. But the

Chinese turned quickly away and placed the chocolates on the shelf of a bookcase behind him.

He looked back hesitantly at Scholefield then began speaking from where he stood, wringing his hands nervously in front of him. 'I am from the People's Republic of China and there are a number of things I have to say. You may be shocked or distressed at what I am going to tell you. If you are, please stop me and tell me to go.' His English was slow and stilted but meticulously correct. He stared down at the floor for a moment, avoiding their eyes.

Nina sat down again on the chesterfield and cleared a space among the Chinese newspapers. 'Wouldn't you like to sit, Mr. Yang?' She shot a quick glance at Scholefield but his face was expressionless, watching the Chinese.

'Hsieh hsieh ni.' He perched uncomfortably on the very edge of the couch, giggling apologetically at his sudden lapse into Chinese, and corrected himself. 'Thank you.' He raised his round, pock-marked face to look at them both briefly before dropping his eyes to the floor once more. 'Before I tell you my story, Mr. Scholefield, I would like you to confirm that you are not a Communist. I do not think you are because you are well-known for your'—he paused, searching for a word—'your objective writing on China. But I could not tell you what I have to say if you were of an extreme left-wing disposition.'

Scholefield noticed that sweat had broken out on his visitor's face. He moved over to his desk. 'Would you like a glass of vodka, Mr. Yang?' The Chinese shook his head quickly without looking up.

Scholefield sat down in the swivel chair, switched on the desk light and pulled pen and paper towards him. 'You can rest assured, Mr. Yang, that my political views are not of the extreme left—or of the extreme right for that matter. Please go on.'

'I am working in Oxford—at an acupuncture clinic. You know there are several student exchange programmes between our two governments. Most of the people I know at Oxford are Communists, extreme leftists or are connected with the Marxist-Leninist Party of Great Britain—which as you know is anti-Moscow and pro-Mao Tse-tung. That is why I am unable to speak openly with them.'

Scholefield nodded. 'I think I begin to understand, Mr. Yang. But you'll have to make yourself clearer.'

Yang nodded quickly. His voice dropped almost to a whisper. 'I am a member of the Chinese Communist Party and I have always supported Chairman Mao. But now I am in some difficulty. I was born in Huang-an County in Hupeh Province in 1934 although I was brought up in Szechuan. I was made an orphan by the war and cared for by the Communists. I was often starving—that is my most vivid memory. But in my country I am now a hero. I served in Vietnam, training the Vietnamese fighters to shoot down imperialist American air pirates. I was decorated for that service and made a hero of the People's Liberation Army. So you see the Party has nourished and nurtured me. My allegiance is to the Party and Mao Tse-tung. I am a patriot.' Yang's voice died away altogether for a moment. 'But now, as I say, I face a very serious difficulty.'

Nina and Scholefield exchanged puzzled glances over Yang's bowed head. Scholefield noticed that the man's hands, which he constantly wrung together, were incongruously delicate in comparison with his squat heavy body—and heavily ingrained with dirt. Scar tissue from what might have been a burn ran from behind his ear and disappeared under the soiled collar of his shirt.

In the silence Yang cleared his throat several times then continued in a more determined voice. 'Over the past year I have discovered something I had not wanted to admit to myself before.' He looked up suddenly, directly at Nina. 'Am I shocking you?'

Nina stared back, disconcerted. 'I'm not sure. No, I'm not shocked yet, I don't know what you're going to say.'

Yang dropped his head in his hands and fell silent. When he spoke again his voice came muffled through his fingers. 'I have discovered here in England that I am—a homosexual.'

Scholefield took a deep breath. Nina continued staring at the bent head of the Chinese with a perplexed expression on her face.

'I think you can understand my dilemma.' Yang let his hands fall away and looked up at Nina.

She leaned towards him, her voice gentle with sympathy. 'Are you saying that this would count against you back home in China?'

Yang laughed humourlessly. 'It would not only count against me, Mrs. Scholefield, there is a chance I would be put to death.' She stared at him, aghast. 'The point is, I am a war hero who risked his life in Vietnam. Look at recent history. Liu Shao-chi and Lin Piao were heroes one day, then the next day they were in disgrace—or worse, dead! So I have this dilemma. I believe in Socialism, in Chairman Mao, and I believe in the People's Republic of China but I have this personal trait likely to result in my disgrace—or even my death. I am very apprehensive of the future!'

Scholefield stood up with a sigh and threw his pen down on the desk.

'Mr. Yang, I'm sorry, but if you're saying what I think you're saying, you've come to the wrong place. There are well laid down channels of approach for people like you. You should go to the British government and ask for political asylum. It's not part of my job to help defectors.'

'No! No!' Yang sprang to his feet. 'I am not asking you to arrange my defection.'

'What then?'

Yang clenched his fists and his voice rose to a shout. 'I am a Socialist, I believe the world is moving inevitably towards a Communist society! I must live in a Socialist country!'

Scholefield looked at the Chinese steadily. 'Any one in particular?'

Yang didn't hesitate. 'Yes, Cuba!'

'Why Cuba?'

'I believe I could live in Cuba because that country is both sufficiently radical to meet my political views and sufficiently broad-minded on other matters to suit my homosexual tendencies,' answered Yang.

Behind Yang's back Scholefield saw Nina shake her head twice quickly in his direction, apparently trying to convey her female disbelief in his story. Scholefield looked back into the Chinese man's pudgy face, to find his narrow eyes watching him intently from under lashless lids. Scholefield sat down again behind his desk and stared at his blotter.

'Mr. Yang, perhaps I might ask you one or two questions.'

Yang moved towards the desk and leaned down towards

Scholefield, his hands resting palms downwards on the leather top. 'Please go ahead.'

'How was it that you only found out about your homosexuality here in England? You are hardly an adolescent if you were born in 1934.'

Yang leaned closer. The light from the desk lamp threw half his tense face into bright relief, leaving the other half in shadow. The one Cyclopean eye visible to Scholefield widened. 'In China and Vietnam I had suspicions about myself because I did not feel as other Comrades did about the opposite sex. But as you know the Chinese Communist Party does not allow its male members to marry until they are thirty-five—and because of this rule I could not be sure. But since I came to England and worked in the acupuncture clinic demonstrating the techniques to your own students I have been constantly confronted with the naked male body—'

Yang paused for breath, blinking rapidly. The perspiration on his brow glittered in the lamplight. His voice sank to a whisper again. 'The problem then became intense. I have also been studying English at Oxford and my tutor there is a homosexual. He wears a badge announcing this to the world. Many others wear badges in Oxford too and it was seeing such things openly flaunted in this way that made me realise and admit finally my own tendencies beyond any doubt.'

'Did you manage to conceal this from your Chinese Comrades from Peking?'

Yang straightened up and looked round nervously at Nina. 'No! Unfortunately not. What you call here "gay" literature was found in my room. Comrades from the Chinese Embassy here in London were called down immediately. I was denounced at a struggle meeting and sentenced to be returned immediately to China. But I escaped their surveillance and made my way here to the capital ten days ago.'

Nina let out a sudden high-pitched squeal and jumped to her feet. 'Good God, just look at that time.' She stared at her wrist in disbelief. 'I should be in Shaftesbury Avenue now.'

She snatched up her make-up bag and ran out of the room. Scholefield followed her into the hall. She wrenched open the door then stopped and turned, twisting her face into an anguished expression of puzzlement and nodding her head mutely towards the study. Scholefield raised his eyebrows in silent mystification in return. She shrugged and smiled, kissing him quickly on the cheek, then on the way out bent and planted another kiss on the nose of the grotesque dragon head on the hall table. 'He'll look after you,' she whispered in its ear, and dashed out, slamming the door behind her.

When Scholefield returned to the study Yang was scrutinising a scroll painting that hung on the wall by the desk. It depicted a group of Ming concubines playing a gentle game in the snow by a winter pavilion. In his hands he was holding a pale green jade figure of a mandarin and as Scholefield watched he turned from the painting and held the figure towards the lamp on the desk, twisting it back and forth so that the light reflected on the translucent stone. He looked up and smiled as Scholefield moved towards him. 'A fine representation of a member of the exploiting classes of the old China, Mr. Scholefield, produced no doubt by the sweated labour of a working class artisan. A good negative example—'

'Mr. Yang.' Scholefield cut in on him with deliberate rudeness. 'Perhaps you would care to tell me why you chose me to relate your troubles to. And where did you hide for eight days while waiting for me to pick up my telephone?'

Yang put the jade figure down. His manner suddenly seemed more confident with Nina gone. 'Your work on China is well-known, Mr. Scholefield. Your articles in the quarterly journals of international affairs analysing our political problems are influential in Western government circles where China policy is set. You are no apologist for China, unlike certain British writers who have made it their business to ingratiate themselves abjectly with my government in Peking.'

Scholefield didn't reply. Yang frowned as though searching his memory.

'You were one of the few English students allowed into our universities in the fifties and made good use of your opportunities to get some understanding of our society. You speak and write Chinese well, you are also fluent in Japanese and you were a Chinese linguist during your National Service in the British Army, monitoring mainland radio broadcasts in Hong Kong.

Your determination to become one of your country's leading Orientalists has also led you to study the "Kyoku-Shinkai" or "Peak of Truth" School of Karate, founded by the Korean, Mas Oyama, who fought fifty-two bulls in his lifetime with his bare hands. You are probably a black belt of the fourth rank—but you keep this to yourself. Your critical academic views on China are widely known through the occasional articles you write for serious Western newspapers and for your work in the broadcasting media of Europe and North America. Isn't that correct?'

Scholefield smiled grimly. 'You seem to know a lot for an acupuncture student from the People's Liberation Army, Mr. Yang.'

Yang smiled easily. 'Chairman Mao has taught that without adequate investigation a Chinese cadre has no right to speak. I have investigated and your qualifications and your background made you the ideal candidate for my purpose.'

'I may as well tell you now, Mr. Yang, I have strong reservations about your story. What exactly was your purpose in coming here?'

Yang looked at him steadily. 'It is precisely as I have told you; I wish to get to Cuba. I know of a doctor in Sweden who will help me to get to East Germany. From there I can go to Cuba without difficulty. But the first step of a long journey is always the most difficult. I must sail from Tilbury to Sweden.'

Scholefield shook his head in disbelief. 'Are you trying to tell me you simply came here to ask for money for your passage from Tilbury?'

Yang stiffened and his eyes flashed. 'I have too much pride to beg money from you.'

'Then what are you after?'

'Your help. I need time to get the money together. Time to work. I need a secret address somewhere in the country. Perhaps you have friends who could help.'

Scholefield's brow crinkled in a frown of suspicion. 'What "work" have you in mind?'

'If necessary I could work in construction.' He looked down at his ingrained hands. 'Hard work, as you know, is unfamiliar to nobody in the China of Chairman Mao. Or I could work in a restaurant.'

'But you have no papers. I couldn't assist you in finding work illegally without breaking the law.'

Yang eyed him calculatingly. 'Or I could help you privately with your work—until I have the money I need.'

Scholefield's face cleared suddenly. He walked slowly towards Yang and paused in front of him considering his words carefully. 'Is this a very subtle way of offering me information privately, Mr. Yang, that would more properly come under the category of "espionage"?'

Yang's blank expression didn't falter and he made no attempt to answer.

'Could it possibly be an attempt on the part of your government in Peking to test me out for some reason best known to themselves or to blacken my reputation—or both?'

Yang still didn't reply. He stared back at Scholefield unblinking.

'Mr. Yang, when you spoke to me on the phone you claimed the reasons for our meeting were very urgent. A matter of life and death for somebody in China, you said. How did you know I wouldn't be away for a month? Was that just a ruse to get me to see you?'

Yang moved suddenly, stepping quickly round Scholefield and hurrying towards the door. Scholefield, taken aback, followed uncertainly. The Chinese turned angrily with his hand on the latch. 'Mr. Scholefield, I will wait until tomorrow for you to make up your mind whether you wish to help me.' He paused. 'If your decision is positive, go to the stall selling Chinese leaves in the corner of the Gerrard Street Market at noon tomorrow. If you are absolutely alone I will contact you there. After that it will be too late. Good night.'

The Chinese swung on his heel and went out, closing the door behind him.

Scholefield hovered uncertainly by the door, wondering whether he should call the Chinese back, or even follow him. He heard the double gates of the lift clang shut outside the door then the painful shriek of its descent. Only when the noise ceased and the sound of the gates crashing closed again echoed back up the shaft did he return to his study. He stood in the middle of the room for a long time looking around himself unseeing, going over in his mind again the conversation of the past half hour.

The label on the box of chocolates that Yang had presented to Nina caught his eye on the top of the bookcase and he shook his head at the banality of the choice. He put a hand to his face and rubbed his eyes hard, remembering suddenly how tired he was from the flight from Montreal. Then he stopped suddenly and went over to the bookcase and picked up the chocolates. The Cellophane wrapping was rumpled and when he turned the box over he noticed it had been refastened with Sellotape. He tore it off and opened the lid of the box.

On top of the first layer of chocolates lay a folded wedge of thin pink paper. He put the box down and spread the sheets out on his desk. There were six large poster-sized pages each covered with a sea of closely-spaced lines of Chinese characters, hand-written in ink. A quick glance told him that the texts had been penned in the simplified characters that had been in use in the People's Republic of China since the early 1950s. The first sheet was headed simply 'Folio Number One', and the rest were numbered up to Folio Six. Scholefield sat down at his desk and began reading the first page.

FOLIO NUMBER THREE

That night they took the bodies away was the first time I ever saw old Tsereng's face. He was one of those Mongols with a high, hooked eagle's nose who look so much like the American Red Indian. The light of the fire in the open hearth on the floor of the yurt danced on the silver ornaments of his belt as he carried the evening bowl of *kumiss* to where I lay half-paralysed on my pile of furs. The fever and delirium were at last dying down and I saw and heard clearly for the very first time the tinkling of the tiny silver bell on its chain.

Old Tsereng must have noticed my vision had cleared for suddenly the belt and its ornaments disappeared from my view to be replaced a moment later by his pitted, lined face. The narrow, dark eyes stared at me in silence for a long time as he squatted beside me. When he spoke, his voice was soft. 'Who are you, Han? Why do your people seek to hunt you down like an animal?'

In my fear I tried to rise up, but he restrained me with both hands. When he had calmed me he made me drink the life-giving mare's milk. Then he told me everything he had seen since he had plucked me out of the burning grass four long nights before. He understood more Chinese than he spoke. He had learned it fifty years earlier in the southern part of the Mongol lands when rapacious capitalist Chinese traders feasted off Inner Mongolia by buying cheap from the nomads and selling dear. He had his people's ingrained historical suspicion of the 'great nation of China'. These horsemen of the grasslands, so different from my own people, had since time began been either defending them-selves against China or attacking her. By comparison the small wandering tribes of Siberia to the north had caused them no trouble, had been of little historical account. That was why the tutelage of the Russians had been so easily accepted by the Mongols and that was why that night old Tsereng committed his life loyally and willingly to my protection and survival—to keep me from the clutches of those predators from Peking he had seen set up a hue and cry upon the finding of my shoe.

THE DEATH OF LIN PIAO

'But why, Han? Why do they want to hunt you?' He always
called me 'Han', the name of my race, and never once asked me
my personal name. In his question he had used his native Mongol
words *soron moljikh*, which are very powerful, meaning 'to draw
towards themselves and gnaw like a bone'. As he waited for my
reply, the lines gouged into his face by time and the fierce wind of
the steppes deepened with concern.

Although weakened and in pain, I tried to explain. I told him
of the great coincidence that had made him pitch his yurt on
the night of 12 September on that point of the world's surface
that was identified on maps by the geographic co-ordinates
111.15 East and 47.42 North. This part of his beloved steppe-
land, I explained, was one of the remotest regions of the populated world. In China all maps of this region were forty years
out of date. This fact had encouraged those in Peking who had
plotted Marshall Lin's death to print false charts indicating that
a large military airfield had been built on the empty desolate
spot where I now lay in his yurt.

As the yak-dung fire spluttered low in the open hearth and the
wind moaned round the felt walls of the tent I explained how
Lin Piao and his wife were put aboard secretly in a closed compartment, unconscious, if not already dead, and how a handful
of others had been duped into flying with him in the doomed
airliner.

I explained how power-mad and ruthless plotters had cunningly
involved other countries—America, Israel and Russia—in their
violent intrigues and that since I had miraculously survived and
was alive to tell of this great treachery I was a danger to the
success of their plans. It was for this reason they would not sleep
easily until my life was terminated and their terrible secret
made completely safe.

Perhaps fortunately I did not know then what I know today.
This awful knowledge that I have would perhaps have under-
mined my very will to recover and survive. But I could not
know then that in 1976 these same vicious demons would be
plotting a greater and more terrible crime—the killing of our
great leader Chairman Mao Tse-tung himself!

On that bleak and windswept night on the Mongolian steppes
in the autumn of 1971, however, old Tsereng in the warmth of

35

his tent listened to my words in silence, nodding his hoary old head from time to time. He lit and relit his slender pipe while I talked, puffing the smoke towards the fire, but never speaking a word. He sat without moving until long after the animals had quietened and his wife and daughter had begun snoring on their beds of fur.

Then he bent over me to make me comfortable for the night and spoke in a whisper in my ear. 'Soon horsemen will come riding up from the south. They will be looking for you. They can travel here from China overland in a three-day journey.' He rested a gnarled hand gently on my shoulder in a gesture of reassurance and grinned a sudden, toothless grin. 'But they shall not find you. We shall move on—and keep moving.' Without another word he stretched himself out then on the ground beside the fire and went to sleep.

When I woke at the next dawn he was gone. He didn't return until the sun was high in the middle of the day and then he reported that he had again been secretly observing the activity around the crashed Trident. At first light he had seen a new group of high-ranking Russian officers arrive. They brought with them a strange man, he said, in crumpled civilian clothes whom he had not seen before. He was a white-skinned European, but he did not have the tense severity of demeanour of the Russian comrades. He was a small, thin, hunched man with a shock of white hair, a shaggy white moustache and thick spectacles. His face was deeply lined and very pale and Tsereng guessed he was almost as old as himself.

Old Tsereng had watched him closely through his binoculars. Immediately on his arrival he had waved his arms and shouted, dismissing all the Russian officers and ordering them to retreat several hundred yards. Then he had wandered very slowly among the wreckage on his own for two hours staring intently at the ground, shaking his head and muttering to himself. All the time he kept his hands in his pockets, touching nothing. He chain smoked, but never removed the cigarettes from his mouth. From time to time this white-haired man drew a flask from his hip pocket and drank from it—old Tsereng again reported this gleefully because it was silver and flashed in the sun. When he had made a thorough inspection of the whole area the man began taking photographs with a tiny camera he carried in his pocket. About this time a convoy of articulated lorries and cranes appeared, rumbling across the plain from the direction of Ulan Bator. They drew up and waited until the white-haired man had completed his inspection. Then he gave a signal and began supervising the removal of the wreckage from the scene. First wooden boxes were brought by the soldiers and he directed them to collect together small fragments of blackened metal and ashes from different parts of the site. Then he motioned the cranes forward and directed them with great care as they hoisted what was left of the main sections of the dismembered aircraft—the two wings, the fuselage and the tail section—onto the lorries. When this was done he gave more orders to the soldiers, and several hundred brushes were issued to them. They lined up in long files across the flat grassland and began moving back and forth sweeping the tiniest shreds of wreckage together and packing them away in canvas sacks.

Finally this white-haired man got back in his car with the officers and led the convoy of low-loaders and cranes slowly away across the steppes to the west. When old Tsereng left his hiding place for the last time, only the long lines of Russian soldiers were left still, slowly sweeping the grassland with their brushes and carefully filling up their little canvas sacks with what was left of the black dust from the Trident.

The rest of that day before dark was spent in making preparations for our departure. The long strips of cheese and solid cream laid out on the roof of the yurt to lose moisture were removed and stored. Belongings were baled and when night fell the yurt was taken down. Other chattels were folded and loaded onto two-humped camels and a litter of tent poles was built for me and attached to an aging and gentle horse. Old Tsereng's two sons, themselves no longer young, also struck their tents, prepared their families and bunched their herds ready for the journey.

We left before the moon was up, travelling south-west. The camels, laden with 500 lbs of baggage each, could easily cover up to twenty-five miles in a night's journeying, but the slow-moving herds travelled more ponderously. The trek was very painful for me. My splinted limbs were jarred constantly. But I was prepared to endure any depths of pain to remove myself from the scene of horror where the Trident had crashed—and where, if I stayed, I would certainly lose my life.

With the coming of autumn, the *arats* usually begin to move their flocks and herds out of the lush river valleys and marshlands to less protected areas where the purifying winds sweep away the autumn insects that otherwise afflict the animals. When winter approaches the herds are moved into sheltered valleys to endure the cold weather there, and do not emerge onto the southward facing slopes of the mountains until spring, when biting winds blow from the north. So although our going was perhaps early and we were travelling at night instead of during the day, the other nomads we encountered accepted our ponderous passage without question, calling friendly greetings from the darkness as though pleased that the rhythmic, shifting pattern of their own restless lives was being reaffirmed afresh for them by our passing.

We travelled only at night and camped by day, because we wished no questions to be asked about why an injured Chinese army man was being dragged along on a litter. In four nights we covered a hundred miles, swinging south-west in a long arc to give the capital, Ulan Bator, a wide berth. Old Tsereng reported gleefully on return to the yurt on the fourth day that our trek was already stirring other herdsmen to strike their camps early. The whole region began to seethe with movement and herds were soon criss-crossing on the plains as they each sought out their favourite autumn grazing grounds. This would make it much more difficult, old Tsereng said delightedly, for pursuers to search the yurt camps that had been pitched in the region of Jibhalantayn Bulag at the time of the crash. All were now quickly dispersing to the four winds across the steppes.

We journeyed on for six weeks without cease, rising night after night over new mountain rims and moving down under clear, star-lit heavens into other plains all speckled thick with their own herds of cattle, sheep and horses. At each summit old Tsereng, an unashamed shamanist, dismounted to place another stone reverently on the neat little piles of rocks that had grown slowly over the centuries in all high places. This was to placate spirits believed to dwell there and give thanks for our successful scaling of each height.

Old Tsereng seemed to grow straighter in the saddle with each ascent. His eyes gleamed with a new fire. His own ancestors and those of the horse beneath him had once conquered their way from Asia to Europe and now he was again taking on the greatest enemy of all from south of the Great Wall in his last struggle! Although it was taking the form of a strategic retreat, his stiffly proud posture as he topped the crest of each mountain pass betrayed the deep satisfaction he felt that he was outwitting and outriding them again across his own fierce grasslands and mountain ranges.

TOKYO, Friday—Rumours circulating here say the Kremlin has strengthened military units massing along the northern frontier of China. American intelligence advice speaks of the movement of at least five and possibly ten new Soviet armoured divisions into the frontier area.

The Daily Telegraph, 26 September 1971

3

The cine camera with the telephoto lens that had been trained silently on the entrance to Scholefield's block of flats for the past eight days began whirring the moment Yang appeared limping down the steps. Mounted by an attic window in a mansion block on the other side of Bentinck Street, it had first begun rolling to record Scholefield's arrival home. It had been restarted to film Yang as he approached hesitantly along the pavement on foot half an hour later, and now the Chinese operating it swung the camera on its tripod to follow him back the way he'd come.

Because the evening was stiflingly humid and the sky overcast, the light was fading early. But the cameraman kept rolling anyway as Yang neared the end of the street and he was rewarded when he picked up a black Mini with smoked windows as it pulled out of a side turning. It drove slowly alongside the limping Chinese and a door swung open before the car had stopped. The moment Yang had clambered awkwardly inside it shot off at high speed and turned right into the one-way flow of traffic heading north up Gloucester Place.

In the shadowy interior a man with a chalk-white face wearing steel-rimmed spectacles was sitting smiling on the back seat. He dropped an enquiring hand on Yang's arm and asked solicitously in Russian how the interview had gone.

'To plan, Comrade Razduhev. I left the folios and offered

the appointment for mid-day at the market.' Yang made his reply in halting Russian, staring straight ahead through the windscreen. He sat rigidly upright until Razduhev had removed his hand from his sleeve. Then he sank back against the upholstery and mopped his sweating face with a handkerchief.

'Did Scholefield seem to rise to the bait?'

'I think so. He can't miss the folios.'

'But you gave him no hint of your real purpose during the conversation?'

'No, Comrade Razduhev.'

The Russian sighed loudly. 'Yang Tsai-chien, how many times must I ask you? "Comrade Razduhev" is not friendly, is it? Be more familiar. We are friends. Although only for a short time more. Listen, I won't even have you call me Vladimir. Call me Valodi.'

Yang didn't reply.

'And Comrade Bogdarin would like you to call him Boris. Wouldn't you, Boris?' The driver of the car nodded and smiled a token smile into the driving mirror without turning.

'We would like to think you remembered your four years in the Soviet Union with some pleasure. Wouldn't we, Boris?'

The driver nodded again and smiled grimly to himself, concentrating on the road.

'There are many worse jobs in Moscow, Tsai-chien, than working as an improver for the Chinese section of the Foreign Languages Publishing House.' He laughed unpleasantly. 'I know you had to work privately in your apartment under constant guard—but it was among the most luxurious and comfortable in Moscow. I hope you feel you were treated in accordance with your high political importance.'

Yang drew a long breath and nodded. 'I feel the strain of the past week and the past hour, Comrade Razduhev. I would prefer to rest quietly now.'

The Russian patted his arm again. 'And so you shall, Tsai-chien,' he said, exaggerating the concern in his voice. 'And so you shall. No more work or worry now until you go to market tomorrow.' The Russian paused and looked quickly at the Chinese. 'We have arranged a little surprise. You will catch a glimpse of your cousin there. In the propaganda kiosk. Just to reassure you that all is arranged.' He removed his spectacles and polished them absently on his sleeve. 'Madame Tan is one of your Party's more attractive comrades, isn't she, Tsai-chien?'

Yang closed his eyes without replying. He slumped lower in the seat and let his head fall backwards as if exhausted. The Russian continued patting his arm unnecessarily. 'It will not be possible of course for you to speak or betray any sign of recognition.' He stopped patting Yang's arm and gripped it with a sudden fierceness. 'You understand that quite clearly, don't you, Tsai-chien?'

Yang's eyes opened wide suddenly with the pain. Not until he had nodded his acquiescence did the Russian relax his grip.

The Chinese at the attic window switched off the camera and turned to pick up a telephone. He dialled the number of one of the illegal basement gambling dens on the south side of Gerrard Street in Soho's Chinatown and settled down comfortably in a chair by the window, prepared for what he knew might be a long wait.

Inside the dingy club a hard-core residue of the afternoon gambling crowd was still hunched round the lino-covered fan tan table, clutching sheaves of purple twenty-pound notes in their hands. The bare stone floor was littered deep with apple and orange peel, broken monkey-nut shells and spilled tea. A bent, arthritic cleaner pushed a broom with painful slowness among the gamblers' feet, going through the motions of sweeping up in preparation for the evening session. Under the garish glare of the naked light bulbs hanging above the table the unsmiling male faces stared transfixed at the little heap of white shirt buttons which the croupier, a thin, hollow-chested Chinese with quick glittering eyes, had just scooped out of a saucepan sunk into the table top. When he glanced round the table the gamblers avoided his gaze.

The telephone began to ring behind a closed door as he concealed a random fistful of buttons under a small saucepan lid. But he ignored the ringing, waiting patiently while the last notes were pushed onto the four chalked squares at either end of the table. When all movement had ceased and a hush of expectancy had fallen over the crowd, he lifted the lid and spread the heap of buttons deftly across the table with a short curved stick, forming two crescent moons. Working with a swift and practised dexterity he slid the buttons rapidly back into the sunken saucepan in groups of four until only two solitary buttons were left on the brown lino. A squat Chinese youth standing at his side quickly paid off those men who had backed Number Two on the chalked squares, then slipped smoothly into the driving seat and scooped up a new handful of buttons as the hollow-chested croupier rose and moved without hurrying towards the door behind which the telephone was still ringing.

The door opened onto an even dingier room that was both a kitchen and a makeshift office. The croupier pushed the door open far enough to pass through, but not wide enough for those around the gambling tables to catch a glimpse of the tall, slender Chinese woman sitting impassively beside the empty table on which the telephone was ringing. He walked across and picked up the receiver without looking at her.

'He's just left Scholefield's flat and been collected by one of the unmarked Soviet trade mission cars from Highgate,' said the voice of the Chinese cameraman in a thick Cantonese accent.

The croupier glanced back at the door as if to make sure he had closed it. 'Good. Dismantle your equipment. And get the film back here quick!'

He replaced the telephone but kept his hand on it and looked enquiringly at the impassive face of the seated woman. A tap with a faulty washer dripped loudly into a cracked, stained sink in one corner and the rattle of the buttons on the table top came faintly through the closed door as he waited.

'Tell the embassy.' She spoke authoritatively without looking up at him.

He picked up the telephone again and dialled the number of the Chinese Embassy in Portland Place. When a voice answered he said quietly: 'It is confirmed. We have film.'

There was a pause at the other end of the line. Then: 'Very well. Continue to gather photographic evidence.'

When he'd hung up he turned to find the squat youth who'd taken over the fan tan table looking at him anxiously from the open doorway. The gambling room behind him was empty, the makeshift table suddenly deserted under the naked light bulbs.

'The American was at the top of the steps,' he said in a sibilant whisper.

The eyes of the silent woman seated at the table blazed suddenly. She gestured furiously through the doorway. 'Get those frightened rabbits back and restart the fan tan. He's *not* police, tell them.'

The youth turned and shouted at the old man with the broom and pointed angrily towards the steps leading up to street level. Then he went out and closed the door behind him.

The croupier sat down opposite the woman. 'What does Peking want us to do now?' He looked respectfully into her broad Han face. Her features were strong and regular and she wore her hair piled elaborately on top of her head, held in place with tortoise-shell combs. She was wearing an expensive leather trouser suit tailored in Hong Kong and a lot of thin gold bracelets and rings decorated her hands.

'Follow the contingency plan! They want the "impostor" returned to Peking alive.' She belaboured the word 'impostor' with heavy sarcasm, then paused. 'And of course they want Scholefield too.'

The croupier grinned a sudden gleeful grin and rose and walked slowly over to the draining board. He picked up a half empty bottle of mahogany-coloured Chinese brandy. He rinsed a dirty glass and poured a measure. 'The Russians *could* have invented him. But couldn't they just as well have been keeping quiet about a survivor for the last five years waiting for the right moment to produce him—' He tossed back the contents of the glass in one gulp and smacked his lips. '—like a rabbit out of a hat?'

The woman watched him with only faintly concealed distaste. 'The Party leadership says there were no survivors.' The hollow tone of her voice was both contemptuous and disbelieving. 'We shall see tomorrow.'

The croupier began grinning inanely again, but the expression dissolved abruptly at the sound of a tap on the door. A moment later the old floor-sweeper poked his grizzled head into the room. He held the door wide to show the same crowd of faces now gathered around the table again. They had taken up precisely the same places as before, like a tableau reformed behind a theatre curtain. All were staring obediently towards the squat youth, trying hard to ignore the crisp, incongruous sound of leather-soled shoes descending the stone basement steps. The buttons had been spread again on the table top but nobody had placed any bets. The gamblers kept their eyes dutifully averted but were obviously following the slow, deliberate footsteps with all their other senses as they came nearer along the bare concrete floor of the corridor outside.

The next moment a tall Caucasian man wearing a pale suit, a straw fedora and dark glasses appeared in the doorway. His lips parted in a broad confident grin as he raised his right hand and mimed a silent knock on the open door. The eyes of all the illegal gamblers swivelled as one man to see if approval was to be given to the stranger.

The woman stared at the tall man for a moment then motioned the hollow-chested croupier quickly from the room. As he hurried out a babble of solid sound rose from the men round the table again as they began placing bets once more.

When she had closed the door behind him, the newcomer offered his hand formally and greeted her in fluent Mandarin that bore only the faintest trace of his native American accent. 'Very glad to see you again, Tan Sui-ling. It's been too long.'

'You are very welcome, Mr. Ketterman.' She spoke formally, moving another rickety chair up to the table that was covered with a frayed and faded oil cloth. She set out the brandy bottle and two clean glasses, and Ketterman removed his hat as they sat down opposite each other.

'Your information was correct, Mr. Ketterman. Scholefield was contacted an hour ago.'

He raised his shoulders and both hands in a silent 'What else did you expect?' gesture. He removed his sun glasses and gave her another crinkle-eyed smile. His steel grey hair was clipped short and his lean alert face and spare frame hinted at hours spent on summer tennis courts and winter ski slopes far from the unhealthy Soho gambling cellar. 'We don't make a habit of passing you "bum" information, Sui-ling, you should know that. Remember Seventy-one.' He smiled broadly again as he injected the crude Americanism deliberately into his easy flow of Chinese, and picked up the bottle. He filled the glass nearest

45

her, but left the other empty and replaced the bottle gently on the table top as if afraid it might explode. 'I told you about Marshall Lin in this very room, right? And this little dilly came from those same Israelis in Moscow too.'

She nodded her head gravely in formal thanks for his courtesy in filling her glass, but left it untouched. Before sitting down she had removed her jacket and her long, slender arms were bare to the shoulders. Although her breasts appeared boyishly flat beneath the sleeveless white blouse, he spent several seconds openly searching the weave of the thin cotton for signs of a brassière underneath. He grinned broadly again when she folded her arms deliberately in front of her. But the level gaze she turned on him was unusually self-possessed for a Chinese woman, betraying no hint of embarrassment.

'And do they really think anyone in the world will believe that this so-called "survivor" is genuine?' Although her tone was contemptuous he noticed that she was watching his face closely.

He grinned again. 'Let's just say we're keeping an open mind.'

'There can be no survivor. The Party leadership made a thorough and conclusive investigation!'

Ketterman raised his hands before his face mockingly as though at gun point. 'Maybe your betters in Peking have never told all, even to people like you.' He dropped his hands suddenly on the table, palms downward, making a loud slapping sound. 'What is the reaction of your comrades in Peking to our information?'

Her dark eyes glittered. 'Those the Soviet revisionists wish to incriminate want this lying imposter brought to Peking to be exposed.'

Ketterman pursed his lips and whistled in wonderment: 'Is *that* all?'

'Yes! And the degree of your assistance in this will be a test of your sincerity.'

He tipped his chair onto its back legs and grinned at her through half-closed eyes. 'Hey, this is England, remember. They have some old-fashioned notions here about individual freedom backed up with real live written laws. The "survivor", whoever he is, might want to stay.'

'Your agency has resources and manpower wherever it has the will to use them!'

'We also have allies closer to our way of thinking, who we love just a shade more than we love Chairman Mao.' Ketterman pulled out a packet of cigarettes and lit one. He threw back his head and tipped his chair again, staring reflectively into the spiralling smoke. Suddenly he let the chair crash down onto its front legs and clapped his hands together in front of him, staring at her. 'Who runs the Triad protection teams around here, Sui-ling?'

She cocked her head curiously on one side. 'A man named Johnny Fei. Why?'

'Where is he now?'

'Outside playing fan tan.'

'Johnny the Fat-boy eh?' said Ketterman softly to himself, translating the name into English. 'Can you get him in?'

She went to the door and a moment later came back followed slowly by a slender, expensively dressed Chinese man in his middle thirties. Without waiting for an introduction Ketterman stood up. 'My face is pale, but my heart is red, Johnny.' He spoke slowly in Mandarin and advanced towards Fei grinning broadly and holding up his right hand with the middle finger extended.

Fei's thick dark hair was slicked smoothly back with oil in the fashion of a Thirties film star. His narrow body had obviously won him his nickname, but his loose relaxed stance as he watched Ketterman approach betrayed a high degree of physical self confidence. His features were sharp and regular but his heavily-lidded eyes gave his hooded face a wary, watchful expression. A pale calfskin jacket was thrown loosely round his elegant shoulders over a floral silk shirt, and crisply tailored check sports trousers. On his feet he wore crocodile skin shoes.

Ketterman stopped in front of him and he eyed the American suspiciously for a long moment without speaking.

'The red rice of our army contains sand and stones. Can you eat stones?' Ketterman's grin broadened and he held his right hand higher in front of the Chinese man's face. 'Can you, Johnny? Huh?'

'If our brothers can eat them, so can we!'

'Attaboy, Johnny.' Ketterman slapped him on the shoulder with his left hand. 'Come on, ask me now where I was born and I'll say "under the peach tree" and where I live and I'll give you

that stuff about the "topmost summit of Five Finger Mountain".'
He laughed uproariously and waved his extended finger in the
air again. 'In that "house that is third from the right—and third
from the left".' He shook his head. 'I *like* that.'

The Chinese watched him silently without smiling. Ketterman
suddenly stopped laughing and put his hands back in his pockets.

'You know Triad ritual well, Mr. Ketterman.'

'I know a Red Stick when I see one, Johnny,' said Ketterman
quietly, his face suddenly serious. 'And fools don't reach that
rank in the Triads. You could be just the man to help me. I might
need one of your chop-chop teams to help me on a little job.'

The Chinese rocked back on the heels of his feet and nodded.
'They're very expensive to outsiders.'

'Sui-ling will stand character reference for me, Johnny. I don't
know what or where the job will be exactly yet.' He took out his
wallet and peeled off five hundred-dollar bills and put them on
the table beside Fei's right hand. 'But I'm prepared to put down
this non-returnable deposit just for you to keep your top team
of, say, half a dozen guys standing by ready at five minutes'
notice over the next couple of days.'

Fei picked up the notes quickly and folded them away inside
the breast pocket of his shirt. He glanced once more at Ketterman
then sauntered casually back to the door. 'If Sui-ling says it's
okay—it's okay.' He shrugged his elegant shoulders once and
swaggered out through the door to join the scrofulous crowd at
the fan tan table again.

Ketterman picked up the brandy bottle and slowly filled his
own glass. He lifted it towards Tan Sui-ling and winked. 'Sino-
American co-operation—lips and teeth!' He bared his gums in
an exaggerated grimace and tapped his teeth then his top lip with
his forefinger to emphasise their close proximity. Then he drank
the brandy straight down and, still grinning broadly, walked out
of the door.

FOLIO NUMBER FOUR

Mongolia in its eastern half is mainly plain, circled about with mountains. But its western half is mainly mountains interspersed only intermittently with flatlands. By November, we had left the eastern plains and entered this western mountainous region. By then my fractured legs had mended sufficiently for me to sit painfully astride a walking horse, and we had begun travelling by day and resting by night. Soon we reached the foothills of the mighty Altai range that provide, in the north-west corner of the country, both a natural barrier and the official border with the Soviet Union. In this region the shallow bowls of the mountain-ringed flatlands are much smaller and the rims of the intervening heights twist and interlock like irregular honeycombs. Here, while the herds grazed on the plains, we found shelter from the winds in narrow dales where patches of green, pleasant woodland stretch down out of the dense mountain forests above. We rested in this region for the winter and gradually I recovered and grew strong again. It was there that I learned to live the simple life of old Tsereng and his family, and began helping with the daily domestic tasks.

It was there too that I began later to take my turn with the herds, holding a long rifle astride a horse through the night, guarding the livestock against the marauding bands of wolves that came down swiftly and silently out of the dark mountain forests. I felt at peace in that remote land. It was not very long before I decided that I wanted no more in life than to repay through such service the debt of gratitude to old Tsereng for delivering me from the holocaust of the Trident. After the constant turmoil and suspicion in China, the harsh, simple life was paradise.

Tsereng's wife and daughter spoke no Chinese and I needed only a very few words to assist them in the simple tasks of sustaining our lives through the bitter winter. But nevertheless, a warm unspoken sympathy grew up among us. His daughter, plump, heavy-hipped and approaching middle age, had once lived in the capital, Ulan Bator. But she had lost her husband and children in a terrible fire that gutted the workers' apartment block where they lived, so she had returned sadly to her family on the grasslands. A silent, inward-looking woman, she carried the tragedy with her always in her eyes. Sometimes at night I caught her unawares, staring at me over the flickering flames of the hearth, and slowly I came to realise, without her saying, that we shared an instinctive fellowship—because I too had escaped death by fire.

Nevertheless I was still astonished when, on the coldest night of the winter, with Tsereng and his wife and the animals grunting and snorting in their sleep, she crawled naked to me across the yurt and slipped silently beneath my sheepskin. Without words and with tears on her cheeks she offered me the comfort of her body. On many nights after that as the screaming wind whipped the bare trees outside, and the wolves howled higher up the forested slopes of the Altai, she came secretly to join me in a mute physical communion that eased her unbearable anguish and brought warmth and refreshment to both our injured souls.

I believed then I would stay with old Tsereng forever. The snows came and went, spring blossomed early and we moved eastward once more. When summer arrived we shifted down into the river valleys and in May and June I assisted in the sheep-shearing and the calving of the cows. At the end of June I joined in the almost celebratory ritual of rounding up and tethering the foals in lines alongside their mothers so that the milking of the mares could begin—and with it of course the vital preparation of the new supply of *kumiss*.

It was only when the second sheep-shearing began at the beginning of September that I realised suddenly a whole year had passed since the crash. About the same time I began to fancy that old Tsereng's daughter, whose name was Kiki, was growing even plumper than before. It was with a sudden surge of pleasure that I began to suspect she might be pregnant with my child.

But it was just then that it all ended, without warning, on a night of torrential rain.

The day had been filled with bright autumn sunshine under a sky of piercing blue, such as I have only ever seen in Mongolia. As we were gathering for the evening meal before the yurt, however, clouds raced up over the horizon, darkening the sky like a hastily drawn curtain. We moved inside to eat and soon a monsoon downpour was hammering loudly on the felt roof. Darkness fell immediately and a dung fire was lit in the open hearth to keep out the damp chill which had descended. Inside, crouched around the fire, we felt secure and warm, and we ate in silence, listening to the fierce beat of the rain. I remember smiling happily at Kiki, and she did a rare thing—she smiled back. I had never seen her smile before. I looked down directly at her thickening girth but she looked away quickly into the fire. I felt sure, with a surge of pride, that she was pregnant.

One of Tsereng's sons had been helping us with the milking and was eating with us. When the force of the downpour and a sudden wind began to shake the yurt, he got up with a laugh and went out to tighten the rope bands bound around it, to prevent it falling in on us. It was his dying scream from outside that gave us our first warning.

The next moment there was a great rending sound and the felt wall beside me was slashed open from top to bottom. I stared in horror at the figure of a man standing outside in the storm. Even though he was drenched with rain and disguised in the clothes of a nomadic herdsman I recognised Chiao Feng, one of Wang Tung-hsing's chief lieutenants from Peking. He held a long curved knife in one hand and a pistol in the other. His lips were drawn back from his teeth in a snarl of triumph—and his eyes held unwavering on mine.

Old Tsereng rose slowly to his feet, his hand reaching for the hilt of the decorated dagger at his belt. But there was a shout from the doorway behind us and we turned to find another dripping figure holding a sub-machine gun pointing in our direction. Old Tsereng's hands fell to his sides and for a moment nobody moved or spoke. The rain on the roof and the shriek of the rising wind were the only sounds in the yurt. Tsereng's wife and Kiki remained squatting motionless on the floor, their mouths agape with fear.

Chiao waved his knife menacingly in the air towards old Tsereng and the women, then stepped warily up behind me. He pinioned my arms quickly and had just begun to bind my wrists when the old man sprang. The long pointed dagger that he'd taken from the dead body of the vanquished camel train leader forty years before buried itself in Chiao's chest above his heart. At the same moment the man in the doorway opened fire with the machine gun.

He held his finger curled tight around the trigger until the magazine was exhausted, turning the muzzle this way and that across the yurt, dragging a broken line of gaping scarlet punctures across the back of old Tsereng and the bodies of his wife and daughter on the floor. Neither of them screamed or uttered any sound as they died. Old Tsereng clung to his adversary for a moment, then his heavy bulk toppled slowly backward to the ground. His hand was clenched so tight round the hilt of his dagger that he dragged it out of Chiao's lung and fell dead with the crimson-bladed weapon still clutched in his right fist.

Chiao's companion was joined silently in the doorway by a third Chinese and together they finished binding my wrists. Then they attended to Chiao's wound and one of them helped him outside into his saddle. I was dragged outside too and thrust onto the back of another horse. The third man mounted up behind me and turned the animal's head back towards the yurt. I could see now that old Tsereng's son was lying dead on the ground outside.

The first of Chiao's companions took a large can of petrol and splashed it around quickly inside the yurt. Then he threw the can inside, lit a large rag-bound torch already soaked in petrol and raced for his horse. He rode to the door and tossed the burning torch inside. As we turned to ride into the driving rain, the interior of the yurt exploded with a thump and began burning fiercely. It continued blazing despite the torrential downpour and faded only slowly into the darkness behind us as we rode away.

WASHINGTON, Sunday—The United States has received what officials here describe as the first 'hard evidence' from Peking that Lin Piao, China's Defence Minister and constitutional successor to Chairman Mao Tse-tung is seriously—and possibly fatally—ill. But they will not disclose or discuss the origin of the reports.

New York Times, 11 October 1971

4

'Do you think Yang himself is the survivor?' Nina turned on her side as she spoke and raised herself up on her elbow. The single sheet covering her slipped, revealing her naked shoulders and breasts. She looked quickly at Scholefield, but he was oblivious. Dressed only in a bathrobe, he was sitting on the edge of the bed with his back to her, staring at the pink folios he'd propped up on the tea tray between the milk jug and the sugar basin.

'That looks like the inference we're supposed to draw.' He spoke over his shoulder and wiped the back of his hand across his damp forehead.

'Couldn't it be true?'

'It's just too damned sensational for words.' He began leafing through the pink sheets again and Nina reluctantly covered herself. Although it was only nine o'clock in the morning the temperature in the room was already in the upper seventies. Outside the open window the low sky glowed with a dull metallic incandescence as if some great burnished tureen cover had been clamped over London to keep the breathless heat trapped close to the ground. A stale, dry, sauna-cabin smell of scorched wood hung in the air outside.

'He did limp badly, didn't he?'

Scholefield nodded without turning his head. 'Yes—and I

don't believe that cock and bull tale about being a bent PLA acupuncture student.'

'It didn't ring true to me either. He doesn't seem the type. But why such an elaborate cover story?'

'I think for some reason I was *meant* to see through it. It could have been a signal to look for something more profound.'

Nina smiled. 'Like the folios in the chocolate box?'

Scholefield stared at the pink sheets of paper without seeing them.

'China is well known for its sexual puritanism—but homosexuality is not a *capital* offence. It's frowned on, of course, politically like rape and promiscuity. They say it smacks of "counter-revolutionary" behaviour from the old, pre-liberation days—but I've never heard of it being punished by death.'

Nina moved towards him and tangled her fingers gently in the hair at the nape of his neck. The sheet fell away again as she leaned closer to whisper in his ear. 'Demonstrate a bit of counter-revolutionary behaviour for me right now, could you, sweetheart?'

He ignored her and poured himself another cup of tea. 'What's more, the Party's recommended marrying ages in China are 28 for men and 26 for women—not 35. If he knows as much as he claims to about me, our devious Comrade Yang would know I should spot that sort of deliberate mistake pretty quickly.'

Nina struck her forehead loudly with the palm of her hand and fell back on the pillows. 'Eureka! Of course, Holmes! This Fu Man-chu's an impostor! Why didn't I see that before?' When she stopped giggling and opened her eyes he was sipping his tea thoughtfully and staring serious-faced at the folios again. She sighed loudly, pulled the sheet right up over her head and held it there, lying rigid, without breathing, in the attitude of a corpse.

Scholefield continued reading and only the dull hum of traffic noise from outside broke the hot silence in the room. Suddenly Nina took a deep breath and arched her back, pressing herself up against the tight-drawn sheet until her nipples stood out like buttons. Her voice came through the sheet, petulant and muffled. 'If only you were half as good a Nina-watcher as you are a China-watcher—'

Scholefield turned slowly towards her. He gazed distractedly at the contours of her body for a moment, then laughed despite himself. He snatched the sheet from her fingers, peeled it back and flung it aside.

'If only I was, then what?'

She pouted at him, still holding the posture. 'You'd know how self-sacrificial I'd been, coming back here last night and finding you in a jet-lagged coma. Then pretending not to notice when you got up every couple of hours through the night to sneak off and read those damned folios in the kitchen.'

He stood up abruptly, unknotting the belt of his bathrobe. She collapsed with a little scream of mock horror as he took it off and walked purposefully round to her side of the bed. He stopped and stood smiling down at her. 'This heat doesn't affect your Irish-Italian nymphomania at all, then?'

She touched his nearest knee with the first two fingers of her right hand and watched them walk slowly up his bare thigh. 'It makes me worse—especially after ten-day symposia on Peking's military strength in Ottawa.' She gazed up hot-eyed into his face. 'My intuitive guess is that maybe China and me have something in common—perhaps we both want something from you.'

He bent over her and the tips of their tongues met between her teeth. They tantalised each other slowly with their mouths and hands until passion finally engulfed them and swept them both into a long and tender frenzy. Afterwards they lay clenched together for a long time with their eyes closed, their minds filled only with the blind sensations of their bodies.

'Christ almighty, sweetheart, you know I really begin to suspect I'm only a year or two away from falling in love with you.' He breathed deeply and pulled back from her, touching the damp hair on her forehead wonderingly with his fingertips.

She shook her head in a little motion of disbelief. Her eyes were bright, her cheeks flushed. When she spoke her voice betrayed more than a hint of her original Irish brogue. 'I'm not entirely indifferent to you either.' She traced a slow pattern in the perspiration on his back with one finger. 'Could it be, do you think, because you're such a beautiful indifferent bastard most of the time? In combination with that devastating academic mind of yours, of course.'

He smiled. 'Maybe that has got something to do with it.'

The traffic hum from outside was growing into a dull roar with the advancing day. They lay contentedly side by side, Nina with her eyes closed, Scholefield staring at the ceiling, drifting into their separate thoughts. For a long time neither of them spoke.

When she opened her eyes she saw his brow was again furrowed in a frown. She raised herself to look into his face. 'What's so important about how Lin Piao died, Richard? If it happened in 1971 isn't it all rather old hat now?'

'In one way it is. But still it happens to be one of the greatest unsolved political mysteries of our times. And if the folios are genuine and he *was* murdered as they suggest *and* those responsible are now plotting to assassinate Mao, there might be the odd crank in Washington and Moscow, not to mention Peking itself, who'd be interested in the details.'

She punched him quickly on the solar plexus with a small fist and he jack-knifed into a sitting position, clutching at her wrist. 'Don't be so bloody sarcastic. The arcane doings of 800 million Chinese may be child's play to you and your clever friends—'

He grinned and dropped her wrist. 'Wrong. If you laid all the Sinologists in the world end to end they still wouldn't reach a conclusion.'

'Why not?'

'Because they just don't know any more than you do about what really happened to Comrade Lin.'

'What do the Chinese themselves say happened to him?'

'For ten months after the Trident crash there was a deafening silence out of Peking. Then suddenly the following July they started to gush out statements saying he had, after all, died in the crash in Mongolia with his wife and son and a few hangers-on when the Trident ran out of fuel. Trying to defect to the Soviet Union, he was, they say, after three bungled attempts to do away with Mao and take over as the great sun in all their Chinese hearts. And they've stuck to that colourful story ever since, through thick and thin.'

She hugged her knees in front of her chest and rested her chin on them, smiling wickedly at him. 'And why do all you smug Sinologists lying end to end think they shouldn't?'

'Because in the absence of any evidence really worth that name there've been contradictions by the score. The Russians got the wreckage and the burned-out corpses—and may still have 'em in some grisly deep freeze under the Kremlin for all we know. But although they've never said anything official about their findings, Kosygin told Pierre Trudeau casually on a trip to Ottawa that they'd dug bullets out of some of the barbecued carcasses. Now, unless all the Chinese comrades suddenly wanted to read the empty fuel gauge at once and started taking pot shots at each other for that sole privilege, that makes Peking's story a bit suspect from the start, doesn't it?'

She reached out a hand and stroked his hair. 'I'd believe anything *you* said, darling. I'm sure you're right.'

He brushed her hand away impatiently. 'The Mongolians and the Russians said the bodies were burned beyond recognition—but Chou En-lai told a group of visiting American newspaper editors much later that Chinese diplomats had gone to the scene and identified Lin and the others on the spot. And buried 'em there, what's more. There's a lot else besides, but do you begin to see what I mean?'

He leaned across the bed to reach for his bathrobe but Nina beat him to it. She wrapped it round her shoulders, danced swiftly out of reach, picked up the tea tray from the bedside table and moved towards the door. As she passed him Scholefield reached out and patted her rump affectionately. 'And what's more, my lissom love, whenever all the evidence available in the West is fed into the big China-watching computers in places like Harvard and the American Consulate General in Hong Kong they just rip their bolts loose and get up off their pedestals and rush round shaking their heads and chanting, "Lies, lies, all lies".'

'I think I'm beginning to get a glimmer, Professor, of why you preferred cuddling those pink folios on the kitchen table all night —though I can't say I admire your choice.' She waggled her hips provocatively at him and disappeared grinning into the kitchen.

He heard her clattering the cups in the sink, then the doorbell rang and she went to answer it. When she returned a moment later she was clipping her long hair up on the top of her head in preparation for a shower. 'It was your uniformed voyeur, Moynahan. His eyes nearly fell out of his head. He said an American left some books for you while you were away. He's going to bring them up.'

Scholefield nodded and began to get out of bed. 'Some new American publications from Harvey Ketterman. He's a State Department Pekinologist. A good chum of mine. You'll meet him, he's over here for a couple of seminars.' He padded barefoot down the hall behind her to the bathroom.

'The mystery of Lin Piao would make a good plot for an old Hollywood B movie, wouldn't it?' she said over her shoulder. 'If it wasn't true.'

'It gets more like that the further you go into it.' He soaped his face and watched her long body in his shaving mirror as she tucked her hair inside a shower cap and climbed under the warm water jet. 'We know what fantasies the Chinese rank and file were asked to believe because facsimiles of their secret documents leaked out to Hong Kong and Taiwan. They make it sound as though Lin had a mixture of Buster Keaton, the Keystone cops and Harold Lloyd as co-conspirators.' He fitted a new blade carefully into his razor and began to scrape creamy lather from the side of his face.

'A soldier deputed to blow up Mao's train is supposed to have gone into a blue funk at the last moment and got his wife, who was a doctor, would you believe, to give him an injection to blur his vision so he couldn't see the train when it went by. Then further up the line they allegedly tried to kill Mao by leaking gas into the train's heating system—but found too late the vents in the Chairman's carriage were blocked. Then another would-be assassin fluffed a stabbing attack because he became totally over-awed by Mao's charisma after tricking his way into the great man's presence in the Forbidden City in Peking.'

Nina drew back the shower curtains and poked her head out. 'A case of first-knife nerves, do you think?'

'Okay, I know it sounds hilarious now. And Chou En-lai practically admitted to another foreign delegation later that all that was bunkum. But we might never know how close China and Russia came to the crunch over it. Or what it might have meant for the rest of us. Kissinger had just made his first secret visit to Peking a few weeks before—and America and China had been sworn enemies for twenty years up to then, remember. The Russians couldn't have been altogether happy about finding an unidentified aircraft heading out of China towards their heartland, in the middle of the night shortly after that event—if they didn't know it was coming.' He put down his razor and turned to wrap a large bath towel round her as she stepped out of the shower.

'But how could the Chinese hush up a plane crash like that in a foreign country for ten months?'

'They didn't hush up the crash itself. The Mongolians and the Russians forced their hand by putting out a bald official news agency report from Ulan Bator. Tass carried it too. But even that didn't appear until seventeen days after the crash—at the end of September. The Chinese had to admit then they'd lost a Trident. But they insisted it was a civilian plane. And they didn't come anywhere near admitting then they'd lost Mao's heir-apparent.'

Scholefield stepped under the shower, opened the cold tap and threw his head back under the stinging spray. He shook the water out of his eyes and shivered, despite the heat. 'We knew all hell had broken loose in China in the middle of September because military radio messages monitored in Japan recalled all China's troops urgently from leave. And the messages were going out *en clair*, not coded. They were obviously at panic stations. The American satellites detected a lot of unusual troop movements, and all civilian flights were suddenly grounded throughout the country. Foreigners in China were just stranded where they were. Then to cap it all the annual Liberation Day parade in Peking on October 1st was cancelled at the eleventh hour without any explanation. Whether it was civil war, or war with Russia, they were worried about—or both—we don't know. But China was certainly standing rather unsteadily on one ear at that time.'

Nina slipped the bathrobe on and stared thoughtfully at her reflection in the mirror. She removed the shower cap, unpinned her hair and began drawing a wire-bristled brush through it with long slow strokes, tilting her head from side to side. Scholefield stayed under the cold shower until his teeth were chattering, then he stepped out and towelled himself vigorously.

'How could the Americans and Israelis come to get mixed up in all this? That sounds a bit unlikely, doesn't it?' She stopped brushing her hair and gazed enquiringly at his reflection in the mirror. 'Has that just been thrown in, do you think, so the Chinese can be sure of selling the motion picture rights of your folios to Hollywood for hard Western dollars when it's all over?'

Scholefield draped the towel round his shoulders and moved up behind her. He smiled at her in the mirror as he slipped his hands into the front of the bathrobe. 'You're a cynical bitch Nina.' Her breasts were still silkily damp from the shower and she shrugged her shoulders in a deliberately provocative movement, her eyes fixed on his in the glass. 'Mrs. Chou En-lai contributed her two-pennyworth of mystery by telling some visiting American ladies rather enigmatically that the CIA had found out about Lin's plotting first. Nobody ever really got out of her what she meant by that. And the CIA haven't exactly been forthcoming on the subject. Perhaps you should ask Harvey Ketterman about it when you meet him.'

'Would he tell me—if he knew?'

'He never told anybody else.' She squirmed back against his chest, still watching his face intently in the mirror.

'But then, who knows? He might succumb to your more obvious charms if you ask him nicely.'

'Does he work for the CIA then?'

'He doesn't wear any badge that says so.'

'I'll ask him for you anyway.'

'He has a very legitimate-looking office at the State Department, so go carefully.' He smiled at her. 'Some Washington rumours did get into the papers, anyway. They said that Israeli intelligence, which has good contacts in the Kremlin, picked up details of Lin's "coup" plans from the Russian end of the "conspiracy". They passed it on and the CIA then tipped off Mao about the plot. All of which was presumably designed to encourage Mao to welcome Nixon with open arms when he dropped in to change the history of the world, as he modestly put it, in one week in February 1972.'

Nina put down the hair brush and covered his hands with her own. She stared at his reflection for a moment, her expression suddenly more serious. 'But do you really believe there's a plot to kill Mao? And could they really want to involve you?'

He shrugged and leaned forward until his face rested against hers, smiling suddenly at her puzzled child's face in the mirror.

At that moment the doorbell rang again. Nina turned and looked up at him over her shoulder with a mischievous expression in her eyes. 'That'll be your books. I think you'd better go this time. I wouldn't trust myself in the mood you've got me into—even with your prurient porter!'

FOLIO NUMBER FIVE

Marshall Lin Piao suffered from a chronic affliction in adult life which, because it was a severe embarrassment to him, was a closely-kept secret known only to those few of us who were close and trusted Comrades. This affliction often prevented him from carrying out official public duties and from making long public speeches or even attending such functions as dinner parties outside his own home. Along with the mental tension it induced, this disability was also an additional handicap in his personal relations with his fellow leaders. It helped cause much confusion too in the minds of the Chinese people and among outside interpreters of Chinese affairs because his erratic pattern of public appearances, which seemed so baffling politically, was almost solely attributable to it. The truth is, Marshall Lin suffered from acute amoebic dysentery and because of his sensitive nature this caused him great shame. Also he knew that the shrunken physical appearance of his wasted body and his unsightly baldness which forced him to wear a cap at all times, even indoors, made him an unattractive figure. Because I loved him and worked closely with him over many years I knew he could be courteous and considerate. But with those outside his circle of close confidants he was sharp and difficult because of his deep inner unease.

But why should I now be prepared to reveal such intimate details of Marshall Lin's personal health after he is long dead? The answer is that a close knowledge of his character and his person is necessary to understand why, and how, he was murdered by the treacherous left-wing clique now plotting to seize supreme power in China. For his death was only the first part of their plans soon to be brought to fruition.

By nature Marshall Lin was neurotic and highly strung. He had suffered more than one nervous breakdown in his life. He was, for instance, a compulsive eater of fried beans. He carried them with him everywhere in his pockets and consumed them constantly. Like many men of great physical courage forced by age towards inaction, he lived increasingly through the written word. All day long he would sit at his desk reading party and army documents, writing memoranda and brooding—and all the time tossing the beans repeatedly into his mouth.

Many times I remonstrated with him about this habit. 'They are nutritious, yes, Marshall Lin,' I would agree, 'but extremely difficult to digest. They do your body more harm than good.' But he would always wave me impatiently away. Other people smoked cigarettes, drank alcohol or chewed gum, he would reply sharply—and he did none of those things.

This bizarre compulsion to bean-eating was only one outward sign of the great internal stresses that knotted his intestines with anxiety throughout his waking hours. He suffered insomnia too, and he developed ulcers to add to the burden of residual pain from his war wounds. But these growing bodily hardships only seemed to temper further the fierce steely spirit at the very core of him— the spirit which had won him the battle nickname of 'Tiger Cat' during the years of his great generalship. Once I entered his study with the translation of a Western press profile that wondered at his magnificent military record of victory in a hundred campaigns against the Japanese and Chiang Kai-shek's armies. As he leafed through it I asked him how he would explain his miraculous successes to the world if a Western newspaperman were sitting before him then.

He raised his pale, gaunt face from his papers and in the greying of his skin I could detect the pain he was suffering that day. But he smiled his curiously apologetic, vulnerable smile. 'It is quite simple, Comrade Yang,' he said. 'Only ever engage the enemy when you can be certain of victory. Make that a rule of your life.'

I have never forgotten that moment. Are those the words of a man who would make three clumsy and unsuccessful attempts on the life of the leader he had loyally supported and fought for unhesitatingly during forty years? Are those the guiding thoughts of a man who would fail in any task he chose to carry out, then flee across the enemy's borders in shame?

Marshall Lin uttered those uncompromising words of advice to me in the late summer of 1970. It was just a week before the fateful August meeting of the party Central Committee in the mountains at Lushan. It was there we discovered beyond any doubt that those evil forces closing around Chairman Mao

Tse-tung had at last managed to poison his mind against Marshall Lin.

On the final day the Chairman himself, who had made no formal speech even at a closed party meeting for several years, astounded everybody by rising to launch a bitter personal attack on us. His intervention was astonishing because he had been unwell for some time and we sat staring in disbelief as he reared up, swaying unsteadily, before the microphone. The nurse at his side was so concerned that she was holding his sleeve, ready to leap to her feet and support him if he should falter.

Despite the large doses of levodopa medication he was receiving for his worsening Parkinson's disease, his palsied left arm was trembling uncontrollably. He stared slowly round the hall and finally his gaze came to rest with obvious deliberation on the places in which we were seated. His face had grown dark with anger and a tense hush fell in the hall. Suddenly he shouted into the microphone at the top of his voice.

'I have never been a genius!'

The effort racked his whole body and the entire gathering stared at him open-mouthed with amazement. He glowered round the hall again, gathering his strength. Then his voice dropped and we barely heard his next words. 'I read Confucius for six years and capitalist literature for seven years. I began studying Marxism-Leninism only in 1918! How can I be a genius?'

He lurched against the podium and it seemed he would fall. But he recovered. Swaying unsteadily on his feet, he glared slowly round the hall, again seeming, as he had always done, to search the soul of every one of us for some terrible hidden sign of guilt. Though sick at heart, I took jotted notes of all he said. I glanced quickly along the row at Marshall Lin. His face was white and he was pushing beans distractedly into his mouth in his agitation. The face of his wife, Yeh Chun, was drained of colour too. Everybody in the hall knew that Chairman Mao, quite out of the blue, was attacking Lin's own loyal description of him given the previous day in a short speech. He had praised the historic ingenuity of Mao's political thought and proposed that in recognition of this he should become both head of state and head of the party now that the Cultural Revolution was over.

I looked across at those sitting on the other side of Chairman Mao. I saw that the features of his wife Chiang Ching were set impassively although many others in the hall were obviously distressed that the Chairman might be on the verge of some kind of collapse. No public audience had ever seen him so enfeebled, so manic and uncontrolled.

But the great mesmeric power of his presence hadn't deserted him even then. His words had already produced an electric atmosphere of awe and apprehension in the hall. When his nurse tried to persuade him to sit down he pushed her roughly away and hunched over the lectern once more, clutching with both hands at the slender stem of the microphone for support.

'They have said one sentence from a genius was worth ten thousand sentences.' He paused and his voice sank again to a fierce, growling whisper. 'But no provision shall be made for state chairmanship!'

Swaying from side to side and breathing heavily, he stood for a long time saying nothing more. For a moment he looked round again in our direction. Then he lifted his head and closed his eyes as though listening to some sound nobody else in the hall could hear. 'A tall thing is easy to break, a white thing is easy to stain.' He stopped and breathed deeply, still keeping his eyes closed. 'The white snow in spring can hardly find its match. A high reputation is difficult to live up to.' In the total silence that followed, the sound of his laboured breathing rattled clearly through the loudspeakers on the walls. He opened his eyes and glared slowly round the hall again. 'Li Ku spoke well five hundred years ago! I use his words now to tell you I will not serve as state chairman. I have said so six times. If each time I spoke one sentence there should have been ten thousand sentences then there were sixty thousand refusals! But still they have not listened to me.'

With an effort Chairman Mao straightened up. Although his shoulders sagged with age and infirmity and his jowls quivered, the fierce pride that continued burning inside him made him a commanding figure still. The hall was utterly hushed and the only sound was the rustle of the mountain pines brushing against the windows in the afternoon wind.

'On the surface they are talking about enhancing my prestige,' he said, speaking softly now and nodding his head repeatedly. 'But who knows what is really in their minds? Could it not be a clever attempt to enhance another reputation?' He paused again and turned very slowly in Marshall Lin's direction. He stared directly at him and spoke this time without taking his eyes from his face. 'Couldn't a certain person be anxious to become state chairman in my place?'

At the back of the hall a cadre in the green uniform of the People's Liberation Army stood up and shouted something unintelligible and waved his clenched fist in our direction. We learned later this incident had been carefully stage-managed by our enemies. But Chairman Mao ignored this interruption. He continued, without taking his eyes from Marshall Lin. 'Couldn't it be that a certain person is anxious to split the Party?'

There was an excited buzz of reaction from the hall, although the soldier who had shouted had sat down again. Mao turned back to the microphone and lifted his good arm above his head in a dramatic gesture calling for silence. When the hall quietened he waited for a moment then raised his voice suddenly in a final quavering shout. 'Could it be that a certain person is really anxious to seize power'—he stopped, looked round quickly at Lin, then turned back to the microphone—'for himself!'

There was complete silence for several seconds. Then Chairman Mao sank down, suddenly exhausted, into his seat. A murmur rose all round the hall as Chiang Ching stood up from her place to run and bend solicitously over his chair. But he waved her and his nurse away and straightened in his seat to stare out belligerently across the heads of his audience. His eyes burned with a feverish brightness in his crumpled face as he swung his gaze triumphantly round the gathering.

The murmur grew slowly and uncertainly into a muted roar of applause and approval. Then above the growing din the single voice of that same soldier who had interrupted earlier from the rear of the hall suddenly rang out again. 'Down with Lin Piao! Down with Yeh Chun!'

Hesitantly at first, then with growing confidence, other scattered voices began taking up the chant.

MOSCOW, Saturday—Medical experts who reconstructed the charred remains of nine bullet-riddled bodies found in a Chinese aircraft which crashed in Soviet-dominated Mongolia last September now feel reasonably certain that two of the bodies were those of Lin Piao and his second wife Yeh Chun—though there still seem to be some misgivings that they could be doubles planted by Peking.

The Observer, 1 January 1972

5

The high-gabled, crimson-brick Victorian fortress on Kensington Gore that houses the half-million maps and written archives of the Royal Geographical Society glowed ominously under the fiery glare of the mid-morning sun, giving off the dull, flesh-searing radiance of a red-hot poker. As Scholefield's taxi pulled into the courtyard the taxi driver cursed the heat humourlessly and lifted a rattling thermos flask of iced water to his mouth. As Scholefield paid him off the breathless voice of a Radio London newsreader on the driver's radio was announcing that Parliament had just passed an Emergency Powers Bill to deal with Britain's worst drought in 250 years—and for the first time in history MCC members at Lord's were being allowed to watch the cricket from the pavilion with their jackets off.

'They ought to be in this bloody cab, that's where they ought to be,' said the driver sourly. Already stripped to the waist, he scowled at Scholefield's perfectly reasonable tip as though it should have been more because of the heat, and roared away without thanking him. Scholefield stepped out of the burning sun into the shadow of the entrance lobby a moment before a mini-cab with a Gerrard Street proprietor's name on it cruised past the entrance and stopped fifty yards along the Gore.

The door porter wrote out a visitor's slip and Scholefield carried it across the polished floor of the main hall, past huge antique globes mounted on ornate wooden pedestals, and into the silent, high-ceilinged map room.

A slender, heavy-breasted girl wearing jeans and a thin cotton T-shirt that had ridden up to reveal several inches of bare back, looked down at him from the top of a ladder propped against a high bookcase and raised her eyebrows. 'Mongolia?' She mouthed the word silently, smiling a warm, conspiratorial smile, and peered round among the maze of oaken map cabinets filling the room below her. Scholefield smiled back and nodded mutely.

The girl climbed nimbly down and brought him a roll of maps she'd set on one side. She looked quickly over her shoulder then leaned across the counter and whispered again. 'What did you say the co-ordinates were—111.15 East, 47.42 North?'

'Yes.'

'There's nothing there, nothing at all—what's it supposed to be?'

'I thought there might be an airfield or something.'

The girl giggled prettily. 'I don't think there were many *aeroplanes* around even, when these maps were made. Let alone airfields.' Her hand flew to her mouth and she coloured faintly as an elderly woman with a severe expression emerged suddenly from one of the little corridors between the map cabinets.

'May I help you?'

'My name is Scholefield. I rang about large-scale maps of eastern Mongolia earlier this morning. I spoke to this young lady here. She's being extremely helpful.'

The older woman shifted her spectacles a notch higher up her nose, to enhance her authority. 'Miss Pepper is new and not qualified yet to assist in research. If you would care to proceed to the adjoining map consulting room I will have the maps brought in for your inspection. If you have any queries I'll try to help you with them after luncheon.'

The girl tucked her T-shirt in at the waist with exaggerated care and picked up the maps without looking at him. Walking with a very straight back, she led the way to a gloomy brown chamber supported by black marble pillars. It was furnished with refectory tables and tubular metal chairs that had seen better days. She put the maps down, pulled an apologetic face and walked out.

Scholefield settled down in a tubular chair and pored over the maps. From the shadowy walls the fading images in oil and bronze of David Livingston, John Hanning Speke, Captain James Cook and Robert Falcon Scott of the Antarctic gazed sightlessly over his head. Outside the tall windows, the Society's neatly-trimmed lawn had been burned brown and arid like the bush grass of Africa through which Speke and Livingston trod in their high days of glory.

Scholefield wiped his sweating palms on a handkerchief then began tracing the co-ordinates across the brown and orange wastes of Mongolia with one finger. He encountered no relevant features of any kind on the first two sheets, and as he turned to the third he sensed a presence at his elbow and looked up.

The girl was standing with one hand on a jutting hip, smiling down at him. 'I told you, didn't I?'

'I thought you weren't qualified to help me?'

'She's gone to lunch, so I'm qualified now. I've got a damned degree, you see, but I'm only here for the holidays.'

She leaned over him and pointed to a tiny block of print in the bottom right hand corner of the first map. 'But I told you, look.'

Scholefield bent over the map until his nose almost touched the paper. 'For use by War and Navy Department agencies only, not for sale or distribution.'

'No, no, silly, the next bit.' She picked up the sheet and screwed up her eyes. '"Prepared 1943 by the Army Mapping Service, Topographic Center, Washington, D.C.—copied from a USSR map of 1937." Unless there was an airfield there in 1936 for the Russian Tiger Moths, that's not much help, is it?'

Scholefield picked up the second map and held the bottom corner close to his eyes. ' "Army Map Service, Corps of Engineers, US Army—Washington D.C., compiled in 1957"—well, that's a bit better, isn't it?'

The girl sighed and shook her head. 'Read on, look: "Copied from Mongolia, one inch to a hundred thousand, Japanese General Staff 1937–40, Japanese Kwantung Army HQ". It's no more modern than the other one. The third one is'—she picked it up—' "Japanese General Staff 1941." '

Scholefield scratched his head. 'The funny thing is that the same places on these charts seem to be in different places on the Russian and Japanese versions.'

'Of course they do. Mongolia's notorious for that. The position of features, even up to the size of small towns, varies enormously. The co-ordinates for the same place can be quite different, depending on the source you use.'

Scholefield drew a long breath of exasperation and tipped his chair onto its back legs.

'Wait a minute. What a fool!' Her voice rose with excitement. 'These are all AMS World Ones, aren't they?'

'What's an AMS World One?'

'Sixteen miles to the inch. I'll go and get the AMS Twos.'

'What are they?'

'Different series. Four miles to the inch.' She ran out of the room, her platform-soled clogs echoing loudly across the polished wood floor.

She was back a minute later. Scholefield looked up at her expectantly but she was empty-handed.

'There aren't any.'

'What do you mean?'

'There just aren't any AMS World Twos for the eastern half of Mongolia.'

'You mean not here?'

'No, not anywhere, they don't exist. You've picked a really obscure area for that airfield of yours. You really couldn't have chosen anywhere more remote if you'd tried.'

Scholefield stood up. 'Thank you very much. You've been extremely helpful.'

She stared at him incredulously. 'But I haven't done anything. I haven't found anything at all for you.'

'You've been more helpful than you know.'

She smiled at him, mystified, and folded her bare arms across the dramatic swell of her T-shirt. 'Don't try to fly into that airfield of yours at night anyway, will you? I'd really feel personally responsible.'

She smiled again and stood watching him all the way to the door. She returned to the map archive only after he'd handed his visitor's slip back to the porter and stepped out into the heat again.

The Chinese sitting in the shade of a tree a hundred yards inside Kensington Gardens on the opposite side of the road stood up suddenly as the walkie-talkie set concealed in his jacket pocket crackled and spoke Scholefield's name. Half a minute later he got into the same mini-cab that had passed the Geographical Society earlier and headed back eastwards towards Soho behind Scholefield's taxi. Like the rest of the traffic stream the two cab drivers proceeded cautiously, the tyres of their vehicles splashing through the sizzling tar that was just beginning to melt again on road surfaces all over London.

FOLIO NUMBER SIX

We left the hall with as much dignity as we could muster and walked out into the cool mountain air of Lushan, the jeers ringing in our ears. The delights of that high resort, made famous by Chinese poets of the Middle Ages, its shady paths, the rapid streams among groves of cedar and bamboo, the magnificent vista of the Yangtze flowing into Poyang Lake far beneath, all suddenly seemed sour in our sight. We could not speak among ourselves but hurried away immediately to our separate villas. In a mood close to despair I paced up and down my room reading and re-reading my notes of what the Chairman had said at the Plenum.

Could it really have happened at last? Marshall Lin in one of his blackest moods of depression had once long ago confided to me his fear that the full fury of the Chairman's psychotic paranoia—diagnosed in 1960 by a doctor who disappeared without trace the very next day—might one day be turned against us too.

But even during the five years of the Cultural Revolution, as the sick brain of our once great leader spread turmoil across the land exhausting the minds and bodies of the people, Marshall Lin had on more than one occasion been at pains to console me—and perhaps himself too. 'Unless he descends into the depths of a raving madness,' he had said, 'he will not forget the bedrock of his philosophy—that political power grows out of the barrel of a gun. While there's reason left in him he will never dare to destroy those of his comrades who command the loyalties of the great armies which brought us to power.'

We had watched him smash the whole party to eradicate men like Liu Shao-chi, of whom he had an utterly irrational fear as a successor. And only when the Red Guard youth and workers armed with stolen weapons were fighting pitched battles in every province of the country and the death toll was rising alarmingly did his insatiable appetite for rebellion at last become blunted. Then and only then was the army ordered to exercise the full weight of its power and restore peace.

But now, after only a year or so of calm, had he finally

descended into the depths of madness? Why else should he attack the man he himself had nominated as his successor, one of the greatest generals in China's history, who could tear the heart from the country if he chose to deploy forces loyal to him in the struggle for survival?

Either it was madness—or the coterie of evil courtiers who supervised his every move behind an impenetrable screen of guards within the walls of the Forbidden City had succeeded in poisoning his fevered mind against us, succeeded in manipulating his nightmare fears of betrayal in order to remove the last obstacles from their own path to ultimate power after his death!

The Central Committee had clearly been bewildered by his tirade. But that was not important. The power-hungry group of extremists behind it knew that soon more voices would be raised in a growing chorus against us—when it appeared for the many to be the only safe road to personal survival. As I paced back and forth in that Lushan room my mind was engulfed with a great sadness. How little China had changed! A great revolution had swept the land, a great new leader had emerged embracing a world-shaking modern creed—but its tenets were still being misused as scurrilously as the classical sophistries of the feudal past. The modern scientific truths of Marxism had become the same empty symbol to be hoisted aloft in the same vicious and unprincipled personal intrigues that had racked the imperial courts. Groups of jealous antagonists still grappled blindly for supreme power because they detested or loved the slant of another's eyes! Much had changed for the better in the lives of the ordinary people. But it was a precarious change. The great unknowing masses were still helpless prey to the caprices of the secret court of the modern Son of Heaven, Mao Tse-tung.

These desolate thoughts whirled in my head like a thousand blind bats, driving me towards a black brink of hopelessness. But the realisation that perhaps Marshall Lin might be suffering a worse brainstorm of despair sent me dashing suddenly from my room to the house where he was quartered.

Yeh Chun attempted to prevent me entering. She said he had retired to a darkened room in seclusion and had given strict instructions to allow entry to no one. In my panic I forced my way roughly past her and broke down the door of his retreat.

73

The curtains had been drawn across the windows and the room was in darkness. In the gloom I saw Marshall Lin slumped over his desk with metal spikes jutting from his head. I ran forward with a cry. He had already taken his life with the aid of some terrible crown of torture, I was convinced. But as I approached he raised his head slowly and stared at me.

He had tied a cloth band tightly round his forehead from which several thin spikes of wood and metal protruded. With a flood of relief I recognised the ancient brain-strengthening device of old China which I had seen him use only once before at a period of great stress during the Korean War. In his despair he had fallen back on his traditional belief that wood, metal and cloth, applied to the head under pressure, can have a curative effect. I reached out and gripped his thin shoulder in a gesture of encouragement. But he didn't move or respond. Then I saw the revolver lying on the desk beside him—that same silver gun given to him by Stalin. He continued to stare blankly in front of him and I picked up the weapon quickly and locked it away in a drawer. I closed the door, then returned to sit down by the desk in the semi-darkness. For a long time we sat together in silence.

When finally he spoke, his voice was hollow and lifeless. 'The enemy have opened their mouths. Either they swallow us up, or we swallow them. There is no other way.'

I placed my hands on his arm, cautioning him to silence. 'The room will almost certainly be monitored,' I whispered.

He didn't seem to hear me. In the pale light filtering through the curtains I could see the wood and metal spikes still sticking out all around the crown of his head. 'This is a life and death struggle now. He's using his old tactics of winning over one group and striking at another. Today he woos A and strikes at B. Tomorrow he will woo B and strike at A. Today he talks sweetly to those whom he wishes to win over, but tomorrow he charges them with nonexistent offences and condemns them to death. A man can be his guest one day but his prisoner the next.'

His voice trailed off and I put my fingers to my lips and motioned him again to silence. But he ignored me, still staring wide-eyed into the empty darkness. 'Has anyone promoted by him escaped a political death sentence later? Has any political force been able to co-operate with him from beginning to end?'

He paused and I could see him shaking his head mutely in answer to his own questions. 'We've all closed our eyes so long to the truth, but his secretaries have all been arrested or committed suicide. All his confidants have been sent to prison.' His voice broke with bitterness. 'Even a son begotten by him was driven insane.'

I rose from my chair and began pacing back and forth across the room in my anxiety that he should say nothing more that could later be used against us. But Marshall Lin seemed oblivious to good sense and his voice rambled on. 'He takes a strange delight in maltreating others, doesn't he? His philosophy is extremism. Once he thinks someone is his enemy he will blame all evil deeds on him.' He stopped and drew a long despairing breath. 'All those who have been dropped by him one after another, as if from a merry-go-round, are actually his substitutes who've been punished for the crimes committed by him.'

In my alarm I ran to the window and threw back the curtain. The sunlight of the August evening streamed in. Seeing him sitting hunched and bewildered at his desk, a frail, pathetic figure wearing that bizarre spiked headband, wrung my heart. He blinked quickly in the light and rose unsteadily to his feet. He removed the band, dropped it on the desk, then walked slowly to the window and looked out at the haze gathering round the high mountain peaks.

It was only then that I saw the dried grass stalks on the other side of his desk. I knew there would be forty-nine strands—I had burst in on him whilst he was consulting the ancient oracle of the I Ching, the Book of Changes.

I went to the desk and glanced down at the hexagrams he had formed. Marshall Lin was standing with his back to me looking out of the window. '"The dragon exceeds the proper limit and there will be occasion for repentance."'

He had intoned the classical description of the divination that had declared itself among the stalks. Now he stood waiting by the window for my response. We had often played this game, testing each other's knowledge and memory of the ancient writings. But I stared at his back dumbly, reluctant this time to speak in interpretation. 'Go on, Comrade Yang,' he said softly, still without turning round.

I cleared my throat and looked down again at the hexagram. 'When things have been carried to extremity...calamity ensues.'

He nodded his head slowly, still gazing out at the mountains. I rushed to his side and gripped him by the shoulders. 'But the calamity need not be ours! It could be his! The army is behind you. Their loyalty would be to you!'

He said nothing for a long time. Then he shook his head. 'I can't fight against him. I have fought for him and by his side in too many battles. China's destiny was in him. If it has gone from him now in his sickness, if he is being used by evil forces, I still cannot turn against him.'

'But to survive, we must!' I pleaded.

He shook his head. 'No. Even though this failure to act means we must die.' His shoulders shook suddenly. 'This time we will *not* engage the enemy.'

He wouldn't turn his face from the mountains then. Though I couldn't see, I knew that in the fading evening light tears were streaming down his cheeks.

WASHINGTON, Wednesday—An astounding report is circulating here which reveals that it was President Nixon who sent Mao Tse-tung the first warning of a conspiracy led by Marshall Lin Piao to assassinate him and set up a new regime of hard-line military men.

London *Evening Standard*, 26 January 1972

6

Outside the red gates of the Soho Market at the end of Gerrard Street the Chinese street photographer was working hard on the lunchtime flood of tourists. Shirtless, and streaming with perspiration, he snapped his shutter and handed out address tickets with an unflagging, metronomic regularity. The amplified output of three or four competing pop record stalls beat the ears of the jostling crowd with a heavy, discordant jangle of noise, and the pungent reek of star anise and other acrid Chinese spices from steaming food stalls assailed the senses in their noses and mouths with equal ferocity.

When Scholefield's taxi drew up at the gates the photographer glanced back along Gerrard Street. He saw the pursuing mini-cab turn the corner and flash its headlights twice. He switched immediately to the second camera slung around his neck. This was fitted with a telephoto lens and while appearing to focus on tourists on the pavement he took several fast frames of Scholefield paying off his driver against the background of the blue and white striped awning over the market entrance.

He watched and waited while Scholefield pushed his way slowly through the throng to where Yang, with his back to him, was buying Chinese leaves from the corner vegetable stall. The man in the rear of the cruising mini-cab lifted a hand in brief acknowledgement to the photographer as the car swung sharply left and accelerated fast away towards Shaftesbury Avenue. Inside the black Mini with smoked windows that was parked on a meter on the other side of the street, Razduhev and Bogdarin were watching Yang and Scholefield so intently that they failed to notice that the photographer was recording several frames of them, too.

Yang wore dark glasses but Scholefield recognised him because, despite the heat, he was still dressed in the dilapidated fawn raincoat. He was holding three pale green, bomb-shaped lettuce plants in his arms, arguing loudly in Chinese with the stallholder about the price, given on a ticket as 16p a pound. Eventually an abacus was produced and Yang received an extra ten pence in change from the disgruntled merchant. He turned with a snort of contempt and found himself face to face with Scholefield. Thirty yards away the street photographer surreptitiously pushed the long telephoto lens through a gap in the chain link fence and got off three shots of the two men facing each other in profile. 'Follow me,' said Yang softly, scarcely moving his lips, and brushed the Englishman aside without giving any outward sign of recognition.

Scholefield stood staring after him as he hurried away between the stalls, dragging his left leg in a shuffling, ungainly limp. He removed his jacket and loosened his tie then started through the crowd in pursuit. Tan Sui-ling, standing in the shadowy interior of a tiny kiosk selling Communist publications from Peking, watched them threading their way through the stalls towards her. Revolutionary figures in bold primary colours strode across posters on the kiosk walls proclaiming 'Socialism Advances in Victory Everywhere—Our Great Motherland is Thriving'. She drew further back into the shadows behind the girl serving and studied Yang's face intently as he approached the stall. Her expression softened suddenly and she saw the faint surprise in his eyes as they fell on the Communist slogans. He paused to look more closely at the books and magazines from the Chinese mainland spread out on the stallfront. He was scrutinising an English paper-backed edition of *Dawn Blossoms Plucked at Dusk* by Lu Hsun as Scholefield approached.

'Have you got this in Chinese?' Yang screwed up his eyes to penetrate the gloom and spoke quietly in English. In the shadows behind the counter he suddenly caught sight of the slender figure of the Chinese woman, standing against a giant portrait of Mao Tse-tung on the rear wall. Scholefield saw his eyes widen suddenly as though in elation. He looked sharply into the shadowy interior of the kiosk—but he was not near enough to see the woman's face. Then almost immediately the expression had gone and Yang placed his purchases deliberately on the counter to leave his hands free.

Tan Sui-ling didn't move as the girl bent out of sight and rummaged for a moment beneath the counter. When she stood up again she was holding a Chinese edition of the book. She dropped it into a paper bag and handed it over. He put down some coins without looking at her. Half turning to conceal his action, he lowered the book below the level of the counter and took a folded wedge of pink paper from his raincoat pocket. He inserted it carefully between the pages then dropped the book back into its bag. 'I'm going into the cinema for an hour to get out of this heat,' he said quietly to Scholefield, and the street photographer managed to get three more frames of them side by side as he thrust the package quickly into the Englishman's hands.

As Yang limped hurriedly away Scholefield pulled the book from its wrapper and studied the Chinese characters on the cover. Then he glanced into the kiosk. He found Tan Sui-ling staring at him intently. His eyes locked with hers for a moment but her broad face, indistinct in the shadow, remained blank and unsmiling. He replaced the book hurriedly in its bag and gazed out over the milling crowd again, looking for Yang. He was nowhere to be seen and Scholefield had to run to the market gates before he caught sight of the Chinese on the far side of the street, hobbling awkwardly round the black Mini and up a flight of steps to a side entrance of the Kowloon Cultural Services Emporium.

The street photographer got two last shots of Yang going through the door that led to a tiny cinema, and a few moments later he recorded two back views of Scholefield as he followed him in. In both shots he had included the anonymous-looking car in which the two Russians were concealed. Behind the Mini's smoked windows Razduhev looked at his watch and smiled grimly. 'Twelve forty-seven, Boris. He's keeping admirable time. I think the Chinese outdo even the Germans when it comes to obeying orders.' He lifted a hand briefly in the direction of the Chinese propaganda kiosk and when he saw Tan Sui-ling nod, he gave the order to Bogdarin to move off.

When he stepped into the air-conditioned gloom of the cinema the wall of cold air struck Scholefield's hot face with a pleasant sense of shock. At the same instant a hand grabbed his sleeve. Because of the sudden darkness he stumbled and almost fell. But Yang steadied him and led the way clumsily towards two seats at the end of the back row. Because of its air conditioning the cinema was almost full. Posters in the foyer had announced a double bill of Hong Kong-made films, *Behind the Lines* and *Massage Girls*, and on the screen two shrieking queens of kung fu were already kicking and chopping their way along the roof of a speeding train aswarm with enemy soldiers. A steady hubbub of Chinese conversation rose above the frantic clamour of the film's vernacular sound track as traders and businessmen closed deals and exchanged gossip in the coolest lunchtime spot in Gerrard Street.

Yang dumped his greengrocery on the floor and lowered himself into the end seat with a grunt. He removed his dark glasses and stretched his deformed leg stiffly into the aisle, then leaned towards Scholefield, speaking softly in Chinese. 'You have decided to offer your help, Mr. Scholefield, I presume.'

In the faint light from the screen Scholefield saw that Yang's eyes were closed in concentration as he waited attentively for an answer. 'I take it we're no longer talking about homosexual acupuncture students defecting to Cuba? I've checked with the Foreign Office. There's no clinic at Oxford and no acupuncture students from Peking in England at present.'

Yang smiled with his mouth without opening his eyes and waved a dismissive hand. 'Oh, before I forget, Mr. Scholefield, your Ming scroll is a fake—a Ch'ing reproduction. Check the signature sometime if I don't have a chance to show you myself. As for last night's subterfuge, I apologise. I could not be sure your apartment was not monitored. Nor could I be sure that you would be sympathetic.'

'What makes you so sure I'm sympathetic now?'

Yang cocked his head to one side as though straining to isolate some important detail from the confused babble of conversation around him. 'I think you have tasted the chocolates I left for you by now, yes?'

Scholefield looked quickly along the row of heads in front of them, but none had turned in their direction. The Chinese waited for his reply with his eyes still closed. 'Mr. Yang, correct me if I'm wrong, but you seem to be claiming that you're the sole survivor of the Lin Piao crash. Is that right?'

The sarcasm was evident in Scholefield's voice and Yang leaned forward suddenly on the arm-rest separating their seats, his eyes dilating in anger. 'Marshall Lin was murdered! Lao Kao was murdered! Look if you don't believe!' He ripped open his raincoat, unbuttoned his shirt and turned round, tugging it back off his shoulders. Even in the half-light the twisted skeins of livid white scar tissue were clearly visible spreading in angry torrents across his shoulders and down his back. He swung round again on Scholefield and refastened his shirt, his eyes blazing. 'Do you still doubt that I have suffered?'

Scholefield looked away and didn't reply.

'Do you still doubt that I want to avenge myself on those animals who are even now plotting to murder Chairman Mao himself?'

Scholefield took a deep breath and turned back to the Chinese. 'You acted the part of a homosexual PLA hero last night. Perhaps you're acting another role now.'

'I want only to save the Chairman and save my country from these monsters!' Yang was forcing the words out between his clenched teeth. 'Why should I want to act?' He turned away and gazed furiously at the screen. One of the lissom kung fu queens had been captured and was about to be tortured in a cellar by enemy troops for what she knew. Yang continued watching as the face of her determined colleague appeared behind an iron grille in the ceiling.

'There are a hundred or so questions I'd like answered before I could begin to believe your story.' Scholefield leaned closer. 'Like how did you get to London? Who's helping you here? And who exactly "killed" Lin and why?'

The ceiling grille crashed inwards in a shower of dust and a female screaming fury launched herself down onto the unsuspecting heads of the torturers with arms and legs flailing.

'You already have some of the answers to those questions in your possession.'

Scholefield stared at him, puzzled. Then, remembering, he glanced down at the Chinese book in the paper bag in his lap. When he looked up again Yang was still staring unblinking at the gaudy kaleidoscopic image of the film. 'Yes, Folio Seven and Folio Eight,' he said quietly.

A long burst of gunfire and mingled screams of simulated Asiatic death rang out. 'In return for those folios, Mr. Scholefield, I want you to do something for me.' The noise from the sound-track grew deafening and Scholefield had to lean closer to catch Yang's words. 'I have conclusive evidence that Marshall Lin was murdered. I wish to make this evidence available to experts in the study of China in Britain and, with the added authority of their approval, to the world at large.' He turned in his seat to face Scholefield. His features, lit only by the glow from the screen, were expressionless. 'I wish to reveal this to those who can influence high-level policy here in London and in other major Western capitals. I wish this to be done very urgently. And you will assist me!'

Scholefield's expression hardened. He stared into Yang's face but the Chinese did not shift his gaze this time. 'That sounds suspiciously like an imperative.'

Yang nodded once, almost absently. 'The East Asia Study Group of the British World Affairs Institute of which you are chairman is a very influential body. I know that leading China academics, Foreign Office and Cabinet Office experts and specialist journalists are all represented on it. Convene an urgent meeting of the Group for five thirty this afternoon.'

Scholefield smiled humourlessly. 'Mr. Yang, your naivety is touching. Members of that group, as you say, are all prominent men in their fields. They can't be produced at a moment's notice like rabbits out of a hat. They aren't your subjugated luminaries from the Academy of Sciences in Peking—or Moscow—who have to come running without a pressing reason when the party crooks its little finger.'

A whole battalion of troops fired blindly into the darkness into which the kung fu maidens, dressed now in black silk pyjamas, had disappeared. Failure to wing them seemed to convince the superstitious pre-Marxist Chinese soldiery that they had encountered supernatural avenging angels and they flung their rifles aside and ran screaming into the darkness where they were methodically cut down by more lightning kicks and chops from svelte female limbs. Yang watched all this then turned slowly back to Scholefield. 'You do have a very pressing reason for summoning an emergency meeting.' The face of the Chinese creased in a sudden glittering smile.

Scholefield frowned. 'Are you making some kind of threat?'

Yang relaxed suddenly in his seat and returned his attention to the film that was now moving towards a noisy climax. 'I have simply taken some small precautions to ensure that you comply with my wishes.'

Scholefield grabbed Yang's left arm and swung him round in the seat. On the screen the nimble kung fu girls were now charging the enemy's munitions depot, holding fizzing explosive charges aloft in their tiny fists. 'What *precautions* have you taken?'

Yang didn't flinch. He glanced calmly down at the watch on his free wrist. 'Telephone your wife. She will give you the details.'

The first small ammunition dump exploded in a sheet of flame. Scholefield grabbed Yang with his other hand and shook him bodily in his seat. 'That wasn't my wife last night.'

Yang freed himself and slowly straightened his coat. 'I am not talking about the actress. Telephone your wife. Ask her about Matthew.'

Scholefield's eyes widened in disbelief as another roar of flame lit the faces of the audience with a fiery glow. 'If you want to see Matthew again, simply convene the meeting. I shall be at the Institute at five twenty-five. Your members will be addressed by the man now sitting beside you on your right.'

Scholefield swung round in his seat as the main arsenal went up and the bright orange glare from the explosion illuminated the man hunched in the seat on the other side of him. Thin, narrow-shouldered and English-looking, he had a big shock of white hair and a straggling moustache stained blonde at the fringes with nicotine. He wore thick spectacles and in the flaring light from the screen Scholefield saw that although the cigarette between his lips had almost burned away, the dead ash still hung from it in a long, bent spike.

'Dr. Vincent Stillman, one of the world's leading aircraft accident investigators.' Yang's sibilant introduction carried over Scholefield's shoulder during a lull in the expanding series of screen explosions. The little man glanced up uncertainly at Scholefield as though embarrassed. Then he nodded diffidently and turned away.

Scholefield swung back to find Yang regarding him calmly. 'Your son will be returned unharmed to his home after the meeting—but only if we are not put under surveillance.' He paused and lowered his voice. 'If you reveal any of this to your security people, you will never see your son again—alive.'

A great surge of music welled up as the delicate female gladiators skipped triumphantly away from the monstrous conflagration they had created. Scholefield leapt to his feet and ran out to the public telephone box in the foyer. When his wife answered he tried to make his voice sound casual. 'I'm just phoning to see how Matthew is.'

'How he *is*? What do you mean how he *is*?' Her voice as usual was cold and hostile. 'I should have thought that you could see that for yourself.'

'How do you mean?'

'He should be with you by now. He left here with his nanny nearly half an hour ago.'

Scholefield gripped the receiver tightly and took a deep breath. 'Who picked them up?'

She made a loud noise of exasperation. 'What on earth's wrong with you? The mini-cab you sent of course. The Chinese driver said you'd arranged a special showing of that Dragon Boat Festival film for them at the Institute this afternoon. Isn't that right?'

The heat in the enclosed telephone booth was suffocating and sweat was running suddenly down his forehead into his eyes. 'Of course, of course, that's right. How long ago did they leave, did you say?'

'I've told you once, about half an hour ago.' The brittle irritation changed abruptly to alarm. 'Is anything wrong?'

He swallowed hard. 'No, the traffic's terrible in town today,

84

that's all! I'm just checking they were picked up all right. I'll
try to have him back by six thirty.'

Scholefield dropped the receiver and ran back into the cinema.
The lights had come on and the audience was already streaming
out. He shouldered his way rapidly through the crowd until he
reached the auditorium. Then he stopped, staring in dismay. The
back row of seats, like all the others, was now empty.

The three bomb-shaped lettuce plants were still lying in the
aisle but there was no sign of Yang, or the little hunched man
with the shock of white hair. The Lu Hsun book in its brown
paper bag was propped up on the arm of the seat where he had
been sitting. He picked it up and pulled the book out of the bag.
Between the pages he found the two folded sheets of pink paper
headed 'Folio Seven' and 'Folio Eight'.

FOLIO NUMBER SEVEN

Trickery was used to force Marshall Lin Piao to board the Trident aircraft for that fateful journey on the morning of 13 September 1971. Deception of the vilest kind was employed, worthy of any of the murderous intrigues perpetrated in the secret precincts of the imperial courts of China in ancient times. They used his daughter Tou-tou to bait the trap and didn't hesitate to cause her physical suffering so as to add realism to their plot. It was typical of their character that afterwards in their faked documents they told the people of China and the world that it was she who had reported her father to the authorities and so ensured the failure of his 'plot' to murder Chairman Mao and seize power.

But it was almost as if by then Marshall Lin was anticipating treachery and did not seek to avoid its snare. He seemed in the end to welcome it passively as though he desired nothing more than the cold embrace of death. Ever since the Lushan meeting he had remained sunk in a deep and unprecedented melancholia. Listless and apathetic, he became a complete recluse in his study, hiding more than ever behind his shaming ailment, and building an impassable barrier between himself and the outside world.

The inevitable process of clothing vicious and petty personal feuds in high-sounding political and philosophical arguments, so little understood by the outside world, began immediately after we came down from Lushan. On the day after his thunderous attack, Chairman Mao resorted to his classic and well-tried tactic of self-effacement. He circulated one of his imperial-style edicts to all who had attended the meeting, professing a humility which he knew would be totally disregarded.

'Those opinions of mine were given only as personal views,' he said, in a note reproduced in the calligraphy of his own hand— a device which he also knew would help imbue the words with a mystical quality. 'They were only casual remarks. Don't draw any hasty conclusions. Let the Central Committee do it gradually.'

The insidious political manoeuvres and the indirect public pillorying in the party press that this was designed to spark off unfolded relentlessly under the Chairman's famous but grossly hypocritical exhortation: 'Learn from past mistakes to avoid future ones, and cure the sickness to save the patient.' But Marshall Lin, true to his vow by the window in Lushan, made no effort whatsoever to engage his enemies.

His son Lin Li-kuo and his wife Yeh Chun worked frantically with his supporters and drew up plan after plan for him to defend himself. But he kept his mind resolutely closed to them. He scarcely read the documents they placed before him. He spoke little, retreated deep into his inner self and never for one moment countenanced any of the suggestions. Later, after his death, snatches of these disregarded proposals were falsified and enlarged on, then embodied in wholly fabricated documents circulated throughout China as proof of Marshall Lin's 'guilt' in planning a coup d'état.

I realised his will had finally broken when he made no attempt to resist the vital reorganisation in January of the Peking Military Region that placed less loyal commanders in key positions in the capital around him. He seemed unperturbed and carried out all his routine duties perfunctorily in the seclusion of his study as though he had ceased to live in the real world beyond its walls.

On many occasions in the early months I entered his room to find him fumbling on his desk top with his divining stalks. But after a while I ceased to ask what the hexagrams foretold. Always the omens were ill. He had succumbed completely, and I'm sure the emanations of despair from his mind and body ensured in turn that no matter how often he consulted the River Map and laid out the stalks they would only ever produce forebodings of calamity.

Only once did he seem to rouse himself from this moribund mental torpor—after the American Kissinger had come secretly to Peking from Pakistan in mid-summer. It was as though sudden fear, for the very survival of the China he had fought to build, revived him. He was deeply apprehensive that the sudden and public offering of China's hand in friendship to the greatest enemy of the Soviet Union would increase the danger of a sudden attack by Soviet forces across our northern borders. His conviction was profound and the fear galvanised him back to life.

For two days he worked frantically and without pause, compiling a detailed draft of his views. The document he produced was a forceful and brilliantly argued exposition of both our nuclear and conventional strengths—or rather weaknesses—compared with the Russians. He rushed copies to the Chairman and Premier Chou En-lai and I was ready to rejoice that this outside threat of danger had brought the Marshall Lin I loved back to life from the brink of the grave.

But many years had passed since our leadership had debated their opinions openly and honestly without fear of recrimination. The poison from a once-mighty mind turned sick had spread its suspicions and jealousies too deep in the Chung Nan Hai. The memorandum was seized by the plotters, distorted and added as fuel to the flames they were already stoking like demons to incinerate Marshall Lin. Within two days he had sunk back deeper than ever before into his terrible apathy.

Even the horrifying reports that were secured by our own military intelligence agents in early September failed to arouse him. They discovered that the left-wing plotters had maliciously passed false 'proof' to the American Central Intelligence Agency via Israeli agents in Moscow that Marshall Lin was planning to murder Chairman Mao. The American spies, although they could not know whether the information was true or false, unscrupulously relayed the information back to Chairman Mao as if it were true. Their aim was to win his gratitude and so persuade Chairman Mao to welcome their head of state, Nixon, with open arms, because he needed the accolade of a successful visit to China to increase his prestige and ensure victory in the coming presidential election.

This was the plotters' master stroke! They knew that no matter how much evidence was produced internally about the suspected treachery of his opponents, nothing would explode with more devastating impact in the persecution-crazed brain of Chairman Mao than a report from the enemy's espionage apparatus of an internal Chinese plot to kill him.

Marshall Lin must have known that this was his death warrant. But still he would do nothing to resist his fate. He seemed to retreat even further into the shell of his resigned inner despair. His eyes saw less, his ears became more deaf to reason. His wife

THE DEATH OF LIN PIAO

and son, now at their wits' end, persuaded him at last to move for his health's sake to the sea resort of Peitaiho, 200 miles from Peking on the Gulf of Laotung. He agreed reluctantly and without enthusiasm, and at the end of the first week in September we all flew there from Peking in one of the four British-built Trident jet airliners which had been bought from Pakistan the previous year for the personal use of the leadership. Because of his family's fears, Lin Li-kuo, from that time onward, used the influence of his Air Force officer's rank to keep the same aircraft standing by twenty-four hours a day in a state of constant readiness in case an emergency should require it.

His plan, which he confided to me, was to fly south to Chekiang where the commander most loyal to his father in the whole of the People's Liberation Army would ensure their safety from intrigue. If necessary he would pilot the plane himself.

But long before, without our knowledge, the plotters had infiltrated their own personnel into key positions in the Peitaiho control tower and among the air and ground staff manning the Trident itself. And as the evening breeze from off the sea began to cool the exceptional heat of the day on 12 September, they struck.

Just as the sun was setting, Marshall Lin's daughter Tou-tou, named affectionately at birth by her father after the beans he loved so well, was strolling disconsolately in the sand dunes beside the shore. She had wandered out on her own, deeply depressed and, like the rest of the family, beside herself with anxiety for her father. She was worried too about the effect his fate might have on all their lives and because of this, she scarcely looked where she stepped. She had taken to walking out alone at that same time each evening since our arrival in Peitaiho and this had obviously allowed our enemies to draw up a strategy.

Because of her distress she took little notice at first when a group of men appeared among the dunes, chasing a dog. As they drew nearer, however, she noticed that the men were shouting wildly and waving their arms. The dog was baying, too, in a most unnatural manner and she first began to be apprehensive when she saw it bounding towards her.

She turned and began to run. But the dog, a powerful animal of the kind used to guard military installations, caught her easily.

It sprang up on her back and she fell screaming to the ground with the dog snarling and tearing at her clothes. Before it was able to inflict more than superficial injuries, however, the crowd of armymen and civilians giving chase arrived and drove the dog off.

Tou-tou, shocked and hysterical, did not resist when one of them carrying a leather satchel with a red cross painted on it declared himself to be a doctor. He told her that the dog was believed to be rabid and that was why it was being pursued. The dog's attack had left scratches and lacerations on her neck and arms and he drew a hypodermic from his bag, explaining that an early injection could protect her against a possibly fatal infection.

Her brother, Lin Li-kuo, had been attracted by the commotion and he ran to her side from the nearby grounds of Marshall Lin's quarters. As he arrived breathless on the scene, the doctor was just withdrawing the needle of the empty hypodermic from his sister's arm. At that moment a volley of shots rang out and the men pursuing the dog cheered as the animal staggered and fell dead in the surf on the beach. Before the bewildered Lin Li-kuo had fully realised what had happened, the doctor had persuaded him that he too should have an inoculation against possible infection, and he rolled up his sleeve on the spot.

Between them he and the 'doctor' carried the shocked Tou-tou back to the house. She was very pale and near to unconsciousness. Because of their great consternation, Marshall Lin and his wife also submitted without demur to the doctor's immediate insistence that the entire household, family and domestic workers, should be inoculated too.

Marshall Lin sat quietly at his desk with his eyes downcast as the needle punctured the slack, scrawny muscle of his left arm. He watched the 'doctor' press home the ounce or two of colourless liquid without knowing it would finally quench the long-indomitable fighting spirit that had made him one of China's greatest-ever warriors. Or perhaps deep within himself he did know—and still refused, because of his courage and his life-long loyalties to the ideals of the old Chairman Mao, to turn aside.

The details of this might have remained unknown to me if Marshall Lin's young cook, Sao Li, had not taken fright as he waited in line in the study with the rest of the staff for his turn under the needle. He was a thin, squeamish youth, and after seeing Marshall Lin injected he suddenly took to his heels and ran from the house without knowing why.

He ran through the town to the Palace of Culture where Lao Kao and I were attending a performance of revolutionary music. We had gone there for an hour or two's respite from the deep pall of unbearable despair that gripped the household. When Sao Li burst into the packed auditorium I recognised his scarecrow figure at once. He stood by the stage staring round uncertainly at the sea of faces in the audience. In the unknowing alarm of his expression I at once read confirmation of my worst nightmares. I pulled Lao Kao to his feet and shouted and waved to the cook. When he saw us we all ran headlong from the hall, heedless of the commotion we caused.

I took the wheel of our car and drove at breakneck speed back to the house. My heart sank as Sao Li related what had happened. I cursed myself again and again in an agony of remorse for leaving Marshall Lin's side. The cook could not explain why he had run out to fetch us. But I think he was as instinctively aware, just as we as outsiders were, that the 'mad dog' hue and cry was just the beginning of some terrible subterfuge.

Lao Kao and I did not exchange a single word. He sat white-faced beside me clutching the dashboard as we raced along the beach road. There was no moon that night, and the surf roared loudly in the blind darkness beside the highway. I expected to find the house ringed with hostile troops and I had quickly become reconciled during that wild drive to giving myself under arrest to them in order to demonstrate my loyalty to Marshall Lin. But when we arrived the house stood dark and silent. At first I thought it was a trap. But once inside we found the rooms empty. Nothing had been removed, nothing packed, no preparations made for departure.

We stood in Marshall Lin's study, the three of us, staring help-lessly at one another. The house was silent as a grave. I picked up an empty syringe from the desk and held it in my hand. I would have jabbed its point into my own heart at that moment in my misery.

Then we heard a groaning from the rear of the house. I dashed through to the kitchen and found the wash amah slumped in a corner, her head in her hands. She tried to look up at us but she couldn't focus her eyes because of the drug that had been injected into her. The cook shook her roughly and asked her where everybody had gone. Had they been taken away by force?

'No, no,' she sobbed. 'Lin Tou-tou became hysterical. She began to suffer spasms and foam at the mouth. The doctor said she must go at once to Shanghai for treatment or she would die.'

I grabbed the amah by the shoulders. 'How did they travel?' I shouted at her.

The woman seemed on the point of losing consciousness. I slapped her sharply in the face and she opened her eyes with the shock. 'The Trident! They are all flying to a hospital in Shanghai. They left half an hour ago.' She groaned something unintelligible and collapsed against me, her face ashen.

At that moment we heard a footstep in the stone passageway behind us and turned to find three soldiers with rifles confronting us. Broad-bladed bayonets jutted from the ends of their weapons and I recognised this 'badge' of the special troops from Unit 8341, Chairman Mao's crack personal bodyguard in the Chung Nan Hai.

I leapt to my feet and backed away, holding the now unconscious amah in front of me. I shouted to Lao Kao to make a dash for the door behind us. It was at the end of a narrow passageway beside the fireplace and from the corner of my eye I saw him fumble with the door for a moment then hurl himself out into the courtyard.

The unfortunate cook tried to flee with us but in his terror he stumbled clumsily against me in the passage and fell to the stone floor. The nearest of the three soldiers lunged forward and speared him through the chest with his bayonet. His shrieking rang loud and long in the hollow kitchen as I struggled backwards along the passage, still dragging the unconscious amah in my arms. Outside I heard Lao Kao start the car.

The soldiers kicked the cook's body aside then rushed screaming towards me along the passageway. At the last moment I dropped the limp form of the amah at their feet and as they stumbled on one another I turned and dashed into the courtyard. Lao Kao already had the car on the move with the rear door swinging open and I flung myself inside. The gates hadn't been closed and we roared out onto the coast road and headed for the airfield.

When we'd caught our breath we realised there were no signs of unusual traffic movement. Only the local peasants wobbled homewards on their bicycles along the tree-fringed roads and it was obvious that the plot had been launched in great stealth to avoid any risk of open clashes between army units that might provoke a wider civil war. Our arrival at the house after the removal of the family by a trick had seemingly not been provided for.

The shock of our narrow escape under the soldiers' bayonets gradually subsided—only to be replaced by the acute fear that we might not reach the airfield before the Trident took off. We drove with our windows open listening anxiously for the faintest sound of engines from the night sky.

The airfield lay in a flat depression inland, and when we rose at last over the hill that brought it into view we saw the Trident was still standing in the brightly-lit taxiing area. But the orange dorsal light on its fuselage was flashing intermittently, indicating that it was about to depart.

It was approaching midnight as we raced down the hill towards the airfield. We could see that there were no more troops than usual on duty—but special signs had been erected under the floodlights by the gates. Sombre black skull and crossbones symbols had been painted on white boards and large black characters announced: 'Danger—Prohibited Contagion Area— No Entry Without Medical Authorisation.'

For a moment I wondered if we were wrong. Could the explanation be a genuine one? At the gate an armed soldier I had never seen before barred our way. Through the windscreen I could see the ground staff starting to remove the gangway steps from the Trident out on the tarmac. Its engines were already roaring as it prepared to move off.

The soldier shouted through the window that the airfield was closed until the emergency medical flight carrying rabies victims had departed. With one hand I took from my pocket the pass proving my status as Marshall Lin's personal aide—and with the other I snatched my service revolver from under the dashboard. I told the soldier I would accompany Marshall Lin on the flight despite the health hazard. And I ordered Lao Kao to drive onto the airfield.

The soldier let out a fierce oath and swung the muzzle of his rifle in through the window. But I knocked the barrel aside with my arm and shot him at point blank range through the chest. At the same instant Lao Kao sent the car surging forward, splintering the flimsy barrier and knocking down another guard. We accelerated fast across the tarmac and closed on the Trident just as the rear hatch was swinging shut.

I recognised Comrade Ma, the cadre in charge of the ground staff. A loyal officer of Lin Li-kuo, he was supervising the removal of the gangway. In the darkness I couldn't be sure who the other men were. As the car screeched to a halt I concealed my revolver and leapt out, yelling for the steps to be replaced. Comrade Ma recognised me instantly and signalled for them to be rolled back against the Trident. I ran to his side and whispered in his ear that there had been a plot against Marshall Lin. He gaped at me in astonishment. Then he looked round and saw Lao Kao racing towards the steps.

'We're going on board,' I told him in a fierce whisper. 'If we fail, try to stop it taking off. Enemies are all around us!' I shifted my eyes mutely in the direction of the other ground staff.

Ma stared at me in disbelief. 'But Comrade Lin Li-kuo telephoned his orders! Then the ambulance came and took them all on board. Comrade Tou-tou was on a stretcher—'

Lao Kao was halfway up the steps. 'Act now!' I shouted in Ma's face. Then I turned and sprinted after Lao Kao. He was hammering on the closed hatch as I rushed up the steps. When it began to swing open he drew his pistol and thrust it through the narrow slit, firing blindly into the interior of the plane. Then he widened the gap with his shoulder and disappeared inside.

The Trident, its engines roaring, began to roll forward as I reached the top platform. I stopped to draw my own revolver, then launched myself across a widening gap of several feet towards the open hatch of the moving aircraft.

7

A long crooked spear of hot ash tumbled from the end of his
cigarette and splashed across the lapels of his crumpled jacket as
Doctor Vincent Stillman stood up. He removed the glowing stub
from his mouth and squashed it in the ash tray beside the lectern,
covering his mouth with his other fist at the same time to smother
the sudden rasp of his smoker's cough. When he'd recovered he
pushed his thick-framed spectacles up the bridge of his nose and
fixed his eyes reflectively on a point above and behind the heads
of the seventeen members of the East Asia Study Group.

'Have you any idea, gentlemen, what sort of velocity would
be required to break a hair from the human head and drive it
like a javelin into a foamed plastic seat cushion to a depth of two
inches?'

The rush-hour roar of the traffic streaming past the pillared
entrance of the British World Affairs Institute in Pall Mall
carried faintly into the stifling, windowless basement lecture
room during the long silence that followed. The front page of
an evening newspaper on the lap of a prematurely bald diplomat
from the Cabinet Office sitting in the front row announced that
it was now officially London's hottest July of the century. The
burning sun that was shrivelling the whole country had again
pushed London's afternoon shade temperature into the middle
nineties—hotter, the newspaper's headline shrieked, than Biarritz,
Malta, Nice, Honolulu and Hong Kong.

But although some members of the East Asia Study Group had resorted to shirtsleeves, the Foreign Office men present, as though to emphasise their separate and exclusive experience, were stolidly defying the tropics that had now come to them on their home ground, by retaining their jackets and ties. Nevertheless, some faces in the audience were beginning to betray heat-induced signs of short temper and irritation as Vincent Stillman's pause for rhetorical effect lengthened. Sensing this he leaned forward suddenly over the lectern. 'Velocities, gentlemen, in the range of five thousand to ten thousand feet per second—and I think you'll agree it would be difficult to conceive anything other than an explosive event being capable of producing velocities of that order.'

Richard Scholefield, who was chairing the meeting, glanced uneasily along the platform to where Yang sat beside Stillman. He wore now the high-buttoned tunic suit which Communist Chinese cadres since 1949 had made their own official uniform, and he was scanning the attendance roster that he had insisted on receiving from Scholefield before starting the meeting. It listed professors and doctors from Oxford and Cambridge, the London School of Oriental and African Studies, La Trobe, Australia, Windsor Ontario, senior members of the International Institute for Strategic Studies and a smattering of London-based journalists specialising in China as well as Foreign Office and Cabinet Office diplomats. Some members had not bothered to conceal their irritation when they arrived to find Scholefield declining to answer questions about the nature of the speakers. He had concealed the tension that had built up during a long afternoon on the telephone in the convenor's office behind a sharp brusqueness of manner, and now he sat propping up his head with one hand, keeping his eyes averted from the faces in front of him.

Only one name was not on the list. Nina had insisted on attending as Scholefield's guest after he confided the nature of Yang's threat. She sat a little apart from the main body of members at the end of the front row nearest the door. She had dressed soberly in a loose grey dress which concealed her figure and had tied a matching band of the same material demurely around her hair. She sat staring at the floor in front of her with her arms folded, trying not to let her anxiety communicate itself to those around her.

'To people who do my job, it's a well known fact that the best places to look for the tiny fragments of metal sent flying in explosions are seat cushions—and deceased human bodies.' Stillman smiled vaguely round the room at nobody in particular. 'Since a corpse wouldn't do anything to sweeten the already somewhat foetid atmosphere in here, I've brought along an example of the former.'

He reached under the platform dais and lifted up a dun-coloured slab of foamed plastic. 'Incidentally, gentlemen, it was much hotter than this in Vietnam where I once spent a couple of weeks examining fifty-seven bodies for fragments. The refrigerators broke down and they were all decaying beautifully long before I'd finished.' Stillman smothered another cough and looked back absently at the plastic cushion in his hand as if he'd suddenly forgotten why he was holding it. 'But of course that's another story.'

Scholefield started in his seat as the door at the side of the platform swung open suddenly. Several members glanced up irritably at Harvey Ketterman as he stood in the doorway, widening his eyes in a silent, theatrical grimace of self-recrimination. He cringed bent double to a rear seat, took off his jacket and mopped his brow. He held up another copy of the evening paper. 'Only hell's hotter today, Mr. Chairman. We're close to your famous English "sticky end", now, I'd guess. My taxi boiled over on the way here! Deepest apologies.'

He winked exaggeratedly then, immediately serious, turned and peered through screwed-up eyes in the direction of Yang and Stillman. The scientist was holding up the seat cushion above his head and gazing myopically over the heads of his audience again.

'This, gentlemen, is a seat cushion from an airliner. It was part of the original furnishings of a Trident IE purchased initially from the British Aircraft Corporation by the Pakistan Air Force in 1967.'

The prematurely bald man from the China section of the Cabinet Office rose suddenly to his feet with a snort of exasperation. 'Mr. Chairman, I feel I must intervene. We've been called here at exceedingly short notice to listen to two people whom you have declined so far to identify for us beyond their fairly meaningless names. We have only your vaguest assurances that they've got some important revelations to make about the death of Lin Piao.' He fanned himself rapidly with his evening paper. 'We know absolutely nothing of what qualifies these men to speak on the subject, which of course makes it impossible for us to evaluate what they say. Since Lin is believed to have died fully five years ago, I fail to see what urgency there can be in detaining us on one of the hottest afternoons London has ever known when we might be cooling off at home in our gardens with iced gin and tonics in our hands.' He stopped and smiled wearily round at his fellow members. 'So before we hear any more from Doctor Stillman about his, I'm sure fascinating, seat cushions, I think we'd all be grateful for a mite more elucidation.'

Murmurs of agreement came from other men in the audience and Scholefield stood up awkwardly. 'I fully appreciate that most of you might share Percy Crowdleigh's feelings. I would probably have reacted in the same way in your place, Percy.' He spoke without looking at the audience, staring down instead at his hands clenched in front of him. 'I apologise for having to ask you to bear with me down what might look at present rather like a blind alley, but—' Out of the corner of his eye Scholefield saw Yang stand up.

'Perhaps, Mr. Scholefield, I may try to help your colleagues.' All eyes swivelled suddenly to Yang. His features were set in a fixed, glassy smile. Scholefield saw that Nina was leaning forward in her seat, stiff with tension. Yang picked up a copy of the Institute's charter that lay before him on top of the dais.

'If I may quote from your founding articles, gentlemen, your Institute was inaugurated during the 1919 Paris Peace Conference "to encourage the widest possible dissemination of information about world politics". Also, I think in the interests of safeguarding world peace, to promote understanding of all aspects of international affairs.' He paused and licked his lips. 'My name is Yang Tsai-chien. I was Marshall Lin Piao's closest personal aide until he was murdered in September 1971. His death created a grave risk of war between my country and the Soviet Union which could have threatened the peace of the whole world.' He paused

THE DEATH OF LIN PIAO

and looked slowly round the hushed room. 'Those responsible for his death are plotting new intrigues in Peking today. That is the cause for urgency!'

Total silence greeted Yang's announcement. After a long, uncomfortable moment the members began shifting uncomfortably in their seats, looking dubiously at one another, unsure how to react. Yang looked briefly along the platform towards Scholefield. 'I have already provided your chairman with a written account of my own part in the events of 1971. But I have not asked that you be brought here to listen to what you might reasonably see as my personal and unprovable testimony. What you are about to hear will be detailed and irrefutable *scientific* proof. And you will hear it from no less an authority than one of your own countrymen, who also happens to be one of the leading aircraft accident investigators in the world.'

Yang nodded in the direction of Stillman. The little grey-haired man was leaning casually on the lectern, gazing vacantly into space. He had lit another cigarette that was already drooping from the corner of his mouth.

'Because the aircraft was British-built and because the revisionist scientists and technologists of the Soviet Union were unable to interpret satisfactorily the readings of the foreign flight recorder in the aircraft, Doctor Stillman was coerced into playing the role he did. To be more explicit, he was kidnapped from his home by the KGB on the night of 14 September 1971 and smuggled to Russia. After completing the investigation of the Trident crash he was detained in Moscow—until last year when he evaded his captors and sought asylum in the embassy of the People's Republic of China in Moscow. With the help of certain people who wish to see the evil plotters defeated in Peking we escaped to Hong Kong and then made our way to London.'

Yang paused and looked slowly round the room. 'Perhaps now, gentlemen, you will be more ready to listen to what he has to tell you about what happened aboard that Trident jet over Mongolia on the dark night of 12–13 September 1971.'

FOLIO NUMBER EIGHT

Because the Trident lurched forward as I leapt from the top of the embarkation steps, I fell sprawling onto the floor of the fuselage inside the hatch. A foot smashed into the side of my face and another stamped on my wrist. My revolver exploded harmlessly into the galley then a hand snatched it up and flung it away. Lao Kao had already been struck down and lay in the gangway with blood running from a wound on his temple.

Our three adversaries were all dressed in long white hospital gowns. They also wore white headcovers and gauze surgical masks around their faces. One of them clutched at a spreading red stain around his left shoulder where a bullet from Lao Kao's gun had found its mark. All were armed with automatic rifles.

I struggled to my knees as the Trident gathered speed and swung out onto the runway. Through the open hatch I could see Comrade Ma driving a ponderous yellow fuel bowser flat out across the grass. Then once again a foot smashed into my face and I fell backwards against a bulkhead. I heard a brief burst of gunfire from outside before one of the white-gowned men slammed the hatch closed. Then I was seized and dragged half-conscious along the gangway and bundled into a seat.

I felt the Trident shudder and gather speed. Through a side window I saw Comrade Ma's fuel bowser veering across the grass towards us. As I watched, Ma leapt from the cab and left the bowser to career driverless onto the concrete runway in front of us.

My spirit soared because I was sure our take-off had been aborted. The guards were flung in all directions as the Trident swerved off the runway. The whole aircraft shook violently as we thundered across the pitted grass surface at high speed. It seemed as if the aircraft must break up. But the pilot succeeded miraculously in swinging round the bowser and steered us back onto the concrete further along the runway. He accelerated frantically then, and moments later, with a great roar, lifted us steeply off the very end of the airfield into the dark sky.

I struggled upright between the seats, trying to grapple

with the nearest guard. But he raised his automatic rifle high above his head and crashed the butt-end down into my face with savage force. As I fell I felt another heavy blow on top of my head and I lost consciousness.

When I regained my senses, my ears were roaring and there was a dull, sick pain in my head. I found a white-masked figure standing in the gangway glaring along his rifle at us. Red PLA flashes were visible on the collar of the tunic under his white gown. His eyes were bright with aggression above his mask and I judged him to be a simple peasant in his first years in the army.

Lao Kao was sitting beside me. Both of us were handcuffed, our arms wrenched painfully behind our chair backs. Another guard, like the first, wearing mask, gown and headcover over an army uniform, stood by the door at the front of the Trident holding his automatic rifle stiffly across his chest. He was older than the peasant boy but his expression was dull and vacant.

Lao Kao's face was caked with dried blood that had run from the wound on his temple. He struggled to smile but was obviously in great pain. 'We've been in the air nearly two hours,' he told me through bloodied lips. 'They say we're going to Shanghai. They say they have some important party members on board suffering from an infectious disease. Their orders are to allow nobody to come into contact with them or their doctor until we land.' He nodded towards the forward compartment at the front of the aircraft.

I looked round at the body of the third guard, slumped across the seats on the far side of the gangway. The red stain had widened to cover all his chest and he lay very still. The peasant boy, noticing my glance, stepped forward and jabbed the muzzle of his rifle viciously into Lao Kao's chest. 'You will pay for that crime when we land.'

'No, it is you who will pay—with your lives.' I spoke very quietly in reply. 'You will pay for a much more towering crime that you have not even committed.'

The simple face of the young peasant soldier clouded. He looked round uncertainly at the other guard at the front of the cabin. 'Have you thought why two junior fighters have been given charge of such an important task?' I had raised my voice deliberately so that both could hear. 'So that you can be made scapegoats for one of the greatest treacheries in China's history!'

They both gaped at me. 'Do you know who is in there?' I nodded towards the forward compartment. They continued to gape and I thrust my right shoulder forward indicating the right breast pocket of my army tunic. 'Inspect my pass!' Although all visible markings of rank were abolished in 1963 the two armymen, like all soldiers, recognised that the four pockets on my military jacket and the fineness of the cotton weave denoted high officer status. The peasant boy reached out and undid the flap. He pulled out my identity card—and his eyes widened immediately. He hurried to the front of the cabin and showed it to his comrade. Then they both stared round apprehensively at the closed door of the forward compartment.

'How do you know you are flying to Shanghai?' I called. 'How do you know your commander Marshall Lin and his family have not already been murdered in that compartment? If they have, you two will be accused of causing their death, when we reach our destination.'

They continued staring open-mouthed, stunned by the enormity of my suggestion. They then looked back at my pass. 'There is a doctor in there.' They nodded diffidently towards the door. 'It is dangerous to enter because of the risk of infection.'

'Call him!' I shouted my words contemptuously. 'Call to him and ask him to confirm who's in there. You have been duped!'

They began shouting immediately. But no reply came through the flimsy partition. The steady roar of the Trident's engines from outside in the darkness was the only sound in the cabin. My head throbbed and the agony of not knowing what had happened to Marshall Lin was making me sick with tension.

At last the two guards both came back to where we sat and stood looking down at us indecisively. 'Break the door down and go in and see for yourselves before it is too late,' I urged.

They shook their heads. 'Our orders came from the office of Chairman Mao himself,' said the senior guard. 'The risk of infection is too great. Nobody may enter.'

'I will go in,' I said softly, 'With my handcuffs on, I will risk infection—to show you.'

They stared at each other for a moment. Then the senior man nodded his head and ordered me to stand up. He forced my hands up painfully behind me until they came free of the seat-back. Then he pushed me ahead of him with the end of his rifle towards the front of the plane.

I stopped for a moment in front of the door to the forward compartment, apprehensive of what I might find there. But the guard was holding the rifle firmly in the small of my back and as I hesitated he prodded me forward again. So I turned quickly and lashed out with my foot. The flimsy door gave immediately and flew back on its hinges. I took two paces into the compart-ment and stood still, staring in horror.

Three white-cowled figures lay strapped into facing seats, their heads jogging lifelessly with the motion of the plane. A fourth figure, similarly cowled, lay strapped to a stretcher that had been propped across seats on the other side of the gangway. I rushed to the stretcher and looked into the white hood, expecting to see Tou-tou's face. But it was empty. I turned my back so that I could use my manacled hands to open the robe. Over my shoulder I saw immediately that it was stuffed only with twisted bandages and pillows. I looked up at the guard in the doorway. He stood gazing open-mouthed at the scene, his face white, his eyes dilating with fright.

I hurried across to look at the three other figures. Their seats had been moved into a reclining position and they lolled motion-less, their faces obscured in the shadow of the loose white anti-infection cowls.

By half-turning I was able to use my chained hands to pull the hoods aside. But even as I did this I could feel that their cheeks were already cold. Their features were the colour of wax and it was impossible to tell whether they were still breathing or not. A great sadness engulfed me as I gazed down at the faces of Marshall Lin and his wife and son.

Lao Kao and the peasant boy appeared in the doorway, staring in. The older guard stepped forward and lifted the lid of a document box lying on a spare seat beside Marshall Lin. The characters 'Top Secret' written in red across the cover of a mili-tary folder were plainly visible. Next to the box lay the silver-plated pistol Stalin had given Marshall Lin. All four of us stared at each other. Even the guards, despite their low intelligence, could see how hopelessly we were all trapped in the faked conspiracy.

'The pilot,' I said dully. 'We must get to the pilot and stop him landing.'

'But where are we?' The peasant boy's voice was shrill with panic.

'I don't know.' I turned and moved quickly towards the door at the front of the compartment.

'Wait! The guard has strict orders to defend the flight deck with his life. Nobody from this quarantine compartment must approach the pilot.' I looked around. It was the older guard who had shouted the warning. His rifle, however, hung loose on his arm, and he clearly had no intention of trying to stop me.

'We have no choice. We must show him.' I lashed out at the door with my foot. It splintered and broke from its hinges and I fell sideways under the impact.

The guard outside was ready for us. Holding his automatic rifle steady in front of him, he took one step forward and opened fire. The peasant boy took the whole burst in his chest and toppled over backwards, screaming dementedly. The older guard had wisely stepped aside and taken cover as I shattered the door. Now he fired carefully from a crouching position behind a seat and the flight-deck guard tumbled forward, dying, on top of me.

The older guard knelt quickly beside the young peasant, then stood up shaking his head. Lao Kao persuaded him to unlock his handcuffs and together they came and moved the dead guard's body off me and helped me to my feet. When my hands were freed I picked up a rifle and we broke open the door to the flight deck.

The pilot looked fearfully round at us over his shoulder. 'Don't shoot! Keep back. We are flying low.'

I stepped up beside him and thrust the rifle under his nose. 'Where are we?'

The pilot didn't answer but continued peering anxiously out through the screen. I followed his eyes and under the pale light from the stars I suddenly saw the vast sweep of the steppes beneath us. A great herd of horses terrified by the noise of our engines close to the ground was stampeding madly across the darkened plain in our path.

'Mongolia!' The word burst from me in astonishment. 'We are across the border.'

The pilot nodded frantically, still straining his eyes into the night. 'We must land soon. I am returning you to your homeland.'

I stared at him in bewilderment. 'Where?'

He jabbed a finger at the projected map display on the panel beside him. I looked quickly and saw the markings of an airfield 200 kilometres east of Ulan Bator, just across the Kerulen.

'The airfield should be somewhere here. I'm sure my navigation is right. But there are no lights.'

'We are Chinese!' He turned and stared up at me. I jabbed the rifle against the side of his neck. 'What are your orders?'

'My orders, from the office of Chairman Mao himself, were to fly three revisionist Mongolian spies back to their homeland.' He pointed again to the map display. 'To this airfield. Then I am to return with three Chinese comrades who were innocently arrested as hostages. We are flying a specially agreed low course for reasons of security.'

'You are the victim of a plot,' I said very slowly. 'Like the rest of us. Turn back immediately. Return home to the People's Republic of China.'

He looked pleadingly up at me. 'I must obey the orders of Chairman Mao's office.'

I pushed the gun roughly against the side of his face. 'Turn now! Or I will kill you this instant and we will all die together.'

He flinched but said nothing. Obediently he made the necessary adjustments to the controls and I watched the compass heading alter as we climbed and banked in a wide arc above the steppes. When it had settled again on a bearing due south-east I moved back and handed the rifle to Lao Kao. 'Ensure he holds that course.'

I turned away to find that the older guard had removed his mask and head covering. I patted him reassuringly on the shoulder. 'We will return and confront the plotters with the evidence of their treachery.'

His simple, puzzled eyes searched my face and, I remember, he nodded uncertainly as I brushed past him. 'I'm going to see if there is anything I can do for Marshall Lin,' I said.

I went out through the door of the flight deck and made my

way into the forward compartment again. As I stepped over the dead guard a sudden, deafening roar engulfed my senses. An invisible force struck my body like a battering ram and a bright orange sheet of flame rose before my eyes. In that instant I passed painlessly into oblivion.

TAIPEH, June 1972—According to a certain source, the nine passengers on the Trident, including the woman, were all under fifty years of age and in the woman's purse was a man's French cap. Since a woman as old as Yeh Chun would not have need of such an article, this suggests Lin Piao and his wife might not have been on that plane.

Issues and Studies,
Journal of the
Institute of International Affairs,
Taiwan,
1 June 1972

8

'The Russians, not to put too fine a point on it, were baffled.' Dr. Vincent Stillman leaned his folded arms on the edge of the lectern and gazed up at the ceiling. Lost in thought, he opened his mouth wide and those members of the East Asia Study Group sitting in the front row were able to see that his teeth, like his ragged moustache, were also stained bright yellow with nicotine. For a moment his head seemed to shake almost imperceptibly on his shoulders.

'The Trident had come in too low, remember, for their radar screens to pick it up. So the first thing they knew of its presence was when it crashed. Their nearest radio-sonde observations from the Soviet rocket base near Choibalsan, a hundred miles away, showed there had been no unusual meteorological conditions. The weather was fine that night with only moderate wind and there was no evidence to indicate the presence of clear air turbulence in the region.'

Scholefield glanced quickly round the room. All seventeen members of the group were listening intently to Stillman now. Harvey Ketterman, he noticed, was leaning forward on the seat in front, his head cocked on one side and his eyes closed in an attitude of intense concentration. For a brief moment Nina caught Scholefield's eye from her seat at the end of the front row. Her face puckered with concern and she shot him a quick, worried smile. A rustle of paper drew his attention back to Stillman and he watched him fumbling with a sheaf of notes on the lectern.

'You'll all no doubt be familiar with Premier Chou En-lai's famous account of what happened to the Trident, given to a group of American newspaper editors in October 1972.' Stillman looked up, then picked the top sheet off the lectern and read from it. '"Its fuel was nearly exhausted," said Chou, "so it had to try a forced landing. It slid a good distance on the ground leaving behind very clear marks. When the plane landed, one of its wings first touched the ground and caught fire and all the nine persons on board were burned to death."' Stillman dropped the paper back on the lectern and bared his yellow teeth suddenly in a crooked smile, directed towards the ceiling. 'I'm surprised that's not been seen in the West for what it is—a modern Chinese fairy story.' The smile faded only very slowly from his face. 'The disposition of the wreckage of an aircraft is one of the most important clues about how the crash has occurred. An experienced air accident investigator can tell a lot from how and where the various bits and pieces come to rest.'

He raised his arm abruptly in a signal to the projectionist behind a small window at the back of the room. The lights immediately went out and an illuminated slide appeared on the white screen behind the dais. It showed the burned-out hulk of an aircraft's main fuselage silhouetted against the sky on a flat, grass-covered plain. In the far distance the rear fuselage, engines and tail unit which had broken off cleanly were visible standing up perpendicularly as though undamaged. One wing, on the starboard side of the main fuselage, was still intact.

'As you can see, gentlemen, the distribution of the wreckage was not inconsistent with Chou En-lai's explanation,' said Stillman's voice from the darkness. 'But it does seem very odd to me that nobody in the West has ever bothered to ask how, if the Trident really did run out of fuel, its empty tanks were able to produce such a fierce fire that it burned all the occupants beyond recognition.'

Everybody gazed in silence at the slide of the crashed aircraft. 'And since, as you can see, the aircraft came down practically intact why didn't anybody manage to get out? They would have had a good chance of remaining conscious in these circumstances. Has nobody ever wondered that?' Again nobody broke the rhetorical silence. 'It takes a good many minutes in a fierce fire, you know, before all the skin and superficial flesh on the human body gets burned to the extent that these fellows were.'

The slide changed abruptly and the starkness of the next image provoked an involuntary murmur of shock around the room. Scholefield clearly heard Nina's separate gasp of horror. On the screen nine charred corpses had appeared, laid out in a row on white sheets. The photograph had been taken by a cameraman standing at normal height and the bodies seemed to resemble poorly-constructed human-sized puppets fashioned from blackened papier-mâché.

The tense silence in the darkened room was broken by the scrape of a match and a tiny bud of flame flowered brightly in front of Stillman's face. His sagging features were illuminated theatrically for a moment as he lit another cigarette. Again his head seemed to quiver momentarily on his shoulders. 'It didn't take the Soviet Army pathologist boys long to discover that three of these corpses had bullets lodged in them,' he said quietly, turning back to the screen. 'Two lots were of rifle calibre and the other one was a smaller revolver bullet. All the weapons were found in the wreckage and matched up with their respective bits of lead by their ballistics boffins. But there were no bullets in the pilot. His body was found at the controls—and this was what worried the Soviets. Because, although there may be *popular* misconceptions nowadays about what happens when you fire guns in pressurised airliners, these were not shared by our Russian friends on the spot. They knew that air pumps are perfectly capable of maintaining pressure differentials in spite of leaks from several bullet holes. You've got to have a fairly massive hole, you know, gentlemen, three or four feet square, before it beats the pumps.' He stopped and removed the cigarette that his audience had been watching jiggle between his lips in silhouette against the light of the screen. 'You could stage the gunfight at the O.K. corral, you know, in the pressurised cabin of a modern airliner and I doubt if even that on its own would bring it down.'

He turned suddenly and noticed that the slide of the charred bodies was still showing. 'Let's lose that now shall we?' he called quickly to the projectionist. 'It's not all that pleasant, is it?' When he was satisfied the screen behind him was blank he turned back to his audience. But he didn't ask for the lights to be switched up again.

'Because of all this, the Soviets really needed at this stage to consult everybody's "spy" on board the Trident—the flight recorder. Or the "black box" as the newspapers tend to call it. They dug it out from the wreckage, all right, but it was a Plessey-Duval, you see. Now, that's a common enough flight recorder in Western aircraft but to their dismay the Soviets found they couldn't make head nor tail of the ruddy thing.'

Stillman took out his cigarette packet again and lit a further cigarette from the stub of the old one. He walked across to the lectern and dropped the old stub into the ash tray. 'Now this has happened before of course. Several times in Eastern Europe, airliners built in the West have crashed and the men who put the first sputnik in space have been embarrassed to find they didn't have the technical equipment to do the black box read-outs. They couldn't, for instance, develop and print your Kodak colour films in Moscow either for the same reasons—but that's neither here nor there. A couple of times in the past they saved their faces by returning the black boxes to their capitalist makers and asking them to send them back with the data in readable form. They always covered up their incompetence by saying they were anxious to demonstrate their desire to co-operate in international air accident prevention. But you can see without my telling you that they couldn't risk returning this particular Trident's black box to the makers.' Stillman laughed suddenly, a short, shrill bark of laughter. 'That's where I came in—or rather, looked at from your point of view, gentlemen—that's where I went out.'

Stillman turned his back suddenly on his audience and stood staring pointlessly at the brightness of the blank screen. He took an audible deep breath in the darkness and this brought on a sudden fit of coughing. When he had recovered he spoke more quietly than before, still without turning round. 'To cut a long story short gentlemen, I was subjected to a considerable degree of physical coercion and taken forcibly to the scene of the crash. I arrived there on the fourth day after it happened, September seventeenth.'

He swung round suddenly and paced with new resolution to the end of the dais where Scholefield was seated. He snapped his fingers and a new slide appeared on the screen showing a sheet of photographic paper covered with a graph grid. Four parallel lines were traced evenly across it. Stillman turned to face his audience again and cleared his throat. 'This, gentlemen,' he said softly, 'is the read-out from the Trident's black box.'

The Group members stared in uncomprehending silence at the screen.

'It's great, just great, Doctor Stillman.' Harvey Ketterman's voice carried cheerfully from the back of the room. 'The trouble is that all of us here may well be staring at the most vital piece of evidence since they took Cain's fingerprints off that asses' jaw-bone east of Eden—but it might just as well be an extract from my granny's pearl and plain knitting book for all I can tell.'

The American's lightness broke the tension and there was a rattle of relieved laughter from around the darkened room. Stillman picked up a long pointer and moved briskly to the side of the screen. 'These four lines are traces from the four channels of the flight recorder.' He pointed quickly to each line in turn. 'The first records the aircraft's heading, whether it's flying north, south, east or west. The second shows its altitude, the third shows when the machine was yawing or pitching—that's backwards and forwards and from side to side, like this.' He stuck out his arms stiffly to make aeroplane wings and swung his body to illustrate the movements. 'And the fourth records negative G. That shows if the plane suddenly drops or goes up in turbulence.'

He turned and looked round over his shoulder at his audience. 'The time scale is along the bottom and the box operates, remember, all the while the aircraft is flying. If these lines all run smoothly you can say with certainty the plane was travelling in a normal way. If it starts to do anything strange these lines will tell you exactly what it was and help you work out afterwards why it happened.'

'These four lines of yours all look pretty steady to me, Doctor Stillman,' said Ketterman slowly from the back of the room, 'for an aircraft that's supposed to have come to a violent end.'

'Precisely.' Stillman turned back to the screen and raised his pointer again. 'You can see that the top line is the only one that gives us variable information. It indicates that there was a steady 180° change of heading from north-west to south-east not long before the lines cease. That proves conclusively the pilot turned and was flying back the way he'd come. But other lines show the altitude didn't change, there was no rising or falling from turbulence and no pitching or yawing.' Stillman slid his pointer back and forth across the screen, illustrating his points by tracing each line in turn. 'All four lines stop dead here abruptly—with the plane in a normal posture.' He pointed to the ends of the lines again. 'There's just these little tick-like kicks.'

He remained silent and continued to hold the pointer against the screen for several seconds, as though anticipating that somebody would prompt him with an obvious question. When nobody spoke he laid the pointer aside and turned round slowly like a schoolmaster exasperated by dull pupils. 'If the Trident, as Chou En-lai claimed, had come in to land relatively successfully, at least as far as getting onto the ground was concerned, we would have expected, wouldn't we, gentlemen, to have found that altitude line descending gradually to zero? And the other lines would have gone on recording the changing postures of the aircraft during the descent, until the very moment it broke up on the ground. Wouldn't they?'

When nobody offered a response, he stopped and signalled for the light to be switched on. He blinked in the sudden glare from the neon tubes and looked round the room. 'Does nobody know then what these straight lines prove?' He brushed perfunctorily at the grey ash that had gathered on the front of his jacket. Still nobody responded. He looked up slowly and stared out above their heads again. 'Well, I'll tell you. It proves that the black box stopped operating suddenly and unexpectedly when the Trident was flying perfectly level at two hundred feet. That means all its electrics were destroyed in a single instant during normal flight.' He paused and spoke very slowly for effect. 'Only one thing is capable of causing that.'

He turned and walked across the dais to where the discoloured lump of foamed plastic was lying in front of Yang. He picked it up and held it out at arm's length. 'And that's where this fellow comes in. This shapeless and rather ugly modern artifact, gentlemen, contains conclusive proof of the crime.' Still holding it he walked back to his chair and bent down and opened the battered leather briefcase that lay on the floor. When he stood up he was holding a thick bunch of long steel knitting needles in his other fist.

'Though I say this myself gentlemen, not everybody would have appreciated the significance of this innocent-looking object. But our "friends" in the KGB'—he stopped and waved the needles in the air stressing the word heavily—'our "friends" were luckier than they knew when they chose to take me on their special Mongolian package tour. In my youth I developed a special knowledge of cushions in my work at the forensic laboratories of the Royal Armaments Research and Development Establishment. Some of you probably know that's a section of the Ministry of Defence that provides certain special services to other government departments. I became a specialist there, gentlemen, in the study of ordinary house cushions that certain citizens were in the habit of wrapping round safes before opening them violently and illegally without keys.' He lifted his head and his discoloured teeth appeared suddenly in another brief smile towards the ceiling. 'Life is full of strange coincidences, isn't it? Out there on the steppes of Mongolia I tripped over this object and saw the same kind of marks I'd first seen forty years ago in cushions taken from a broken bank vault in the Mile End Road.'

He placed the slab of foamed plastic on the lectern in front of him and began inserting the long steel knitting needles one by one into holes in its surface. 'This was a back-rest cushion in the Trident. I picked it up a good half mile from the site of the main wreckage. It wasn't burned like everything else.' He bent closer peering shortsightedly at the plastic to find the entry points for the needles. 'The first thing I noticed were these holes. The human hairs I mentioned earlier showed up in another cushion from a facing seat when I got all the stuff back to the laboratory they'd set up for me in the Academy of Sciences in Moscow.'

The two dozen or so steel needles jutting out from the surface had begun to form a funnel-shaped cluster tapering to a point like the bare poles of an Indian wigwam. 'But as soon as I stuck these ordinary Russian knitting needles into the holes, I knew.' He picked up the cushion, turned it over and held it out towards his audience in both hands. The cluster of needles now hung down from its underside, converging towards a common point beneath the cushion. 'The seat-back you see was reclined to its maximum. These holes were clearly made by tiny objects passing upwards through the cushion. You only have to trace their trajectories to see that all the little objects, whatever they were, radiated from a common source underneath the seat-back.' He paused and peered triumphantly round the room. 'Are you beginning to get a glimmer, gentlemen, of what that common source might have been?'

He was still holding the cushion and its hanging cone of needles in front of him, when there was a quiet knock on the door. Because Stillman's demonstration had engaged the rapt attention of everybody in the room, nobody moved at first. The knock was repeated and Nina, after a questioning glance towards Scholefield, got up and opened it.

The aged porter from the Institute's front reception desk upstairs stood in the doorway holding an expensive-looking brown leather document case. He peered round the room until his eyes lighted on Scholefield. 'Pardon me, Sir, but a Chinese gentleman asked me to deliver this immediately to a Mr. Yang. Some reports for distribution to the meeting, apparently.'

Scholefield motioned him in and he hobbled across to where Yang was sitting. He set the document case down by his chair and they heard the Chinese man's quiet 'Hsieh hsieh' as he thanked him. Then the old man turned and left, closing the door noise-lessly behind him. Yang nodded apologetically towards Schole-field and gestured with his hand for Stillman to continue. Outside in Pall Mall Razduhev's black Mini slowed and stopped to pick up the Mongolian diplomat in a black Chinese cadre's uniform as he emerged from the Institute's front door. Once he was inside, the car edged out from the kerb once more and merged inconspicuously into the rush hour stream of traffic flowing down towards St. James's Palace.

Inside the basement lecture room, Stillman, who had held the foamed plastic cushion pointedly in front of him throughout the entire interruption to emphasise his displeasure, lowered it with exaggerated slowness onto the lectern again. He lit another cigarette and lodged it in the corner of his mouth, screwing up

THE DEATH OF LIN PIAO

his eyes against the smoke. 'To prove beyond doubt what that mysterious "common source" was, gentlemen, I X-rayed this cushion from all angles and found literally hundreds of tiny fragments of metal still inside it. About the size of specks of dust, they were, that's all. They didn't weigh much more than a milligram. Some of 'em in fact weighed much less. Just like the hairs driven into that other cushion on the facing seat, they'd been forced in to a depth of two or three inches by a very high velocity indeed. Many of these specks of metal when we put 'em under a stereoscan electron microscope were found to have fused with the plastic when they came to a standstill. This proved they were hot when they went in. What's more, most of the little jiggers turned out to be made of a mild type of steel which hadn't been used at all by the British Aircraft Corporation in the construction of the aircraft.'

He stopped and looked up to see how this information was being received. In the front row, Scholefield noticed, Percy Crowdleigh from the Cabinet Office had begun to shift restlessly in his seat again.

'To make absolutely sure at what velocity these bits of metal and the hairs had been driven into the cushion, I got the Soviets to fix me up a gas-launcher and using a replica of our friend here'—he patted the foamed plastic cushion with something approaching affection—'I fired minute steel pellets into it. I used my maths to scale the sizes down and came up with a provable conclusion that the real bits in this cushion—like that human hair I found—must've gone in at a rate of above seven thousand feet a second. Now—'

Crowdleigh jumped up suddenly, waving his evening paper again and shaking his head in irritation. 'Doctor Stillman, this is all very fascinating, but at the risk of appearing ignorant I have to confess you're beginning to lose me.' Other voices around the room murmured agreement. 'This may indeed be all very convincing but I feel obliged to ask whether we're going to be provided with any documentary evidence to support this highly sophisticated scientific hypothesis.'

Stillman half turned towards Yang, his eyebrows raised in enquiry. 'I think I can say that copies of my full report have now been brought here for distribution.' Yang nodded quickly and indicated the document case that had just been delivered.

Stillman turned back to the man from the Cabinet Office. 'There is your answer, Sir. My purpose tonight is to give you a popularised and readily understandable introduction to my report. You will be able to take it away and study it at your leisure and no doubt subject it later to analysis by experts.'

The diplomat nodded with ill grace and sat down again still fanning himself with the newspaper. Stillman pushed his spectacles up onto his forehead, rubbed the sockets of his eyes with two clenched fists, and peered out unseeing at his audience through screwed up eyes. 'As I was saying, seven thousand feet per second, gentlemen—there is one thing and one thing only that will produce such a velocity and that is an explosion.' He pursed his lips as though about to savour some invisible culinary delicacy. 'Not to put too fine a point on it, gentlemen, an explosion brought about by the detonation of a bomb.'

The members of the East Asia Study Group stared back at him, accepting his announcement in total silence. Then slowly Harvey Ketterman rose to his feet, scratching his head. 'What you're saying, Doctor Stillman, unless my unscientific American mind isn't very much mistaken, is that Lin Piao's Trident couldn't possibly have crash-landed after running out of fuel. You say that it was quite definitely blown out of the sky by a deliberately planted high explosive bomb, put aboard secretly by persons unknown before it left China. Is that it, in a nutshell?'

Stillman nodded. 'Just so.'

'And you claim that your scientific evidence is conclusive beyond any shadow of doubt whatsoever?'

Stillman nodded again. 'When you come to read my report you will find it runs to some 250 pages. There are more than a hundred photographs showing everything I have told you in tabulated detail. All my conclusions about the explosion are borne out by diagnostic microtopography.'

Ketterman, still on his feet, leaned forward easily on the chair in front of him, grinning broadly. 'If that's some kind of new scientific religion, I have to tell you right away Doctor Stillman I'm going to reserve my judgement until I've had a chance to put your full report under some of our own highly agnostic microscopes.'

Stillman bared his yellow teeth in a tolerant grin then poked another cigarette under the straggling fronds of his moustache. 'There's a great deal I haven't told you yet, gentlemen,' he said quietly. 'I haven't told you about how the pathologists dug the big fragments that made those needle-sized holes in the cushion out of the charred back muscles of the body lying strapped to the seat.' He stopped and drew hard on the cigarette. 'I haven't told you about the mock-up of the Trident's fuselage that I had the Russkies build for me to prove my theories beyond doubt. I simulated the explosion from the same place underneath the seat, you see. I deduced from the velocities and the position that it was a three pounder packed in a cold steel tube that had been exploded with a military "pencil" detonator. It blew a four-foot hole in the side of the fuselage, gentlemen, and ripped open an underfloor fuel tank at the same time, starting an immediate fire. The controls to the tail were smashed too, locking it horizontally. That's how it glided in to land.

'The blast even ripped the cushions from the nearest seats and they were sucked out of the hole—which explains why, quite remarkably, they survived the fire.' Stillman's eyes glittered and again Scholefield noticed that in his excitement his head was wagging slightly on his shoulders.

'All that, gentlemen, is in my report—and more. I found evidence of other incendiary devices that had ensured that the fire started by the bomb would spread rapidly. The pathologists' report, which appears as an appendix, will show you that the victims all died by inhaling flames directly into their lungs—except the pilot, who died more slowly of carbon monoxide poisoning.'

'Doctor Stillman, your scientific expertise is most impressive.' Scholefield spoke quietly from his chair without rising. 'But it's all entirely irrelevant, isn't it, unless you can prove something else that nobody else has managed to do positively so far—that Lin Piao was actually on the plane?'

Several of the other men in the room stirred in their seats, watching Stillman's face carefully to see how he dealt with the question.

'I'm an aircraft accident investigator, not a medical expert.' Stillman paused and lit another cigarette. 'The Soviet pathologists produced dental charts which they say they had kept since the Thirties when Lin spent several years in Moscow undergoing treatment for war wounds. These dental charts are presented side by side with a matching chart of the teeth from one of the nine charred bodies, in an appendix to my report.' He tapped the document lying on the lectern in front of him with a note of finality. 'That is all I have to say on the subject. Comrade Yang will distribute my report.' He picked up his sheaf of papers and sat down, glancing at Yang, who had sat through most of the address staring expressionlessly in front of him.

Yang nodded and reached for the case. He began unfastening the brass locks, using both hands. As he opened it, Scholefield heard Nina's stifled scream. He looked up and saw she had risen to her feet. Her face was clenched in an expression of alarm and she was staring at Yang pointing with an outstretched arm towards the case whose lid was now raised in her direction, giving her a view of its contents. She shouted something unintelligible and the Chinese looked up in astonishment as she flung herself towards him.

For Scholefield the room tilted suddenly and he felt himself tumbling backwards off his chair. He fell, it seemed, only very slowly towards the floor. All the time his eyes were riveted on Nina, Yang and Stillman, although the rest of his body seemed to spin rapidly around the axis of his vision. All movement outside himself seemed to take place haltingly as though already recorded by a slow-motion camera and he saw the Chinese dive very deliberately for the cover of the heavy wooden dais. Then he felt an unbearable pressure squeeze his ear drums tight inside his head. Stillman and Nina, who had first of all been flung together in a violent, unwilling embrace, separated abruptly and began to glide apart above him in opposite directions as the great roar burst inside his brain.

He hit the floor and at the same time saw Stillman floating jerkily away from him towards the ceiling, like a ping-pong ball on a fairground rifle range being propelled erratically upward by an invisible jet of water. He heard very clearly the heels of his shoes knock against the perforated acoustic tiles of the ceiling. Then great cataracts of plaster and other debris began cascading down all around him. A confused babble of shouting reached him through this curtain of grey, roaring fog. Then abruptly it ceased and he heard, and saw, nothing more.

PART TWO

The Death of Mao Tse=tung

LONDON, Friday—Ten months after Mao's chosen successor Lin Piao, his wife and four top military leaders vanished into the night—or into a Mongolian hillside, if indeed they were passengers in that mysteriously vagrant Trident jet—the Chinese have offered no official explanation of the event.

The Economist, 8 July 1972

9

'Ring by eleven—and your coffin's flying by seven! That's what we promise at Jarvis's, Mr. Ketterman.' The dapper little cockney, dressed all in black, standing at the American's elbow in the noisy crowded bar of the Black Horse in Marylebone High Street, looked up into the blank smoked lenses that covered Ketterman's eyes and opened his mouth wide in expectation. His tongue flickered briefly out of the dark void like a stunted red antenna seeking reaction to the motto he had just chanted.

When Ketterman didn't reply he turned abruptly and sank his nose into the froth on top of the pint of bitter the American had just bought him. 'You won't find another FD in London who can match Arthur Cooper for speed—your consular officer tell you that, did he?' He wiped his mouth and nose on the sleeve of his black jacket and set the pint mug down on a counter already awash with spilled drinks. 'Should have done, if he didn't. I've lost count of the cases I've handled for your embassy.'

Ketterman nodded absently as he picked up his own half-pint tankard. His face twisted in disgust as he sipped the warm beer, and he pushed it away. He leaned back hard against the noisy crush of bodies that was threatening to squash him against the bar and looked down speculatively at the narrow-shouldered little funeral director. He could see from the discoloured roots on the crown of his head that he'd dyed his white hair black to match his undertaker's clothes.

'All the pubs are running out of ice about this time every night, y'know, in the heat. Must be terrible for you Americans. You live on it, don't you?' He took another sip of his beer. 'Here, what's happened to you then, Mr. K? Looks as if you've had a nasty knock. There's a lovely bruise turning out on your cheek, isn't there?'

'I had a fall earlier this evening.' Ketterman waved a dismissive hand. He slipped a sealed foolscap envelope from the inside pocket of his jacket and handed it to Cooper. The little man looked up into his face with a puzzled expression. 'Take it to the washroom and count it,' said Ketterman softly.

Cooper picked up his beer with his other hand and took a long gulp. 'You were lucky to catch me so late, Mr. Ketterman,' he said loudly. 'It's thanks to this little fellow of course.' He pulled a bleeper, of the kind carried by doctors on call, out of his top pocket then slipped it back again. 'If I hadn't been out at the airport on another rush case for the Sudan, I'd have been at home in Potter's Bar long ago.'

Although all the windows and doors were wide open, the air inside the pub was hot and dank and condensation dripped occasionally from the ceiling onto the heads and shoulders of the drinkers. 'Excuse me then,' said Cooper with a leering wink, 'I'll just go and shake hands with the wife's best friend.' Ketterman leaned on the bar and watched the little man push his way through the crowd to a door beneath an illuminated 'Gentlemen' sign.

Outside in Marylebone High Street the last flush of light was fading from the sky. The traffic had died to a trickle and even the swallows wheeling and swooping above the rooftops seemed to be moving slowly and listlessly through the heavy, humid air. Ketterman watched Cooper coming back through the crowd in the mirror. The envelope and the money were nowhere to be seen. Under cover of the dark glasses he watched the funeral director mop his glistening brow with a grey handkerchief. With sweating fingers he pushed the already greasy knot of his black tie tight against his bulging Adam's apple and stepped forward to tug at Ketterman's elbow. 'That's four times what it would cost for us to airfreight the deceased urgently to Washington for you, Mr. Ketterman, did you know?' His voice was a hoarse whisper and his mouth opened wide again revealing the tip of his tongue dickering hopefully in its frame.

Ketterman put a cigarette in his mouth and immediately, with a deferential gesture born of his profession, the little Londoner produced a silver-plated lighter from his pocket. 'That's the first instalment of a personal and private retainer for you,' said Ketterman quietly as he bent his head close over the proffered flame. 'Your firm's account will be settled separately through the embassy.'

Cooper closed his mouth and the lighter with a simultaneous snap. He screwed up his watery blue eyes and stared at the American. 'Your consul said on the phone you were a government officer and you would want my personal attention for the urgent transhipment of very important remains, Mr. Ketterman.' He stopped and looked round to see if anybody was listening. 'I'm not averse to doing a bit of "overtime" in return for a backhander. But a tenner's the most your embassy's ever slipped me for running out to the airport for a night flight.' He looked round uneasily again and leaned close. 'Nobody, Mr. Ketterman, has ever offered me *two thousand quid.*'

Ketterman raised his eyebrows significantly. 'That's only ten per cent of your eventual gross—if you do the job to my satisfaction.'

'Ten per cent?' Cooper's mouth opened wide again and this time stayed open. He cocked his head on one side, looking at the American like a loyal but puzzled puppy. 'Whose corpse is it?'

It was Ketterman's turn now to look carefully around him. But the roar of conversation and laughter from the crowd swirled unheeding around their heads. 'I don't have a corpse, Mr. Cooper. I want to rent one from you.'

'Rent a corpse?' Cooper's eyes widened in disbelief.

'Let's say an elderly, white, Anglo-Saxon, embalmed male. For an hour or so in the morning. Long enough to get the right legal documentation so the coffin can go out on the six p.m. flight to Washington.'

Cooper suddenly straightened up, squaring his puny shoulders. 'Mr. Ketterman, it's more than my job's worth to do anything illegal.'

Ketterman signalled to the barman and ordered another pint

of bitter for Cooper. When he'd paid for it he turned back to the little undertaker, removed his dark glasses and smiled. 'You've been in your line of business for forty-nine years, Mr. Cooper. Shipping coffins out of London since before the war. Only about six a year went out by sea then, right? Now you fly out around a thousand a year all over the world—up to a half dozen every day. Almost all of 'em are tourists who die visiting Britain or sickly Arabs who come to Harley Street for medical treatment. You use metal-lined coffins and wrap them in hessian sacking so pilots and passengers don't get unnerved by the idea of flying with the dead. And when you put your hermetic seals on the zinc inner box at your embalming premises, as the law requires, and swear a written declaration that there's only a cadaver inside, the customs men, who don't like looking in coffins any more than anyone else, know you well enough to feel certain that's going to be true. Because you personally and your company are highly respected and want to stay in business. Right?'

Cooper sipped his fresh pint of beer and stared apprehensively at Ketterman, nodding wordlessly.

'And you can get documents too—fast. Death certificate from Caxton Hall, certified permission to take remains abroad from the Westminster Coroner, a no-contagious-diseases clearance from the Medical Officer of Health in Victoria. All those officers know you and trust you personally. And the coffin has to be in the airlines cargo area four hours before take-off. You're the only people who can do it. "Ring by eleven—fly by seven." Right?' Cooper nodded quickly again and Ketterman lowered his voice. 'That's the kind of back-up, Mr. Cooper, that's worth twenty thousand to me.' Cooper stared transfixed at the American, his face flexing and unflexing with indecision.

Ketterman watched him for a moment longer. 'You retire, Mr. Cooper, six months from now. And although you've been a loyal servant to Jarvis's for forty-nine years your pension won't top three thousand pounds a year after tax.' Ketterman drew on his cigarette, looking steadily at the undertaker through narrowed eyes. 'You won't refuse, Mr. Cooper.'

The little man swallowed hard and took a deep breath. 'How do you know all this, Mr. Ketterman?'

The American replaced his dark glasses and smiled again. 'Call it careful forward planning.'

Cooper's eyes narrowed. His mouth opened again and his tongue flickered calculatingly. 'If I agree to help you out, when will the rest of the cash be handed over!'

'At ten o'clock tomorrow morning you'll deliver your "goods" to an address near Grosvenor Square. Then you round up the documents. When we seal the coffin at mid-day at your premises—just you and me alone, no other staff around—you'll get another instalment like tonight's. When I'm satisfied the casket's safely on board the six o'clock Pan Am flight to Washington in the pressurised hold I'll hand you the other sixteen thousand.'

Cooper's eyes took on a haunted look. He raised himself on his toes and leaned close to Ketterman. 'Only one of the four holds on the 747 is pressurised, Mr. Ketterman. Why must it go pressurised?'

Ketterman looked at him steadily but didn't reply.

Cooper stared at him in growing alarm. 'I have no control over what happens to the casket after I deliver it to the cargo bay, you see! They work out the cargo distribution by computer, so the weight's evenly spread. The cargo supervisor is the one who does all that.'

Ketterman placed a reassuring hand on Cooper's sleeve. 'We are looking after the cargo supervisor.'

'But what's going in the casket?'

'Relax, Mr. Cooper. You'll see—at mid-day tomorrow before you seal it for me.' Ketterman glanced through the open door as a taxi with its illuminated sign switched off and pulled up at the kerb. 'Why not take this taxi home and get a good night's rest?'

He took the little undertaker firmly beneath the elbow and steered him through the crowd out onto the pavement. He opened the door of the taxi and helped him in. The driver, a black West Indian wearing a tartan cap and dark glasses, stared stolidly ahead and didn't even turn his head to receive directions. As Cooper sank uncertainly onto the back seat, Ketterman leaned inside, smiling faintly. 'You mustn't worry, Mr. Cooper, if the doors and windows of the taxi won't open from the inside on the way home. You may find your telephone at home isn't working either. But we've only cut the wire as a precaution. My colleague here will spend the night with you to see you don't leave home suddenly, or contact anybody else. He'll escort you to pick up the body tomorrow and show you where to bring it. Sleep well.'

Ketterman stepped back and slammed the door as another unlit taxi pulled up behind. He got in quickly and as the first cab began to pull away, he saw Cooper frantically trying the locked doors. Then his white face appeared staring out through the smoked glass of the taxi's rear window. His mouth was open wide and his tongue protruded visibly between his teeth. The expression reminded Ketterman of the futile snarl of some small furry animal—he couldn't remember which one—suddenly finding itself helplessly at bay.

YENAN, PEOPLE'S REPUBLIC OF CHINA,
Friday—Communist Party members here and in
Kwangchow, Soochow, Nanking, Shanghai and
Peking have been told that Lin Piao's Trident jet was
shot down over Mongolia last September, killing
all aboard—his demise in fact appears to have been
nothing short of an aerial execution.
Far Eastern Economic Review, 22 July 1972

· 10

Ketterman closed his eyes to shut out the sight of Cooper's face
and slumped back in the corner of the taxi's rear seat. His driver,
a young man with shoulder-length fair hair wearing a denim
shirt and jeans, piloted the vehicle with ostentatious care through
the light traffic on Wigmore Street and Baker Street then swung
west onto Oxford Street. He drove as far as Marble Arch, taking
pains to observe strict lane discipline before turning south into
Park Lane. Only when he was safely established at thirty miles
an hour in the solid tide of cars rippling down the wide, grass-
flanked mile towards Hyde Park Corner did he slide back his
glass partition and address Ketterman over his shoulder.

'I bought the Pan Am cargo supervisor for two thousand.'

His English accent had the faintest trace of Boston vowels.
'Got to him in a pub near Hatton Cross outside the airport. Told
him we were an obscure Mormon sect who didn't believe the
soul departed from the body finally until forty-eight hours after
the moment of death. He seemed to swallow it. Grabbed the cash
fast enough anyway.'

Ketterman nodded his head wearily without replying. He lay
back drinking in the cool air provided by the cab's air
conditioning.

'I spent another two hundred persuading one of his loaders to
let me work his shift tomorrow afternoon so I can see it into the

pressurised hold. Documents are copying his security pass for me now. Means I gotta get me a haircut.' He laughed pleasantly.

'Great work.' Ketterman's tired voice made the remark almost sound like a sneer. He didn't pull himself into a sitting position again until the driver changed down to allow the cab to be sucked smoothly into the swift millrace of vehicles that sweeps dizzily around Hyde Park Corner almost twenty-four hours a day. Then he twisted in his seat to stare out through the rear window at the faded Georgian elegance of the pillared hospital standing dark against the fading pink of the sky along the western edge of the Corner. 'Which room's Yang in?'

The driver watched the skeins of traffic around him intently as they broke up to skirt the walls of Buckingham Palace along Constitution Hill and southward to Victoria. 'Fourth floor—the tall lighted window between the middle pillars of the portico.'

Through the gathering gloom Ketterman spotted the silhouette of a man standing at the edge of a tall green screen, looking out into the night. 'They've got a guard at his bedside.'

'And two on the front door below—on the steps. There's another two at the Casualty entrance around the corner in Grosvenor Crescent. What they've got on the ward door and in the corridors we don't know.' The driver leaned on his horn and mouthed an explosive American obscenity as a red TR 6 sports car cut impudently across his bows. Then he swung to the inside lane to begin his turn north past the dilapidated pillared frontage of St. George's Hospital. 'The Russians are using their two television repair vans. Blue ones, parked on meters in Grosvenor Crescent, opposite the Casualty entrance. We think we've spotted most of their pedestrians watching the window, too. They cross every few minutes around the Royal Artillery Memorial opposite the front steps.

Ketterman glanced out of the taxi at the pale stone barrel of the stubby 9.2 howitzer guarded by massive-legged, black metal artillerymen in First World War rain capes and tin helmets. 'Where are the Chinese staked out?'

'Not sure yet, Sir. We've been watching a small furniture van in a residents' parking bay in Belgrave Square. No movement in or out so far, though. Two Japanese "tourists" in plastic macs have been taking pictures of the Quadriga on the Wellington

Arch all evening with very long telephoto lenses. They've shot it nine times so far from different angles—always with Yang's window in their view finders.'

'Are Scholefield and the others in the same ward?'

'No sir! Major Accident Procedures in St. George's don't run to clearing wards right down like, for example, the Middlesex. It's 250 years old, remember. They just absorb the casualties into other wards. Mr. Scholefield's on the third floor, front.'

The taxi crested the rise at the Knightsbridge corner and swung towards Piccadilly Circus. The driver nodded out of the window. 'The British are using the Wellington Arch police office as a reserve area. They've got half a dozen Special Branch men in there, at least, in walkie-talkie contact with the man at the bedside.'

Ketterman could see the tiny lighted windows of London's most discreetly disguised police station inside the base of Wellington's triumphal arch. High above, on its summit, floodlights had already come on illuminating the prancing horses of war and the angel of peace who, in an ideal world, reined them in. Below, in the inner curve of the arch itself, the great, black, wrought-iron gates bearing the Queen's arms were closed. Ketterman made out two or three shadowy figures watching the windows of St. George's through the gaps in the decorative ironwork. He turned back to the driver. 'Take a turn around Belgrave Square, so I can give the rest of the opposition the once over before I visit Comrade Yang.'

The ornamental Victorian wrought-iron gas lamps on both sides of Constitution Hill blossomed yellow suddenly in the gathering darkness, turning the summer foliage of the trees a pale, translucent green, as the driver completed a second circuit of the crowded Hyde Park Corner race track and swung round the side of the hospital into Grosvenor Crescent. The two dark blue television repair vans were still standing back to back on parking meters opposite the Casualty entrance. Nobody was visible behind the blacked out windows and Ketterman scarcely gave them a second glance. He stared across the road instead into the cobbled mews that ran along the back of the hospital. 'Is anybody holed up there?'

'No sir. It's been checked out twice.'

Ketterman studied the cream-painted wrought-iron fire escapes that ran down the side of the eighteenth-century hospital. 'Drive up there.'

'Grosvenor Crescent Mews is a blind alley, Sir,' warned the driver as he swung the cab deftly across the road in its own length in a U-turn. 'It's also a private road of the Grosvenor Estate. They close that little white metal barrier at the entrance at midnight. I guess that's why our Russian and Chinese friends aren't using it.'

He pulled cautiously into the narrow cobbled lane and drove slowly between rows of vehicles parked outside motor repair workshops. In a side spur two empty ambulances were parked in a bay reserved for the hospital. A hay fork stood propped against yellow-painted double doors further along the mews beside a sign advertising 'Hacking in the Park—horses at livery.' At the far end a white stone wall, with climbing creepers hanging thickly, closed off the mews. The creepers almost obscured a narrow door that gave access to pedestrians.

Ketterman leaned forward, staring up the mews through the front windscreen while the driver reversed carefully back to the street again. Then he fell back into his seat, deep in thought. He scarcely glanced at the suspect furniture van that the driver pointed out in Belgrave Square and when he got out of the cab in Knightsbridge three minutes later he strode away towards St. George's Hospital without another word.

The two plainclothes men on the front steps of the hospital inspected his State Department pass then allowed him in after checking on an internal telephone. He encountered no other guards on the stairs or in the corridors, but at the entrance to the ward on the fourth floor a uniformed policeman barred his way. Through a glass panel in the ward door he could see the civilian security guard he'd glimpsed from the taxi standing by the window. High green screens stood all round the bed in which Yang was lying. A doctor and a nurse emerged from behind them as he watched and began walking towards the door. 'Nobody at all is allowed in, Sir, unless carrying express written permission signed by Mr. Percy Crowdleigh of the Cabinet Office.'

Ketterman shrugged as the policeman returned his pass. While he waited for the doctor to emerge, he studied the duty roster for the ward nurses on the wall behind the policeman. When the doctor came out through the door, he held out his pass. 'I was present in the room where the explosion occurred tonight, doctor.' He indicated the bruise on his face. 'I was one of the lucky ones. Can you tell me how Mr. Yang is?'

The doctor looked from the pass to Ketterman's bruised face, then at the policeman. 'I suppose there's no harm in your knowing that Mr. Yang has had a very fortunate escape. He suffered considerable lacerations which have now been stitched. He may have a perforated ear drum and he's had a small blood transfusion. He's under sedation and observation, of course, because he's still in shock. But otherwise it was a rather remarkable escape. It's a miracle more people weren't killed.'

The doctor returned Ketterman's pass and hurried away down the corridor. The policeman stolidly motioned for Ketterman to follow.

The American gave the policeman a friendly smile and complied. But once out of sight he deliberately took a wrong turning and hurried downstairs to the third floor at the back of the building. He peered out into the dusk through an emergency exit leading onto the iron landing of a fire escape. Through the dusty windows he could see the dim street lamps illuminating the cobbled mews below. He checked that the corridor behind him was empty before quietly easing open the latch on the door. Then without hurrying he retraced his steps and took the lift down to the ground floor. He strolled slowly past the X-ray section, making a mental note of its location, and walked out of the front door into the stifling night air. He nodded and smiled at the Special Branch guards then went slowly down the steps and sauntered back along Knightsbridge to the Berkeley Hotel, whistling softly to himself as he went.

LONDON, Saturday—In a symphony of official confirmation almost a year after Lin Piao ceased to be officially mentioned, Chinese spokesmen in Peking, Algiers, Paris, and London yesterday acknowledged that the former Defence Minister died in an air crash in Mongolia on September 13 1971 while fleeing the country as a traitor and frustrated assassin.

The Guardian, 29 July 1972

11

The pale blue five-ton enclosed van with 'New Savoy Hotel Laundry' stencilled on its sides rolled slowly down the Strand past Charing Cross Station and halted at the westward-facing traffic lights in an almost deserted Trafalgar Square. It didn't attract a second glance from the routine police patrol car parked by the base of Nelson's Column. Its driver, the young American with shoulder-length hair, leaned casually out of his open window to look back at the illuminated blue and gold clock face on the tower of St. Martin-in-the-Fields. It showed three-twenty.

When the lights changed, the driver eased the truck smoothly away into Pall Mall so as not to unseat the six Chinese crouching uncomfortably inside on narrow benches that had been fitted on either side of a stretcher trolley. They wore white gauze masks, close-fitting headcovers and surgical gowns down to their ankles. The interior of the truck was equipped with a comprehensive array of casualty treatment aids, including oxygen cylinders and blood plasma bottles rigged on racks ready for use. Johnny Fei and the five other men sat staring expressionlessly at each other across the empty stretcher, listening only for sounds from outside.

The truck drove slowly into Pall Mall and past the anonymous windows of the British World Affairs Institute. There was no outward sign of the explosion that had wrecked its basement lecture room nine hours earlier. Because the royal boulevards of the Mall and Constitution Hill are permanently forbidden to commercial vehicles the driver had to take the long slow climb up St. James's to Piccadilly. By three-twenty-five the truck was dipping down right on schedule into the mouth of the Hyde Park Corner underpass. A minute later it resurfaced from the Knightsbridge end of the tunnel and immediately swung left across the road into the narrow cul-de-sac of Old Barrack Yard.

There it stopped and turned, and backed up to the shuttered outlet of the Berkeley Hotel laundry chute. The driver switched off the engine and headlights, jumped down from his cab and walked slowly out onto Knightsbridge. He lit a cigarette and stood for two minutes on the pavement smoking and looking carefully in both directions. The only vehicles on the road were isolated taxis and occasional long-distance transports making a long dash through the heart of the sleeping city. When he was satisfied the street was deserted, he signalled towards the darkened truck with an urgent upraised thumb.

Immediately the slatted back of the truck flew up. The white-gowned figures slipped out and ran silently on plimsolled feet to the white, creeper-covered wall protecting the end of Grosvenor Crescent Mews. Finding the tiny door already locked, they swarmed quickly over the top. By the time the driver returned to the truck they had all disappeared. He took a crowbar from the cab, crossed to the wall and quietly broke open the door. As he eased it ajar he caught a glimpse of the last man scaling the wall round St. George's Hospital at the other end of the mews. One had separated from the others and was crouched by an ambulance parked in the bay on the other side of the lane, working on its locks. He watched until he saw the last of the five climbers swing from the top of the wall onto the iron fire-escape. Then he ran back to the truck, restarted the engine and reversed across the yard, positioning the open back end of the mobile surgery flush against the open doorway in the wall. When he'd switched off the engine he opened a panel behind the driving seat and climbed through into the back. He picked a sawn-off shotgun from a rack on one wall and settled down on the end of the stretcher trolley, holding the gun across his knees.

At the other end of the mews the cream-painted iron fire-escapes on the western wall of the hospital were in deep shadow.

But Fei made all his men wriggle up the steps on their stomachs so they couldn't be seen above the balustrades. Outside the third floor emergency exit unlocked earlier by Ketterman he produced a knife and slipped it in the crack between the door and its lintel. It came open without resistance and the five men slipped quickly through, still bent double on hands and knees. Because of this, the men from the Russian Embassy watching from the closed television repair vans on the other side of Grosvenor Crescent saw nothing at all of their entry.

Inside, the five men immediately split up. Fei and one other went openly up the stairs to the fourth floor, two began searching for a stretcher trolley, and the last man remained crouching in the shadows by the emergency exit.

As he neared the last blind junction on the fourth floor leading to Yang's ward, Johnny Fei produced a clipboard and pen from under his white gown. He made a quick gesture to his accomplice to hang back out of sight, and strode confidently on around the corner. Without breaking his stride he nodded formally to the policeman, now seated somnolently on a chair at the side of the corridor, and pushed open the ward door. Most of the lights were out and only the faint muffled sounds made by sleeping patients disturbed the silence. Swinging his clipboard in his hand the Chinese walked briskly down the darkened ward towards the tall green screens.

The policeman had risen uncertainly to his feet and was still staring indecisively after him through the glass panel of the ward door when the second Chinese ran silently round the corner of the corridor and clamped a hand over his mouth from behind. In the same moment he hit him in the side of the neck with the heel of his other hand. The Chinese used the momentum of his fall to drag the policeman bodily into the ward sister's empty ante-room. Footsteps sounded immediately outside in the corridor and he looked up to see the other two Chinese arriving at the door with the stretcher and trolley.

Inside the shadowy ward, the Special Branch guard at Yang's bedside rose to his feet with a friendly nod as he saw the man in a doctor's gown approaching with a clipboard. 'We've decided to do a final set of investigatory X-rays right away, just to be on the safe side,' said Fei quietly in perfect, unaccented English. 'So we'll need to have him in the X-ray department on the ground floor for half an hour.'

The guard's face clouded. 'In the middle of the night, doctor?' He spoke in a whisper and glanced down incredulously at his watch. 'It's half past three. And besides, he's under sedation, for God's sake.'

The Chinese nodded briskly and signalled towards the door. 'All the better for him. X-ray is quiet now. It's got to be done—as a precaution.'

The men advancing down the ward pushing the trolley kept their heads bent to hide their features. They pulled the screens quietly aside and aligned the trolley with the bed. They had begun to lift the unconscious form of Yang onto the stretcher before the guard spoke again. 'If you're going down to X-ray, I'd better come too, doctor.'

The Chinese was already starting away down the ward. 'Of course, of course, you must come,' he said quietly over his shoulder. At the end of the ward he opened the doors and waited as his two assistants approached, pushing Yang on the trolley. He held them open long enough for the guard to pass through, then followed him into the corridor.

The Special Branch man stopped in his tracks when he saw the empty chair where the uniformed policeman should have been sitting. He turned suddenly, an expression of alarm spreading across his face. 'What the hell's going on here?'

Fei lifted a warning hand and opened his mouth as though to explain. In that moment the door of the ward sister's room opened and the other Chinese leapt at the guard's back, his arms raised high above his head. He chopped viciously downwards with both hands and the double blow delivered at the base of the neck collapsed the detective to the floor without a sound. Between them they dragged him into the ante-room and dumped him beside the unconscious policeman. Without hurrying they locked the door behind them and walked calmly to the lift. The other two men had already moved Yang inside on the trolley and they all descended to the third floor.

The lookout left by the emergency exit had removed all the bulbs from the lights in the rear section of the corridor and under cover of the darkness all five men unwound long canvas straps from their waists and bound the unconscious form of Yang tightly to the stretcher.

As Fei pushed open the exit door the engine of the ambulance in the parking bay on the other side of the mews coughed and started up. It was the sudden roar of the engine in the silent, locked mews that first alerted the Russians watching from the television repair vans on the other side of the street. They saw two Chinese run ahead down the fire-escape and leap nimbly outwards to straddle the high wall. They watched them lean backwards and guide the stretcher onto the top of the wall, preparing to slide it down to the driver waiting by the now open back doors of the ambulance.

Razduhev, in the front of the first van, gabbled rapidly into his walkie talkie as he watched the five Chinese slithering down the wall. When he'd finished he ordered the driver to start his engine in preparation for giving chase. Within seconds the stretcher had been run smoothly into the rear of the ambulance. The five men jumped in behind it and the ambulance driver flung himself behind the wheel, leaving the rear doors open.

The puzzlement of the Russians at this turned to astonishment when the ambulance, instead of crashing out through the barrier onto the street, shot away backwards up the darkened mews. The Chinese driver leaned out of his seat, peering behind him as he reversed the cumbersome vehicle at speed between the rows of parked cars on either side of the cobbled lane. The horses behind the yellow double doors of the riding stable whinnied in fright at the sudden noise as the ambulance shot past, its engine roaring in reverse, and it was halfway along the length of the mews before the back doors of the Russian repair vans opened to disgorge four men. They flung themselves across the road, leaping the metal barrier one after the other, and dashed headlong after the retreating ambulance.

The Chinese driver kept his foot on the accelerator until the ambulance slammed hard against the wall at the top of the mews, buckling the open rear doors and throwing the men inside to the floor in a tangled heap.

Only the stretcher bearing the unconscious Yang remained in its place, held by three canvas straps that had been attached to the trolley. Within moments the men were on their feet. They freed the stretcher and slid it quickly through the doorway in the wall to the waiting American in the back of the laundry truck. He laid aside his shotgun and clamped the stretcher quickly into place on the trolley. Then he climbed back through the hinged panel into the driving seat. The engine had been idling from the moment the ambulance started up at the other end of the mews and by the time the last of the five men had scrambled through the wall and onto the narrow side benches, he had the truck moving slowly forward across the yard.

Because the driver of the ambulance had been peering backwards up the mews throughout his frantic drive, he didn't see the pursuing Russians until after he'd switched off the engine and lifted his head to look out through the front windscreen. The urgent clatter of their feet on the cobblestones, and the aggressive crouch of their bodies as they ran, left him in no doubt about their intent.

Drawing a knife from a sheath inside his shirt he threw himself out of the open door. The four Russians, with Razduhev at their head, were at that moment still twenty yards short of the ambulance. Above the racing engine of the laundry truck on the other side of the wall he heard the frantic voices of his comrades, calling to him in Chinese. He lunged desperately towards the back of the ambulance. But the twisted metal of the crumpled rear doors had been ground deep into the brickwork. All access to the gap in the wall, except from inside the back of the ambulance, had been cut off.

From the close rush of feet behind him he knew the four men were almost upon him and without turning his head he leapt for the top of the creeper-covered wall. But even while his fingers were still scrabbling for a hold among the vines he felt hands close around his ankles. He lashed out wildly with both feet and managed to free himself as they dragged him back to the ground. He fell on all fours, trapped and at bay, his back to the wall, his teeth bared, the knife clutched before him in his right hand. The Russians hesitated in an uncertain semi-circle, then on a grunted order from Razduhev began advancing slowly as one man towards him.

'Ch'u pa! Ch'u pa!' The trapped man screamed the two Chinese words repeatedly over his shoulder as the Russians closed in. He didn't stop until he heard the slatted back door of the laundry truck slam shut on the other side of the wall. A roar of rapid acceleration followed, then the truck's racing engine began to fade rapidly as it shot across Old Barrack Yard and out into Knightsbridge.

The Chinese grinned triumphantly round at the Russians confronting him. But his expression changed immediately to one of alarm as one, on a barked order from Razduhev, took a sudden flying leap at the top of the wall in an attempt to catch at least an identifying glimpse of the departing vehicle. The Chinese twisted sideways and flung himself at the climbing Russian in a suicidal attack, plunging his knife again and again into his unprotected lower back.

The stabbed man flung back his head and his guttural scream of agony echoed round the mews. The reflex of pain tightened his grip among the gnarled tendrils of the vines and he was still hanging on the wall when one of his companions drew out a silenced pistol and, stepping close, shot the Chinese four times in the chest from point blank range.

The knife clattered to the cobbles and the Chinese twisted round, staring wildly at the man who had shot him. Then his eyes misted over and he sank slowly into a foetal crouch at the foot of the white wall, coughing blood onto the cobbles.

The stabbed man's wailing ceased suddenly and for a moment the silence was broken only by the sound of the laundry truck's engine fading into the night. Then lights began to come on in the upper windows of some of the mews houses. One of the Russians cursed softly and moved to lift the stabbed man down from the wall. Razduhev spoke a fast volley of words into his walkie-talkie handset, then, a moment later, carrying the injured man between them, they all turned their backs on the dying Chinese and rushed away into the shadows, anxious now only to regain the safety of their closed vehicles.

On Sloane Street, the innocuous-looking laundry truck was heading south towards the Thames at a steady, respectable speed that would attract no attention. Within five minutes it would cross the river over Chelsea Bridge, and long before the police alert was put into force it was swallowed up with its human cargo inside one of the anonymous, grime-covered industrial warehouses beside the river at Nine Elms.

PEKING, Friday—Chairman Mao Tse-tung has broken ten months of official silence on the fate of the former Defence Minister Lin Piao by telling two foreign statesmen who have visited him in recent weeks that Marshall Lin was killed in an air crash while fleeing the country in the wake of an attempted coup.

Toronto Globe and Mail, 29 July 1972

12

Harvey Ketterman, wearing a black tie of mourning with his sober Ivy League suit, was standing at an upstairs window of a house in North Audley Street at ten o'clock when a plain white van with 'Ambulance' painted in red on its sides drew up at the kerb. Another undertaker would have recognised the windowless vehicle immediately for what it was—a collecting van for the newly-dead, disguised to save the feelings of those inmates of hospitals and old people's homes still fighting the battle to stay out of it.

When Ketterman saw Arthur Cooper climb from behind the wheel, he started quickly down the stairs to the front door. Cooper, who was dressed in the same shiny black suit he'd been wearing the night before, waited obediently while an empty taxi drew up behind the van. When the black driver in the tartan cap who'd been his shadow for the past twelve hours alighted, he unlocked the rear doors of the van and together they lifted out a maroon fibre-glass collecting coffin. Fastened with two snap clips clamped to the lid, it looked like the carrying case for some grotesque musical instrument. They hoisted it quickly to their shoulders and hurried across the pavement to the front door of the house which Ketterman was by this time holding open.

In an upstairs bedroom he watched them lift out the pale

shrunken body of an old man with bushy grey hair. 'First one in this morning, Sir,' said Cooper cheerfully. 'Died during the night. Cardiac arrest.' As they positioned the body on the bed, the young American, his shoulder-length hair now cropped short, entered carrying a flash camera in one hand and a new, garishly-coloured American shirt still sealed in its Cellophane packet in the other.

Ketterman pointed to the shirt and nodded to Cooper. 'Put that on the corpse and prop him up as naturally as you can in that chair by the bed. Hold his head from behind. We can lose your hands.' He handed the little undertaker a pair of horn-rimmed spectacles from his pocket. 'And put those on him too, it will help the retouchers with his eyes.'

Ketterman walked over and stared out of the window into the sun-drenched street while the photographs were being taken. When the flashes ceased he turned round and took a worn American passport from his pocket. He held it out towards the fair-haired man. 'Fix the retouched photograph in there. And be back in half an hour.'

When he'd gone Ketterman took a new pair of pyjamas from a chest of drawers and Cooper and the Black between them manhandled the dead man between the sheets. Ketterman watched uneasily as Cooper dressed the body in the pyjamas as if it was a stuffed doll, then pushed it down under the bedclothes.

'Wait here please, Cooper.' Ketterman motioned to the negro driver and they went out of the room and down the stairs leaving the undertaker alone with the body. He sat down obediently by the bed, staring at nothing and listening to the hum of the traffic in the hot street outside. Twenty minutes later he heard the front door open and the voice of the young man who'd taken the photographs floated up the stairs as he talked quietly with Ketterman. At exactly half past ten the doorbell rang and moments later Ketterman led a corpulent, arrogant-looking man dressed in striped trousers and black jacket into the bedroom.

He scarcely glanced at the passport of Marshall Symonds which Ketterman handed him. The undertaker, looking over the doctor's shoulder, saw that the retouched photograph of the bushy-haired corpse lying dead in the bed had already been inserted open-eyed and bespectacled in the travel document.

Keeping his eyes averted from both Cooper and Ketterman the doctor put his bag down by the bedside table and clipped a stethoscope behind his neck. Then he shot his cuffs with great deliberation before searching irritably under the sheets for the dead man's wrist. He gazed blankly at the ceiling with his mouth clamped shut, breathing noisily through his nose as he went through the motions of searching for signs of a pulse. Then he dropped the arm carelessly back onto the bed and unbuttoned the corpse's pyjama jacket. When he'd taken several careful soundings he returned wordlessly to the table where his bag was standing and took out a pad of death certificates. Details had already been entered in the top one and Ketterman saw the doctor switch his gold-plated ball-point pen into his left hand before completing the final flourish of a signature. He replaced the stethoscope in the bag with elaborate care then slipped the certificate between the pages of the passport and handed it to Ketterman.

'You've been most helpful.' Ketterman smiled fixedly, but the doctor was already on his way towards the door, the stiffness of his posture making it clear he had not the slightest interest in the American's remarks. Ketterman followed him out and in the hall below the doctor stopped and turned a severe gaze on him.

'Within the hour I shall report to the police the discovery of a break-in overnight at my surgery.' He nodded to the passport in Ketterman's hand. 'If attention is ever attracted to that death certificate for any reason whatsoever, I shall remember that the pad from which it was extracted was among articles missing in the burglary and denounce the signature which is sloped left-handed as a deliberate forgery.' He stood waiting in a pointed silence until Ketterman took a bulky envelope from inside his jacket, then accepted it without a word of thanks. He didn't speak or even look at Ketterman again. When he'd put the envelope in his medical bag he walked stiffly down the steps to the pavement and hurried away in the direction of Oxford Street without looking back.

Five minutes later Ketterman opened the door to welcome a harrassed-looking middle-aged American, who arrived from the direction of Grosvenor Square. He shook him briefly by the hand and took him straight up to the bedroom.

'Hello, Sir!' Cooper smiled eagerly at the newcomer and stood up. His manner had become enthusiastically professional again. 'Done a lot o' jobs together for the embassy, haven't we?'

The newcomer nodded distractedly and peered anxiously towards the bed.

'Mr. Cooper is going to get Mr. Marshall Symonds embalmed super-fast and shipped to Washington tonight on Pan Am,' said Ketterman lightly. He handed the passport and the death certificate to the consular officer. 'Go with him now to Caxton Hall to register the death and he'll be back in your office within the hour with the Coroner's export certificate and all the other documents for you to sign and seal.'

The diplomat took a slow breath and looked down at the dead man's face, comparing it with the picture in the passport. Then he closed the passport and glanced uneasily from Cooper back to Ketterman. 'I don't know what's going on here Mr. Ketterman. I hope you know what you're doing, that's all.'

Ketterman ignored him and opened the door. The black driver reappeared and together he and Cooper lifted the body into the fibreglass case which had been hidden under the bed. The fair-haired man was already behind the wheel of the mock ambulance when they came out through the front door, and as soon as the coffin was loaded he drove away. The negro led Cooper and the consular officer to his taxi to drive to Caxton Hall and Ketterman ran back upstairs for the last time to check the bedroom.

He picked up the now discarded new shirt and its wrappings, retrieved two fallen packing pins from the carpet, dropped all the bits and pieces into his briefcase, then, after a final glance round the room, ran back downstairs. He locked the front door, and dropped the bunch of keys into a stout envelope that was addressed to an estate agent and already contained a cheque for a week's rent. He posted it in a pillar box twenty yards along the street before flagging down a bona fide taxi. Two minutes later he was heading past the gold and concrete frontage of the American Embassy in Grosvenor Square on his way once more to St. George's Hospital.

MOSCOW, Saturday—The plane carrying Lin Piao, his family and comrades was heading back towards China when it crashed in Mongolia last September, killing all on board, according to a new theory here. At the last minute, the theory says, someone on the plane decided to return to China and changed his mind about seeking refuge in Mongolia or the Soviet Union.

The Observer, 6 August 1972

13

At eye level outside the open third-floor windows of St. George's Hospital the four black horses of war on the Wellington Arch seemed to beat frantically at the burning sky with their raised hooves. To Richard Scholefield, as he lay with his bandaged head propped against a broad wedge of pillows, they looked as though they were fighting vainly to stir the scorched, stagnant air around them into a cooling breeze. He dabbed at his own damp forehead with a paper tissue and turned his gaze slowly away from the windows as he heard footsteps approaching his bed.

He saw Harvey Ketterman's sweating face set in an enquiring expression of earnest concern. The bruise on his cheek was multi-coloured and edged now with a rim of jaundiced yellow. Instead of shaking hands he squeezed Scholefield's limp forearm considerately in a gentle gesture of greeting.

'How are y'feeling today Dick?'

'Concussed—in a word.' Scholefield raised his eyebrows ruefully as a substitute for a smile. 'I like your black eye. It reaches down to your chin.'

Ketterman grinned and peered anxiously into his face. 'No bones broken though, huh? You're all of a piece, right?'

Scholefield nodded.

'Thanks be to God and the solid British craftsmanship of that pre-war oaken dais at the Institute!' Ketterman and Scholefield both turned at the sound of the voice of the bald, bespectacled Cabinet Office diplomat who'd sat in the front row at the meeting the previous night. He marched pompously to the bedside and patted Scholefield on the shoulder, causing him to wince momentarily. He swung a visitor's chair away from the wall and lowered himself heavily into it, mopping his brow with his handkerchief. He wore striped grey trousers and a black jacket but despite his efforts to sustain his usual airy manner, his face was pinched and pale from the after-effects of shock. He continued breathing heavily even after he'd sat down.

Scholefield looked at Ketterman. 'Harvey, do you know Percy Crowdleigh?'

The American stood up and offered his hand. 'Only by reputation until now.'

Crowdleigh offered a perfunctory handshake without looking directly at the American and without getting up. Instead his eyes stayed on Scholefield's face. 'Richard, you'll be relieved to know Matthew's now at home safe and sound. None the worse for wear either.' Scholefield stared at him as though he'd suddenly recalled something temporarily forgotten.

'I wish in heaven's name you'd told us about it.' Crowdleigh removed his glasses and dabbed with his handkerchief at eyes shrivelled small by powerful lenses.

'I thought it best to do things the way I did.' Scholefield's voice had taken on a note of irritation. 'Where was he found?'

Crowdleigh breathed on his spectacles and polished them carefully with his handkerchief. 'He was brought back and dropped off in a street close to your ex-wife's home with his nanny—about eight-thirty last night. They'd spent the afternoon locked up in some house in North London. Fed, allowed to watch television, well treated apparently. Several different people all of Chinese appearance involved.' Crowdleigh tipped his head forward and glowered suspiciously round the ward over the top of his spectacle frames. When he was satisfied with his survey he let his eyes come to rest steadily on the American's face for the first time. 'But that's not all I came to tell you. There's a D-notice on all this, of course, from the explosion onwards. That's why you haven't got wind of it from the papers. If the press had got hold of it, it would be all over the front pages now.'

He paused and drew a long breath. 'Because Yang's gone!'

Ketterman cocked his head in puzzlement. 'Gone? You mean he's died?'

Crowdleigh's eyes never left the American's face. 'No, Mr. Ketterman.' He spoke very slowly and deliberately. 'He was abducted from this hospital at three-thirty precisely this morning.'

'By whom, for chrissakes?' Ketterman's eyes had widened in amazement.

Crowdleigh studied the American in silence for a long time. 'We don't know. He's disappeared without trace.'

'But what happened to his guards?' asked Scholefield incredulously.

'They were overpowered by a group of men of'—Crowdleigh hesitated, choosing his words pedantically—'of Asiatic appearance. Yang was spirited away down a fire-escape into the mews behind the hospital and driven a short distance in an ambulance. He was then passed through a wall into another unidentified vehicle which proceeded to disappear into the bowels of London.'

Ketterman whistled. 'So it looks like a Chinese Embassy job?'

'I'd prefer not to advance into the realms of speculation at present,' said Crowdleigh shortly. 'Even though a man of Chinese race was found dead by the abandoned ambulance with four bullets in his chest.'

'From the embassy?'

'They say not. They hotly deny all knowledge in fact. And the police think he might have been a member of one of the Soho Triads.'

'The Hong Kong heroin gangs?' Scholefield's voice rose in disbelief.

'The modern descendants of a Chinese secret society fifteen hundred years old,' said Ketterman crisply. 'And frequently in their long history, you might remember, they've mixed political intrigue with their more orthodox criminal activities.'

'Who killed him then?' asked Scholefield quickly. 'The police?'

Crowdleigh closed his eyes and clutched both hands round one knee. 'The abduction was organised and executed so quickly and efficiently that it attracted no police attention beyond Yang's ward on the fourth floor. Both guards there were overpowered.

The police think there might have been another group of "persons unknown" disputing for possession of Yang in the mews below. This could have resulted in the Asian's death. Some commotion was heard by people living in the area.'

Ketterman lowered himself slowly into a sitting position on the end of the bed and stared distractedly out of the window.

'Who in hell's name is trying to do what to who?'

'I suppose what we're meant to think,' said Scholefield reflectively, 'is that the Peking moderates have smuggled out survivor Yang. Although the folios I showed you before the meeting don't name names specifically, and neither did Dr. Stillman, the clear implication is that Mao's radical supporters led by his wife are now fighting to secure their right to succeed him. We're being presented with what appears to be first-hand "proof" that they were thinking along these lines as long as five years ago and that they murdered Lin Piao. Yang's the moderates' trump card to smear the radicals and stop them taking over.'

Ketterman turned back slowly from the window. 'If Yang's batting now for the moderate "good guys" then by an extension of that theory it would be the radical bad guys who tried to blow him up last night, along with the rest of us at the Institute, to shut him up. And having failed to kill him publicly, presumably they would want to snatch him—and finish him off somewhere quietly, wouldn't they?' Ketterman looked from Crowdleigh to Scholefield and back again seeking support.

'Using a strong arm squad of the Triad drug smugglers?' Crowdleigh's tone was offensively sarcastic. 'The Chinese do happen to make some pretty clear distinctions about who they regard as true revolutionaries. Some of the best organised crime gangs in the world gorging themselves on the carrion of capitalism haven't been among them so far. Or hadn't you noticed, Mr. Ketterman?'

Ketterman scowled. 'They're all goddamned Chinese, remember.'

'I wonder,' said Crowdleigh dryly, 'why you are turning your face deliberately away from the more obvious explanation?'

A wary look came into the American's eyes and he sat straighter on the bed.

Crowdleigh folded his arms and this added a new pedagogic rigidity to his demeanour. 'Richard used a felicitous phrase just now. He said, "What we're meant to think". It was probably subconscious, but let's consider who would have·the most to gain from humiliating the radical group in Peking. They're steeped in Mao's extremer creeds, aren't they? They would make China more independent, more xenophobic, more of an isolated rogue elephant on the international scene. More dangerous to those whom Mao dislikes. And who does he dislike more than anybody else? The great unloved neighbour with four thousand miles of common frontier, who made the historic mistake of patronising him! So who would have most to gain if these anti-Soviet acolytes of Mao lost out in the power struggle after the old man dies?'

The other two men watched Crowdleigh in silence, waiting for him to answer his own rhetorical question. 'The Russians! So who is it that is most likely to have regurgitated an imaginary survivor from Lin Piao's long-lost Trident that crashed into the mists of history five years ago?' With slow deliberation he unfolded his arms and placed his hands palms downward on his knees. 'No ideas at all? Our old friends in Department "A" of the First Directorate of the KGB in Moscow. The "dezinformatsiya" fiction writers! Those folios Comrade Yang gave Richard the other night may be their best bit of creative writing ever. And Stillman's report and his involvement could as easily have been fabricated by the same people.'

Ketterman dabbed at his forehead with his handkerchief, wincing as he touched a tender area of the bruise around his left eye. 'Okay—but that still doesn't tell us who bombed out Yang at the Institute, and why.'

'Speculative discussion about such short term imponderables as who planted the bomb on Yang is futile at present.' Crowdleigh paused and looked deliberately again at Ketterman. 'Or indeed who has kidnapped him—although in both cases the obvious scapegoats to choose would be the Peking radicals. What for me is beyond question is the unmistakable style of the initial operation. Taking Matthew hostage, putting vicious pressure on Richard here and the whole sly backdoor method of trying to filter out disinformation through respected Western academics, specialist writers and what have you. It all reeks far too powerfully of something cooked up in the rancid cauldrons of the Kremlin's kitchen. Especially the stuff about the Mao death plot. The Chinese don't really have enough international self-confidence in the twilight zone to do things quite that way. It's a bit too other-worldly for them. And that's exactly the kind of blind spot which always gives the Kremlin away. It didn't occur to them that it was all too sophisticatedly cynical for Peking to have conceived it. The Chinese simply think and act differently.'

Crowdleigh got up suddenly and went over to the window. He sucked deeply on the still, hot air outside for a few moments then turned with his hands in his pockets and leaned precariously backward on the unprotected windowsill.

Ketterman stirred impatiently on the end of the bed. 'Haven't we learned anything about our late friend Stillman that tends to authenticate what he said? Could he have been suborned and taken to Mongolia?'

Crowdleigh rocked backwards on the windowsill. 'I've had only one preliminary report on the poor devil, which of course is classified, but I suppose I can tell you he was dismissed from his post with the Royal Armaments Research and Development Establishment ten years ago on account of alcoholism.'

Scholefield snapped his fingers suddenly. 'That's the gesture I remember, the wagging head. The sure sign of the alcoholic. It bothered me vaguely all through the meeting.'

Crowdleigh nodded impatiently. 'He worked for a couple of years after that on retainers for various city insurance under-writers investigating air crashes abroad for them as a freelance. Then he was black-listed by them, too, for his drinking and he moved lock, stock and barrel to Yugoslavia. He'd done a few jobs in Eastern Europe and it was through those air accidents that he got to know a few influential Communist intelligence types in the Warsaw Pact countries.' Crowdleigh rocked backwards again at an alarming angle, lifting both feet off the floor. 'That was in 1970. Whether Belgrade will co-operate in further investigations of his "career" or not remains to be seen. His British pension has been drawn regularly through a transfer arrangement with a Belgrade bank ever since—but if the Russians wanted to snap up a tame Western aircraft accident investigator they certainly had one available as a sitting duck in Belgrade circa September 1971.'

A nurse appeared silently behind Ketterman. Crowdleigh stopped talking abruptly. She began straightening Scholefield's pillows. 'I think, gentlemen, Mr. Scholefield should rest now,' she said firmly.

Ketterman stood up and looked uncertainly at Scholefield. 'I must dash, Dick. Got several things to do before I go to the airport this afternoon. Washington wants to put the folios through the computers.' He grinned, then hesitated, again holding his briefcase in both hands in front of him. He seemed to be on the point of walking away but didn't go. He looked uncomfortably across at Crowdleigh who was still balancing precariously, hands in pocket, on the open windowsill. Finally he stepped up beside Scholefield, bowed his head towards him and grasped his forearm again in an awkward parting gesture. 'Dick I'm real damned sorry about Nina. You know that, don't you?'

Scholefield nodded quickly without looking up. Ketterman opened his mouth as if to say something else. Then he changed his mind and hurried away.

Crowdleigh smiled perfunctorily at the nurse and let his feet fall slowly to the floor. 'My deepest condolences, too, Richard, of course.' As he went away down the ward behind Ketterman he turned back and lifted one hand in a silent, parting salute.

OTTAWA, Wednesday—Soviet officials probing
the plane crash in Mongolia in which Lin Piao was
said to have been killed found evidence that pistols
had been fired on board. Soviet premier Alexei
Kosygin was understood to have told Pierre Trudeau
this when he was here a month after the episode.
Canadian Press News Agency, 30 August 1972

14

The five-ton truck moved cautiously at walking speed along a
street pitted with potholes in a wedge of bleak industrial waste-
land carved out of North London by the recent passage of a
stilted urban motorway. The hotel laundry letterwork had now
been replaced with 'Genders' Light Removals' and the whole
vehicle had been resprayed a muddy brown colour. A row of
derelict houses lined one side of the street, their smashed windows
staring sightlessly out over the desolate rusting wreckage of a
scrap dealer's yard on the other. Dust and grit swirled up from
under its wheels and hung in a cloud around the truck as it jolted
slowly towards a grimy railway arch at the end of the road.

A corrugated tin fence closing off a municipal refuse tip
between the scrap yard and the bridge had been decorated in
lurid poster colours. But the hundred-yard panorama of green
hills, bright flowers and grazing nursery cows was darkening
with grime too. A group of youths playing cricket against a
wicket whitewashed on the fence swore obscenely at the truck as
it enveloped them briefly in its gritty dust cloud. One threw a
large stone which thumped against its side, leaving a visible dent.
The young fair-haired American swore quietly to himself inside
the closed driver's cab as he swerved to avoid an emaciated
German Shepherd dog which rushed barking wildly from the
refuse grounds to retrieve the stone.

At the far end of the street the West Indian had parked his taxi in the shadow of the railway bridge a few yards short of the only building in the street in good repair. Its bright modern brickwork contrasted sharply with the blackened, crumbling masonry of the railway viaduct. A low, square complex of modern offices and workshops, it was fronted by a carefully swept forecourt, and two neat bay trees in tubs stood either side of the white-painted double doors. On a black frieze above the doors, freshly painted gold lettering embellished with discreet Gothic serifs spelled out 'H. Jarvis & Sons Ltd. Funeral Directors since 1897.'

Arthur Cooper was sitting inside the back of the parked taxi clutching a plastic folder of sealed documents. He turned an anxious face to look at the truck as it drew up behind, but the black driver shook his head meaningfully. A minute later another taxi arrived and Harvey Ketterman climbed out. The West Indian driver unlocked the doors then to release Cooper and together they hurried up the steps between the potted bay trees.

At that moment the scratch cricket game against the fence along the street was interrupted again by the arrival of a television repair van. It parked outside the row of derelict houses and two men in overalls climbed out carrying metal tool boxes. They ignored the obscene abuse howled at them by the cricketers and hurried off towards the railway bridge and the funeral parlour, keeping close to the front of the gutted houses.

Inside Jarvis & Sons' offices the last of the administrative staff were leaving for lunch and Cooper led Ketterman quickly through towards the embalming workshops at the rear of the premises. The doors were already locked but Cooper produced a bunch of keys and motioned the American ahead of him. Ketterman stopped abruptly inside the door at the sight of a dead Arab on an embalming table, covered to the waist with a white sheet. Three or four more bodies covered with black blankets were lying on stretchers that seemed to have been deposited carelessly in the first convenient place their bearers had found among the clutter of collecting coffins, polythene canisters of embalming fluids and empty caskets.

Cooper smiled nervously as he locked the door behind them. 'That gentleman's ready to go home to Tripoli tonight.' He nodded towards the waxen face of the Arab. 'The Imam is coming after lunch to wash him. Their religion demands it.'

But Ketterman was already walking quickly round the racks of coffins that stretched from floor to ceiling, checking that nobody was concealed in the room. 'Are all these damned things empty?' 'Most of 'em are full.' Cooper leaned closer to read a label. 'This one's waiting shipment to Beirut next week.'

Ketterman hurried over to the sliding doors that formed the far wall. He hauled them open and looked out into a large garage filled with black hearses and collecting ambulances. The doors to the street were padlocked on the inside. He bent down and peered under a row of carpenters' benches, but saw only a clutter of wood and metal shavings, acetylene gas cylinders and scattered tools. As he stood up the coffins began to tremble on their racks. A distant rumble of sound built up rapidly to a roar as a train raced across the railway viaduct outside. For several seconds the workshops were filled with a deafening clamour of noise. When the silence returned Ketterman walked slowly back to Cooper. Beads of sweat stood out on the undertaker's forehead although the atmosphere in the embalming room was chilled.

'I thought our "Connaught" would suit best, Mr. Ketterman. It's always been popular with you Americans.' Cooper pointed to a large ornate casket carved out of dark mahogany that was lying open on two low trestles. With a shaking hand he stroked the quilted interior. 'Zinc-lined, then white satin and flannellette. Our best finish.'

Ketterman glanced into the pristine cleanness of the casket's interior and nodded. 'Perfect. Let's get on with the holes, fast!' Cooper blinked uncomprehendingly at him. 'At least a dozen.' Ketterman strode over to a workbench and picked up a one-inch brace and bit. He thrust it impatiently into the little man's hands and began indicating spots around the casket where he should drill.

'But we only make holes in caskets to be buried at sea'— Cooper caught sight of Ketterman's threatening expression and bent quickly over his task, winding frantically on the handle of the drill—'to make them sink, of course.'

Ketterman ignored him and turned to pick up the zinc inner lid that stood propped against the wall. It had a little window of plate glass eighteen inches square let into it at about head height. 'That's for identification purposes, Mr. Ketterman.' Cooper, panting with exertion, was trying to watch Ketterman over his shoulder as he worked. 'Your embassy doesn't do it any more. But most of 'em still send diplomats down here to identify the body from the passport once it's been sealed in—' Cooper broke off suddenly in alarm and turned to stare up at the window in the wall behind him. He could see nothing through the frosted glass but something had deflected the light momentarily. He looked quickly towards Ketterman for reassurance. But the American was still staring thoughtfully at the identification panel in the inner lid.

'They make us solder that on. If a dead body isn't aspirated properly, you know—the gases build up inside it. A corpse can explode and blow the lid off an ordinary coffin, if there isn't an inner metal lining with a soldered lid.' A hint of hysteria had crept into Cooper's voice and by now he was turning constantly to glance over his shoulder at the window. 'If that happens in an aircraft hold all the other cargo can get contaminated. It's happened more than once. The French for instance are terrible embalmers. Bodies from France often reek to high heaven.'

Ketterman laid the panel carefully aside and walked over to the bench where Cooper had left the file of sealed documents. He picked them up and began to inspect them minutely.

'They're all there, you'll find, Mr. Ketterman. The top one's the affidavit I swore at your embassy. Just a simple affidavit, that's all you need now if you don't send someone to identify. The Russians and the East Europeans still come through. They don't trust anybody. We have to put extra screws in the top of the coffin and drip sealing wax on them so they can stamp them with their seals—' Cooper stopped and swung round towards the window again. This time he caught a glimpse of a blurred shadow through the frosted glass, before it ducked away out of sight.

'The Israelis are the most careful though, Mr. K.' Cooper was almost sobbing now. 'They always come, never miss. Feel all round the body and underneath it. Search the whole coffin with a fine tooth comb before it's sealed. Nobody else does that.'

Ketterman finished scrutinising the documents and tossed them onto the bench. He watched as the point of the drill broke through the zinc lining then put a restraining hand on his shoulder. 'Okay Cooper, that's enough. Now open up the garage door.'

Cooper licked his lips nervously and hurried over to the garage door. When he'd opened it Ketterman slipped through and waved a signal to the driver behind the wheel of the truck. A minute later it had been reversed into the garage. Cooper replaced the padlock with hands that were now trembling violently. His face twitched as he watched the black taxi driver and the fair-haired man climb up into the mobile surgery to lift the stretcher out. It was covered with a white sheet but the outline of a man's figure was discernible beneath it. The two men manoeuvred it carefully down into the garage, then looked enquiringly at Ketterman.

At that instant Cooper glanced up over his shoulder at the window behind him for the hundredth time—and found himself staring into the distorted face of Vladimir Razduhev. Ketterman swung round as Cooper let out a shriek of fright. The Russian was peering through the narrow strip of clear glass at the top of the frosted windows, his face unrecognisable under the pressure of a nylon stocking. As Ketterman looked up at him he dropped quickly out of sight.

The American shouted and waved frantically to the two men holding the stretcher. Immediately they lowered Yang to the floor and slid him beneath the heavy carpenter's bench. Ketterman snatched a pistol from his briefcase and backed against the bank of refrigerators that lined one wall, covering the window where Razduhev's head had appeared. The black taxi driver and the fair-haired man drew hand guns from inside their jackets and dragged Cooper down behind the carpenter's bench.

In the silence that followed Ketterman pointed mutely to an empty stretcher and motioned towards the embalming table where the dead Libyan was lying. The two men nodded quickly and dashed bent double across the workshop. They lifted the dead Arab between them, dropped him onto the empty stretcher and pulled the sheet up to cover his face. Then they ran back across the workshop to where Ketterman had set up two more empty trestles beside the open casket and lowered the stretcher hurriedly onto them before dropping behind the bench again.

For a moment there was silence, broken only by Cooper's

intermittent whimpering from behind the bench where he was hiding. Then the distant rumble of another train approaching along the overhead track began to make the coffin racks tremble once more. Ketterman glanced up suddenly and caught sight of Bogdarin's face watching these preparations intently from a small square window in the opposite wall above the refrigerators. But he dropped from sight too as the sound of the train thundering onto the viaduct became a deafening roar. A moment later the sound of the glass shattering was drowned in the roar of the train's passage and the barrels of the sub-machine guns that Razduhev and Bogdarin had carried dismantled in their tool boxes burst through the windows and began stitching uneven threads of bullets along the racked coffins a few feet above the ground.

The Americans pressed themselves to the floor beneath this lethal barrage and watched helplessly as one of the Russians directed a long burst of fire at the stretcher beside the open casket. The body under the sheet leapt and jerked spasmodically as the bullets slammed into it and eventually the trestles broke and collapsed under it. The attack lasted about fifteen seconds in all, and the shooting ceased as abruptly as it had begun when both Russians dropped out of sight.

Gradually the noise of the train faded slowly into the distance. The coffin racks stopped shaking and silence settled slowly over the chilly embalming room once more. Even Cooper's whimpering which the others had heard intermittently throughout the attack, had stopped at last.

15

For a full minute after the Russians disappeared Ketterman allowed nobody to move. Then he stood up slowly himself and, still watching the windows carefully, walked over to where the stretcher had been concealed. He took hold of Yang under the armpits and dragged him out from under the carpenter's bench. The black taxi driver took his feet and together they lifted him gently into the open "Connaught" casket. The expression on the face of the Chinese was peaceful and relaxed. His eyes were closed and his breathing was even. A puzzled frown creased Ketterman's brow for an instant and he glanced up uneasily at the window where he'd caught sight of Bogdarin's face. Then he shrugged and returned his attention to the job in hand. When they had settled Yang satisfactorily with a pillow under his head, Ketterman looked round for the little undertaker.

Silent and apparently even now petrified with fright, he was still crouched motionless behind the carpenter's bench. 'Okay Mr. Cooper, the bully boys have gone,' said Ketterman soothingly, 'you can come out now.'

When Cooper didn't move Ketterman walked over and patted him consolingly on the shoulder. The instant the American's fingertips touched him, Cooper pitched forward. His head thudded dully against the stone floor and he rolled slowly onto his back. When Ketterman saw the ragged hole above his left eyebrow he lifted both hands to his temples and stood motionless with his eyes closed for fully half a minute. When he opened them again the fair-haired man and the black taxi driver were standing looking at him expressionlessly, waiting for instructions.

'One of the individual refrigerators I guess.' He waved a hand wearily over his shoulder. 'And make sure you lock it. It's far from ideal but it might just give us the time we need.'

Ketterman walked over and lifted the sheet covering the dead Libyan. The fusilade of bullets had done surprisingly little damage to the bloodless corpse. Dry puncture marks spread thickly across the trunk of the body but the face and neck were unmarked. 'There's a casket addressed to Beirut in that rack by the door. Drag it out and open it up with this.' He picked up a plumber's chisel from the workbench. 'Put our bullet-riddled friend inside and dump the Lebanese on the slab. We just gotta hope the Imam won't notice the difference when he comes to wash him.'

Ketterman took off his jacket and picked up the zinc inner lid for Yang's casket. He lowered it carefully over the face of the Chinese and fitted it into the side grooves. He watched with satisfaction as the unconscious man's breath fogged the glass of the identification window a few inches above his face. Then he connected up the acetylene gas cylinder to a burner, picked up a foot-long strip of solder and directed the flame onto it until it began dripping into the runnel around the edges of the zinc panel.

When the other two men had opened up the coffin bound for Beirut they undressed its corpse and removed it to the embalming slab. Then they put the bullet-riddled Libyan inside and using another acetylene set, soldered a new lid into place. Ketterman told them to turn round all the coffins that had been raked by the gunfire so that the holes wouldn't be discovered immediately. They also cleaned up the glass from the broken windows and fitted sheets of opaque polythene over the missing panes with sticky tape.

When he'd finished soldering, Ketterman stood looking down at the face of the Chinese beneath the inspection panel. Yang's breath was still misting the glass regularly as he exhaled.

'What in God's name happens to him if he wakes up while he's still sealed in?' asked the black driver in an awed voice. 'It would take me all of thirty seconds to go permanently insane in there.'

'Sedation will last him twenty-four hours,' said Ketterman crisply.

They lifted the wooden coffin top into place and screwed it down, then tugged the tailor-made hessian cover around it. They checked to make sure that it wasn't torn and that none of the breathing holes were visible. Then the fair-haired man sewed up the end with a long string bodkin. With the hessian stretched tight around it, the casket looked, as was intended by those who made the rules, like any other innocent freight package. They loaded it into the back of one of the collecting ambulances and Ketterman drove it out. The fair-haired man took the five-ton truck and the black driver followed in his cab along the quiet, lunchtime street.

Two miles away near a junction with the M4 motorway Ketterman handed over the ambulance to the black driver, who took it to Hatton Cross and delivered the coffin on behalf of Mr. Arthur Cooper of Jarvis's to the Pan American cargo supervisor, at five minutes to two. The fair-haired man parked the truck in a car park of a nearby public house and checked in for his shift using the fake identity card he'd carried with him in his stolen Pan Am overalls. Ketterman took a taxi to the Post House hotel, close to the Heathrow passenger terminals, and booked into a single room.

At five o'clock he left again, took a taxi to Terminal Three and checked onto the six o'clock Pan Am flight to Washington. Because of the long queues for routine security checks on hand baggage and body searches, the Boeing 747 didn't trundle out onto the taxiing runway until six-thirty-five. When it finally made its long lumbering run along the southbound runway ten minutes later, Ketterman was sitting in a seat in the first class section, sipping a glass of chilled champagne.

Somewhere beneath him in the underbelly of the aircraft a partly-tranquilised dog in a straw-lined crate raised its head and howled in fear when it detected faint but unmistakable signs of human life coming from the box lying beside it.

Half an hour later as the airliner headed out over the Irish Sea the dog cocked its head again to listen. Against the dull background roar of the engines it heard the noise of a man crawling clumsily across the floor of the darkened hold and it began to whine once more. It heard the scrape of metal on metal as the fair-haired American struggled among the closely packed freight cases, carrying a torch in one hand and a knife in the other. When he found Yang's casket he cut away the hessian until he had uncovered the screw heads countersunk into the lid. He removed these with the knife and eased the lid aside. By the light of the torch he saw the viewing window in the zinc panel had now misted over completely. He quickly fitted suction pads from his pockets onto all four corners and cut round the edge of the glass with a diamond tipped cutting tool. Then he lifted the glass and touched Yang's forehead with his fingertips. His skin was burning hot and his breathing was fast and shallow.

The American took a pad of cloth soaked in surgical spirit from a small medical satchel strapped around his waist inside his overalls and wiped the perspiration from Yang's face. Then he extracted a flat vacuum pack of ice cubes from the satchel, wrapped several inside the cloth, and held them gently against the Chinese man's burning forehead. With his free hand he loosened the cloth around his throat to ventilate his body as far as possible.

As he worked he turned his wrist slightly so that he could read his watch in the light of the torch. He drew a long, careful breath, then exhaled very slowly. It would be more than six hours before the 747 touched down at Dulles International Airport outside Washington.

PEKING, Thursday—Lin Piao was killed when his plane ran out of fuel in Mongolia, Chou En-lai has informed visiting American newspaper editors. 'I have told you everything, it's much clearer than your Warren Report on the assassination of J. F. Kennedy,' the Chinese Prime Minister said.

United Press International, 12 October 1972

16

When the groaning lift shuddered to a halt outside his flat, an unseen hand pulled open the outer gate before Scholefield could move. Taken aback, he peered cautiously into the pitch blackness through the iron lattice of the inner gate. Then he smelled the whisky, and in the faint fluorescence from the dim bulb in the roof of the lift he made out the grinning features of Moynahan.

As he stepped out onto the landing, the porter took his arm and drew him quickly along the passageway. The reek of spirit on his breath made Scholefield wince as he leaned close to whisper conspiratorially in his ear. 'Glad to see you back, Mr. Scholefield. You're as popular as ever with the ladies, I see.'

The porter's features creased into their familiar lascivious leer. Scholefield passed a hand wearily across his brow. 'What the devil are you talking about this time, Moynahan?'

The porter raised his index finger urgently to his pursed lips, motioning him to a silence. He tried to pull free of the porter's grasp, but failed. Moynahan, suddenly feeling the bandages around the wrist he was holding, peered close into his face in alarm. 'You're hurt, Mr. Scholefield.'

'I was involved in a slight accident, Moynahan, yes, but I'm fine now, I've just come from the hospital.'

The porter drew him along the darkened landing a pace or two until they were out of earshot of the flat door. 'Is it your drinkin' arm or your lovin' arm, Mr. Scholefield, eh?' Moynahan nudged him with his elbow and giggled lewdly. 'I hope it's not your lovin' arm because there's a real dilly of a Chinese lady awaitin' you. Paid me to let her wait inside, she did. Gave me a tenner, no less. Thought you'd want me to let you know that.'

Scholefield stared at him uncomprehendingly in the darkness. 'What sort of Chinese "lady", Moynahan? And what the hell are you doing letting strangers into my flat when I'm out.'

'She's no stranger, Mr. Scholefield. Said she's an old friend of yours. Wearing one of those lovely green silk dresses with big slits up her thighs. A cheongsam, d'you call it? Hair all piled up on top of her head with combs like one of those geisha girls, eh? Real dish, Mr. Scholefield. Said you was expectin' her.'

Scholefield could see in the faint light coming from the lift that he was holding out his hand. His voice had taken on a wheedling tone. 'Did I do right, Mr. Scholefield?'

'How long ago?'

'Ten minutes, quarter of an hour.'

He pushed him aside and strode to his door. The porter was still cursing him softly in the darkness as he shut the door behind him. Inside, the entrance hall was in darkness but there was a line of light showing under his study door. He opened it and found the green-shaded desk lamp was lit, casting a pool of bright light on his empty blotter.

As he closed the door behind him the high-backed leather swivel chair at his desk rotated slowly to reveal the impassive seated figure of Tan Sui-ling. Her hair was dressed on top of her head in an elaborate high coiffure and she sat relaxed and at ease, her bare arms spread along the arms of the chair. Her feet were primly together on the carpet so that the divided skirt of the cheongsam fell straight, revealing nothing but her ankles.

He stared at her, a puzzled frown wrinkling his forehead. Then his face suddenly cleared. 'You were behind the kiosk counter when Yang bought the Lu Hsun book.'

She nodded slowly.

He crossed the room to where he'd left the bottle of vodka on a side table two nights before. The unwashed glass he'd used then was in the hall and he poured himself a large measure and gulped it straight down. The arm that had been damaged in the explosion had begun to throb and he rubbed it with his uninjured right hand. 'What do you want?'

'To talk to you about the so-called folios "Comrade Yang" brought to you.' She laid heavy ironic emphasis on the name and tossed her head contemptuously as she spoke.

'Who showed you them?'

She hesitated and smiled faintly. 'Your "friend" Ketterman.' Again the heavy irony, again the little toss of the head. 'He knew about it all in advance.'

He looked up at her for a long time without speaking, then poured himself another drink. He took it back to the chesterfield and sat down. 'So you've come to give me Peking's official answer to Yang's fake folios?'

She didn't reply. The relaxed curve of her slender body in the chair, the wide slow-blinking eyes in a broad, high cheek-boned face gave her, he thought, the air of a sleek, watchful cat.

'You're going to tell me the Russians are running Yang, are you?' Scholefield emptied the glass and put it down on the floor with unnecessary care.

'He was landed at Blakeney on the North Norfolk coast two weeks ago in an inflatable dinghy towed ashore from a Russian fishing trawler by two KGB frogmen. Even the CIA know that.'

'Who are you?' Scholefield got to his feet again and walked over to her chair.

She tucked an imaginary strand of hair back away behind her ear. 'My name is Tan Sui-ling. I have come from Peking.'

He bent over suddenly and leaned both hands on the arms of the chair, trapping her in the seat. His breath came out between his clenched teeth in a sudden, sibilant hiss. 'So it was you who organised the bomb at the World Affairs Institute last night— to silence the Russian imposter!' He grabbed her by the shoulders and shook her bodily in the seat. 'Two innocent people died in that explosion—' His voice trailed off suddenly and he stared into her face.

She offered no resistance but waited passively in his grip watching his face patiently until the rage subsided. 'No Chinese were involved in that incident,' she said quietly. 'It was the work of the Russians. Now that he has planted his poisonous propaganda they want him eliminated.'

She winced as the pressure of his grip on both arms suddenly tightened. Then he flung her back in the seat and stepped away. 'And having failed to blow Yang to pieces your Russians snatched him from the hospital during the night with the help of a gang of Triad hoodlums, I suppose?'

She rose suddenly to her feet, her eyes blazing in turn. 'Again you are wrong. Your CIA "friend" Ketterman masterminded that treachery. The Americans have got Yang now.'

He stared at her incredulously. 'Why should Ketterman and the Americans want Yang if they know he's a fraud?'

Instead of replying she walked straight-backed to where she had left a bamboo-handled handbag on the floor by the chair and bent to pick it up. When she turned round again she was holding the bag in front of her in her right hand. 'Lin Piao did have an aide by the name of Yang Tsai-chien. But his was one of the bodies positively identified by the Comrades from Peking who visited the scene of the air crash in Mongolia. It was indisputable—they checked his fingerprints. This man posing as "Yang" was brought here from the Soviet Union!'

'The fact that Yang was brought here from Moscow doesn't prove by itself that he's a fake.' Scholefield sank down on the corner of his desk and nursed his injured arm with the other hand. 'The dead remnants and the wreckage of that air disaster in Mongolia finished up in Moscow—why shouldn't a living survivor?'

She gave a snort of derision. 'Why have they waited five years then to produce him, if he is genuine?'

'Perhaps they were waiting for the moment when they could use him to best advantage. Large parts of the folios seem to me to have a ring of truth, despite some decorative lies to disguise the fact that the Soviets found him in Mongolia, not your comrades. And the report of the dead air accident investigator, Stillman, is standing up to analysis so far by British experts.'

She made another contemptuous noise and moved towards him again. 'The KGB are expert forgers. They have gone to great pains. The folios and the accident report were designed to stand up to close analysis.'

He looked at her without speaking for several seconds. The only sound in the room was the intermittent buzzing of a dying fly against the window pane. There was a distant hum of traffic from the street far below, but it was muffled and muted as though stifled, like everything else, by the oppressive weight of that unnatural summer heat. She had dropped her eyes and was idly toying with the jade figure of the mandarin on the side of the desk. The silence lengthened.

' "A member of the exploiting classes of old China, produced by the sweated labour of a working class artisan." '

She looked up at him frowning, still holding the green jade figure.

'That's what Yang called it.'

She stared at him uncomprehendingly.

'Yang was moved to handle it too when he was here—that's how he described it.' Scholefield nodded towards the figurine.

She put it down suddenly as though it had become red hot. 'Jade should be touched. It is for handling, not simply admiring with the eyes.'

'That sounds dangerously like an expression of bourgeois sentiment. It wouldn't come under the heading of socialist realism in your art appreciation.' Scholefield broke off suddenly and stood up. He stared at the wall by the desk, then strode over and picked up the desk lamp to give himself better light. He leaned towards the scroll painting of the Ming concubines, and peered at the verses inscribed in Chinese calligraphy by the artist above his signature in the top right hand corner of the picture.

Tan Sui-ling saw him stiffen and lean closer to inspect the vertical column of script. After several seconds he turned to face her, still holding the lamp above his head.

'Your "Comrade Yang" also had more than a trace of bourgeois sensibility in his love of traditional Chinese art, didn't he?' Scholefield nodded towards the painting behind him. 'He admired this Ming painting as well as the jade—and to my considerable disappointment informed me it was a nineteenth-century Ch'ing dynasty "reproduction" in the Ming style. I bought it in Peking thinking it was genuine Ming.' He watched her begin frowning in irritation. 'But one of the first things he said to me at the Soho cinema was a reference to this painting.'

Suddenly she was listening intently, her head cocked slightly to one side in concentration.

'He said the artist's signature gave it away.' He paused, watching her reaction carefully. 'Now a second signature has been added with a felt tipped pen since I last looked at it.'

She made as if to go to inspect the painting herself but Scholefield lowered the lamp quickly and walked back to replace it on his desk, leaving the wall in deep shadow once more. 'It was your picking up the jade figure that made me remember. Does the name Li Tai-chu mean anything to you?'

The only sign of reaction to his question was a slight tightening of her knuckles on the bamboo handle of her bag. Before she spoke he noticed she exhaled slowly as though she had previously been holding her breath. 'The name means absolutely nothing to me. Nothing at all.'

She took a sudden quick step towards him. 'Mr. Scholefield, I have yet to reveal the main purpose of my visit.' She hesitated for a moment, then hurried on speaking with a new intensity. 'Chairman Mao Tse-tung is an old man. His health is ailing now, but he is still in touch with day to day events. He has been told of the Russian plot to plant false evidence about China in the minds of the world outside. He knows even that *you* were chosen to be the focus of this plot by the Kremlin.'

Scholefield sat straighter suddenly on the desk. She had opened the bamboo-handled bag and was fumbling inside it. When she withdrew her hand it held a long white envelope sealed in several places with red sealing wax. 'For several days he has been asking for all intelligence reports to be submitted to him. He has taken a detailed interest. Now, in view of the vicious nature of the Soviet plot, he has decided to intervene personally.' She held the sealed envelope towards Scholefield. He looked at it with suspicion for a moment then smiled sarcastically. 'A personally written folio by Chairman Mao himself, is it? Giving his version of events?'

Her watchful, cat-like eyes gazed back at him unblinking. 'It is not a joke, Mr. Scholefield. And it is more than an explanation.'

There was a long silence in the room broken only by the sound of the fly buzzing drowsily on the windowpane in its final death throes.

'Open the letter. You will see then it is genuine.' Again she held it towards him.

He took it but had difficulty breaking the seals. In the end he had to slit two sides of the envelope to extract the single sheet of thick cartridge paper inside. He held it under the desk lamp to study the scrawl of Chinese calligraphy that spread erratically across the page. His name and '24 July 1976' were typed in English in the top right-hand corner. At the foot of the page a large red circular seal embracing China's national symbol of five stars above the Gate of Heavenly Peace was impressed in the paper, surmounted by a ring of characters that spelled out 'Office of the Chairman of the Communist Party of the Chinese People's Republic'.

He leaned close over the paper, his body suddenly alert, his eyes intent on the inscription. Eight vertical lines of four characters had been scribbled seemingly in haste beside the almost illegible three-character signature. With difficulty Scholefield traced each scrawled ideogram with his finger, his lips moving as he went. Then he took a pencil from a jar on the desk top and began jotting down a translation of the inscription on the blotter. When he'd finished, he sat back and re-read what he'd written. It said:

Amid the frowning shades of dusk
Riotous clouds are racing, swift and terrible
The hostile northern bear clambers foolishly upward to his doom.
Let us now ensure his fall from perilous peaks!

He picked up the blotter and stared at the words in silence.

'Does the distinctive hand and style convince you now of the authenticity of this personal message?'

At the sound of her voice he looked round sharply, almost as if he'd forgotten she was there.

'If this is another hoax it's commendably elaborate.' He shrugged wearily and dropped the blotter back on the desk. 'Those few lines have all the right ingredients: Mao's poetic hatred of the Russian "bear", his reputation for eccentric calligraphy—it even looks like the writing of a tired old man.'

She gesticulated impatiently towards the note once more. 'Read the back.'

He picked it up and turned it over. On the reverse side the same almost illegible signature and the imposing red seal had again been appended under a block of characters imprinted by a Chinese typewriter. They said: 'Give assistance and safe passage. The bearer, Richard Scholefield, is invited to Chung Nan Hai to talk with Chairman Mao Tse-tung.'

He was still staring at the message, reading and re-reading it, when he heard the click of the outside door. He looked up then and found the room empty.

17

Harvey Ketterman swung the long nose of his red Chevrolet Malibu sharply to the north at the junction of M Street and Wisconsin Avenue and, because tension was beginning to tighten his reflexes, accelerated too fiercely up the hill towards the heart of Georgetown. A sharp summer shower was giving way to bright evening sunshine again and the tyres of the car skittered dangerously across the impractical cobblestones that Washington's history-hungry citizens had never been able to bring themselves to tear up from between the iron streetcar tracks.

The tourists thronging the old tobacco port's boutiques and bistro restaurants, under heavy garlands of red, white and blue bicentennial bunting, glanced indifferently at the skidding car for a moment, then resumed their cow-like window gazing. Other sober-suited escapees from the vast administrative bunkers along the capital's main avenues mouthed silent obscenities at him from behind their tightly closed windows and pressed on their accelerators with almost as much impatience as they neared the end of the long north-west haul up Pennsylvania to their bijou hilltop dormitory. Ketterman ignored them and eased across to the inside lane as the bow-fronted windows of the Georgetown Inn came in sight.

The moment he swung the Malibu in under the arch, a doorman, top-hatted and liveried in deference to bygone days of carriages and horse-drawn streetcars, hurried over to park it for him. Ketterman passed him a dollar bill and strode quickly through the tiny lobby into the hotel's dimly-lit modern American drinking lounge. He made straight for the grand piano which doubled as a coy little leather-rimmed musical bar in the centre of the room. Razduhev was sitting on one of the swivel stools placed round it, his elbows on the piano, apparently lost in the rapture of the syncopated selections from *The Sound of Music*. He opened his eyes as Ketterman approached and lifted a small glass of clear liquid slowly to his lips. He offered no greeting as the American eased into the swivel seat beside him.

For a moment the two men looked at each other without speaking. Then Ketterman suddenly grinned broadly and gripped Razduhev's forearm in a genial gesture. 'You know Yuri, if I ever have the offer of reincarnation in the after-life I'm going to grab it and come back as a KGB "overseas".' He glanced over his shoulder into the gloom. The faint glow from the pink candles in the over-large crystal chandelier above the piano gave insufficient light to identify anybody but an immediate neighbour. But he had chosen the bar because he knew the pianist's roundly struck chords would preclude them from being overheard at least, and he turned back to the Russian, still grinning. 'You wouldn't change places with a member of the Kremlin politburo, would you? Chief of Mission in London, all your kids' schooling paid for at home, a dacha at the beach outside Moscow, expensive Persian rugs on the floor of your apartment overlooking Hyde Park, all expenses paid to the best hotels of your choice in the Western world.' He punched the Russian lightly on the arm, then turned to signal to a passing waiter who came immediately. 'Two vodkas. Polish, not Russian. Large ones please.' He turned back again to Razduhev, still grinning. 'Never touch Russian vodka, Yuri. You might poison a year's supply just to get me, huh?' He laughed uproariously at his own joke then leaned away to speak to the piano player.

As the drinks arrived the pianist wound up 'The Sound of Music' with a flourish and went straight into a lachrymose rendering of 'Midnight in Moscow.' Ketterman smiled broadly at Razduhev and lifted his glass.

Razduhev left the new drink untouched. 'Washington is like

an elephant's asshole,' he said in wooden English. 'Very big and very unattractive.'

Ketterman nodded appreciatively. 'Only in Washington twenty-four hours, Yuri, and already making with the wise-cracks. That's good. You'll tell me next you've proof that Rock Creek Park *isn't* a South Korean intelligence agent.'

'I didn't come here to swap wisecracks.'

'I know Yuri, I know. You want Comrade Yang back—and you're gonna have him, yes sir.' He broke off and looked at his watch. 'I can't get him to you here this minute, you understand, Yuri, but if you'll give me an hour I'll try to have something for you. . . .' He looked up with an eager, boyish grin on his face. 'Will you do that for me, Yuri? Give me an hour?' Ketterman smiled broadly again but Razduhev continued to stare at him stony-faced.

'Could you be at the intersection between 34th and P Street in an hour, Yuri, do you think? It's here in Georgetown, you can walk. It's just a few blocks north-west of here. I'll meet you on the corner myself, okay?' He stood up, dropped two bills on the tray of the waiter as he passed and told him to give the piano player a drink. Then he turned back, still grinning, punched Razduhev on the upper arm again and hurried out.

At the hotel entrance Ketterman hung back until he was sure the doorman who had parked his car wouldn't notice him leave, then hurried through the arch onto Wisconsin Avenue. He turned north and walked quickly towards the junction with P Street. As he turned west at the intersection he took a guide book from his pocket and, carrying it ostentatiously in his hand, began sauntering slowly along the narrow pavement under the trees looking about him as if admiring the elegant frontages of the town-houses decked with their clusters of bicentennial flags. The unshuttered windows revealed glimpses of brass-stemmed lamps, heavy colonial furnishings, potted rubber plants, gilded mirrors. Cocktail-hour drinks were being downed in some of the houses by little knots of neatly dressed men and women. From time to time Ketterman stopped and bent close to peer at the wrought-iron work on gates or railings, turning his head surreptitiously as he did so to look back along the street.

As he approached the junction of P Street and 34th, he stopped and gazed up at a white colonial Georgian villa with black shutters, standing back from the street on high, sloping lawns. Black metal fire-escapes ran down the side of the building from dormer windows in the curved mansard roof and ugly air-conditioning boxes jutted from several of the finely-proportioned windows. On the front steps under a white portico an old rusting bicycle was chained incongruously to the hand railings. Ketterman put the guide book in his pocket and began whistling loudly, as he gazed up at the house, as though appraising its architectural features. Then he turned and set off westward again at a brisk pace.

A hundred yards further along the street he turned abruptly and walked back, stopping once more opposite the three-storeyed villa. The rusty bicycle had now disappeared from the front porch and when he saw this, Ketterman crossed the street and ran lightly up the front steps. The door opened from inside as he reached the top and the black man who had driven the taxi in London closed it quietly behind him. He was no longer wearing the tartan cap or his dark glasses.

Together they went into a small room off the front lobby and peered at a bank of closed-circuit television screens. All of them from different angles showed the junction of the tree-lined streets outside. Ketterman bent over a console and twiddled a knob which panned the cameras individually inside the fake air-conditioning boxes on the outside of the windows. He studied all the screens showing the four approaches to the house in turn but, with the exception of an occasional car passing, the crossing remained empty. Ketterman nodded his approval to the black man and they walked quickly out into the vestibule and entered an elevator that had been tastefully concealed behind a broad, panelled door, opened by a porcelain doorhandle decorated with roses. When he stepped out on the top floor, a white-coated doctor was waiting for him.

'How is he, Doc?'

The doctor fell into step beside Ketterman as he set off along the broad corridor towards a white door at the end. 'Surprisingly well for what he's been through. He's out of shock now—asks frequently where he is—in English. I haven't told him, of course —but he should be told something soon to help him re-orientate.

The left ear-drum's definitely perforated—but he's hearing okay with the other one. Other lacerations stitched in London are healing okay.'

They stopped outside the door and Ketterman motioned the doctor to wait. Then he knocked quietly, and went in. Yang was lying stiffly in a hospital bed, his head and shoulders raised on a bank of pillows. The high-ceilinged room was furnished over-elaborately with gilded red-velvet French antiques. A pale Indian carpet covered the centre of the polished wood floor and vases of summer flowers and bowls of fruit had been carefully arranged on side tables. A Handel concerto was playing softly from concealed speakers.

Yang's round, moon-like face was drawn and pale and he watched Ketterman approaching with a suspicious stare. The American pulled a straight-backed chair to the bedside and sat down. He smiled and waved a hand vaguely round the room. 'I hope you feel we are looking after you well here, Comrade Yang.' He paused, 'In Washington.'

Ketterman had spoken Mandarin and he watched Yang's eyes widen in surprise.

'How did I get to Washington?'

'Let's just say I had it arranged.'

Yang was silent for a moment, his narrow, lashless eyes studying Ketterman's face. 'You were at the Institute,' he said slowly, 'the American who came late.'

'Right! Harvey Ketterman, US State Department.' He held out his hand towards Yang. When the Chinese ignored the gesture he dropped it and, still grinning, gripped his right forearm through the sheet instead.

Yang turned his head angrily in the direction of the black guard pacing ostentatiously back and forth outside the window on the fire-escape. 'So after four years as a prisoner of the socialist imperialists in Moscow, I am to be held captive now by the American imperialists.'

'Wrong, Comrade Yang. That guy out there is one of several affording you protection from your "friends" from Moscow. They tried to blow your brains to pieces in London. They very nearly succeeded—and they did kill Dr. Stillman and Dick Scholefield's friend, Nina Murphy.'

Yang's angry glare faltered for only an instant. 'It was not the Russians. The culprits were the radical faction in Peking whom I have exposed!'

'You're still trying to sell your bum folios, huh, Comrade.' Ketterman stood up and walked slowly to a fake antique chiffonier standing against the wall at an angle to the bed. He removed the vase of flowers, lifted the false top and turned down the volume of the Handel concerto in the control panel of the concealed tape deck inside.

'Your fraternity brothers Razduhev and Bogdarin took the bomb in the briefcase to the World Affairs Institute. Dressed up a minor diplomat from the Mongolian Embassy in a Peking-style cadre's uniform to deliver it, of course, to make it look like a Mao-job.' Ketterman opened the doors of the chiffonier to reveal a built-in 29-inch television screen. He switched it on and stepped back to study the picture that immediately appeared of the intersection outside the house. A car drove slowly across, followed by two girls on bicycles. After that the screen remained devoid of activity.

Ketterman turned back to find Yang looking at the screen with a baffled expression. 'Sorry the programme isn't more fun, Comrade. It's just so we can see which people try to pay a call on you. You're a popular guy right now. You could have a whole stream of visitors coming up here all day long if we'd let 'em.' He closed the doors of the chiffonier, leaving the set switched on, and turned round grinning.

'Why was I brought here from London?' Yang winced as he shifted his position slightly in the bed.

'There are an awful lot of shepherds running around the field looking for one lost sheep right now, Comrade. Three-quarters of the intelligence services of all Russia and China, I'd guess, are working twenty-four hours a day to locate you.'

A faint tap on the door interrupted him and Ketterman opened it. The fair-haired man who had driven for him in London handed him a slim leather document case and quickly closed the door again. Ketterman unzipped it and took out two large folded sheets of pink paper. He opened it and held it out in front of him at arm's length, running his eye rapidly over the handwritten Chinese script.

Yang's features twisted into a sneer. 'And why should you care whether I am safe or not? Have the rabid capitalists of America suddenly become concerned with the sanctity of life of every single communist, worldwide?'

'Fair question,' said Ketterman calmly, 'to which the answer's "No". We just want to keep you in one piece long enough to counteract the lies your buddies from the Kremlin have cooked up with you in those folios of yours.'

'They are not lies!' Yang raised his head from the pillow, his eyes blazing. 'They tell the truth.'

'The whole truth and nothing but the truth, Comrade?' Ketterman raised an eyebrow and walked back to the chiffonier again. He took an unmarked tape cassette from the document case lying on the chair beside it, stopped the Handel and removed it. He slotted the new cassette into the deck and turned up the volume. Yang sank back on the pillow listening as a crackle of static came from the concealed speakers.

Above the interference a Chinese voice shouted a call sign first in Mandarin, then in English. 'Trident 256 to Irkutsk control ... Trident 256 to Irkutsk control ...' Yang's face clenched tight suddenly as he listened. 'Cleared take-off Peitaiho, heading Irkutsk ... Marshall Lin safely on board ... Repeat Marshall Lin safely on board ... Anticipate no interception at border with People's Republic of Mongolia ...'

The static and background roar took over again and Ketterman softened the volume. He turned and looked questioningly at Yang.

'It's a fabrication!' The Chinese glared at Ketterman from the pillows.

The American smiled patiently. 'Comrade Yang, our satellites don't lie. We know every time Chairman Mao leaves his zip-fly undone—and how many workers you've got on the nuclear night shift at Lop Nor.' He spread his hands wide and hunched his shoulders. 'The National Reconnaisance Office has four or five hundred pieces of junk bumping around up there in the sky over the Soviet-Chinese land mass—and we've got B29's flying around with basketball nets on their noses catching the tape decks jettisoned from those birds—that's how we get such clear reception on your signals. The National Security

Council employs eighty *thousand* guys around the world intercepting radio signals and playing them through the largest computer complex in existence anywhere in the world. Its budget is twice the CIA's. With outfits like that we don't even have the *time* to fake up signals.' He walked over to the bed and dropped his arms to his sides, grinning hugely again. 'Besides—your Szechuanese accent is a dead give-away—you're mixing up your third and fourth tones, as usual.'

'If the interception of the radio signal by your satellite is genuine, why is there no response from Irkutsk control?'

'Peking's a difficult bull's-eye to hit, Comrade, with those spy-birds. For a start if we get the angle of launch wrong from Vandenburg Air Force base in California, the satellite just burns up. We've lost a lot trying to throw them up onto the precise "hook" in the sky so that they orbit constantly right over your Chung Nan Hai.'

A movement outside the window caught his eye and Ketterman acknowledged a hand signal from the black man with a faint nod of his head. 'Even when we get it right the slant range gives us a fairly good pick-up over a radius of only about a hundred miles around Peking—that's why the first signal was clear. But out at 150 or 160 miles from the centre, the pick-up is down to thirty-five percent. That's the reason we never registered anything at all from the Irkutsk end. Okay?'

Yang looked away. He winced and shifted his position painfully in the bed again.

'So the boys in the Kremlin definitely knew you were coming —they were in on the plot. We've known that all along, Comrade Yang.' Ketterman grinned. 'So the crap about dodging in under their radar screen without their knowledge we read straight away as a pure Kremlin snow-job to clear them of any complicity in Lin Piao's activities. We know too you didn't come out of China. We know the KGB put you and Stillman ashore in an inflatable raft on the North Norfolk coast two weeks ago because the Israelis in Moscow tipped us off—just like they tipped us about the Lin plot in Seventy-one.'

Yang lay silent staring at the ceiling. Ketterman walked over to the bedside and stood looking down at him, holding the large square of folded pink paper in his hand.

'We're pretty sure, too,' said Ketterman quietly, 'that Marshall Lin Piao was still alive and living in Peking in January 1972—four months after he's supposed to have died in that Trident.'

Yang's head turned slowly on the pillow until he was looking up into Ketterman's face.

'We picked up radio messages by satellite that Lin's supporters were sending to you out in Mongolia. I can play them to you if you'd like.' He delved into the document case, drew out a sheaf of papers and dropped them on the bed. 'Here are the transcripts of the Trident signals and the messages to you on the steppes. We knew somebody survived that crash—and with a back-pack radio transmitter and receiver intact. We believe he was *meant* to survive it.' Ketterman pulled up the chair, sat down and waved the pink paper in front of Yang's face. 'Your options have run out, Comrade. Officially you're dead. We know Yang Tsai-chien died in that crash, his body was fingerprinted. The Russians who've sprung you to here obviously want you dead now—whoever you are, if that bomb in London is anything to go by. To stay alive, you have to remain here.'

Yang's head jerked towards the window in alarm as the silhouette of the black man suddenly reappeared on the fire escape outside and tapped urgently on the glass. Ketterman waved him away with an impatient gesture.

'If you want to stay, we want two things from you—first, some more lies.' He opened the sheet of pink paper out so that Yang could see the Chinese handwriting.

'What is that?'

'The Ninth Folio.'

Yang gazed at it blankly.

'It begins,' said Ketterman, reading from the opening paragraph, "'Now that I am free after four years' imprisonment in the Soviet Union and about to start a new life at a secret address in the West, I wish to state that I was forced to invent a terrible tissue of lies that have been presented as the truth in Folios One to Eight written by me.'" The American paused and smiled. 'There's a lot of detail telling how the Russians encouraged Lin Piao in a plot to murder Mao, how they offered him a safe sanctuary—and how they sent up MIGs to shoot his Trident down over Mongolia to cover up their treachery when he failed.'

'But that isn't true!' Yang's voice was barely a whisper.

'Sure it isn't true,' Ketterman agreed blithely. 'We know they scrambled no MIGs. Our satellites would have picked them up if they had. This faked Ninth Folio is an antidote to the other eight. If the Soviets try to get their bum information broadcast around the world, we produce this one in your calligraphy signed by you and with your thumbprint on the bottom right hand corner, right, just exactly like the others.' Ketterman was grinning affably at Yang again. 'The other thing we want is the truth about the Trident. We believe maybe even the Russians themselves don't fully know what happened. We think even now they believe a lot of that bullshit you've written in the Folios—that you've held out on them right under their noses in Moscow for four years. But most important of all, we want to know why they've mounted this elaborate operation.'

Yang swallowed hard. His skin had taken on a grey pallor, but his eyes still gleamed bright with defiance. 'I won't co-operate!'

Ketterman stood up suddenly, his smile gone.

'Even though you torture me!'

'You're in the wrong country if you're looking for something as unsubtle as torture.' Ketterman rubbed the side of his nose with his forefinger, gazing down coldly at the Chinese. Then he turned on his heel, walked briskly to the fake chiffonier again and opened the doors. He looked at the closed-circuit picture for a moment, standing deliberately in front of the screen. 'I think an old friend of yours is arriving to see you, Comrade Yang.' He stepped aside so that the Chinese could see the picture of the intersection from his bed.

Yang raised his head to look. On the screen a car had halted at the kerb on the far side of the street and a man had climbed out. He stood uncertainly on the pavement looking about him, taking care to hold the passenger door of the car open. Elsewhere in the house an unseen hand operated a control switch that set the telephoto lens of the concealed camera revolving in a steady zoom to close-up on the man beside the car. Within a few seconds Razduhev's chalk-white face filled the screen.

'He seems to have forgotten your flowers and grapes,' said Ketterman.

Razduhev was squinting through his wire-rimmed spectacles in the late evening sunlight as he peered about him in all four directions in turn. Once his eyes seemed to look directly into the room as the lens caught him scanning the windows of the house. Ketterman folded his arms, settled himself comfortably with his back against the wall beside the cabinet, and waited. Yang stared at the screen transfixed.

'Sign and thumbprint the Ninth Folio, Comrade, and I'll run down straight away and show it to your fraternal Marxist ally.' Ketterman smiled jocularly again. 'It's a life-saver, don't you see? Once the Ninth Folio is authenticated by you, the other eight are invalidated—even if they kill you! Think of it as your *life* warrant. You can copy it out in your own handwriting later to do the job properly—after that socialist imperialist jackal down there has been sent away with his tail between his legs.'

'These pictures are a trick! I still refuse.'

Ketterman shrugged. 'Okay. You have a free right to choose in a democratic country, Comrade—and you've chosen wisely. You're free to go right away.' He eased himself away from the wall and strode across to the window. He opened it and spoke loudly to the black guard. 'Okay fellah, stand down now—and tell all the other security guards to disperse immediately. Only the medical staff need stay on. And go tell Razduhev I'll be right down to talk to him about Comrade Yang.'

He closed the window and stood gazing out abstractedly across the sunlit lawns for a moment. 'This is a private clinic, and of course visitors are allowed any time day or night—no embargoes.' He was speaking out towards the gardens, his back to Yang. 'Really concerned friends can use the fire escape as a direct means of entry, even after dark.' He turned and pointed to the screen on which the black guard could now be seen crossing the street to talk to Razduhev. A group of half a dozen broad-shouldered young men followed him out from the house and sauntered away along 34th Street. Ketterman watched the screen intently as Razduhev and the black man exchanged a few wary words. 'You see, Comrade, it's no trick.' He gathered up the document case and walked over to the bed. Slowly he took out a pen and inserted it in Yang's right hand. After a final glance round at the screen he smoothed the pink folios out on the face of the document case and held it at a convenient height in front of Yang's chest.

The Chinese hesitated for a whole minute. Then he signed both copies, without looking up. Ketterman removed the pen smoothly from Yang's hand, then dipped into the document case again and drew out an ink pad. He opened its lid and pressed it against the unprotesting thumb of the Chinese. Then he held the case under the folios once more while Yang impressed his print on the bottom right hand corner of each copy of the Ninth Folio. Ketterman inspected both documents minutely in turn then replaced them in the case and hurried out. A minute later he appeared on the grey screen walking towards Razduhev. The camera moved into another telephoto close-up and Yang saw what appeared to be anger contorting Razduhev's features as he scanned the paper Ketterman had thrust into his hand. He saw the American laugh and punch the Russian lightly on the arm. Then he walked back towards the house, looking up into the camera and grinning hugely.

Razduhev climbed angrily back into the car which immediately shot away out of the picture, leaving the intersection quiet and still once more. A minute later the black guard re-appeared on the fire-escape outside the window and dropped into a squatting position, surveying the gardens below, as before. Almost at the same moment Harvey Ketterman re-entered the room. He went directly to the chiffonier and switched off the closed-circuit picture of the street outside. He put the Handel cassette back into its slot in the tape deck and immediately the soothing strains of the sixth Concerto Grosso swelled gently from the concealed speakers. The same switch activated another concealed tape machine hidden behind a panel beneath the headboard of the bed and Ketterman picked up the chair again, swung it round and sat down resting his chin and elbows along its back, smiling genially at Yang.

'Okay Comrade, so much for the lies—now let's hear what really happened on the Trident. And perhaps as a bonus you'd like to tell me the truth about this new "plot" to kill Chairman Mao. If it's really good we'll see what we can do about finding you a new identity and a new life in the land of the free.'

WASHINGTON, Friday—American intelligence experts today expressed strong doubts that Marshall Lin Piao died in an air crash in Mongolia. The belief here was that he either died of natural causes while imprisoned or was shot trying to escape.

New York Times, 28 July 1972

18

When he pulled the woven red curtain aside Richard Scholefield could see, through the plastic foliage of a vase of everlasting carnations, the steps leading up from the canopied D Street entrance to the State Department. As he shifted the vase along the window-sill to give himself a less restricted view, a female voice behind him asked, with an irritable note of reproof, if she could help him. He turned to find an unsmiling middle-aged waitress in beige slacks and a loose gaudy blouse of synthetic material holding her order book pointedly in front of her with a pencil poised over it.

He glanced at the slip of card tucked into the handle of a wire basket of pink sugar-substitute sachets on the table. It announced that for the pleasure of his dining the Governor Shepherd Restaurant invited him to try a carafe of Californian wine— Hearty Burgundy, Chablis or Sauterne, all at a dollar fifty. He chose the Hearty Burgundy. But when the waitress brought it he wished he hadn't—it tasted like raspberryade spiked with warm water. He left the rest of the carafe untouched and gazed out of the window again.

The communications mast and radio antennae on the State Department roof stood out in silhouette against the fading silver light of the southern sky. Among them a large yellow-painted funnel structure shaped like an old-fashioned ear-trumpet suggested that headquarters was adapting some of the early principles of the phonograph era to pick up signals from its far-flung space-age embassies. Behind him little groups of State staffers who had been working late were snatching belated, inexpensive dinners and muted desk officer gossip about incoming telegrams and policy points drifted to his ears in fragments. At the next table an efficient-looking harridan with greying hair scraped back tight above her ears was moaning to a female companion about her husband. 'Then I asked him how many crepes he thought 200 people would eat, and he said about three or four each, so I spend hours making them—and everybody ate just one. I was furious!'

Scholefield stared out of the window, watching without seeing as the Virginia Avenue traffic signals chopped and packaged the mid-evening traffic flow with steady precision, halting, accumulating, then releasing the cars to run on down towards the West Potomac Park in well-spaced, neatly tied bundles. From time to time he rubbed his hand over his face or massaged his left wrist lightly through its bandage. But always his eyes returned to the entrance under the canopy which he knew the Research Bureau staff used.

He turned in his chair when the door opened to admit a man in a blue suit with his left arm in a sling. One of a group of four men seated by a bank of plastic ferns greeted him with a loud remark which set the table laughing uproariously. The woman with the scraped-back hair made a disapproving sound with her tongue, and her haughty expression didn't change even when the man came over and pecked her sheepishly on the cheek, before lowering himself gingerly into an adjoining chair.

At that moment Scholefield saw her coming up the steps. He recognised her at once, even though the light was beginning to fade. She was dressed in a flame-coloured corduroy trouser suit tailored tightly round the hips that on anybody less startlingly attractive would have looked vulgar. The tall heels she wore accentuated her height and she moved with the easy, stalking grace of her race. He watched her swinging across the grass in front of the mounted statue of Bernardo Da Galvez, her face set in an unconscious half smile as if the very sensation of movement pleased her. She ignored the pedestrian crossings and slipped across the two lanes of Virginia Avenue, between the halted cars. Several drivers turned to watch her progress and missed the change to green which set horns blaring loudly in the ranks further back. Conversation stopped and heads turned as she paused inside the door looking round the tables. Even the woman who had made too many crepes turned to stare. Some of the male diners greeted her politely, as though pleased to be favoured, as she made her way across the restaurant.

At Scholefield's table she stopped and stood looking down at him with a sad, rueful smile on her face, saying nothing. When he stood up, she put an arm on his shoulder and leaned her cheek against his in greeting. 'Dick, I'm terribly sorry, you know that.' She sat down and placed her handbag on the window-sill beside the plastic flowers. She peered into his face with concern, then leaned across the table and put a hand on his arm. 'You were very lucky to get off so lightly, weren't you? Harvey's still got a black eye down to his goddamn navel.'

'Where is he, Katrina?'

'He's very tied up right now. Where, I don't know. He was amazed when I told him you'd rung from the airport and were coming to Governor Shepherd's to wait for him. He thought you were still in hospital.'

'Thanks to him, I might have been.' He sucked breath in angrily between his teeth.

The pale gold smoothness of her brow crinkled into a worried frown. 'I don't get you. But if you're having a "hate Harvey Ketterman" week, welcome to the club. That makes two of us.' She took a packet of cigarettes from her handbag and lit one. 'By the way, the bastard said I was to take great care of you till he can get here. See you have anything you want.' She raised an eyebrow archly and squeezed his arm. 'And that really means "anything" Dick. I've always liked your English cool, you know that.'

Scholefield turned away to look out into the gathering dusk. The cars were turning on their headlights and they reflected on his face as he gazed out of the window.

'How long had you known Nina?' She asked the question in a quiet, compassionate voice.

'About six months.'

'Were you in love with her?'

Scholefield didn't reply. He turned to look at her carefully for a long moment, made as if to say something, then took a deep breath and looked out onto Virginia Avenue again. During the silence that followed, the conversation of two other black girls with skins darker than Katrina's drifted across from the table behind them. 'I saw Frank Sinatra on television last night—he just can't sing any more. My mother was really cut up. It's like for us I guess when we turn on TV one day and see the Beatles in wheelchairs. Then we'll really know it's all over.'

Katrina was staring at Scholefield with a strange expression in her eyes. 'I wish Harvey-the-bastard-Ketterman would say something even half as eloquent about me.' Her voice had a catch in it.

'Comparing you to a Beatle in a wheelchair, you mean?' asked Scholefield, frowning.

Katrina didn't smile. 'I'm talking about that expression on your face when I asked you if you were in love with Nina. Eloquence doesn't always require words.'

Now it was her turn to look away and stare out of the window.

Scholefield studied her profile. The tight curls of her short-cropped hair and the proud way she held her head gave her a self-contained look. 'He's still giving you a tough time then?'

She let out a long slow breath. 'He still runs home every goddamn weekend to the wife and kids in Greenwich. Sailing and tennis at the club in summer, skiing and paddle tennis in the winter. "Just till the kids get into school then it's all up", he used to say. Now it's "When the kids are through school".' Her voice suddenly became bitter. 'Next it will be "When they're through college"—Harvey Ketterman betrays people like other guys drink bourbon—as a matter of course.'

'Why don't you ditch him?'

She shrugged and continued staring out of the window. 'I guess I've got something of the baby goose in me. A gosling thinks the first thing it sees when it comes out of its shell is its mother, right? Maybe the first male thing an oriental studies major sees when she emerges from the shell of the Asian Department has to be her man for life, whether she likes it or not.'

'Parrots do the same,' said Scholefield absently.

If she heard him she ignored him. 'Especially when it's a man like Harvey-the-bastard. Not everybody you meet was a junior OSS military attaché with enough of a brass neck to get to talk to Mao, Chou En-lai *and* Chiang Kai-shek in Chungking during the war. Not many "suspect" China scholars survived the McCarthy purges to come back and head up the State Department's Bureau of Intelligence and Research. Not too many men these days are as together as he is, know where they've been and where they're going.' She drew so hard on her cigarette that the end glowed a fierce red, burning down fast into a sharp spearhead. 'I'm just a whole damned bunch hung up on him, it's as simple as that, Dick. But I'd sure as hell like to hurt the bastard right now. So if you'd like to come up to my apartment upstairs and let him come back to find us rolling around in bed together with our legs wrapped round each other, that's fine by me. I'd only be following his instructions.'

'Where is he now?' asked Scholefield gently.

'I don't know, Dick, honestly, I don't. He treats me and the rest of his staff like mushrooms—you know, keeps us in the dark all the time and opens the door just occasionally to throw a bucket of shit over us. I think he went up to Georgetown earlier this evening. He drove off that way at least. He asked me specially to stay on in the office. When he rang in I told him you'd called and he told me to come and meet you because he had to go urgently to the White House, would you believe?'

'Shouldn't you perhaps believe him, this once?'

'He's addicted to complex cover stories, Dick. It's a compulsion with him. All those goddamn lies mean is that he's got not just one fancy whore but two—one at either end of Pennsylvania Avenue—and his pride in his machismo compels him to service them both on the same evening.'

'Why not get away somewhere for a bit, if it's eating you up that much?'

She turned and looked at him levelly with wide dark eyes. 'Where can I go to get away from Katrina Jackson? I did go away once, remember, for two years, and what happened? I got myself married to a rich, boring guy who talks people into lining their houses with aluminum sheeting for a living. So I came back. The world is full of dummies, Dick, and whatever else Harvey-the-bastard is, he isn't a dummy.'

Scholefield poured some of the Hearty Burgundy for her. She tasted it, pulled a face and pushed it away. Scholefield toyed uncomfortably with the stem of his glass for a moment. 'Katrina, you don't have to concoct an elaborate front for me. Although I've known you and Harvey for a while, I know that you must respect office confidences.'

'Dick, I genuinely haven't the faintest notion what's going on. If his lies are true, then it is something big.' She lifted her shoulders in a shrug and held them there looking at him, the pale palms of her long slender hands turned theatrically upwards.

Scholefield leaned his elbows on the table suddenly, his chin resting on the clasped knuckles of both hands, as if coming to a sudden decision. 'Katrina, I want you to help me.'

'Anything, Dick, like I said, is anything.'

'I want to check a name—quick!'

'Is that all?'

'It's an obscure name.'

'Chinese?'

He nodded. 'It needs to be an exhaustive computer check—tonight.'

She lifted her wrist and looked at her watch. 'The son of a mega-millionaire who owns every second barrel of oil in Texas is into the China thing in a big way at Harvard right now and Daddy's bought him the biggest and best computer there is outside of Langley. I could call one of the guys who operates it for him, he's an admirer of mine I guess you could say. He'd run the check for you. They've put everything into it that was ever known about anybody who's ever been anybody in the People's Republic—right down to the laundry marks on Chou En-lai's underpants when he was a student in Paris.'

'That sounds terrific,' said Scholefield quickly.

'We can go up to my apartment to make the call—it's right here in the Governor Shepherd block overhead.'

Scholefield shot her a quick wary look. 'Can we do it from the phone booth over there in the corner? If you get through I'll take over and tell him what I want.'

She smiled slowly. 'Don't trust the bugging boys not to listen in on my line, huh Dick?' She got up and made her way to the telephone in the corner of the restaurant. He remained at the

THE DEATH OF MAO TSE-TUNG

table and watched her dial. She spoke into the receiver quietly for about a minute then waved Scholefield over and handed him the receiver. 'Go ahead. My friend's name is Larry.'

Scholefield took the phone and introduced himself. 'The name I'd like checked out is'—he paused and glanced round the restaurant—'Li Tai-chu.' He repeated the name twice, describing the characters visually to the man at the other end, so there would be no mistake, drawing them out unconsciously with his index finger on the wall above the telephone as he spoke. 'No other clues. Just see if he exists—or if he is simply a figment of my imagination.'

'Sure. I'll call you right back.'

Scholefield hung up and walked back to where Katrina was sitting. She had ordered a hamburger and he sat down and watched her lift its lid and decorate the interior of the bun liberally with ketchup from a plastic squeeze bottle. She wore a large pearl ring on her left hand, he noticed now, and a gold band around the base of her throat.

She picked up a crinkle-cut French fry between her finger and thumb, dipped it into the ketchup inside the hamburger and slid it sideways into her mouth with a delicate movement of her wrist. All the time she smiled suggestively into his eyes. Somewhere not far away a pianist began belting out a jazz version of 'How High the Moon.' He watched her eat the hamburger in silence. Once he picked up the glass of Hearty Burgundy, then remembered, and quickly put it down again. They both looked at each other and laughed suddenly. Gradually the restaurant emptied. The woman who'd made too many crepes led her husband out. Then the girl haunted by the idea of Beatles in wheelchairs left with her friend.

When Katrina had finished eating the hamburger she stood up and picked up her bag from the windowsill. 'When you've had your phone call, come on up,' she said softly. 'You can relax up there—whichever way you like.' She leaned over him and smoothed her hand affectionately over his hair. Then she turned and walked to the door without looking round.

Ten minutes later the phone rang in its booth and Scholefield hurried across the restaurant to answer it. Larry's voice came apologetically on the line.

'Only the very slightest of references, Mr. Scholefield, I'm sorry to say. And a very old one at that.'

Scholefield held his breath. 'Well what is it, for God's sake?'

'Way back in 1964, I'm afraid. Not a report, just a picture caption on the back of a May Day edition of the *People's Daily*. A back page photo montage. I've had to fish out the appropriate number of the paper to check, that's why I've been so long. Li Tai-chu is one of several minor functionaries listed—on a pre-May Day platform with Marshall Lin Piao.'

Scholefield tensed. 'What's Li Tai-chu look like?'

'The picture is the usual blurred *People's Daily* quality, you know.'

'Can you describe Li to me, for Christ's sake? This is important!' Scholefield shouted in his impatience, and then apologised immediately.

'He's not much of a looker,' the voice at the other end said at last. 'Short and dumpy, I'd say . . .'

'Describe what you can see very carefully, please.'

There was a long silence. Then a sigh of professional frustration. 'It really is hard to say from the quality of this shot. He's got a roundish sort of face. I guess you'd say, kinda cherubic for a Chinese.' There was another long pause. Then Larry's voice came on again slightly more excited. 'I've just taken a magnifying glass to the caption and picture and it looks as though his face does have one distinctive feature—he's got bad skin. Kinda pock-marked, I'd guess. So Li Tai-chu, I think you could surmise, is or was a round-faced heavy acne victim and a one-time supporter of the late Lin Piao.'

'Thank you, Larry. Thanks a million. I'll tell Katrina you've been a great help.'. Scholefield hung up and stood looking indecisively at the door through which she had made her exit ten minutes earlier.

TAIPEH, Sunday—More than 37,000 Chinese Communist military personnel have been arrested for being involved in an alleged plot by Lin Piao to overthrow Chairman Mao Tse-tung, according to secret Communist documents smuggled into Taipeh.
Central News Agency, Taiwan, 5 November 1972

19

Harvey Ketterman paid off his taxi at the corner of Pennsylvania and West Executive Avenue and walked quickly to the security blockhouse inside the north-west gate of the White House. The guard behind the reinforced glass gave a nod of approval as soon as he announced himself and pushed a numbered, plastic-covered security pass through a flap at the bottom of the window, even before he went through the formality of ticking Ketterman's name on the check-list of invited visitors.

Ketterman fixed the pass into his lapel and hurried along the path that curved away between lawns and shrubs towards the National Security Council offices in the western basement. Before he'd gone ten yards the guard in the blockhouse had telephoned the China specialist on the National Security Council in the Old Executive Office Building on the other side of West Executive Avenue. He immediately left his desk and hurried through the underground tunnel to the White House.

He arrived at the security guard's desk inside the basement door at the same moment as Ketterman and he offered his hand gravely in greeting. Despite this show of recognition, the guard with a gun on his hip insisted on inspecting Ketterman's pass before allowing him inside. They walked by a sign on the wall announcing 'Situations Room' with an arrow pointing in the opposite direction and entered a lift. No conversation was exchanged as the NSC man led him out of the lift and along a carpeted corridor on an upper floor and opened a door into an office that faced south over open parkland to the Potomac.

Through the window the floodlit monuments of the capital were already glowing brightly in the deepening darkness. Although the three men standing by the window had their backs to the room looking out, Ketterman recognised all of them immediately. The Director of the Central Intelligence Agency was on the right, the burly, hunched figure of the Secretary of State on the left, and in the middle, with his hands thrust deep into his pockets, stood the President of the United States. They had been talking quietly in low voices as the two newcomers entered and now they stopped and turned round. After a quick flurry of handshakes, all five men sat down at a small circular table.

The President sat with his back to the reinforced window and the two distant red eyes in the top of the pointed stone hood of the Washington Monument winked alternately over his shoulder at the men facing him. The President nodded at Ketterman and turned the palm of his right hand upward, inviting him to begin. Ketterman glanced round at each of the four faces watching him in turn, trying to gauge their mood from their expressions. Then he cleared his throat. 'Mr. President, gentlemen, you are already familiar with the contents of the eight folios that the man known as Yang presented to Richard Scholefield in London as a true account of the Lin Piao incident.' He nodded to the translations of the folios which were lying open on the table in front of the President and the Secretary of State. 'And you are also aware, I think, of the existence of the "Ninth Folio" which I prepared, to counteract them in case the Soviets pressed their efforts to get the original eight disseminated publicly. Well, as you know, I have just completed an interrogation of the man calling himself Yang who says he is a survivor of the Trident crash. He's told me what he claims is the full story of the incident. He also gave me his interpretation of why Moscow has now decided to try and disseminate these lies, some of which he helped cook up.'

Ketterman paused and looked slowly round the table once more. 'The upshot of his information is, gentlemen, that there is a Russian plot to kill Chairman Mao Tse-tung in Peking.

What's more it's been timed to coincide with the breaking of his false story from London.'

The President who had been watching Ketterman with his chin resting on one hand straightened in his chair. The owlish eyes of the Secretary of State blinked quickly behind his heavy hornrims, but nobody attempted to interrupt.

'The first thing you will want to hear from me, gentlemen, I'm sure, is my assessment of the reliability of Yang's "testimony". Well, in answer to that, I can only say that although his version of the Lin Piao incident is more fantastic than anything yet suggested, it does check out fully with the information we gathered at the time by electronic surveillance methods.' Ketterman paused and drew a long breath. 'The layers of deception in this whole affair have sometimes seemed endless, Mr. President. But my guess is that, at last, through Comrade Yang we've finally hit bedrock.'

'What does your friend say the Soviet motive is in attempting to assassinate Mao?' The Secretary of State put the question in a matter-of-fact voice, while subjecting the fingernails of his right hand to a minute scrutiny.

'He claims the cost of keeping a million and a half troops, who can't be used anywhere else, on the Chinese border is proving an intolerable strain on the weak Soviet economy. Yet another failure of their agriculture has sharpened the problem—in addition to which they're not too keen on the prospect of China's constantly improving rocketry being able to take out Moscow with increasing accuracy as time goes by. For these reasons they've decided to make a big throw for a rapprochement with their Communist brothers now. With a change of regime due any moment with Mao sinking fast, they see the chance receding rapidly if they don't grab it now. They want to prevent the anti-Moscow supporters of Mao—the radicals led by his wife Chiang Ching—from taking over at all costs. Hence, the plot to kill Mao and the elaborate ploy built around "Yang", the ace they've been holding quietly for four years, to blame it all on Mao's radical supporters.'

The NSC China specialist, a distinguished Harvard academic who had the bull-like shoulders of a college football player and cropped steel grey hair that looked like wire wool, nodded several times and looked at the President over the top of his glasses. 'That's a totally logical prognosis, Mr. President.'

'How, precisely, do the Soviets plan to carry through the assassination?' The CIA Director put the question in a dispassionate voice, but even so it failed to conceal his burning curiosity about the practical planning of such an operation.

'Yang said he knew no details of the actual assassination plan, beyond the fact that they have the capability to place an unsuspected Chinese assassin in Peking.' Ketterman touched the bruise on his cheek absent-mindedly with the fingertips of his right hand and stared over the President's shoulder at the burning eyes of the Monument. 'Yang is a very tough customer indeed and has been playing a deep game. I believe he managed to hold them off for four years in Moscow without telling them what had really gone on with that Trident. I think he agreed to help them in this plan or maybe even suggested it, for two reasons. First their aims to bring down the radicals probably coincided with those of his old boss and himself—and second it was his one sure escape route out of Moscow. He seems to think he was going to get political asylum in Britain. He didn't see that they would never allow him to live once he'd done their dirty work. I don't think he realises how lucky he is to be alive.'

'What does he say really happened on that Trident, Mr. Ketterman?' It was the first time the President had spoken since Ketterman entered the room. His tone was unnecessarily formal, as if he was nervous of having his office and his person involved closely with matters of low intrigue so soon after Watergate and so close to the election.

'A lot of stuff in those folios is probably true. Yang's line is that Lin *was* depressive and apathetic. His son contacted Moscow, Yang says, as a last resort to ask them if they would provide sanctuary if Mao moved against his father. Somebody among Lin's enemies *did* discover the plan to flee to Moscow and they *did* infiltrate the Trident ground staff at Peitaiho to plant a bomb. Now whether it was the "radical" group as we know it today, or Mao himself or Chou En-lai's moderates or simply Wang Tung-hsing's secret police, it's impossible to say. Alliances in the Forbidden City form and reform like cloud in a windy sky with everybody jumping hastily on the "antis" bandwaggon when someone is obviously heading for the chop . . .'

'*But* what, where's the "*but*"?' The Secretary of State's quick interjection betrayed his irritation, as if he thought Ketterman was taking too long to get to the point.

'But,' said Ketterman slowly, refusing to be hurried, 'what Yang didn't tell anybody until now, not even the Russians, is that the Lin Piao group discovered the bomb plot against them long before it was executed.' Ketterman looked round the table again. All eyes were attentively on him. 'And decided to try to turn it to their own advantage. They went ahead and prepared a defection party to fly out to the Soviet Union—but Lin Piao himself wasn't in it.' He paused again, noting the attentive silence with satisfaction. 'They substituted a "look-alike" and such embellishments as his silver pistol anticipating that the radicals would denounce Lin as a traitor and a defector after his fake death when he could offer no defence. Lin Piao was kept in hiding in China with the intention of bringing him out when the denunciations had been completed. Then, his supporters hoped, shocked out of his apathy, he would create an enormous stir, denouncing the plotters in his turn, rally army support and claw his way back to the top of the pile.'

'But the Russians had ways of identifying even the charred corpse of Lin,' the Director of the CIA protested. 'They had dental casts of his mouth from the time he was treated in Moscow during the war.'

'No, it was all successfully faked up. The look-alike's finger-prints were surgically removed. His dental history was fabricated. Unless the Russians had a whole-head X-ray of his jaw they couldn't run a reliable check. And it's highly unlikely they would have taken whole-head X-rays during the last war in Moscow.'

'Doesn't all this sound a little'—the NSC China-watcher searched for an apposite word—'far-fetched, over-fantasised?'

'There are precedents,' said Ketterman evenly. 'Remember the corpse of the pilot with the false D-Day landing plans the Brits dumped in the Channel so that it was washed ashore in France. Fingerprints removed, teeth fixed, and so on.' Ketterman paused but nobody challenged him in the silence he offered. 'It was a ruthless plan admittedly. The "look-alike" had to be put aboard comatose not knowing what fate awaited him. They couldn't put him on board dead because the time of death had to coincide with the bomb going off. The rest of the doomed party on the plane, with the exception of Yang, didn't know what was going on. They were sacrificial lambs to Lin Piao's future survival. It was only when one of them stumbled on Yang getting into his parachute ready to desert the about-to-explode ship that the gun-battle broke out—that's why the bodies had bullet holes when the Russians found them.'

'Parachute?' The Secretary of State's eyebrows threatened to disappear in his hairline. 'So Yang *jumped* before the bomb went off?'

Ketterman nodded. 'That's what he told me. He jumped and broke his hip. He did, as he says in the folios, run into old Tsereng Toktokho on the ground, who took pity on him and took him under his wing. All that's true—except he was found by the Russians who shot up the yurt and burned it—not the guards from the Chung Nan Hai.'

'The KGB disinformation department must have enjoyed writing that into the scenario,' murmured the CIA chief.

'How did Yang explain the bullets in the corpses to the Russians? Presumably he didn't admit to baling out.' The NSC man leaned forward eagerly on the table.

'He told them at the last minute some of the party funked it and wanted to turn back. He and the KGB together concocted the rabies fable to hide Moscow's involvement in Lin's plot.'

'So why did it all fail to work?' Again the President's tone implied a distaste for the subject. He asked the question as if forced.

'Lin's hideaway in China was discovered. He was taken by his opponents and held under strict house arrest outside Peking. Yang says he died in the spring of 1972 of what are termed natural causes while under arrest. His chronic ill-health was probably worsened by his depression and dejection. That's why it took the Chinese a year to come out with the official story of Lin's death while defecting. It took them that long to establish that there had been a plot within a plot. By then however they felt that if there had been enough faked evidence for them to believe for a time, after sending men to the spot, that he really was on board, there was enough for the rest of the world to be told that same story. And it had the double advantage that it was more damaging to Lin—and covered up the treachery of those who tried to kill him.'

There was a long silence in which all the men round the table sat looking wonderingly at each other. The Secretary of State shook his head slowly, a faint smile of incredulity twisting the corners of his mouth downward. 'It all sounds incredible—but it would all fit.'

'The thing we've got to decide,' said the President brusquely, 'is whether to tell Peking about the new death plot. And what do we do about Yang?'

'That's one curious thing I've not mentioned, Sir,' said Ketterman quickly. 'We know he's not Yang Tsai-chien. At least the Chinese insist that the man of that name was positively identified by them at the crash site by his finger prints. Yang consistently refuses to divulge who he is. We know he was on that Trident but his identity remains a mystery.'

'It's not really important, is it?' said the President irritably. 'More important is, do we tell the Chinese we believe the Russians are planning to kill Mao on the strength of these claims?'

'It's not entirely against our interests to have a regime in Peking that hates the Muscovite guts of Brezhnev and his friends.' The NSC man smiled as he spoke to emphasise his heavy irony. 'If they ever do roll back into the arms of the Russians we'll have to rethink a lot of our current precepts.'

The President nodded, frowning. 'It's not our damned job anymore to try to decide which governments should be in power in foreign countries. We've gotta do our best to rub along with whichever of those that come out on top.'

'Mr. President, I have decided to recommend,' said Ketterman slowly, 'that we ought to hand Yang back to the Russians once we had extracted the truth from him. There is a certain amount of continuing interface between us at the intelligence level, the detail of which needn't bother you. Now we've stymied their plans with the Ninth Folio they're pretty damned anxious to get him back, I can tell you. And they're making unmistakable threats about what might happen if they don't.'

'What threats exactly, Mr. Ketterman?' The President's voice was coldly hostile now.

'The Soviet ramrod handling this is a guy named Razduhev, KGB head of station in London. He's very senior and *he* says the Politburo is going to put pressure on all round if we don't hand Yang back. They're ready to push the Cuban troops now in Angola into Rhodesia, they're making dark hints about stepping up their activity in the Horn of Africa to turn Ethiopia and Somalia to the hammer and sickle. They might refuse to co-operate over any force reductions at all in Eastern Europe, work to rule on the SALT agreements. He implied there's hardly a damned thing they won't do if we hang on to Yang.'

'If we grant Yang asylum we offend not only the Russians, we offend the Chinese too.' The Secretary of State directed his words idly towards the ceiling as if musing aloud. 'They'll claim he should be returned to them to be dealt with in their own way.'

'If we return him to the Russians the Chinese will take considerable umbrage, you can be sure of that, Mr. President,' said the NSC man earnestly. 'We're suppressing the Folios to save Peking the international humiliation of being made to look like liars over the original Lin Piao affair. Shouldn't we be consistent and follow through in Peking's favour?'

'At my level, Mr. President, a certain amount of even-handedness is essential,' Ketterman insisted. 'The Soviets saw us lean very definitely towards Peking in seventy-one when we tipped Mao off about the Lin Piao plot that we heard of out of Moscow, If we appear to be throwing our lot too far in with the Chinese again over intelligence and security the Russians could begin to feel dangerously isolated.'

There was silence in the room for a moment.

'I'm meeting Razduhev at the Lincoln Memorial at midnight,' continued Ketterman, lifting his wristwatch into view from beneath the table. 'He's expecting to hear what arrangement will be made to return Yang to them.'

The President jerked forward in his seat suddenly and leaned his forearms on the table, looking directly across at Ketterman.

A pugnacious glint came into his eyes. 'The information we gave Peking in 1971, Mr. Ketterman, was to say the least unsubstantiated by any incontrovertible evidence. If we tip the Chinese about another death plot against Mao, we could make fools of ourselves again—and give them a basis on which to build more lying propaganda. We can kill two birds with one stone here. We don't really know beyond any shadow of doubt the truth behind it all, despite what you've told us, and we don't want to grant Yang asylum.' He paused and glowered round the table. 'So let them make up their minds for themselves about his story.'

The President stood up suddenly and looked round in turn once again at the NSC man, the Secretary of State and the Director of the CIA. Each returned his gaze without sign of dissent and he ignored Ketterman. 'Okay,' said the President, turning rapidly on his heel and heading for the door. 'Ship Yang back to Peking—but quick.'

PEKING, Wednesday—Teng Ying-chao, the wife of Chou En-lai, the Chinese Prime Minister, disclosed here yesterday that the American Central Intelligence Agency got to know of the death of Lin Piao, Chairman Mao's heir apparent, even before the Russians. But she did not disclose how the CIA got to know so quickly.

The Daily Telegraph, 19 June 1973

20

The hand-written poster nailed to the trunk of a tree at the corner of Ashmede and 20th Street on the edge of Washington's diplomatic quarter was headed 'Dog Lost'. Its message scrawled in orange and blue crayon said: 'Small, black, shaggy poodle (female) wearing pink and red coat and bright orange collar lost around 10 p.m. on 25th July, 1976. Finder please call urgently. She is under medication. Thank you.'

Harvey Ketterman read it a second time, closed his eyes briefly to test his memory of the telephone number added at the bottom, then returned to his car. He drove slowly back to Connecticut Avenue, glancing as he passed at the windows of the former 300-bedroom Windsor Park Hotel which Peking had bought in its entirety in 1972 after the diplomatic thaw brought on by Richard Nixon's visit. It had been converted now into an urban fortress named 'The Liaison Office of the People's Republic of China.' The ground floor windows had been reinforced with heavy concrete frames and thick black-painted steel bars protected the glass. Above the double doors of the old hotel a light illuminated the circular red and gold symbol of Communist China—five stars floating above the Gate of Heavenly Peace. Only a few slivers of light showed dimly through closed curtains on the upper floors of the squat eight-storey building that served as home, office, and recreation area to its Chinese diplomats. The floodlights however had been left lit on the empty basketball and badminton courts enclosed behind stout black iron railings at the rear.

Ketterman stopped his car at a telephone booth higher up the Avenue and got out and dialled the number on the poster. The voice that answered spoke English with a heavy Chinese accent. 'I think I've found your missing pet,' said Ketterman slowly. 'It answers to the name of "Yang" and is still under medication. How would you like me to return it?'

There was a long silence on the other end of the line. In the office of the Central External Liaison Department's head of Washington station on the fifth floor of the old Windsor Park Hotel a Chinese in a high buttoned cadre's uniform put his hand over the mouthpiece of the telephone and turned to shoot a stream of excited Mandarin at Tan Sui-ling, who was sitting quietly reading a copy of *Time* magazine on a sofa on the other side of the room. She got up quickly and took the receiver from the man. 'What is your name please?' she asked in English.

'I answer to "Ketterman".'

She sucked in a quick breath. 'Are you sure that what you have found complies exactly with the description of what we are seeking?'

'Positive!' said Ketterman. 'And I can have it back to you within the hour. No rewards sought.'

Tan Sui-ling covered the phone and consulted the man at her side in rapid Chinese. Then she uncupped her hand from the mouthpiece once more. 'We shall open the gates onto the basketball court in forty-five minutes time.' She spoke the words crisply and hung up without waiting for a reply.

Ketterman walked slowly back to his car and lowered himself wearily into the driving seat. When he'd turned its nose south again he leaned over the dashboard and picked up the hand microphone for the two-way radio. 'Our friend is expected in forty-five minutes from this time.' His voice was tired. 'Deploy three ambulances with one patient in each. Maximum security precautions are to prevail at points of departure and arrival. Contact me at Katrina's to confirm.'

'Your message read and understood,' said the voice of the young fair-haired man from the Georgian villa on P Street.

Ketterman replaced the hand microphone in its cradle and had to swerve wildly to avoid an oncoming car because he'd drifted into the centre of the road while sending his message. The Governor Shepherd restaurant was in darkness when he reached it and he left his car at the kerbside next to a No Parking sign and opened the street door to the adjoining apartment block with his own key. He took the lift up to the eighth floor and used a latch key to open the door of the apartment. In the sitting room he found Richard Scholefield sprawled in an easy chair with his jacket off, balancing a cup of coffee in one hand. Katrina was sitting by his feet on a white goatskin rug, her arm resting casually on his thigh. She was naked and her flimsy black brassiere lay crumpled on the rug beside her. She looked round and smiled sweetly up at Ketterman but didn't move.

He stood in the doorway looking expressionlessly from her face to Scholefield's and back again. She made a little shrugging movement with her shoulders and nuzzled the swell of her breasts closer against Scholefield's knee. 'You look tired and old and grey-faced, Harvey, you bastard,' she said, still smiling sweetly, 'where the fuck have you been?'

'Working my ass off to save the goddamned Western world, as usual—for no thanks.' Ketterman turned and closed the door and shrugged out of his jacket.

Scholefield didn't get up. He sat watching the American carefully, still holding the coffee cup in his right hand.

Ketterman draped his jacket over the back of an easy chair and lowered himself into it with a weary groan. 'Nice to see you, Dick. Even if it is a helluva surprise.'

'I wish I could say the same, Harvey.'

Ketterman appeared to study the long dark curve of Katrina's naked back for a long moment. Then his gaze strayed to the flimsy undergarment on the rug before returning to Scholefield's face. 'What brings England's most celebrated sinologist to Washington, may I ask?'

'You.' Scholefield's voice had a hard edge to it.

Ketterman leaned over suddenly and rubbed his hand quickly over Katrina's tightly frizzed hair. 'A Jack Daniels and ice, Kat, please.'

Katrina smiled dazzlingly into his face. 'Get it yourself, Harvey.'

THE DEATH OF MAO TSE-TUNG

Ketterman stood up slowly, looking first at Katrina then at Scholefield. Then suddenly he grinned. 'Hey, what the hell goes on here? The hunter's home from the hill and all he gets in his tepee is unmitigated hostility.'

'His squaw's tepee,' corrected Katrina, turning to smile brightly at him once again. 'On a nine thousand-year mortgage maybe, but technically his squaw's, not Harvey's.' She sipped her drink, still looking into his eyes and still resting her elbow on Scholefield's thigh. 'Maybe it's got something to do with what the hunter was doing on the goddamned hill. If there was a popularity contest in the wigwam right now he'd get no votes out of two.'

Ketterman rubbed his eyes with both fists and went over to the tray of drinks on a side table. He dropped some ice into a glass and poured himself a large bourbon. While his back was turned Katrina stood up. She plucked her bra from the rug and stood dangling it from one hand, resting the other on a jutting hip. 'I guess I'll go and slip into something *less* comfortable now you're here, Harvey.' When she knew he was watching her, she turned and minced out on her toes, waggling her hips exaggeratedly and swinging the brassiere around her finger. She looked both vulnerable and desirable in the same moment.

Neither man spoke for a long while after she had left the room. Ketterman finished his drink and stood looking at Scholefield indecisively, holding the empty glass in his hand. The Englishman returned his gaze steadily. Eventually Ketterman turned away to get himself another drink.

'You knew all about the Yang thing in advance, Harvey.' Scholefield's voice had a hostile, accusing note, and when Ketterman turned round he found he'd stood up.

The American took a long pull at his drink, then continued to inspect the contents of the glass intently, avoiding Scholefield's eyes. 'So what, Dick?'

Scholefield put down his coffee cup and took a step towards him, his fists clenching at his sides. 'So if you had told me what you knew in London, Nina might still be alive.'

Ketterman lowered the glass and looked at him. 'I didn't know they were going to bomb the poor bastard out.' He lifted a hand to his bruised and swollen check as if in corroboration.

'But you knew about the whole jar of worms beforehand from the Israelis in Moscow—and you let it all run smoothly to schedule even though I was being used as an oily rag!'

'How the hell do you know that?' Ketterman stopped and looked round at Katrina, who had reappeared in the doorway dressed in a long white kaftan. He spread his arms suddenly in front of him in a defensive gesture. 'For Chrissakes, this is no place to discuss—'

Scholefield's left shoulder dipped suddenly and his body swung back and down through a low arc as if beginning a discus throw. His bunched right fist came up fast out of the flat, stiff-armed swing and caught Ketterman squarely between jaw and cheekbone, propelling him bodily across the room. The glass flew from his hand and smashed against the door. He slid backwards down the wall onto the carpet, his eyes glazed with shock and a dribble of blood running down the centre of his chin from a cut inside his mouth.

At that same moment the Russians, watching from a car parked fifty yards along P Street in sight of the white Georgian villa, saw the first stretcher coming down the front steps. The two men carrying it hurried to the open rear doors of an ambulance parked at the kerb under an ornamental wrought-iron street lamp. The driver of the Russian car started the engine as the two men slid the stretcher inside and closed the doors. Then Bogdarin, who was sitting beside him, let out a muffled curse and pointed through the windscreen to a second ambulance nosing slowly out across the intersection from 34th Street. By radio, he alerted the back-up car parked round the corner in Volta Place, then watched with a dark scowl disfiguring his features as a second stretcher borne by two more men appeared at the top of the villa's front steps.

The driver had pulled out of the line of parked cars and was easing towards the intersection when Bogdarin spotted the third ambulance coming slowly south down 34th. He cursed again, more loudly this time, as it swung round in front of the villa and stopped well out from the kerb, blocking the way westward where the other two ambulances were already moving off.

Two more figures descended the steps of the house with a third

THE DEATH OF MAO TSE-TUNG

stretcher and quickly ran it into the back of the third ambulance and closed the doors. They strolled back up the steps into the house, without looking back at the Russian car although the driver was leaning on its horn in frustration at being blocked in. The back-up car, seeing what was happening, accelerated frantically away down 34th and swung westward along O Street with a loud scream from its tyres, clearly hoping to pick up the track of the other two ambulances by making a detour to the southwest.

The third ambulance moved slowly off followed by the Russian car. Once it was under way the fair-haired young man threw back the blanket covering him on the stretcher and crept to the windows in the back door to look out. When he saw Bogdarin through the windscreen of the car cruising slowly behind him, he waved and grinned, picked up a hand microphone from its rest on a side wall of the ambulance and asked to be connected to Katrina Jackson's number.

When the telephone rang inside Katrina's apartment, she was bending over Ketterman where he'd fallen with his back jammed against the wall. She dabbed gingerly with a damp sponge at the blood running from his mouth, then thrust the sponge into his hand and rose to answer the telephone. Scholefield stood watching impassively from the other side of the room, finishing his coffee.

Katrina carried the telephone across to Ketterman and pushed the receiver into his empty hand. The voice of the fair-haired young man was exuberant, but correct. 'Departure procedure carried through correctly, Sir,' he said quietly. 'The vehicle transporting "lost dog" is on its way unimpeded. Estimated to arrive at its destination in seven minutes from now.'

Ketterman grunted his thanks and handed the telephone back to Katrina. He looked at his watch then wiped some more blood from his teeth with the sponge. He rose unsteadily to his feet and looked balefully at Scholefield.

'You'll live, Harvey. That was just to relieve my feelings enough so I could talk to you. If I'd really wanted to hurt you I would have used my feet.'

'Thank you,' said Ketterman, feigning gratitude. 'Thanks a million.'

Scholefield put his coffee cup down. 'Where's Yang, Harvey?'

Ketterman massaged his jaw slowly with one hand. Instead of replying, he walked over to the drinks table and began pouring himself another bourbon. 'That's a question, Dick, that goes far beyond the bounds of our unspoken understanding on exchanges of academic interpretation.' Ketterman spoke over his shoulder without turning round.

'Letting Yang and his friends abduct Matthew so you could watch the pot boil up and check the validity of Israeli information was way outside that mark too, Harvey.'

Ketterman swung round. 'Okay, Dick, okay, you feel aggrieved. But, so help me, I never foresaw things turning out this way.'

'You're a lying bastard!' Scholefield stepped quickly towards him again. 'In the course of doing whatever it is you do—"protecting justice and freedom for the Western democracies" is no doubt how you'd describe it to yourself—you use other people like paper tissues—to do all the dirty jobs you don't want to soil your own fingers with. You betray every damned moral principle—loyalty, honesty and decency—that's supposed to lie at the heart of what you're defending.'

Ketterman closed his eyes and held up his palms towards Scholefield. 'I don't have a pat answer ready for that right now. Let me work on it, will ya?' He opened his eyes again and looked round at Katrina for support. But she stood watching him expressionlessly, holding the blood-soaked sponge limply in one hand. 'Hell, this is like one of those arcane Greek tragedies where everybody double-crosses everybody else so many times you lose count.' He shrugged wearily. 'The only trouble is there's nobody here to come to the front of the stage from time to time to tell me which are the good guys and which are the bad.'

The telephone jangled at that moment beside Ketterman and he picked it up. 'The lost dog's safely back on the basketball court,' said the voice of the young fair-haired man.

'Thank Christ!' said Ketterman explosively and hung up. His shoulders sagged as he dropped the receiver. He looked dully at his watch and moved off towards the door. Scholefield and Katrina stood watching him but he went out without turning round.

* * *

Inside the back door of the former Windsor Park Hotel, Tan Sui-ling stood beside the Central External Liaison Department's station chief as two junior diplomats wheeled the stretcher bearing Yang across the basketball court. Against the glare of the floodlights they were gawky silhouettes. Behind them the American ambulance reversed towards the gates in the high fence. As they watched, it stopped in the gateway, and the black driver jumped out and ran back to the doorway. The CELD man went forward to meet him.

'The special Japanese Airlines flight J 719 scheduled to leave Dulles in 90 minutes will be held for him,' he said tersely. 'Customs and security at the airport have been primed to allow him through unconscious. The Japanese have agreed to co-operate for this one flight to Tokyo to make a connection to Peking with no questions asked. If you don't get him out tonight, we give no further guarantees.' Without waiting for a response the black man turned and ran back to the ambulance. He jumped in and moved the vehicle out onto Connecticut Avenue. The gates were slammed shut behind it and the floodlights on the asphalt basketball court suddenly blacked out.

The two diplomats pushing the stretcher trolley manoeuvred it carefully in through the double doors and the CELD man stepped forward to inspect Yang's face in the overhead passage light. A moment later he picked up his right wrist and felt for a pulse. He stood with his head on one side for fully half a minute, checking his watch. Then he dropped the wrist and nodded briefly to Tan Sui-ling, before swinging round to lead the way along the corridor towards what had once been the hotel's service lift.

Tan Sui-ling walked beside the stretcher, with her back to the two men pushing it. As the party moved down the dimly-lit corridor, Yang's eyes flickered open. The first thing his gaze lighted on was Tan Sui-ling's face. Shielding the movement from the men pushing the trolley with her body, Tan let her hand fall on Yang's arm. She applied quick, gentle pressure with her fingers and smiled at him. Immediately he closed his eyes again.

PARIS, Friday—Scores of men and women supporters of the late Lin Piao who led an abortive coup
against Mao Tse-tung in the autumn of 1971 have
been executed during the past few weeks in Nanking,
according to French businessmen recently in China.
                    The Daily Telegraph, 10 May 1974

21

Scholefield lunged down the stairs two at a time, ran across the
lobby and wrenched open the door to the street. Then he stopped.
Harvey Ketterman was standing stock still at the kerb. He had
given himself up entirely to a foul and fluent stream of cuss-words
which only ceased when he noticed Scholefield standing beside
him.

'It was right here, dammit!' He pointed foolishly into the
empty gutter. 'I left it right here and the bastards have towed it
away.' Another torrent of four-letter words escaped his lips in an
unbroken flow. 'Christ, if this isn't my lucky day!' He rubbed his
jaw again and glared at his watch. It was ten minutes to midnight.

'Your bio-rhythms have obviously all hit zero at once, Harvey.
You should go home, go to bed and stay there till there's an
upturn.'

Ketterman ignored Scholefield and stepped off the kerb. He
ran across in front of two fast-approaching cars, coming dangerously near to cannoning into the front fender of one of them.
The wail of blaring horns from two drivers, more relieved than
angry at having narrowly avoided slaughtering another insane
jaywalker, faded fast into the night as they rushed on down
Virginia Avenue.

Scholefield waited for a safe gap in the traffic then ran after
Ketterman. He caught him up on the grass by the mounted

statue of Bernardo Da Galvez and fell into stride beside him. They rounded the western wing of the State Department and turned south down 23rd Street. A high grassy bank rose abruptly on the western side of the street topped with a chain link fence and barbed wire. A signboard announced that they were passing the Naval Bureau of Medicine and Surgery.

'Have you got Yang in there, Harvey?' Scholefield nodded towards the sign. 'Pumping truth drugs into him and shining bright lights in his eyes?'

Ketterman didn't reply.

'I know you flew him to Washington after the Russians brought him to England on a submarine-and-rubber-dinghy package tour. Then you used a friendly Triad gang to snatch him from St. George's.'

Ketterman stopped suddenly and turned to face Scholefield. 'Why did Tan Sui-ling approach you?'

'To complain about your treacherous ways, Harvey, of course. What else? Everybody's doing it these days.' Scholefield's tone was deliberately offensive. 'The Chinese, the Russians—even Katrina. And certainly Percy Crowdleigh and his friends aren't going to be very pleased when they find out you smuggled Yang out of the country under their noses.'

'She wouldn't give you that information without some special motive!'

'Maybe the Chinese are growing tired of their perfidious superpower friends and are looking to a reliable third force in dear old Europe.'

Ketterman put a hand on Scholefield's shoulder in a confiding gesture. 'Look Dick, I'm genuinely sorry I can't throw more light on this. But this isn't a matter of swapping notes on a *Red Flag* editorial any more. It's up as high as the White House roof right now—and those who don't know you like I do would say, "How the hell do we know he isn't working for the Chinese?"'

Scholefield shook his head slowly in disbelief. '"Deceit makes the world go round", is that your motto, Harvey? To you nothing seems what it really is. I'm surprised you can tell who *you're* working for any more.'

The two men glared at one another for a moment without

speaking. In the brief silence a police siren wailed distantly then grew stronger. Above their heads the disembodied landing lights of an aircraft swung slowly down the sky heading into the National Airport.

Ketterman spread his hands outwards suddenly in a gesture of resignation. 'Okay Dick, I'll give you a picture, right? It won't be everything because as I've told you this whole thing is in the White House now. And I can't compromise any of that.' He took Scholefield by the elbow and guided him down the hill towards Constitution Avenue and the park. 'Yes okay, I talked to "Yang". That's not his real name. He won't say what it is. But he claims he's a genuine survivor and old Toktokho did give him succour and sustenance—that part at least of his folios seems true. I've had him sign a Ninth Folio that counteracts the other eight which he concocted together with the KGB's disinformation fairy-talers. A lie for a lie, a truth for a truth—but it blocks the goddamned Russkies, okay?'

Scholefield was listening intently, his head bent as he walked. 'What really happened on that Trident?'

'We think Lin's men got to know it was going to be sabotaged by the radicals so they put a Lin-Piao "look alike" on board and kept the genuine article at home, meaning to produce him later. Yang went along to supervise the spoof—and jumped on a parachute before the bomb went off. He kept the Russians in the dark about that for the four years they held him.'

Scholefield let a long breath whistle out between pursed lips. 'So what are the Russians trying to pull out of the hat now with the folios?'

They had come out onto Constitution Avenue at the foot of the hill and the fast flow of traffic halted them abruptly at the pavement's edge. Ketterman stared across at the bright flood of white light illuminating the Doric colonnade of the Lincoln Memorial. The dark matchstick-sized figure of a man was visible standing silhouetted against the white stone between the massive middle pillars of the northern face of the monument. Ketterman stiffened for a brief instant. 'Yang says they're planning to assassinate Mao in Peking any time now.' He had to shout to make himself heard above the roar of the traffic rushing through the green light. 'They're using Yang and the folios as a smoke screen to hang it all on the radicals. They want to cool the border thing, he says, and bring home a million and a half boys to work in the refrigerator factories and on the farms to build a Soviet fatherland running with milk and consumer goods.'

'Where's Yang now?'

The lights changed suddenly and the flow of traffic screeched to a standstill. Ketterman immediately hurried across. Inside the park it was quieter. 'I'm sorry Dick, I can't reveal his whereabouts to you—now or ever.' He looked at his watch and quickened his pace again.

They walked on in silence for a minute then Scholefield stopped in mid-stride. 'You're handing the poor bastard back to Peking!'

Ketterman swung round, studying Scholefield's face intently, but saying nothing.

'It was a guess, Harvey,' Scholefield nodded silently. 'But I know from your face it's right. It fits your style—and the White House, too. You're beyond disgust.' They stared at each other in silence for a moment. Then Scholefield's brow furrowed into a frown. 'But I can't help wondering whether you haven't both miscalculated. Has it occurred to you that the Russians may *not* have been trying to kill Yang at the Institute—but just trying to give that impression? He dived for cover pretty smartly—almost as if he knew what was coming.'

Ketterman's eyes widened suddenly. 'Jesus! And they missed him at the mortuary too, even though they saw me switch him!'

'What?' Scholefield gazed at him mystified.

But Ketterman was staring distractedly towards the Memorial again. He turned back and opened his mouth as if to say something more then seemed to change his mind. 'Let's discuss it later.' He glanced at his watch and there was an uncomfortable silence for a moment. Then the American looked unaccountably embarrassed. He gazed down suddenly at his shoes. 'Look Dick, Katrina was just kidding me, wasn't she? She's a helluva kidder, you know. The best thing is to ignore her, not encourage her, not give her any satisfaction, am I right?' Scholefield didn't reply. After a moment Ketterman looked up at him, with his eyebrows still raised in mute enquiry.

'Before I answer that, Harvey, just give me one piece of useless information first,' said Scholefield slowly. 'Just to prove you have a single redeeming feature.'

Ketterman glanced impatiently at his watch again and nodded absently as if he really wasn't listening.

'Tan Sui-ling is probably our Chinese lady-friend's workname, right?' Ketterman nodded again. 'What's her real family name?'

Ketterman shrugged carelessly. 'Li Kwei-min, why?'

Scholefield shrugged too. 'Just curiosity, Harvey, just curiosity.'

The American waited a moment then nodded his head impatiently. 'Well, okay, Dick, okay, you got *your* answer. Now tell me, Katrina was just horsing around back there without her clothes, right?'

Scholefield stared straight at him for a long moment. Then slowly he shook his head.

Without another word Ketterman spun round and marched away towards the steps leading up to the Memorial. Scholefield stood watching him go. The American's broad shoulders were hunched around his ears in a curiously defensive attitude, his tall, angular body a stooping silhouette against the bright glow of the marble temple. As Scholefield turned away he saw him slip between a row of tourist buses and begin running across the circular approach road.

Razduhev saw him running too, from his concealed position at the foot of one of the giant Doric entrance columns high above the road. He watched him trotting up the steps beneath him then stepped back quickly out of sight. He walked inside, checking his watch as he went, and stopped and gazed up at the Second Inaugural Address, chiselled into the stone of the north wall.

The twenty-foot marble figure of Lincoln, massive and craggy-jawed on its great stone throne, faced out towards the distant floodlit rotunda of the Capitol above the trees, dwarfing Razduhev and the swarm of midnight sightseers to tiny matchstick figures. Flashguns on the tourists' cameras flared constantly but as Ketterman toiled up the last few steps most of the milling crowd were beginning a ragged retreat from the awesome scale of the god-figure down towards the small, acceptably mundane buses that had brought them. Ketterman stopped at the top to get his breath and let the crowd pass by. Immediately he spotted Razduhev and walked over to him. 'While the First Inaugural Address was being delivered from this place,' he whispered over his shoulder, reading from the quotation, ' "insurgent agents were in the city seeking to destroy it without war—seeking to dissolve the Union and divide effects by negotiation." Is that your favourite American quotation, Yuri, huh?' He grinned and banged Razduhev heartily on the back with his right hand while he slipped a key into a pocket of the Russian's jacket with the other. 'No offence, Yuri, no offence meant, fellah.'

Razduhev looked at him contemptuously for a moment then brushed by him and walked away. He paused, gazing up at the mural depicting an angel freeing a slave above the Gettysburg Address on the south wall, then he turned and slipped abruptly into the shadows beyond the Ionic columns flanking the statue.

Ketterman scanned the faces of the few remaining tourists carefully and when he was satisfied that nobody was paying him any attention, he turned and sauntered casually into the shadows after Razduhev, making for the lift in the east wall. He pressed the call button and the door opened immediately. Only when he was sure the doors had closed behind Ketterman did Bogdarin step out from the deep shadow in the three-foot gap behind the base of the Lincoln statue and follow in the same direction.

When the muted bell announced the arrival of the lift Bogdarin moved quickly inside before the doors were fully opened. At the bottom he stepped out and glanced to the right along the passage-way towards the rangers' offices. They were silent and deserted. Inside the lift shaft the groaning of the lift motor indicated it was rising again. Bogdarin edged along the wall and peered round the side of the spectators' window that gave a view of the massive concrete bowels of the monument. A concrete walkway with steel handrails linked the great square concrete piles that had been driven sixty-five feet into the earth to hold up the thousands of tons of marble overhead. Heating and air conditioning ducts snaked among them and Bogdarin could see Razduhev and Ketterman standing on the gantry in the shadow of the ducts, absorbed in a heated conversation. Razduhev's face was purple with anger and he was gesticulating fiercely with one hand as he spoke. Bogdarin dropped to his knees and crawled bent double beneath the window as far as the door to the men's washroom. Inside he tried the handle of the maintenance door that opened onto the gantry but found it had been carefully secured by Ketterman from inside. Bogdarin drew a lock-picking tool from his pocket and began working silently on the door. As he worked he heard the lift motor whir into life again.

The raised voices of the two men inside penetrated faintly through the door as their argument grew more acrimonious. Thirty seconds later Bogdarin grunted with satisfaction as the lock tumblers yielded. He reached inside the waistband of his trousers and drew out a short-bladed knife and began to turn the handle at the same moment that the faint 'ping' of its bell announced the arrival of the lift once more.

A moment later Richard Scholefield, still breathing heavily from his run up the steps of the Memorial, opened the door to the washroom to find Bogdarin hunched in a half crouch with the knife clutched in his free hand. The Russian already had the maintenance door half open but he remained frozen in a moment of indecision looking at Scholefield, his eyes wide with the apprehension of discovery.

Scholefield began moving towards him immediately in a reflex action and at the same instant caught sight of Ketterman and Razduhev. The American's back was still turned towards the door and the hum from the ducts and the lift motor had clearly covered the sounds of the door opening behind him.

'Watch your back, Harvey!'

Scholefield screamed the warning and lunged towards the Russian's knife hand at the same moment. Bogdarin tried to fend him off with his free hand but slipped and fell to his knees. Ketterman swung round, his face suddenly white with alarm, to find Scholefield and the Russian writhing in the open doorway in a desperate contest for the knife. He turned back but although he began to duck away as soon as he saw the silenced .22 hand gun in Razduhev's right fist, he was too late to avoid its first shot. The Russian had aimed for the heart but because of his sudden movement, Ketterman received the tiny slug between his second and third ribs, low down on the right side of his chest. He staggered back towards the doorway clutching the wound with both hands, staring at Razduhev in disbelief. The Russian extended the gun in front of him to make more sure of his aim—and as he moved slowly towards Ketterman, cursing him softly in his native tongue.

Scholefield freed himself from Bogdarin's grasp at that moment and struggled upright. He swung his left foot high and brought the heel down squarely across the fallen Russian's throat. The knife flew from his hand, slithered across the steel gantry and fell over the side into the darkness between the foundation piles.

Scholefield spun round to see Ketterman folding up slowly over the top guard rail. He was coughing and clutching at the centre of a large and growing blood stain spreading over his lower ribs. Even though he was bent practically double he still stared help-lessly aghast at Razduhev, who was continuing to advance on him holding the tiny gun at arm's length.

In desperation Scholefield threw the only thing that was to hand and Bogdarin's lock-picking tool caught the Russian a glancing blow on the cheek before clattering to the floor of the steel gantry and dropping away into the darkness. Scholefield followed in fast behind the throw, twisting sideways and aiming a high, two-footed yoko-tobi-geri at the Russian's gun hand. The gun recoiled soundlessly the moment before Scholefield's feet struck and the second lead pellet hit Ketterman in the left shoulder three inches from his jugular vein. The impact knocked him to his knees and the top half of his body slipped slowly sideways through the first and second bars of the safety rails.

Scholefield's double kick broke Razduhev's arm and his gun flew into the air in a high arc. Scholefield ducked closer and chopped hard at his throat with the edge of his right hand. The Russian took the full force of the blow directly on the Adam's apple, staggered two steps and toppled backward over the rails. The strangled shout of pain and shock ceased abruptly as he hit the dirt floor of the foundation chamber twenty feet below.

Scholefield flung himself to the floor and grabbed the tails of Ketterman's jacket in time to prevent him slipping over the edge. When he had untangled him from the railings and dragged him into a sitting position he was still coughing and flecks of blood had appeared at the corners of his mouth. He stared wide-eyed at Scholefield. 'Christ almighty, Dick . . .' His voice was barely a croak and he was unable to manage anything further before his eyes clouded with pain and he began coughing again.

Scholefield bent and got his shoulder under the American's armpit and half carried and half dragged him off the gantry. He stepped over the unconscious body of Bogdarin and struggled with Ketterman as far as the rangers' offices. He broke the door open with his foot and stretched Ketterman on the floor while he used the telephone.

Four and a half minutes later the whoop of sirens and the blue glow of revolving lights announced the arrival of police and an ambulance at the foot of the Memorial steps. But by that time Harvey Ketterman was dead.

PEKING, Tuesday—Concern grew here today about the health of Chairman Mao Tse-tung after he failed to receive a visiting head of state for the first time in fourteen months. An official Chinese spokesman told Reuters: 'The Central Committee of our Party has decided not to arrange for Chairman Mao to meet foreign guests.'

Reuters, 15 June 1976

22

The blue and white Boeing 707 of the Civil Aviation Administration of China throttled back its engines as though pausing for one last deep breath, then plunged its nose into the sea of stagnant cloud pressing on the flat plain beneath it. A clammy grey fist clutched immediately at the tilting aircraft and from his window seat inside it, Scholefield watched glistening pearls of moisture grow quickly on the leading wing-edges. As it lost height they began to tear themselves free and explode in translucent streaks of light across the outside of the windows.

The Boeing sank slowly through to the bottom of the grey fog and gradually the ancient, shaded patchwork of the landscape below began to reveal itself in fleeting, distorted glimpses through the scarred Perspex. Scholefield watched this disfigured image of China glide slowly up towards him for a full minute, then turned his eyes away. Flight CA 922 from Tokyo was three-quarters empty. It carried only a delegation of twenty Japanese businessmen in charcoal grey suits, a handful of Chinese government cadres in their high-buttoned uniforms and a group of European diplomats and wives returning to their Peking base from a long weekend in Japan.

During the flight Scholefield had studied all their faces carefully. None of them had been on the plane from New York. He'd watched embarking passengers carefully at Anchorage but no one had seemed to take any special interest in him. Nobody had approached him in fact on either aircraft, although he had been constantly prepared for a surreptitious contact.

The Chinese stewardesses, in dark blue boiler-suit jackets and ballooning trousers, were hurrying to finish clearing the last remains of a savoury buffet they had offered with Chinese beer and erh-kuo t'ou, the local red wine. They had treated everybody with a polite correctness, taking obvious care not to show any signs of obsequiousness to the foreigners. Their best smiles they reserved for the Chinese government cadres on board.

Scholefield had been looked after all the way from Tokyo by a tall skinny girl with a pinched-looking face. Her blue boiler suit hung about her bony frame like a collapsed tent and her mouth had remained set in a thin, unsmiling line throughout the flight. She had acknowledged his 'hsieh hsieh ni's' only with curt nods of the head. As she leaned close across him now to remove his tray he noticed that more had disappeared than just the red silk jackets he had seen on China's smart air girls when he'd first flown into Peking in 1959. The crimson ribbons, with which they had decorated their long glossy braids then, had now been replaced by functional elastic bands doubled several times over their short bunches of carelessly cut hair. Ten years after it erupted, he reflected, the Cultural Revolution was still demanding a heavy toll in proletarian drabness.

Outside, the evening light beneath the clouds had become grey and luminous. One wing of the plane dipped suddenly and it banked to the right giving Scholefield a distant glimpse of paved runways. As its engines throttled back a snatch of subdued conversation reached him from the two nearest Japanese business-men. Scholefield leaned close to his window trying to identify, in the village below, the tunnel entrances they were discussing.

China and Japan had fought a great battle in the Second World War here in the Shunyi district, a middle-aged man was explaining to a younger colleague. Chinese peasants had con-tinued a fierce, unyielding resistance in tunnels linking the villages and the international airport had been built close to this old 'underground battlefield'. But it was better to make no mention of the fact, he advised the young man earnestly—not even in praise to their hosts who would meet them on the runway.

214

The thin stewardess chose her moment carefully, waiting until Scholefield had turned his head to look at the Japanese who was speaking. He giggled in sudden embarrassment at Scholefield as though realising, too late, he had been overheard by someone who spoke his language. At that instant the stewardess dropped the blue canvas holdall onto Scholefield's lap. He turned back in surprise but by then she was moving away along the aisle, reaching down coats and parcels for other passengers from the overhead racks.

He half rose to hand back the case but the stewardess swung round in the aisle and stood looking meaningfully at him. She neither nodded nor shook her head. Her face remained expressionless but she held his gaze long enough to make it clear the case had not been given to him inadvertently. Scholefield settled back into his seat and pulled open the zip.

The note tucked inside on top of a khaki cotton jacket instructed him to go immediately to the lavatory compartment at the rear of the aircraft before the seat belt sign was switched on. He looked up to find the thin stewardess watching him impatiently from the front of the cabin. He rose from his seat immediately and hurried to the rear of the aircraft. As the door closed behind him the stewardess gave a signal to the pilot behind her and straight away the illuminated seat belt signs came on above each seat to the accompaniment of a single warning chime from the airliner's intercom system.

Inside the lavatory Scholefield bolted the door and took out the white card. The unsigned note had been handwritten in English. On the back, a further message instructed him to dress in the clothes contained in the bag and put his own suit and shoes inside. He was then to wait where he was, the note said, until his name was called in English through the door.

From the curtained rear seat of a dun-coloured Public Security Bureau Warszawa, Tan Sui-ling watched the Boeing float slowly down, stretching its undercarriage with a blind man's caution towards that first invisible moment of contact with the ground. She wore an official dark blue tunic suit now and her long hair had been cut and scraped close to her head beneath a soft-peaked worker's cap. Opaque green curtains of elasticated nylon were stretched across the rear and side windows of the car so that she and the two men sitting on either side of her in Public Security cadre's uniforms could watch the plane's arrival from an impenetrable, submarine gloom.

The hollow-chested croupier from the Soho cellar, sitting on her left, shot a quick sideways glance at her as the airliner's undercarriage brushed the runway, then settled and took weight. 'Hao, hen hao,' she said softly and gave a little nod of satisfaction as the now earthbound Boeing rushed smoothly towards where they were parked on the taxiing apron.

The man on her other side was taller than the average Chinese. He stared straight ahead through the windscreen, watching the plane slow down, the top of his cap brushing the plastic-lined roof of the Warszawa. When he moved, his heavily muscled arms and shoulders bulged under the thin jacket, stretching it tight across his broad back.

The driver of the ten-year-old Warszawa started the engine and moved the car close to the bottom of the disembarkation steps as they were rolled up against the stationary Boeing. But nobody got out. From the shadowy interior they watched the Japanese delegation descend to be met by half a dozen Peking officials of the Foreign Trade Ministry. The Japanese bowed and giggled and pumped hands for several minutes before letting the Chinese whisk them away in shiny black official Hung Chi cars. By then the last of the foreign diplomats and their families had disappeared inside the single terminal building and the pilots of the Boeing and their cabin crew had departed on a rickety transport bus.

Tan Sui-ling watched the baggage gang emptying the aft hold. When she saw the last piece of luggage thrown onto the open truck she nudged the hollow-chested man beside her. He climbed out quickly and without hesitation plucked a brown-leather suitcase tagged with Scholefield's name from the rear tailboard. When he had stowed it in the boot of the Warszawa she nodded to the big man beside her and he got out and followed the smaller man briskly up the steps into the fuselage of the Boeing.

During the two minutes which elapsed between their disappearance and the re-emergence of the hollow-chested cadre at the top of the steps, her eyes never left the open doorway. She watched him glance once round the airport then start quickly down the steps, followed by the bigger man, who now carried a blue canvas holdall. Both kept their heads bent forward so that only the tops of their khaki caps were visible. They got into the car quickly from different sides and the driver had the Warszawa moving before the doors had closed.

In the sickly green gloom of the rear seat Scholefield stared out at her from under the khaki peak of the Public Security Bureau cap. His face was gaunt with tension. He opened his mouth to speak but she motioned him to silence with a quick gesture as the car sped across the airport towards a side exit.

HONG KONG, Thursday—Since the death of
Premier Chou En-lai in January, events in Peking
have unfolded like a plot from a Ming dynasty
court intrigue.

New York Times, 18 June 1976

23

Scholefield knew that the twenty-foot, single-character sign-
boards spaced at fifty-yard intervals along the airport approach
road spelled out one of Mao Tse-tung's thoughts on the inevit-
ability of international revolution. But they flashed by him now
in an unreadable red and white blur as the driver accelerated the
rattling Warszawa rapidly towards its maximum speed of eighty
miles an hour.

Once out on the wide, arrow-straight forty-kilometre highway
leading into Peking the driver kept his foot on the accelerator
and his hand on the horn and rushed headlong down the centre
of the dusty, tree-lined road. Oncoming cyclists swerved from
their path screaming abuse and sweating mule drivers hauling
commune produce into the city on tottering, net-covered carts
took off their straw hats and waved them in fury in the thick dust
clouds thrown up in the wake of the speeding car.

The driver didn't slow until they reached the outer suburbs of
the city. By then the light was beginning to fade and Tan Sui-ling,
after checking the road behind them, leaned forward and tapped
him once on the shoulder. He throttled back immediately and
drove more carefully among the cyclists pedalling unlit machines
several abreast on both sides of the broad street.

Because of the clammy heat, occupants of the apartment blocks
that stretched like red brick cliffs along both sides of the street

were squatting in the dust on the unpaved sidewalks. Many of the men were stripped to the waist and the women and girls had rolled their baggy trousers up above their knees in an effort to keep cool.

Scholefield took off the khaki cap and mopped his sweating face. He could feel the cotton jacket sticking to his back but when he wound down the window on his side the fetid air that entered through the nylon curtain carried the sickly reek of drains. Suddenly the oppressive heat, the press of sweating bodies around him in the cramped car, and the fatigue of eighteen hours flying sent a surge of anger through him. 'Do all Chairman Mao's guests in Peking get this cloak and dagger welcome?' He spoke the words fiercely in Chinese and swung round to face Tan Sui-ling.

She ignored the question completely and they drove for several minutes more in a brittle silence.

'You were selected quite arbitrarily, by the socialist imperialists in Moscow, to propagate lies about China.' She spoke quietly at last without turning her gaze from the road ahead. 'Because of this Chairman Mao took the unprecedented step of inviting you to Peking—on my recommendation—to hear the truth.' She turned her head slowly to look at him. 'But these are unsettled times. The leadership of China is not united. You will perhaps be surprised to find Chairman Mao, when you meet him at midnight, in a mood of apprehension.'

Scholefield stared at her. 'Were you following his instructions in offering me disguise before I left the aircraft?'

She looked away into the gathering dusk and nodded. 'It was commanded by Chairman Mao himself that for your own safety your movements in China should be conducted under conditions of maximum security. Such meetings are not unprecedented. There has been trouble before.'

The Warszawa was passing through Wai Chiao Ta Lou, Peking's foreign diplomatic quarter, and Scholefield watched a British Ford Escort with diplomatic plates, driven by a young haughty-looking man, swing across in front of them. The Warszawa had to brake sharply to avoid the car, and the driver shook his fist after the Escort as it sped away towards the British Embassy, now fully restored after its destruction by Red Guards at the height of the Cultural Revolution.

'The American journalist Snow came several times to Peking to talk with Chairman Mao. But always there was opposition—although he had penetrated the Nationalist blockade in the Thirties to reach Yenan.' She shrugged. 'Chairman Mao's wife spent sixty hours with an American woman sinologist in 1972 revealing her life story. This too was opposed by her enemies and therefore had to be conducted in secret.' She paused and smiled a brittle humourless smile. 'Because of our historical experience at the hands of foreign exploiters there is a deeply-ingrained suspicion in China of intimate contact with outsiders. Such things can be magnified as serious political misjudgements, indiscretions which may be used as a basis for all-out attacks by political opponents.' She smiled bitterly again. 'My own experience with your friend Harvey Ketterman leads me to share that suspicion.'

'Harvey Ketterman is dead.'

For a fraction of a second she was unable to disguise her surprise. Then she looked quickly away. 'He deserved to die,' she said in a barely audible voice.

'The Russians killed him.'

She nodded once more. 'It is right.' She made no further attempt to explain herself.

The Warszawa swung onto Chang An, the ten-lane Boulevard of Eternal Peace which bisects Peking east to west, and immediately the driver began leaning heavily on his horn again. But its voice was immediately lost in the already deafening symphony of noise coming from the red and cream trolley-buses as they nosed through the rapidly-failing light, honking furiously at the undisciplined droves of cyclists all around them. The thick crowds thronging the wide pavements under the trees on either side of the boulevard were barely moving, as if the stifling humidity of the approaching night had already sapped their last dregs of energy.

With a muttered curse the driver of the Warszawa swung out towards the centre of the highway to find a clear passage. As he accelerated Scholefield saw through the windscreen a great ragged mass of purple-black cloud spreading like spilled ink across the evening sky behind the Great Hall of the People. It snuffed out the last flicker of light with a surprising suddenness, and in the brief moment before the trolley-buses switched on their headlights a deep, breathless darkness gripped the city. Then the street lamps began coming on, and Scholefield caught a glimpse of the giant floodlit portrait of Mao high on the vermilion walls of the Gate of Heavenly Peace just before the Warszawa swung into Nan Chitze and began running north beside the moated east wall of the old Forbidden City.

'Where are we going?'

Instead of replying she unbuttoned one of the breast pockets of her tunic and handed him a plastic-covered document. She switched on an interior light and he saw that the green security pass was inscribed with his name written in both Latin and Chinese characters above one of the photographs taken at the Soho market. In the bottom right-hand corner it bore the signature and photograph of Wang Tung-hsing, Deputy Minister of Public Security and head of Unit 8341, the elite army group responsible for guarding Chung Nanhai and the person of Mao Tse-tung.

'That and your letter from the Chairman should ensure your safety here in Peking—if your presence is not too widely advertised.' She reached out and switched off the light. 'You will remain only a few hours. Your departure has been arranged at dawn on the first flight to Tokyo—for your own sake.' He tucked the pass into his pocket and glanced anxiously out of the window again. The car was threading through one of the narrow, cluttered streets of drab grey-roofed houses huddled beneath the high walls of the Forbidden City. 'It was an imperial edict that ensured that the common people of Peking paid architectural as well as physical obeisance to the golden roofs of the emperor's palaces from these humble homes of no more than a single storey.'

Puzzled by the heavy irony in her voice, Scholefield turned back from the window to look at her. Her features were barely visible in the suffused glow of the dim street lights. 'But since liberation we have allowed the building of higher walls—especially to contain the enemies of the Party.' She was staring past him through the front windscreen.

He looked out in time to see the street sign at the entrance to a narrow rutted alley between two rows of single-storey houses. He read it aloud to himself and turned back quickly to look at her. 'Tsao Lan Tse Hutung—Grass Mist Lane. Your notorious prison for foreigners!'

She laughed shortly. 'The detention centre of the Peking Bureau of Public Security, if we are to be perfectly correct, built on the site of a poetically-named Buddhist monastery. But it is not just for foreign spies—it is for counter-revolutionaries of all kinds.'

The headlights of the Warszawa flared into two large yellow circles on a massive iron gate in a twenty-five foot wall and a uniformed guard stepped out of the shadows holding a rifle. He inspected the driver's pass then held his arm in through the window for Scholefield's. He returned it without comment after reading it in the light of headlamps, then checked those of Tan Sui-ling, the Chinese, and the hollow-chested cadre. The guard walked slowly back to a sentry box at the side of the gate and there was a rattle of chains as the gate was wound up precisely to a height that would allow the Warszawa to enter.

Immediately the car had passed underneath, the iron gate thumped back into its beaten earth base and Scholefield watched as the headlights searched across an inner compound. Another gate in another twenty-foot wall swung open as they drove towards it and Scholefield caught a glimpse of two more armed guards in khaki jackets standing in the shadows on either side as they went through. Inside they stopped at a third gate, which eventually parted in the middle and swung slowly open after another inspection of their passes. The Warszawa bumped through across rutted mud and halted in the inner courtyard of the prison.

Scholefield's door was immediately wrenched open from outside. As he stepped out into the shadowy compound the fierce saturated heat of the night flooded into his throat, making him gasp. A long, low growl of thunder rumbled slowly across the sky to the north and as he looked up towards the sound he noticed for the first time the electrified barbed wire strung round the top of the high walls. Four dimly-lit machine-gun emplacements had been built into the corners and the silhouetted head and shoulders of the four men manning them were clearly visible, gazing watchfully down into the yard. There was a damp, sour smell of rotting vegetation in the compound and when the thunder died away, the distant night screech of cicadas was the only sound that penetrated inside the walls.

'You will act precisely in accordance with my instructions!'

Scholefield felt a hand seize his right arm and he was swung bodily round. He found himself staring into the face of a heavily-built Security Bureau man. He released his arm and snapped his fingers in Scholefield's face. 'Your identification document!'

Four or five guards armed with rifles stood grouped behind the man who had spoken. Scholefield noticed as he handed over the green pass that the man wore an officer's jacket with four pockets. One of the guards shone a torch so that the senior man could make the inspection while two others moved quietly round to take up station on either side of Scholefield. The document was subjected to a minute scrutiny lasting two full minutes. Then the officer looked up at Scholefield. 'Remove his cap!'

The cap was snatched from his head from behind and the guard with the torch shone it full on Scholefield's face. The officer stared at him for a long moment, then looked back at the photograph on the pass. 'Hao-li,' he said at last, and put the pass into one of his jacket pockets. Without another word he turned and started off across the compound. The two men at his shoulder grunted and nudged Scholefield with their rifles, indicating that he should follow. He looked quickly round at the Warszawa. The doors were closed and the curtains remained drawn. Neither the driver, Tan Sui-ling, the Chinese, nor the hollow-chested cadre had moved from their seats.

The two guards began walking and because they stood shoulder to shoulder behind Scholefield he was forced to start forward across the yard to prevent himself falling. As he walked he heard the Warszawa's engine start up and the creak of the gates opening to allow it to depart. Ahead of him a square of light appeared at the bottom of the wall on the far side of the compound as the senior officer pulled open a door and stepped into a dimly-lit passage. He waited until Scholefield and the two guards were inside, then closed the door and shot heavy bolts into place top and bottom. Scholefield stopped, looking round uncertainly. He saw the senior officer casually unbutton the leather holster on his belt and pull out a heavy Colt .45 revolver. He motioned along the corridor with one flick of its barrel and waited until

Scholefield had begun walking before falling into step behind him. The two guards with rifles followed.

They walked in silence, the scuff of their regulation-issue canvas-and-rubber slippers echoing softly in the empty passages. Occasionally they splashed through puddles of condensation dripping onto the bare concrete floor from rusting overhead cold-water pipes. The air within the building was hotter and more rancid than in the compound and the choking humidity magnified the mingled stench of human excrement and sweat given off by incarcerated men. Scholefield felt the perspiration begin trickling down the inside of his arms and legs as he walked. They passed a series of heavy, unpainted wood doors with only a spyhole at eye level and he fancied he heard the faint dragging movement of a body shifting behind one of them.

They came to a brightly-lit deserted lecture hall with a bare wooden floor and chairs stacked at the sides. A huge coloured portrait of Mao Tse-tung hung above a dais at one end. The officer nudged Scholefield in the back with the barrel of the revolver and all four men crossed the hall at a fast walk.

On the other side, the passage was narrower and lit at infrequent intervals by single naked bulbs. The officer caught the sleeve of Scholefield's jacket and motioned him to stop beside a plain wooden door without a spyhole. He produced a key and opened it. Scholefield saw a narrow flight of steep red brick steps. One of the two guards produced a torch and flashed it into the darkness. The officer motioned Scholefield ahead of them and the group started downward.

At the bottom an iron door blocked the staircase. The officer produced another key and opened this. The steps continued on the other side but the passage was narrower and Scholefield's shoulders began to brush the walls on either side. Behind him all he heard was the soft rustle of the guards' rubber-soled slippers on the brick steps.

At the bottom there was a short stretch of airless passageway leading to a wooden door reinforced with heavy iron cross members. Suddenly the air became unnaturally hot. Scholefield stopped but the officer forced him forward again until he was almost touching the door. Then he drew a whistle from his pocket and blew a piercing blast.

The door, opened soundlessly from inside, flew back suddenly on its hinges. Scholefield saw a final flight of half a dozen steps leading steeply down through a narrow opening. The officer and the guards propelled him through it and he stumbled forward and halted, staring.

The confined space was lit by an orange glow from the coal brazier in one corner. The heat from this and the glowing red hot chains suspended above it was intense. A hinged and jointed torture bench with leather straps for wrists and ankles stood along one wall and on a table beside it were laid out metal thumbscrews, mallets, bamboo splinters, jugs of water and sodden towels that steamed slowly in the heat. As Scholefield's eyes adjusted to the glare of the fire he noticed for the first time a hunched figure manacled by the wrists into a heavy wooden chair in one corner. The man's head was sunk on his chest and his features were indistinguishable in the gloom.

'The bench was used to start with. It was a toss-up whether the hips or the vertebrae of the spine splintered before other bones in the body.' The officer spoke quietly in Chinese, his voice cold and matter-of-fact.

Scholefield dragged his eyes away from the torture instruments to look at him. He was standing by the fire, stirring the coals idly with a pair of iron tongs. His lips were drawn back from his teeth in a sneering smile. 'The infamous water torture you are no doubt familiar with, Mr. Scholefield.' He pointed to the towels and the jugs. 'The towels were pressed over the prisoner's face and the water poured on little by little. He had three choices: suffocate, drown—or talk.' He paused and lifted a few links of red hot chain from the hooks above the brazier. 'What do you think the prisoner did, Mr. Scholefield?'

The officer's face shimmered with perspiration. In the flickering light from the fire his features seemed constantly to liquefy and merge, then reform again. 'In the People's Republic of China, we have found there are two basic types of human reaction under interrogation—those of the toothpaste tube and the water faucet.' A short laugh escaped his lips. 'The "Faucet" needs only to be twisted sharply at the beginning for everything to gush forth. But the "Tube" must be squeezed frequently to get at what's inside. And every time you squeeze, a little more of what you want comes out.' He gazed down reflectively at the red hot chains for a moment before replacing them carefully on their hook. Then he turned and signalled to one of the guards standing quietly by the foot of the narrow flight of steps. 'You will no doubt be interested to know Mr. Scholefield that the man we have brought you to see turned out to be a Water Faucet.'

The guard holding the torch switched it on and swung the beam into the corner. It illuminated the bent head and shoulders of the man manacled to the chair by his wrists. As Scholefield watched, the other guard stepped forward and grabbed him by his close-cropped hair. The head was jerked back and Scholefield found himself staring into the round, pock-marked face of the man he knew as Yang.

WASHINGTON, Tuesday—*U.S. News and World Report* said Monday that US Intelligence believes Chairman Mao Tse-tung of China is fading fast— but groups contending for power are determined to avoid civil war.

Associated Press, 21 July 1976

24

The Warszawa was flagged down twice at the road blocks set up along the northern boundary of the Square of Heavenly Peace. But Tan Sui-ling held her pass out at the window and when the soldiers and Public Security Bureau cadres manning the barricades saw the tiny photograph of Wang Tung-hsing in the bottom right-hand corner they hurriedly waved the car through.

Before it had halted at the rear of the long column of shiny black official Hung Chi limousines parked in front of the Great Hall of the People, Tan Sui-ling had jumped out and was running up the steps towards the vast twelve-columned entrance to the megalith. She stopped however when she caught sight of the rotund figure of the man whose face decorated her pass, hurrying down towards his car. She waited until he had reached the lower tier of the steps just above her before calling his name.

'Comrade Wang!'

He halted and waited impatiently for her to approach. The drivers and guards standing beside the cars stiffened rigidly to attention as one man when they saw him. She ran across the steps and put a hand breathlessly on his arm.

'Has the Standing Committee meeting finished so soon?'

'It has been adjourned—there is an emergency!' He spoke in a fierce whisper and nodded towards his bulky briefcase. 'Reports of natural phenomena coming in from all over the north-east are

227

disturbing. Well levels have fallen up to two feet on twenty different communes in Hopei alone in the past hour. Other reports are still coming in from the peasants' observation and prediction groups. I'm on my way to see the Chairman urgently.' His beetle brows knitted in a grimace of exasperation. 'Nobody dares risk panicking a hundred million people with emergency measures without his authority.'

He turned as if to continue his rapid descent of the steps, but she caught his arm again and looked directly into his face. 'He called me personally to his bedside at three a.m. this morning for a verbal report on the Soviet smear campaign in London. He looked very ill.'

Wang Tung-hsing shook his head. 'He sleeps rarely, if at all. There is great deterioration. Look!' He opened his briefcase and she caught a glimpse of the dark outline of a revolver on top of the white papers.

'His paranoia is reaching a crisis. He demanded that I bring him a gun for his personal use tonight—I, who have guarded him faithfully for forty-two years. He distrusts even his own shadow now.'

She turned and moved down the steps alongside him, smiling sympathetically. 'He asked me to report to him again tonight. I was coming to clear the visit with you. Would I be intruding if I were to accompany you now?'

'Of course not, Comrade Tan. Your visits, I know, are among the few things that have pleased him recently.' He smiled back at her, revealing his uneven teeth and put his right hand solicitously under her elbow. She leaned very slightly against him as she allowed him to guide her down the steps and into his car.

Inside the curtained, air-conditioned Hung Chi he removed his cap and used it to mop away the perspiration that was streaming down his heavy-jowled face. Tan Sui-ling unfastened the top two or three buttons of her tunic and fanned herself with one hand, turning at the same time so that he could see she wore no blouse beneath. 'If only this terrible storm would break. I am suffocating.'

As the car shot away across the square towards the Tien An Men he leaned towards her and let one hand rest on her thigh for a moment. 'The storm and the heat are both unnatural. And there are other bad omens, not just the wells—a plague of rats has been

reported in one suburb of Tangshan.' He shook his head. 'Pray
the storm doesn't break, but passes over us here in Peking!'

The driver sent the Hung Chi careering across the broad
expanse of the Boulevard of Eternal Peace at more than sixty
miles an hour and screeched to a halt at the New Gate entrance
to the walled compound of Chung Nan Hai. Wang wound his
window down and started to show a plastic covered pass. But
when the young sentry saw his commander's face he waved the
car on without further checking. Wang immediately stopped the
car and leaped out, yelling at the top of his voice.

'Check all passes, you vile turtle's egg! Leave nobody out.
Search every single car—there can be no exceptions! The life of
China's greatest hero in all history is in your careless hands!'

The other guards grouped beside the gate shrank back under
the lash of his tongue. 'What kind of fighter would I be,' the
youth protested, 'if I could not recognise the man who personally
guarded Chairman Mao in the caves of Yenan?'

Wang's voice sank to a menacing growl. 'Don't give me my life
biography, you filthy toad! Give me a security check. Quickly.'
The soldier made a frantic body search of Wang where he stood
while his comrades hurriedly went over the car, and the driver.
Then they checked Tan Sui-ling's pass and searched her gingerly
for weapons. As the car roared away, brushing beneath the
hanging willows that marked the margins of the palace lakes,
the soldier Wang had abused drew a deep breath of relief. He
looked around red-faced at his fellows. 'The "Devil's Clutch" is
living up to his name tonight.'

Inside the car Wang sank back into the cushions of his seat and
mopped his brow again. He stared out over the dead, viscous
waters of the lakes searching the ornamental terraces and pavilions
beyond with screwed up eyes. 'Perhaps his paranoia is contagious.'
He turned and smiled another broken-toothed smile at Tan
Sui-ling. 'I, too, think I see shadows moving on every balustrade.'

The car skidded to a halt outside a single-storeyed pavilion with
a golden-tiled roof. It was one of a group of dwellings built
originally to house an emperor's mandarins which since 1949 had
served as the official living quarters of the Party Politburo. Wang
clambered out with his bulky briefcase and hurried up the steps
past four more guards to the front door. Inside, his face darkened

when he saw only one soldier standing outside the study. 'Where are your three comrades?' he thundered.

The guard flew to attention and shouldered his rifle. 'Chairman Mao Tse-tung is not here, Commander Wang!'

'Not here?' The veins on his temple bulged in his fury. 'Where is he?'

'He descended to his retreat in the tunnels—an hour ago. He ordered the deputy commander and a detachment of men to move him. They are down there with him now.'

Wang swung on his heel and hurried along the corridor to the lift. He pressed the call button and when the door opened he stepped inside, followed by Tan Sui-ling.

The doors closed noiselessly and the lift descended for a half a minute. When they opened again Wang dashed out into the brightly-lit concrete tunnel that was broad enough to allow the passage of a jeep. He muttered angrily over his shoulder as he lumbered along at a half trot. 'Why must he choose tonight of all nights to bury himself a hundred feet under Peking? And without consulting me!'

He ignored the sentries as they slapped their rifles and came to attention at the guard points set at regular intervals along the passageway. The floor of the tunnel sloped steeply downward for fifty yards and finally entered a broad arch guarded by four more soldiers. Wang insisted irritably that they inspect his pass and Tan Sui-ling's, and search them both, before moving through into a carpeted antechamber which had empty chairs placed around the walls. Tan Sui-ling hung back as Wang exchanged greetings with a general of the Unit 8341 who stood alone beside a heavy leaded door. The officer, she noticed, never removed his right hand from the butt of the holstered revolver at his waist. As they moved forward she smiled at him, but he did not return the greeting. He unlocked the door with a large key which was chained to the wrist of his other hand and stood back, his face impassive. Wang turned and beckoned to Tan Sui-ling then hurried through the door, which the officer immediately locked behind them. As their footsteps died away inside he picked a telephone receiver from its hook on the wall and spoke their names softly into it.

Most of the room inside was in shadow. Book-shelves crammed

with pale-spined books and bound files, many of them flagged with reference tags, glimmered faintly in the gloom. The shelves lined three of the four walls from floor to ceiling and other books and papers were piled in haphazard working disarray on low tables and chairs. A high-backed leather couch raised high off the floor had been placed with its head against a fourth wall. A single lamp on a cluttered desk beside it focused a bright pool of light onto the sunken features of the dying man propped up on two large white pillows.

On the other side a medical trolley supported an array of bottles, pill-boxes, trays and surgical instruments laid out in neat rows. The head lay on its pillows at an awkward angle, its features collapsed in concentric lines about the sagging, half-open mouth. The one sound in the room was of faintly laboured breathing. Only the darkly glittering eyes, watching intently through half-closed lids, still burned with the angry spark of life, following their progress watchfully every step of the way to the couchside. A gnarled hand from which the flesh had retreated clutched a black-covered volume anonymously downward on the covering rug.

'Ni hao, Tung-chih.' Wang spoke softly, at the same time bending and laying his hands briefly on both the older man's bony shoulders.

Tan Sui-ling waited a moment then stepped forward into the circle of light and removed her cap. She reached out, lifted one bony claw from the rug and held it tightly for a moment. The watchful eyes widened into the beginnings of a crumpled smile, looking down wistfully at the firm round hand of the young woman. 'The fire in the flesh has already died.' He stopped and lifted his head to look up at her. 'But the hand of a pretty woman still warms an old man's heart.'

He spoke in a sibilant whisper and she had to strain to catch the sense of his nasal Hunanese. For a moment she covered the palsied hand with both hers then let go and stepped back.

'Comrade Chairman.' Wang paused and snapped open his briefcase. His raised voice had taken on an urgent, formal note. 'Reports of traditional phenomena from all over the north-eastern provinces are giving great cause for alarm. Indications have reached me from twenty separate communes in Hopei alone that well levels have fallen two feet in the past hour.'

He pulled a bulky manilla file from his briefcase, tapped it quickly and laid it on the desk beside the couch. 'Seven reports of pigs consuming their young on different communes. Twenty-nine reports throughout the north-east military region of cockerels flying to roost in trees. A plague of thousands of rats has appeared in a suburb of Tangshan, the heartland of our coal industry—' He broke off and looked at his watch. 'And the night shifts have been underground for two hours already.'

The eyes in the emaciated face had turned inward. With an effort he pushed his shoulders backward against the pillows and sat up. He wore a grey tunic buttoned close beneath his scraggy chin and he fumbled now in one of the breast pockets. He drew out a crumpled packet and placed a cigarette rolled in dark paper between his lips. Wang lit it with matches from the desk and listened to the smack of his lips as he sucked the smoke into his lungs. 'What reports do you have from the Peking region?' He asked the question slowly in a quavering voice without looking up.

'None of significance. On a map the majority of critical criteria are clustered to the south-east halfway between here and the coast.'

They watched him sink thoughtfully back into the pillows, holding the cigarette between his lips with his left hand. 'To put all your trust in ancient superstitions and omens is not good.' His voice had sunk to a half whisper again.

Wang tapped his file again more urgently. 'There are reports too, of bees swarming in great numbers and stinging livestock to death. Bats are gathering in great flocks also—they are sensitive to ultra-sonic vibrations, changes in the electrical fields of earth and atmosphere. There is a clear scientific base to these ancient signs ...'

The grey jowls of the man on the couch shuddered in a sudden fit of rage. When he turned his head to look up at him his eyes were ablaze. 'Enough of this talk! Are even you turning against me too? Where is the weapon I commanded you to bring?'

Wang bent hurriedly and picked up his briefcase. He tugged out the heavy revolver and, after a moment's hesitation, laid it beyond the old man's immediate reach on the desk.

'Is it fully loaded?'

Wang hesitated. 'No.' He reached into his briefcase and drew out a box of ammunition. 'I thought it better that—'

Again the jowls quivered, the incandescent anger flashed. 'Load it immediately—and place it within my grasp!' The effort of shouting wracked the wasted body.

Wang hurriedly broke the gun and dropped shells into all six chambers. When he had finished, he applied the safety catch. The black-backed book slipped to the floor as the gnarled hand that had been holding it reached towards him. 'Give it to me!'

Wang held the revolver by its barrel and guided the butt into the trembling, crooked fingers. The hand fell back clutching the gun on top of the coverlet where the book had lain before. He continued holding the cigarette to his mouth with the other hand, screwing up his rheumy eyes against the curl of the smoke.

'In view of the reports I would urge you, Comrade Chairman, to return to your quarters above ground immediately! You are in danger here!' Wang leaned earnestly towards the couch, trying to penetrate the trance-like detachment of the dying man.

'I will remain here!' His eyes shone suddenly. 'Let those who wish to flee, like lesser vermin before the omens of pigs and rats, do so. I shall continue to lodge here in the ancient heart of China.' He raised his head imperiously. 'Leave us now!'

Wang took a step nearer as though to speak again. But the eyes of the old man stared deliberately unseeing at the air above his head, indicating that he had already been dismissed. Wang bent to pick up his briefcase and hurried out. One claw-like hand reached out and depressed a push-button on the edge of the desk and the red-lacquered door swung closed behind him.

After a long silence he beckoned Tan Sui-ling nearer. She approached and leaned over him until her ear was close to his mouth. 'What new intelligence of the Russians do you bring?'

'They killed the American Ketterman in Washington because he sent Yang back to us. They are clearly furious that their meticulous campaign to vilify you and your supporters has collapsed and humiliated them instead.'

The hoary head with its thin wispy grey hair nodded with a slow and obvious satisfaction.

Under interrogation, 'Yang has confessed everything concerning his four years imprisonment in Moscow. I will arrange for him to be brought before you in chains within the hour to explain himself and offer personal atonement.'

His head turned slowly to look at her. 'And the Englishman? Has he arrived in Peking?'

She nodded. 'Yes, Comrade Chairman. He is here, waiting to be called to your presence.'

'Is his arrival in the capital widely known?'

She shook her head quickly. 'Only a few men loyal to me know he is here. Even Wang Tung-hsing is ignorant of the fact.'

His eyes closed and his deeply lined face lapsed again into an expression of intense weariness.

'I shall bring him—and later Yang—through the tunnel for greater security if that is your wish. You will inform your personal duty guard?'

He nodded again slowly without opening his eyes.

She turned to go. At the door she stopped and looked back. His eyes remained closed and he appeared already to be sleeping. As the door swung shut behind her, leaving him alone in the room once more, the claw-like fingers of his right hand tightened convulsively round the butt of the black revolver.

PEKING, Sunday—A decline in public discipline, growing tension, a sense of unease. . . . China is awash with rumours and secondhand accounts of what is going on, and foreigners have been accumulating individual experiences that add up to a picture of a troubled country.

Toronto Globe and Mail, 25 July 1976

25

'You were perhaps deceived for a moment, Mr. Scholefield.' The crackling coal furnace illuminated the Public Security Bureau captain's face from below with a demonic glow as he moved round behind it towards the Englishman. His lips retreated from his teeth in another sneering smile. 'You were possibly not aware you were paying a visit to a museum.'

Scholefield didn't reply. He looked round again at Yang who was slumped back now in the interrogation chair, his head twisted to one side in an effort to escape the direct glare of the torch beam.

'We find it quite effective to bring such prisoners as the renegade Yang here to remind them of the horrors that were once perpetrated by the Nationalist scum of Chiang Kai-shek.' The captain stopped close beside Scholefield. 'These cellars below ground level were part of the original foundations of the Buddhist monastery. This was one of several isolation cells used by the monks. When the Nationalists razed the monastery to build a prison here in the nineteen thirties they hit upon the brilliant idea of incorporating them as torture chambers.'

The captain took a key from his pocket and leaned over to unlock the manacles on the arms of Yang's chair. Scholefield noticed then that his ankles were also chained together. Yang stretched his cramped arms with difficulty and chafed at his wrists, still keeping his head turned away from the light. The captain signalled to the guard holding the torch to turn the beam aside, then swung back to face Scholefield. 'It is part of our educative process in the prison to allow difficult prisoners to contemplate what might have happened to them if they were not being dealt with under the humane socialist principles laid down by Chairman Mao and the Party. We find it helps them realise their responsibility to be truthful.'

'The first twist of the "Faucet" in Yang's case.' Scholefield spoke the words contemplatively, almost to himself, not troubling to hide the disgust in his voice.

The officer looked steadily back at Scholefield for a moment, then his features broke into another slow, dangerous smile. But he said nothing. Instead he turned suddenly and shouted at Yang. 'Now tell the Englishman why you and your Russian masters implicated him in your treacherous plot!'

Yang lifted his head slowly to look at Scholefield. His face was haggard with fatigue. 'When I approached you in London, I was acting on the orders of vile revisionist traitors who have long since abandoned the socialist path of Marx, Lenin and Mao Tse-tung—'

Yang's voice was little more than a croak and Scholefield had to move nearer to hear clearly what he said. 'They had held me prisoner in Moscow for four years, waiting for the moment when they could employ me for their own evil ends.' Yang coughed suddenly and lifted his sleeve to wipe the perspiration from his face. The captain signalled quickly to the second guard who filled a cup from one of the water torture jugs. Yang took the cup and drained it greedily, spilling a lot of water down his tunic front.

'You see, Mr. Scholefield,' said the Public Security captain softly, taking the cup from Yang's hands, 'we use water not to torture a man's body but to refresh it, to encourage his mind towards correct socialist thinking.'

'Your subtle Thought Reform techniques are well enough known to the world,' replied Scholefield sharply, without turning round. 'The instruments you use to disfigure the mind have the obvious advantage that they are invisible. Future generations will find no trace of your racks and branding irons—but that's only because you're better versed in deceit, not human principles.'

The Public Security captain's hands clenched suddenly at his sides. He took a quick pace towards Scholefield. 'Do not forget that your personal safety in Peking rests in only a very few hands.'

'They used drugs to addle my mind and turn me against Chairman Mao Tse-tung.' The sound of Yang's voice resuming his confession broke the tension between the two men. They turned to see him staring obliviously into the fire. 'They believed that if they could plant false "evidence" on Western governments through China specialists showing that the Chairman's close supporters murdered the traitor Lin Piao—and were also planning a greater crime, the murder of Chairman Mao himself—then the bourgeois rightists in positions of some power in Peking would be emboldened to try to seize power by a coup d'etat. The Kremlin plotters believed this would produce a new leadership in China more favourable towards them and thus help to foster a false and treacherous new friendship with the Chinese Communist Party.' Yang paused and wiped his brow again. 'This is an urgent requirement for the Soviet socialist imperialists because the ordinary Soviet people are deeply dissatisfied with their wasteful preparations for war along the border with China. The economic sacrifices these war preparations demand are enslaving the Soviet peoples. Also the Soviet leaders anticipated that rapprochement with China would deal a severe blow to Sino-American friendship and put Washington at a global disadvantage.'

Twenty feet above their heads, at ground level, the headlights of the Warszawa carrying Tan Sui-ling and the hollow-chested cadre turned once again into the mouth of Grass Mist Lane. The driver eased back to a crawl over the uneven surface of the hutung and as the vehicle swung and creaked on its inadequate springs the cadre beside her plucked at Tan Sui-ling's sleeve in the curtained darkness of the rear seat. In the gloom she watched him unzip a document case and take out a dried bamboo leaf fan. He waved it once or twice in front of his face and grinned. Then, still grinning, he held it, stem first, towards her. The moment she grasped it, he pulled the flat leaf sharply back towards himself.

In the half darkness they both stared at the narrow tapering shaft of steel left protruding from her fist.

'Hsieh hsieh.' She nodded her thanks perfunctorily and he giggled inanely by way of response. Then he re-fixed the body of the dried leaf carefully back round the blade of the stiletto and with great care placed its shaft once more in her hand. He reached into the briefcase again, and after checking ahead through the windscreen that there was still time, he took out a broad roll of flesh-coloured adhesive tape and a tiny pair of nail scissors. These she tucked into the pockets of her baggy blue trousers. When the car pulled up at the outer gate of the prison, she handed out her pass for inspection and sat back in her seat, perfectly composed, fanning herself quietly. 'We have returned to visit the prisoner Yang,' she told the guard without looking at him.

Two minutes later the car passed through the third gate into the inner courtyard and she got out, to be met by the same four guards who had been on duty earlier. They led her to the door on the far side of the compound and with one guard in front and two behind they escorted her along the hot fetid passageways, across the empty echoing lecture hall and on down towards the cellars. As she walked she continued to fan herself with the dried leaf of the bamboo.

Scholefield looked speculatively down at Yang. The Chinese had stopped talking and was sitting with his head bowed in the flickering light from the fire.

'If you were the loyal supporter of Marshall Lin Piao that you first claimed,' said Scholefield quietly, 'why did the Russians need to use drugs to poison your mind against Mao Tse-tung? Surely the fact that you had to flee with Marshall Lin because of persecution by Mao and his supporters left you with a natural antipathy towards the Chairman.'

When Yang raised his head he wore a wary expression. He looked quickly at the Public Security captain then back at Scholefield. 'I was forced to fly on the Trident with the traitor Lin Piao,' he said softly. 'He had been deserted by all his followers with the exception of his close family. Members of his staff like myself were forced onto the plane at gunpoint. We did not want to accompany him. We wished to stay and give loyal support to Chairman Mao but were prevented from doing so.'

'So all the folios you wrote were complete lies? The new "plot" to kill Chairman Mao was a fiction?'

He nodded, keeping his eyes averted. 'They were the sole work of the Russians. They threatened me with death if I did not act out my role. I am ashamed now to admit that I agreed to do this in the hope of saving my own worthless life.' His head dropped onto his chest and his voice became muffled. 'I wish now too late that I had chosen death instead of treachery.'

In the silence, the sound of several pairs of slippered feet pattering quickly down the narrow steps reached them from above. A moment later Tan Sui-ling and the three guards appeared in the narrow opening into the torture chamber. She stood looking down, moving the bamboo fan slowly back and forth in front of her face. 'Within the hour,' she announced in a ringing voice, 'you will have the opportunity to ask Chairman Mao personally to grant you a speedy death to atone for your treachery.'

Yang stared blankly up at her. She returned his gaze with a sneer of contempt twisting her face, then paced slowly down the remaining steps. 'Has he given a sufficient explanation to the Englishman?' She addressed her question to the Public Security captain, in a peremptory voice making her superior rank plain.

He nodded quickly. 'He has repeated his confession in full, Comrade Tan.'

She turned to Scholefield, smiling faintly. 'You now have, I hope, a fuller understanding of the Kremlin's vicious nature.'

Scholefield smiled a sudden grim smile. 'I have learned, I think, above all else, that nothing in China is what it seems to be at first sight.'

She looked at him with a startled expression for an instant. Then she turned back to the captain and motioned towards Yang. 'Handcuff him again immediately and take the Englishman up to the car! I wish to be left alone with Yang for a moment to instruct him on how he should conduct himself in the presence of Chairman Mao.'

The captain nodded obediently and motioned for Scholefield

and the others to leave. He fastened the cuffs on Yang's wrists and locked them, then turned and followed the others up the steps. Only when the noise of the iron-clad door slamming shut echoed back down the narrow passageway did she turn to face Yang again.

They stood looking at each other for a moment in silence. Then without taking her eyes from his face Tan Sui-ling withdrew the long knife slowly from the stem of the bamboo leaf fan. Its polished blade shimmered red suddenly in the dying glow of the coal furnace as she pushed it towards him.

They both stared at the knife, their faces clenched in awe, as if it were a symbol of deep mystical significance. She laid the fan aside and with her free hand began to unfasten the buttons of her tunic. When the jacket hung open to the waist she jerked the knife towards him, breaking the spell that had gripped them both. She reversed the blade and he raised his manacled hands awkwardly in front of his chest to receive it, handle first.

The silence in the cellar was broken by coals shifting in the furnace and a flurry of sparks spluttered up towards the low roof as she shrugged out of the jacket and stood facing him, naked to the hips. He watched the firelight casting its dappled patterns across the smooth bareness of her small breasts for a moment, then turned his eyes away. She said nothing, waiting quietly until he raised his head. When he did she reached out and covered his chained hands gently with her own and they clasped their hands tight together for a long time as though in mute supplication. With an effort she gathered herself at last and swung abruptly on her heel.

Fumbling in her pocket she took out the flesh-coloured roll of adhesive tape. With the nail scissors she quickly cut off five strips of equal length and attached them to the edge of the torture bench. Then she turned to take the knife from him and passed back the first strip with her other hand. Turning away she twisted her right arm behind her back holding the stiletto by its point, so that the handle rested against her spine between her shoulder blades. Moving his cuffed hands with difficulty, he fastened the first piece of tape horizontally across the blade just below the hilt and pressed it against her skin on either side.

She handed him the four remaining pieces of tape in turn and he pressed them carefully into place, one below the other, until a secure scabbard for the knife had been formed which left the handle standing free of the tape in the small of her back.

When he had finished, she picked up her jacket and slipped it on. She buttoned it up and turned her back to him so that he could survey the results. The knife had been taped so close to her skin that no hint of its shape disturbed the line of the loose cotton jacket between the sharp jut of her shoulder blades. The chains linking his ankles clanked as he moved round in front of her and nodded. She picked up the remainder of the reel of adhesive tape and dropped it into the fire along with the pair of scissors, then she peeled away the joints that had held the knife in the bamboo fan and dropped them into the fire too. Flapping the innocent leaf in front of her face, she walked to the far side of the cellar and turned and stood looking at him. After a moment she began walking slowly in his direction, fanning herself as she came.

She stopped three feet away and spun around, dropping the fan as she did so. She unfastened her jacket, shrugged out of it, and took two paces towards the bench, all in the same movement. Yang rushed forward, simultaneously raising his manacled hands to pluck the knife from its sheath between her shoulder blades. As she felt him grab the knife, she stepped smoothly to one side and with a loud clank of his ankle chains, Yang moved past her in a fast shuffle, the knife held high above his head. With one great lunge, he brought it down two-handed with all his strength and buried the blade deep in the wood of the torture bench.

He crouched over the low table for a moment, breathing noisily. Then slowly he straightened up, and together they stood gazing at the still quivering knife. Then she looked at him and nodded. After a moment he nodded his head slowly too.

He remained standing, breathing deeply through his nose to regain his composure while she tugged the knife free. She handed it to him and he returned it carefully to its sheath between her shoulder blades. She made him check its position once more before replacing her jacket. Then when she had buttoned it up, she led him, manacled hand and foot, up the steps and out of the cellar.

PEKING, Wednesday—A powerful earth tremor shook Peking early today sending thousands of people rushing onto the streets, smashing windows and cracking walls. The tremor began at 0345 local time and lasted about two minutes.

Reuters, 28 July 1976

26

Although midnight had long passed, the clammy breathless heat of the streets had not abated. To Scholefield, as he sat in the back of the moving Warszawa staring out of the open window at the low-roofed houses, the heat if anything seemed to have intensified. The houses had obviously become intolerable ovens in the darkness and everywhere their occupants were sprawled outside the doors on stools and chairs, or on the ground itself, stripped down to their underclothing. A slow-moving night soil collection cart edged down the street in the opposite direction leaving a rank, ammoniac stench hanging heavily on the air in its wake.

In the shadowy entrances to several hutungs, Scholefield caught a glimpse of determined-looking groups of men and women who had obviously set themselves apart. Their demeanour was more alert and the long wooden truncheons they carried marked them out as members of the People's Militia, the para-military force built up by the radical wing of the leadership. Thunder grumbled in the far distance once more as the car swung south onto Wang Fu Ching, Peking's main shopping street. It was almost deserted because of the hour and Scholefield immediately recognised the entrance to the East Wind Bazaar, the covered market of six hundred stalls where he had often hunted for jade and lacquerware bargains during his student days. The mandarin figure on his desk in London that Yang had admired, he remembered suddenly, had come from the market. A giant coloured portrait of Mao, flanked by two of his quotations in gold lettering on red boards, decorated the entrance now. The street itself, he saw from a signpost, had been re-named Street of the People as a result of the Cultural Revolution. The car slowed as it passed the Peking Department Store and the New China Bookshop's main depot and turned into the mouth of a narrow hutung at the end of which stood a tiny, old-fashioned shop now labelled 'The Peking No. 3 Watchmaker's'.

A light went on behind its grimy windows the moment Tan Sui-ling rapped on the door. It was opened by a bent, wizened Chinese who didn't look at them but kept his eyes averted, staring deliberately towards the floor. In the dim light from a single bulb above a cluttered workbench, all that Scholefield saw of him was the top of a hairless head, wrinkled and furrowed like the shell of a walnut. He wore a leather apron over a black tunic and trousers and he handed Tan Sui-ling a torch after closing the door behind them. Once they were inside, he turned and pretended to busy himself with a wristwatch on the bench, peering closely at its workings through the jeweller's glass screwed into his eye.

Tan Sui-ling led the way quickly to the rear of the shop without addressing the watchmaker and pulled a lever outwards from the wall. A section of the floor slid silently open and she stepped down immediately onto a flight of steps that was revealed. The hollow-chested cadre had stayed in the car outside and Scholefield heard it move off as he followed her down through the trapdoor into an unlit tunnel below. The light in the shop above them was immediately extinguished.

She switched on the torch and led the way into the darkness. The tunnel was about eight feet high and five feet wide and the roof was coated with thick white plaster which deadened the sound of their footsteps. Air-scrubbing ducts snaked along the roof and telephone points had been fitted at regular intervals. He followed her and they walked for five minutes in silence before coming to another door. 'This door is air-tight and blast-proof,' she said over her shoulder as she fitted the key in the lock. 'We are entering now the labyrinth of tunnels that lead us under the

Chung Nan Hai. If any of Wang Tung-hsing's guards should challenge the validity of the pass I have given you, produce your letter. You understand?' He nodded and she opened the door and motioned him through.

The passageway on the other side of the door was wide enough for them to walk side by side. She left the torch in a niche beside the door and soon they began passing labelled side-tunnels leading off at intervals to storerooms and generating plants. Scholefield began to recognise street name plates on the tunnels corresponding to streets above ground level. At major junctions in the tunnels, clusters of signs pointed the way to hospitals and canteens, assembly rooms, ammunition dumps, armouries and grain stores. Machine gun emplacements had been built at all strategic points with firing slits covering all approaches.

'A whole alternative city underground, no less,' said Scholefield quietly, looking around in wonderment.

She nodded. 'You are fifty feet underground here. These tunnel networks have taken us eight years to build. But now four million people, the population of the entire city, can go underground in six minutes. An underground road system which we are now completing ensures that they can be evacuated to the western hills ten miles outside Peking without coming to the surface.'

Scholefield shook his head as he stared round at the brick walls and concrete floors of the tunnels as though he still didn't believe the evidence of his eyes. 'They're an impressive manifestation of Chairman Mao's paranoia, if nothing else,' he said quietly. 'He's certainly communicated his fear of war with the Soviet Union to his people.'

'War is only inevitable while no effort is made to ward it off.' The sudden vehemence of her reply took him by surprise. 'Somebody must act to prevent these tunnels being used for their terrible purpose.' He turned sharply to look at her but found her staring expressionlessly ahead. They had reached the bottom of a long, sloping ramp and at that moment they came in sight of the first guard post.

Scholefield's pass provoked no questions, but the fresh-faced peasant soldiers stared hard at his Caucasian features under the Public Security Bureau cap before waving them through. As they walked on, Scholefield heard them whispering animatedly to each other. Then a telephone receiver was lifted. When they had passed out of earshot round a bend in the now steeply sloping tunnel she shot him a warning glance. 'You will need to show the letter too at the next checkpoint. We are descending into the maximum security area a hundred feet beneath Chung Nan Hai.'

At the next guard post Scholefield produced his pass and the letter. The guards read and re-read them several times, but finally waved him through without comment. They passed a third checkpoint without incident and no body search was demanded until they reached the four guards standing by the archway where she had been checked through earlier with Wang Tung-hsing. The same guards were on duty and they searched only Scholefield. His letter of safe conduct produced a marked lessening of hostility and when the search was over they directed him politely into the carpeted antechamber beyond the archway.

But there the general, beside the leaden door, greeted them with a hostile stare. He barked an order to them to stand with their backs against the wall and called in two of the guards from outside. He watched closely while Scholefield was searched again. They removed his shoes and inspected the lining of his cap, then one guard worked carefully inch by inch up both legs, after checking all his pockets and both sleeves. Finally he felt inside his jacket under each armpit. When he had finished the general nodded sourly towards Tan Sui-ling. 'Nu-jen!' he snapped. 'Now the woman!'

She glared back at him and the younger guard hesitated. The general returned her stare with equal hostility and nodded peremptorily for the guard to start at her feet. Without taking her eyes from the general's face, Tan Sui-ling took a step back and kicked off both her slippers. When he was satisfied with his inspection of them the guard pressed his hands inch by inch against her legs moving upward from her ankles. She continued staring at the general, her face contorted in fury. 'I will report your actions in full when I am inside. Your attempt to humiliate a trusted comrade of the Chairman will not go unrewarded!'

A shadow of doubt puckered the general's brow and she saw it. When the guard had reached her thighs Tan Sui-ling suddenly unfastened the buttons of her jacket and ripped it off. 'Perhaps this is what you really wish to see! You sexual pervert!' She shouted loud enough for the guards outside to hear and there was a stir of consternation from their direction.

'Come on.' She backed against the wall and tossed her head scornfully at the general in invitation. 'Search my body personally with your own filthy hands if it will satisfy your twisted mind.'

The young guard crouching in front of her at her feet stared up at her open-mouthed. The general, thoroughly disconcerted by the sight of her naked breasts, shouted an order for her to replace her jacket immediately and turned away. He waved the two guards off to join their comrades then swung back and stood glowering at Tan Sui-ling. In his confusion, his right hand had fallen from the butt of his revolver and he stood clenching and unclenching his fists spasmodically at his sides. He waited until she had refastened the jacket then turned scowling and unlocked the lead-covered door. Without looking at her directly he stood back and angrily waved them inside.

At that moment the Warszawa cruised to a halt in the narrow deserted hutung outside the Peking No. 3 Watchmaker's shop for the second time in half an hour. The hollow-chested cadre got out, followed by two other guards from the Grass Mist Lane Prison. They pushed and dragged the manacled figure of Yang across the pavement and when the wizened watchmaker opened the door, they propelled him quickly inside. The cadre took the proffered torch and hurried to slide back the door to the tunnel. A minute later the light went out in the shop and the manacled figure of the lone survivor of the Trident crash in Mongolia began clanking slowly and painfully along the darkened underground passageway following the light of the torch towards his appointment with the Chairman of the Communist Party of the People's Republic of China.

PEKING, Wednesday—Heavy damage was reported in the wake of two major earthquakes that struck the heavily populated Peking-Tientsin area of north-east China early today. The first shock was the most powerful anywhere in the world for twelve years.

International Herald Tribune, 28 July 1976

27

'If you have studied the Chinese classics you will know of Chung Kuei!' His head had fallen slackly to one side on the snowy-white pillow and his clouded eyes seemed to roam the thickly packed bookshelves in the shadows on one side of the subterranean library, as though vaguely seeking a confirmatory reference for his statement.

Scholefield found he had to strain to catch the meaning of the slurred Hunanese tones. He moved a pace nearer the couch and glanced up at Tan Sui-ling, standing on the other side by the cluttered desk. 'Chung Kuei was a legendary scholar of the seventh century whom the emperor Hsuan Tsung met in a dream.' Scholefield spoke slowly and quietly, exaggerating his enunciation of the Chinese words for the sake of clarity. 'Chung told the emperor he possessed the power to repel ghosts and evil spirits. When the emperor awoke he described him to the court painter and the likeness of the scholar he sketched became a symbol that was hung above the door throughout China at New Year to ward off invasions of ghosts.'

The silence that followed lasted a full minute. The head on the pillow didn't move. Scholefield was about to repeat his reply when the eyes in the sunken face swivelled suddenly to look at him for the first time through their veil of pain.

'The Kremlin revisionists chose well. Your knowledge of

China is not insignificant.' He paused considering Scholefield intently. 'I was transformed into Chung Kuei by my enemies in the Party. My images had outnumbered Chung Kuei's by tens of millions. But I was never a god. I was made one against my will.' His tongue flickered out to moisten bloodless lips and his voice rose suddenly to a shrill note of complaint. 'The higher a thing is blown, the greater the destruction at its fall. It is impossible for the people of China to cast aside the emperor-worshipping habits of three thousand years in a single generation. My enemies have constantly used this stratagem in their efforts to isolate me, to break me to pieces. I have always been the target of everybody, always standing alone—tell that!'

He lifted his left arm suddenly from under the coverlet and pointed into the shadows. Scholefield turned to follow the direction indicated by the trembling finger. In the gloom above the door through which they had entered he could see a framed portrait. He walked over to it and looked up at the likeness of a pigtailed Chinese scholar, capped and gowned in loose-sleeved court robes. He studied it for a moment then walked back to the couchside. 'You bear no noticeable facial resemblance to Chung Kuei,' he said softly.

'Nor was I able to repel the spirits of demons.' His arm fell back onto the coverlet and his voice shook suddenly. 'But even if the entire Politburo and Central Committee are against me, the earth will go on rotating. The truth is always on the side of the minority.' He was quiet for a moment. 'But I am fearful now that even the power of Chung Kuei is no longer sufficient for my protection.'

Another long silence settled over the room, broken only by the steady rasp of his breath. 'I once said when I was a young man I believed I could live two hundred years and sweep three thousand li. I was haughty in appearance and attitude. But always secretly I had doubts. For instance I lack education, I speak no foreign languages—' He raised his eyes slowly to look at Scholefield. 'It is well known that when tigers are absent from the mountain, the monkey professes himself king. It was just such a king that I became.'

Scholefield looked up from the notebook he had been writing in. 'Insincere humility was one of the great deceits of old China.

But perhaps it was that appearance of unshakeable arrogance, not genuinely felt, that incited the advanced Western "barbarians" to the merciless plunder of your country. Perhaps that same false arrogance now inflames Russian sensibilities too, with such dangerous consequences for yourself and China—and for the whole world.'

The fearful eyes closed wearily in their sunken sockets. 'I am old and exhausted with illness. My best strength was spent fighting twenty years of war with Chiang Kai-shek and the Japanese. I wish above all to have it known that I have been treated by others as a god. In my mind I have been first conscious of my mortal shortcomings. Tell, too, that the supreme irony of the greatest power is that at its end wait only the greatest feebleness and fear—tell that!'

His head sank back deeper into the pillows, and it was a long time before he opened his eyes again. 'There are more than a hundred different parties in the world calling themselves "Communist". But few any longer believe in Marxism. Some people say my brain is made of granite and therefore cannot change... I agree with them. But even Marx and Lenin themselves have been smashed apart. Why shouldn't I face their fate too? My body will be whipped even after I am dead.' His eyes closed once more and he grimaced as though in sudden pain.

'You have presided over a great historic change in China,' said Scholefield quietly. 'Nothing, not even the hatred of your enemies, will alter that.'

His shoulders shook suddenly and his breath rattled dryly in his throat. 'Little has changed. And the changes themselves are as lasting as the brush of rouge upon a young girl's cheek.' His eyes grew hazy again and he stared into the shadows beyond the ring of light cast by the lamp. 'Eighty per cent of all China's people live in the countryside. They revere only sun and wind, storm and flood. They endure and accept the government that rules them as they endure and accept the calamities visited on them by the great forces of nature. A great many are still illiterate, or in only the first stages of literacy. They still hide their savings in a sock under the mattress... Their rulers are as remote from their daily lives as the forces that explode thunder and lightning from the heavens.'

The soft click of the door opening beyond the shadow of the entrance arch reached Scholefield's ears and he looked up quickly at Tan Sui-ling. She met his gaze without moving from her place in the shadow by the desk. He glanced over his shoulder but there was no movement in the darkness and no further sound.

'Yes, their strength can be harnessed for great works, they change the course of rivers—the muscle power of eight hundred million human work-horses is truly great. But their passivity of mind makes the Chinese people the most compliant on earth. So even today the ambitious few who fight to high places of power still pursue their petty intrigues on the head of a pin in these imperial precincts.' There was a note of bitter despair in his voice and one wasted hand began clenching and unclenching convulsively on the edge of the coverlet. 'Despite Marx and Lenin, intrigue remains an endemic disease in the Chinese brain. In three thousand years nothing in China has really changed.'

As Scholefield's pen raced across his notebook, a soft footfall behind him made him turn suddenly. In the darkness the indistinct outline of a woman was visible standing motionless beneath the archway. Scholefield turned back to the couch to find the eyes in the sunken face staring intently in the same direction. 'Several years ago the Americans warned me of the treacherous assassination plot formulated by Lin Piao.' He spoke in a rising tone, as though suddenly he was making a public speech. 'Now the Russians say that my own closest supporters intrigue against me.' He paused, gathering his strength, and his voice fell to a whisper. 'They say that even my wife is involved in the plotting.'

His breathing had become fast and shallow and he raised his head and shoulders suddenly from the pillow with a visible effort. 'The burden of leadership in China has always been too weighty for a single mind to bear! I said many times I have felt like a man attending his own funeral—enduring veiled glances, the whispers behind a hundred hands!' His rheumy eyes widened and he stared up slack-mouthed towards the blank ceiling. 'Now I know the feelings of a man dying in the sands of the Gobi! Watching the vultures swing down out of the burning vault of heaven, their open throats stretching for his living flesh!'

Twin circles of reflected light flashed on her spectacles as the woman stepped forward out of the shadows. She stopped at the foot of the couch and stood looking down without speaking, her face a mask of fury. She drew breath quickly as though preparing to speak—then stepped back with a cry of surprise as the dark coverlet was suddenly flung aside. Scholefield found himself staring at the black revolver clutched in a claw-like hand. The muzzle of the weapon was pointed directly at her throat.

'To be rid of the gun, you must take up the gun!' He uttered the words in a rasping whisper, holding the revolver steadily in his right hand, his arm at full stretch. His eyes burned again with the sudden unnatural brightness. 'If I had to obliterate all the truths I have written, save one—I would choose to preserve those few characters.'

The double gleam of the lamp mirrored in both lenses of her wire-rimmed spectacles hid her eyes as she stared transfixed into the mouth of the gun barrel. The fleshless finger began to tighten on the trigger and she opened her mouth to scream. But no sound came out. Then abruptly the hand began to tremble and the long black barrel wavered. With a great effort he steadied his aim and brought the muzzle to bear again. But the moment the talon-like finger in the trigger guard contracted a second time, the hand shook wildly once more. And this time the trembling became uncontrollable. The revolver swung erratically from side to side for a moment then slipped slowly from the palsied fingers and clattered to the floor.

He moaned and his chest heaved as he struggled for breath. His feverish gaze remained riveted for a moment on the motionless figure at the foot of the couch. Then his eyelids fell and his head sank forward onto his chest.

A hand touched Scholefield's arm and he looked up to find Tan Sui-ling motioning him silently to leave. He turned to find the door already open. The vestibule under the archway was empty. The shadowy figure of the woman had departed as silently as it had come.

PEKING, Wednesday—A strong earthquake occurred in the Tangshan-Fengnan area in east Hopei Province, north China, at 0342 hours on July 28th. Comparatively strong shocks were felt in Peking and Tientsin. Damage of varying degrees was reported in the epicentral region.

HSINHUA
(New China News Agency),
28 July 1976

28

Scholefield heard the clank of his heavy ankle chains before Yang himself came into sight. A moment later he appeared round a bend in the tunnel, shuffling painfully forward a foot or two at a time, his wrists manacled in front of him. His head was bent forward, his eyes cast down watching the ground. The hollow-chested cadre and the two guards followed close behind.

Scholefield stepped aside to let him pass. The close-cropped head of the Chinese remained bowed as he moved slowly on down the tunnel. He did not raise his eyes to look at Scholefield or Tan Sui-ling as he edged past them.

The four guards at the archway halted Yang with a shouted order and immediately began searching him. Scholefield watched them rip at his jacket, pushing and pulling him roughly back and forth between them. One of the younger guards spat contemptuously in his face.

'The Chairman is resting,' said Tan Sui-ling crisply, turning to address the hollow-chested cadre. 'He is to receive us again after he has talked with the prisoner Yang. You will escort Scholefield to his quarters and post the guard outside for his security!' She turned to check on the progress of the search on Yang. 'I will remain here to conduct the prisoner into the Chairman's presence.'

The cadre nodded. He motioned to Scholefield to follow him and set off up the slope of the tunnel. Scholefield hesitated, looking back at Yang. He saw the guards stand back respectfully as Tan Sui-ling approached. She snapped orders to two of them and walked on stiff-backed, through the archway. Yang raised his head sharply as she passed him. For a fleeting instant his eyes lost their defeated, hangdog look and he gazed fiercely at her retreating back until she disappeared through the arch. Then immediately he dropped his eyes, hunching once more into a submissive crouch as he shuffled forward between two guards.

Scholefield's escort nudged him roughly with their rifle butts, and gestured impatiently in the opposite direction. Reluctantly he turned away and started up the long slope. They climbed in silence for three or four minutes and when they reached the top, the hollow-chested cadre turned off into a dimly-lit accommodation tunnel lined with numbered doors on either side. They walked on for a further quarter of a mile then halted outside a door without a number. The cadre produced a key, unlocked the door and stood back, motioning Scholefield inside.

The floor and walls of the room were rough, undecorated concrete. A tier of metal-framed bunks stood against one wall and there was a plain wooden table and four chairs in the centre. In a smaller, connected room Scholefield could see a sink with taps and a lavatory pedestal. The rooms were lit by a buzzing fluorescent tube fixed to the ceiling. On the table stood a large thermos flask decorated with red Chinese characters spelling out a quotation from the Collected Works of Mao Tse-tung.

'You will remain here until you are summoned again!' The cadre waved towards the flask on the table. 'There is boiled water to drink. The two guards will be stationed outside. I shall lock the door—for your own security.'

He went out quickly and slammed the flimsy, wooden door behind him. Scholefield heard the key turn in the lock. There was a murmured burst of conversation between the cadre and the two guards, then silence. Scholefield looked at his wristwatch. It was exactly three-thirty A.M. He pulled out one of the rough wooden chairs from the table and sat down. He took out his notebook, opened it on the table and closed his eyes for a long moment. Then he plucked a pen from his pocket and began writing rapidly.

*   *   *

The ten thousand seats in the main assembly auditorium of the Great Hall of the People stood silent and empty as Wang Tung-hsing hurried across the rear of the red-draped podium. He was taking a short cut from his office to the little-used chamber reserved for formal meetings of the Standing Committee of the Party Politburo. The auditorium was almost in darkness. Only the twin spotlights, lodged against the high ceiling to illuminate the giant coloured portrait of the Chairman hanging above the podium, were lit.

Wang came out onto a high, broad, marble-floored corridor, turned left and stopped outside a closed door guarded by two 8341 soldiers with fixed bayonets on their rifles. Even though they were standing motionless, beads of sweat stood out on their faces in the suffocating heat. As he lifted his left hand to knock, Wang glanced at his watch. It was three-thirty-two. He rapped once crisply on the door and entered without waiting for a response.

Although the four men and one woman seated round the table inside looked up at him warily as he entered, no greetings were exchanged. He walked briskly towards them and dealt five bulky, buff-coloured files quickly round the table onto their empty blotters. While they were still in the act of opening them he began talking rapidly. 'Reports are continuing to proliferate from all quarters of the north-east. The communication systems of the public security apparatus are fast becoming clogged by the reports. In addition to the animal behaviour anomalies, fluctuations in the telluric current, changes in the radon content of well water and other macro-seismic phenomena all point to the same conclusion.' He turned and hurried to one wall covered with large-scale sectional maps of the People's Republic of China. He reached up and jabbed a finger onto a map of the northern provinces halfway between Peking and the Yellow Sea coast. 'The epicentre could be somewhere here—and time is running out fast.' He glanced down again at his watch. The minute hand had crept round to three-thirty-five.

He looked up to say something further but his gaze lighted suddenly on a tray of glasses and bottled mineral water on a side table. He waddled quickly across the room, twisted the stopper from a bottle and emptied its contents into a glass. When the last drop of liquid had dripped out, he turned the bottle upside down on the table, balancing it on its slender neck. He looked up at the five members of the Standing Committee to find them watching him intently. 'May I suggest that if the bottle falls of its own accord,' he said quietly, 'we evacuate the building immediately— but go outside at ground level. Do not use the underground tunnel route to Chung Nan Hai.'

There was an intense silence in the room for a moment.

'It is not the most scientific instrument for predicting an earthquake and it does not give a great deal of advance warning— but it is one the peasants in my home province have used for many centuries.'

'What instructions did the Chairman give to the man who has been his beloved bodyguard since those romantic far-off days in the Yenan caves?' The sharp, sarcastic question came from the bespectacled woman. There was a sneer on her face and her voice was half scornful, half resentful.

Wang walked slowly back to the table, his face stretched tight with anxiety. 'The Chairman refuses to be moved from Peking. He declines to flee before what he calls "the omens of pigs and rats".' He directed his words at the tabletop, avoiding the eyes of all those watching him. 'I urged him at least to remove himself from the tunnels to ground level. But he insists absolutely on remaining where he is.'

'Perhaps he is too busy receiving clandestine foreign guests'— Wang looked up sharply—'and shackled prisoners in clanking chains.' Her eyes glittered behind her spectacles and she smirked in triumph when she saw the surprise on his face. 'It seems his confidences with Comrade Tan, his empress of foreign intelligence, are withheld even from his old and trusted chief bodyguard.'

Wang drew a deep breath and with an obvious effort directed his gaze into the empty air above their heads. 'The Chairman intimated that he was prepared to permit his authority to be lent to whatever emergency action this meeting may decide—even mass evacuation. The issue is now extremely urgent, in my view.' He glanced down quickly at his watch once more. 'With your permission I shall now absent myself from your presence for a moment to allow you to deliberate in confidence on your decision.'

Without waiting for a response, he turned and hurried from the room. As soon as he had closed the door behind him, to the amazement of the two sweating guards outside, he broke into a lumbering, flat-footed run down the centre of the broad corridor.

The uniformed general, standing by the leaden door a hundred feet beneath the foundations of the Forbidden City, stared hard at the hunched figure of Yang as he shuffled into the light of the outer vestibule, dragging his ankle shackles noisily across the concrete floor. Tan Sui-ling stood aside waiting, her chin held high, watching him approach with a coolly contemptuous expression in her eyes.

Yang hesitated as he reached the edge of the carpeted area, but didn't raise his eyes from the floor. The general barked an order for him to advance and gestured for the two guards behind him to remain where they were. 'He has been given a thorough body search?' The two guards nodded vigorously in affirmation, shouting their replies dutifully in unison.

When Yang was only three or four feet from him, the general ordered him to halt. Drawing his pistol from its holster, he stepped forward and grabbed the chain linking Yang's handcuffs with his free hand. He tugged at it roughly, checking its strength, then shouted at Yang to raise his arms in front of his face. He pressed the pistol into his ribs and inspected every link of the wrist manacles individually, holding them inches from his eyes. When he was satisfied, he barked another order at Yang to lift his arms higher, then dropped to one knee and jabbed the muzzle of the pistol roughly into his groin while he inspected the steel bands around his ankles. Again he tested each link of the chains joining them, as he had done with the handcuffs, before rising to his feet once more.

He looked coldly across at Tan Sui-ling. For a moment their eyes locked in a stare of mutual hostility. Then with slow deliberate movements, the general unhooked the key chained to his left wrist and inserted it into the lock. Before turning it he hesitated and glanced back over his shoulder once more at Yang, as though beset by a last moment of uncertainty. Yang, however, was still standing with shoulders hunched, staring down at his shackled wrists.

The general eyed him in silence, then as though making up his mind finally, slipped his pistol back into its holster. He unlocked the door with a quick movement then turned and stepped to one side so that Yang could shuffle past him. Tan Sui-ling followed him through the doorway without looking left or right, and together they disappeared slowly into the gloom inside. After a last glance at Tan's retreating back the general closed the door and locked it carefully behind them.

MENLO PARK, CALIFORNIA, Wednesday—
No foreshocks were recorded by American instru-
ments here before today's massive earthquake in
China which registered 8.2 on the open-ended
Richter scale—worse than the shock which destroyed
San Francisco in 1906.

Reuters, 28 July 1976

29

The sweat running down his forehead into his eyes forced Scholefield to stop writing. He laid his pen aside and wiped the back of
his hand across his face. As he did so he caught sight of his watch.
It was three-forty. The only sound in the room was the buzz of
the faulty fluorescent tube in the ceiling. He stared round at the
unrelieved greyness of the concrete walls for several seconds then
unscrewed the plastic cup on the thermos flask and filled it to the
brim. But the boiling water scalded his mouth and he flung the
beaker against the wall with a curse. He watched it fall to the
floor and roll slowly into a corner before turning back to his open
notebook. He ran his eye over what he had written and for a
moment his brow furrowed in thought. Then slowly his eyes
closed and he began massaging both temples wearily with the
tips of his fingers. He sat like this for perhaps a minute, his
shoulders hunched around his ears.

Then suddenly his head jerked up out of his hands. He rose to
his feet, knocking the chair backwards with a crash, and stood
staring wide-eyed at the blank wall in front of him. But he saw
nothing of the grey concrete. Instead, for the first time, in a star-
burst of realisation, his memory was matching the retina-image
of the sudden blaze of savage hope in Yang's eyes a few minutes
before as he gazed at Tan Sui-ling's retreating back in the depths
of the tunnel. Greatly magnified in intensity, it had mirrored what

he now knew was the fierce joy of recognition, quickly stifled, that he had first seen in the shadow of the Soho kiosk! Li Tai-chu and Li Kwei-min! Brother and sister? Cousins? It didn't matter which, the intimacy of intent in their fleeting facial signals was indisputable.

Other elusive inconsistencies tumbled into place with a rush like a picked lock yielding of a sudden all its secret resistance. The false Russian attempts to kill Yang at the Institute and the mortuary that made it seem so highly desirable for him to be saved by the White House for Peking, the otherwise senseless killing of Ketterman when he had just stumbled across this logic —they only made sense if the folios and the revelation in London of a plan to kill Mao had not been ends in themselves, but the very means of moving the assassin who had announced his own intent into place for his kill! Scholefield shook his head quickly in wonderment. And the final fake confession in the torture cellar had taken Yang over the last barrier into his victim's presence. Desire for revenge by Lin's admirers had been harmonised by the Kremlin with their ambition to thwart the radical successors to Mao. Evidence implicating them would no doubt be pressed on the Western outsider whom the Chairman had been persuaded to summon by his murderess! 'Yang' had presumably concealed his real identity to avoid identification with his cousin—but in a weak moment, haunted by the fear of an anonymous death before the plan had been carried through, had he scribbled his real name on the Ch'ing scroll in London?

Scholefield looked round frantically, picked up the fallen chair and darted across the room. He swung it wildly against the flimsy wooden panels of the door and let out a high, keening scream. One of the upper panels shattered under his assault, and outside in sudden close-up he saw the shocked, alarmed faces of his two guards. Scholefield backed off quickly, then ran a few quick steps before jumping into a two-footed yoko-tobi-geri which shattered the remaining panels of the flimsy door. He landed on all fours in the tunnel outside in a storm of splintering wood, sending one of the guards sprawling to the concrete floor under the impact of his rush. He flailed the shattered chair-back at the head of the other guard, stunning him, and was running fast along the tunnel fifty yards away before either of them scrambled to his feet.

*   *   *

Yang did not allow himself the luxury of raising his bowed head until he had hobbled as far as the edge of the circle of light cast by the single lamp. Then he looked up for the first time at the shrivelled, waxen face sunk into the snowy pillow. His shackles ceased to rattle as he stopped and stared, transfixed. The eyes of the man he had come so far to kill fixed on him with a feverish intensity as he raised his head from the pillow on the wasted stalk of his neck.

'This is the loyal servant of Lin Piao.' Tan Sui-ling made the introduction in a flat, detached voice, giving no emotional weight or colour to any of her words. As she spoke she moved quietly forward until she was standing between the couch and the emergency call button on the edge of the desk.

The burning eyes of the dying man swivelled frantically in their sockets and he gazed at her for a moment in stupefied disbelief. She had deliberately omitted the ritual adjectives of vituperation that should have accompanied any reference to Lin! His lower jaw sagged suddenly and a dribble of saliva ran out of his mouth and down his chin. The pitiless mask of her features had confirmed for him beyond any doubt the shock of betrayal. After a moment of total silence he turned his head and stared at Yang as though hypnotised.

'For five long years in the wastes of Mongolia and in my Moscow "prison" I dreamed of this moment.' Yang whispered the words in a shaking voice. 'I served Marshall Lin Piao loyally for many years and was powerless to prevent you destroying him, as you destroyed a host of other great men loyal to you and your ideals.' His voice died away and his face contorted as though in pain. He raised his manacled hands and clenched his fists. 'I have come here not to seek atonement but to avenge the countless good men of China on whom you have rained ruin and destruction.'

The chief night supervisor of the Party Communications Centre in the Great Hall of the People looked up in alarm as Wang Tung-hsing sent the door crashing back on its hinges and lunged past him towards the nearest telephone switchboard. He ran across and asked if he could be of assistance but Wang ignored him, snatched an operator's head-set from a hook beside the board and dialled a single digit. His shoulders rose and fell convulsively as he fought to regain his breath. When the general outside the leaden door came on the line he had controlled his breathing sufficiently to speak and he tried to make his enquiry sound casual. 'How is the Chairman?'

'He is rested, now,' said the general warily. 'He interrupted his talk with the foreigner in order to rest.'

Wang's face twisted into a scowl. 'Is he alone?'

'No, the personally authorised audience of the prisoner Yang and Comrade Tan of the Central External Liaison Department has just begun.' The general paused and his voice took on a faint note of alarm. 'You were aware of these privately-arranged visits, Comrade—'

Wang's reply was barely audible. 'Of course.' He closed his eyes. 'Permit no further visits of any kind. I shall be there in less than two minutes.' He flung the head-set to the floor and turned and dashed out into the passageway.

The clamour of the two guards shouting for him to halt echoed along the confined passageway behind him as Scholefield came out at the top of the steeply pitching ramp leading to the maximum security areas under the Forbidden City. He tugged the letter from his pocket as he ran, and when he rounded a curve in the downward tunnel he slowed and held it out towards two guards manning the first wooden barrier. 'I have been ordered to return immediately!' he yelled in Chinese, pointing beyond the barrier.

The same soldiers had been on duty when he was escorted through earlier and they recognised him and the letter immediately. They hesitated for a moment and Scholefield, taking advantage of their indecision, accelerated past them, hurdled the low barrier and rushed on down the slope.

The next guard point was two hundred yards further on and although the curve of the tunnel hid him from his pursuers, as he ran he heard the shouts of the guards growing louder behind him. Then a volley of shots rang out and the whine of bullets ricochetting along the smooth walls filled the tunnel. There had been enough time for a warning to be telephoned ahead to the next checkpoint and when Scholefield rounded the last bend in the tunnel he found four armed guards confronting him before the barrier. He ran straight at them and leapt feet first in another side-jumping kick, striking out simultaneously right and left with the flattened blades of both hands. One man went down under the onslaught but the other three used their rifle butts to block the blows and crowded him quickly to the ground.

HONG KONG, Wednesday—A total of 655,237
people were killed and another 779,000 injured in a
devastating earthquake which hit north-east China
last July, according to a highly classified Chinese
document just obtained by a Hong Kong newspaper.
London *Evening News*, 5 January 1977

30

'Your death by violence is necessary to return China to the path
of sanity.' Tan Sui-ling whispered the words as she unfastened
the top button of her jacket. 'A few minutes from now the
Englishman will be brought here to look upon your lifeless body.
He will be given evidence that you were murdered by your
own supporters—and he will take that evidence to the outside
world.'

The dying face collapsed suddenly inwards on itself. Toothless
gums gleamed wetly in the sunken cavern of his mouth and his
jaw sagged in a mute shout of horror. She saw an enfeebled
hand begin to grope ineffectually towards the revolver under the
coverlet and leaned quickly over him and wrenched it from his
limp fingers. She slid it away across the desk top then turned
back to look at him. Her face clenched suddenly into a glittering
smile of hatred and without taking her eyes from his face she
ripped off her jacket and laid it aside. A sharp inhalation of breath
made her small, pouting breasts rise suddenly as she stepped closer
to the couch. Half turning her shoulders, she leaned backwards
from the waist towards Yang, offering the small of her back to
his shackled hands.

She watched his eyes bulge from their sockets as he gazed up in
terror at her naked body. Yang's hands eased the long-bladed
knife slowly from its sheath between her shoulder blades and

she saw his gaze following it hypnotically as it rose slowly into view behind her. She stepped quickly aside as Yang lifted his arms high above his head.

'Sha! Sha!' She breathed the order to kill in an urgent whisper and turned back to watch the face of their victim.

Yang's ankle chains clanked noisily as he took two quick steps to the couchside. He stretched his arms upward until they were straight above his head, holding the long knife tight in both fists. An unarticulated moan of emotion escaped his lips and he swayed slightly on his feet. He hesitated for a moment then suddenly his arms bent at the elbows and he leaned backwards, beginning the convulsive downward thrust he had rehearsed beside the bench an hour earlier in the prison cellar. Tan Sui-ling watched the bulging eyes of the man on the couch flinch and close in anticipation of death.

At that moment the upturned bottle on the table in the Great Hall of the People began to rock very gently from side to side. The five members of the Standing Committee of the Party Politburo looked round at it in alarm. It settled again for a moment and they sat staring at it in an electric silence. Then, without further warning, it toppled and rolled slowly across the table. The explosive sound of it smashing to pieces on the marble floor rang through the silent room like a pistol shot. Immediately the four men and one woman rose to their feet and rushed from the room.

At the instant the bottle broke Wang Tung-hsing was halfway down the steps beneath the twelve entry columns of the Great Hall. The first sensation he noticed was a shifting unsteadiness in the steps beneath his feet. He stopped running immediately and stood still. The steps seemed to tilt and roll very gently first in one direction, then the other, like the deck of a ship answering the groundswell before a storm at sea. In the sky he heard a distant, muffled sound that resembled the gently subdued roar of surf on a remote beach. It grew gradually louder like a slow-rising wind. But the dank, stagnant air of the night hung as heavy and still over the capital as ever.

*   *   *

The general on duty outside the leaden door in the maximum security tunnel below the Forbidden City heard the shouts of the four guards on duty beyond the arch moments before the tremor began. He drew his revolver from its holster and stepped warily into the passageway. He saw the soldier stunned by a blow on the side of the neck rise slowly to his feet, shaking his head, then begin advancing menacingly towards Scholefield who was being restrained in a double arm-lock by the other three guards. He was aiming a kick in the direction of Scholefield's groin when the general fired. In any other place he would have raised the gun above his head but the low roof at that point was only three feet above him. So he aimed high along the tunnel and the bullet grooved the walls and ceiling as it shrieked along an erratic trajectory, before flattening itself against the impenetrable concrete of the end wall.

The guards and Scholefield gaped round at the general as the roar of the shot died away. He was standing in the middle of the tunnel, feet astride, fanning the gun in a threatening arc over the whole group. Scholefield was the first to recover from the shock of the explosion in the confined space.

'Yang is an assassin!'

He yelled the words over and over, struggling wildly, and succeeded in his frenzy in freeing one arm. The four guards cursed loudly as they fought to restrain him. The general was still shouting at the top of his voice to make himself heard when the floor of the tunnel began to tilt sharply beneath their feet.

In the silent room on the other side of the leaden door, Yang stood frozen in a moment of indecision. He gazed down at his victim, a demented snarl distorting his features. His knees were bent, his shoulders hunched forward, and he held the knife suspended in the air above his head. The floor of the chamber seemed to quiver slightly and Tan Sui-ling looked up at him sharply. But Yang was oblivious.

The face beneath him had dissolved into liquid lines of fear, misshapen already beyond recognition by the primal, animalistic horror of death. Slowly but with great deliberation Yang brought the knife down in front of him with both hands until its needle-sharp point rested against the base of the scraggy throat. His breath came unevenly now in sobbing gasps and his hands shook slightly.

'Never before have I seen such naked terror in the eyes of a man!' The sobbing grew louder on every indrawn breath. But suddenly he stopped and his eyes widened. 'Marshall Lin will be better avenged by allowing you to live out the short hours and days left to you with this fear!' He nodded his head frantically now, the tears streaming from his eyes mixing with the rush of perspiration down his cheeks. 'Fear of death will be a greater punishment for you than death itself—for every tortured second that you live on!'

The concrete floor shook itself suddenly like an angry snake and a deep rumbling sound rose from beneath their feet. Yang closed his eyes for a moment. Then he lifted the knife quickly, and holding it in front of him in both hands, turned and shuffled rapidly away from the couch. He hobbled as fast as the length of his shackles allowed, moving straight towards the blank wall between the bookshelves. He lifted his arms stiffly in front of him as he neared the wall, as if to fend it off. But he did not check his momentum. Instead he turned the knife and lodged the base of its handle against the concrete, so that its blade jutted out and upward like a climbing spike. He made no sound as he hurled himself forward like a sprinter lunging in despair for the final tape.

For an instant his whole body stiffened in spasm. Then he relaxed and fell to embrace the wall limply. He slid slowly down, face forward, into a crumpled kneeling position at its foot. Above him on the grey concrete a broad smear of blood marked the passage of his body.

Tan Sui-ling's scream of anguish rose above the rumbling of the earthquake as the door from the darkened vestibule burst open. She snatched up the revolver from the desk and swung round, levelling it at the couch. The general yelled frantically from the doorway and dropped to one knee, at the same time raising his own pistol to fire.

As Wang Tung-hsing's Hung Chi raced across the deserted Square of Heavenly Peace the roar of the earthquake reached a crescendo and a great blaze of white light lit Peking and the surrounding countryside as brightly as the sun at mid-day. The ground shook constantly and the darkness that followed this first elemental release of energy was deeper than before because no electricity installations survived the shock.

A moment later a second incandescent glare illuminated the capital and in the suburbs terrified people began running into the streets, screaming that the Russians had launched their long-feared hydrogen bomb attack. Buildings swayed and cracked and in the densely populated mining towns of Hopei, a hundred miles to the south-east, entire streets of buildings were crumbling like playing card houses. Hospitals and high apartment blocks fell into the earth up to roof level and were crushed to rubble as the cracks closed. In the underground coal seams many thousands of miners were dying as the earth settled itself afresh, filling instantly the puny underground holes driven by man-made machinery. Great tracts of farmland were becoming inundated with sand and foul liquids that gushed up out of the fractured earth. Nearer the capital an entire train bound for Peking toppled into a vast black ravine as the earth gaped open suddenly in front of it, then snapped its jaws closed once more.

As Wang's Hung Chi limousine dashed along the shores of the Chung Nanhai in Peking, the waters of the lakes that had earlier lain stagnant under the heavy pall of saturated air were aboil with turbulence. At the very moment the car screeched to a halt outside the yellow-roofed pavilion, the black heavens broke and a great deluge of water began flooding down onto the trembling city.

A hundred feet under Chung Nanhai the cosmic roar of the earth's movement drowned the sound of the general's gun exploding and Scholefield, crowding into the chamber behind him with the four terrified guards, saw the slender figure of Tan Sui-ling spin rapidly round like a pirouetting ballet dancer. She flung out her right arm and fired a single shot in the direction of the couch before tossing the black revolver high into the shadows. The lead slug from the general's pistol had taken her in the right shoulder and the force of it lifted her bodily backwards across the room.

A wide crack opened up suddenly in the wall above where Yang lay huddled and the shock of the tremor knocked Scholefield off his feet. The air was filled suddenly with a choking yellow dust. Through the foggy gloom Scholefield saw the general lifting the head and shoulders of the shrunken figure on the couch. He waved his free arm and screamed for the four soldiers to come to his assistance. The floor heaved again and two long bookcases pitched forward from the walls, hurling their contents about the room. Scholefield scrambled to his feet as the general and the soldiers rushed past him towards the door, bearing the couch and its helpless occupant between them. He staggered across the chamber to where Tan Sui-ling lay face down. She was half covered with books that had spilled from the bookcases and she lay perfectly still. He grabbed her by the shoulders and turned her over. A large bloodstain covered the front of her jacket. Her eyes opened as he looked down at her and her lips moved. But he was unable to hear her words above the growing roar of the earthquake.

Thick dust clogged his throat and eyes as he bent to pick her up and he began coughing and retching as he staggered across the chamber towards the door. Outside in the tunnel there was no light at all. The dust was thicker there and he scrambled blindly on, over piles of rubble and fallen blocks of concrete that he could only feel in the total darkness. By instinct he was making for the upward slope, carrying the now unconscious Chinese woman in his arms. As he went the crack and roar of the tunnel works splitting open around him in the pitch blackness added their awful clamour to the deeper rumble of the moving earth.

PEKING, Thursday—Chairman Mao Tse-tung, 82-year old leader of 800 million Communists, is dead. Radio Peking gave no indication of the cause of Mao's death but it was widely believed he had suffered a series of strokes in recent years and was a victim of Parkinson's disease.

London *Evening News*, 9 September 1976

31

The antiquated lift cage groaned and creaked as its worn, nineteenth-century pulley-system cranked it ponderously up to the fourth floor. The bulb on the landing was still not lit and Moynahan hung back in the shadows, peering expectantly between the lattice-work of the spring-loaded gates as the head and shoulders of the man inside rose slowly into view. His face was hidden by an open copy of the *Evening Standard* he was reading and in the dim glow of the lift's interior light Moynahan watched the massive, two-word headline stretched across the front page in heavy black type shifting steadily up towards his eye-level.

The greased bicycle-style chain rattled noisily in its pipe and the light inside went out abruptly as the lift stopped and the gates opened. A muffled curse accompanied the crash of the gates slamming shut again in the darkness and Moynahan darted forward and bent down to free the trapped trouser leg.

'All right, all right Moynahan! I can manage, thank you.'

'Sorry sir.' Moynahan's voice was crisply respectful and he stood up quickly when he saw his help wasn't needed. 'Surprised to see you here, sir.'

'I'd like to have a look in the flat for myself, Moynahan.'

'Right sir, of course.' He pulled out his key and inserted it in the lock. 'I thought for a moment, sir,' he said over his shoulder, 'it was Mr. Scholefield himself coming back.' He swung the door open and reached inside to switch on the light.

Percy Crowdleigh stepped past the Irishman into the lighted hall without answering and stood staring irritably down for a moment at the torn cuff of his dark striped trousers. He made a loud clicking noise with his tongue for several seconds then slowly folded the paper he was holding and laid it on the hall table. He waited until Moynahan had followed him inside and closed the door before speaking.

'He's dead.'

'I know, sir. I heard it on the news.' Moynahan grinned suddenly and nodded down at the big headline on the evening paper. 'Still, he had a good run. Eighty-two's not a bad age for a guerrilla revolutionary, is it?'

'I'm not talking about Mao Tse-tung!' Crowdleigh's voice was still testy. 'Your assignment here is finished.' He waved a hand vaguely towards the paper. 'Page seven, two paragraphs from Singapore, refers.'

Moynahan picked up the paper and opened it. He read the brief agency item at the bottom of the foreign news page under its Singapore dateline, then looked up at Crowdleigh questioningly. 'September the eighth? Yesterday—and nobody in the whole world of journalism wondering why a British sinologist should be the victim of a hit-and-run accident in the Singapore bar district at three o'clock in the morning.' Moynahan's accent had suddenly become less pronounced. He stared at the Cabinet Office man a moment longer.

'The post mortem showed his lungs were clogged with dust,' said Crowdleigh dryly. He considered Moynahan with a bored expression on his face. 'Some time we may assign you, Moynahan, to break into the crystal casket in which they will no doubt enshrine the Chairman's remains, and bring back samples of the contents of his lungs too.'

Moynahan gazed back at his superior uncomprehendingly. Then he laughed uncertainly at what he assumed was another of his over-elaborate jests. 'For myself, I can't say I'm sorry to be moving on to something else, Sir. The last six or seven weeks since Scholefield left have been as quiet as the bloody grave here, Sir, if you'll pardon the—'

Crowdleigh interrupted him with a peremptory gesture. 'Did you get his papers?'

'Yes sir.' Moynahan reached inside the black jacket of his porter's uniform and pulled out a long buff envelope. 'His bank manager was very reluctant. Refused point blank even to consider opening the strong box just on the strength of a Special Branch card. We wouldn't have them now if I hadn't told him to ring you—and he wants them back by quarter to three.'

Crowdleigh took the papers from him and walked into the study. He paused in the middle of the room for a moment, looking round. The half empty vodka bottle and the unwashed glass still stood on the desk. He walked over to the Chinese scroll near the desk and raised his spectacles to his forehead to peer closely at the double signature at the foot of the inscription. He drummed his fingers absently on the envelope in his hands as he leaned closer. 'Take a couple of shots of this, please,' he said quietly over his shoulder.

While Moynahan was photographing the signatures with the miniature camera he had taken from his pocket, Crowdleigh prised open the envelope and shook the papers inside onto the blotter. He pushed his spectacles up onto his forehead again and peered at the photostat of the poem in Chinese calligraphy. Behind him the clicking ceased and Moynahan put the camera back in his pocket and stood waiting beside the desk. 'Was anything found on the body that would give a clue as to what happened?'

Crowdleigh continued gazing at the convoluted Chinese characters for a long time before he looked up. Then he stared absently at Moynahan as though he had forgotten who he was. 'There was a notebook in his pocket with a lot of detailed notes in it, yes, and a few other papers. We're doing our best to check them out.' He reached up to his forehead and readjusted the spectacles on the bridge of his bony nose. 'Do a couple of pictures of all the papers in that envelope, then get 'em back to the bank, fast.'

He wandered off idly across the room, picking up the jade mandarin figure from beside the vodka bottle. He carried it across to the window and held it towards the light. He stood for a long while gazing absently out into the street, stroking the pale green stone. 'We're beginning to get a picture, piece by piece.

And if only the damned Americans didn't try to do everything on their own. . . .' He spoke quietly to himself without looking up from the jade figure, as if the room was empty.

Moynahan looked up from what he was doing, but Crowdleigh did not complete the sentence. When he had finished his photography, Moynahan returned the documents to the envelope and re-sealed it with some gum from a bottle in the desk. He held it up for Crowdleigh's inspection and the Cabinet Office man nodded quickly and led the way out into the hall. He waited while Moynahan opened the door for him. He was almost out of the door when he leaned back and picked up the evening paper from the hall table. He looked at the picture of Mao Tse-tung and the headline for a moment, then raised his eyebrows at Moynahan as though in silent self-congratulation that they had not been careless enough to leave it behind. He tucked it away in a pocket of his trousers, drew back the heavy metal gates of the lift and disappeared inside, without any parting salutation.

Moynahan stood listening to the moan of the lift as it sank slowly down towards the ground floor. Then he turned back and switched out the light inside the hall of Scholefield's flat. He locked the door carefully behind him, leaned against it once to make sure, then walked off into the darkness of the hall and down the stairs.